JULIA LONDON

SUMMER
of TWO
WISHES

POCKET STAR BOOKS

New York   London   Toronto   Sydney

"We aren't through yet."

Finn kissed Macy possessively, sending a thrill through her.

"Finn, I—"

"Not this time, Macy. I'm going to do what I should have done the moment I got home and show you just how much I missed you, how much you mean to me."

Macy's blood raced, making her so weak with longing that she was powerless to do anything to stop him.

"Look at me," he quietly commanded her. "I don't have much that means anything to me anymore. Only you."

Also by Julia London

Pocket Star Books
A Division of Simon & Schuster, Inc.
1230 Avenue of the Americas
New York, NY 10020

This book is a work of fiction. Names, characters, places, and incidents either are products of the author's imagination or are used fictitiously. Any resemblance to actual events or locales or persons, living or dead, is entirely coincidental.

First Pocket Star Books paperback edition September 2009

POCKET STAR and colophon are registered trademarks of Simon & Schuster, Inc.

For information about special discounts for bulk purchases, please contact Simon & Schuster Special Sales at 1-866-506-1949 or business@simonandschuster.com.

The Simon & Schuster Speakers Bureau can bring authors to your live event. For more information or to book an event contact the Simon & Schuster Speakers Bureau at 1-866-248-3049 or visit our website at www.simonspeakers.com.

Cover design by Lisa Litwack.
Cover photo illustration by Melody Cassen.

Manufactured in the United States of America

10 9 8 7 6 5 4 3 2 1

ISBN 978-1-4165-4708-2
ISBN 978-1-4391-6417-4 (ebook)

In memory of a pair of yellow labs who enriched my life beyond measure for many years. I miss them very much. I have two wishes: That they are in a better place, and that they are not forgotten.

Maude
January 15, 1995–February 10, 2008

Hugo
January 15, 1995–January 11, 2009

SUMMER
of TWO
WISHES

1

The first time two U.S. Army Casualty Notification Officers came looking for Macy, it was to tell her that her husband Finn had died in Afghanistan.

Suicide bomber, the taller officer said. Nothing left but a half-burned dog tag.

Macy didn't remember much after that, except that she had been getting groceries out of the car when they'd arrived, and the taller officer's eyes were the exact shade of the head of iceberg lettuce that had rolled away when she'd dropped the bag.

Three years later, when the third Casualty Notification Officer came to see Macy, she would remember Finn's black lab, Milo, racing in between the tables they'd set up on the lawn, pausing to shake the river water from his coat and spraying the pristine white linen tablecloths. She'd remember thinking, *Don't panic, don't panic*, over and over again as she stared at those dirty brown spots on the tablecloths.

Everything else would be a blur.

The officer found Macy at her Aunt Laru's limestone ranch house just outside of Cedar Springs, in the Texas

Hill Country west of Austin. It was a beautiful spread, forty acres of rolling hills covered in live oaks, cedar, and blooming cactus on the banks of the Pedernales River.

Laru Friedenberg had married and divorced three times before the age of forty-five. The marriages had left her a little bit jaded and a little bit wealthy, and when Laru had learned Macy was hosting a luncheon, she'd insisted that Macy host it at her house. The luncheon was a fundraiser to benefit a nonprofit organization, Project Lifeline. Macy and a friend had founded the charity to help families of soldiers who'd been wounded or killed with financial aid or services. The organization was a success thus far, and Laru was eager to help.

"I didn't put up with Randy King for six years to sit and look at this view by myself," Laru had said with a flip of her strawberry-blonde hair over her shoulder. "Have the luncheon here, Macy. A pretty setting and plenty of liquor will open up those wallets faster than the devil in a white suit."

As it was June and not yet miserably hot, Macy had decided to have it on the grassy riverbank and had set up three large round tables beneath the twisted limbs of the live oaks. She'd dressed the tables in linen, littered them with rose petals and rose centerpieces, and set them with fine china from Laru's second marriage. She'd enlisted Laru to make batches of her signature white and red sangria, and had food catered from Twin Sisters, which specialized in "discriminating palates."

"If by *discriminating* they refer to gals who won't pass over a single morsel that isn't nailed down, then

I think we've got the right caterer," Laru had quipped.

The day was overcast and a slight breeze was coming up off the river. An hour before the guests were due to arrive, Laru insisted on tightening the halter of the pink sundress Macy had found on sale for the occasion. "You look so cute!" she said at last, her hands on her waist. "Very hostessy. Has Wyatt seen you in that?"

"Not yet," Macy said as she donned the pearl earrings and necklace he'd given her. He was always giving her gifts: Pearls. An iPhone. A boat.

"Best make sure he doesn't see you until after the luncheon. He's likely to tear it right off your body."

"Laru!" Macy said with a laugh.

"What?" Laru asked innocently. "It's no secret that every time that man looks at you his eyes get as shiny as new pennies."

"Well, he's not invited. It's ladies only. *Rich* ladies, and as we both know, that's not his type," Macy said, pointing at herself and making Laru laugh. "Besides, he's in San Antonio for a couple of days."

Satisfied with her appearance, Macy walked outside to check on everything once more. Ernesto, Laru's handyman, was out front, sweeping the flagstone porch. "If you see a bunch of women in fancy hats, send them on around, will you?" she asked, indicating the walkway around the side of the house. "*Gracias!*"

Macy followed the path around the corner of the house. Laru was right—the setting was truly lovely, and her tables looked perfect. But as Macy stood there admiring her work, Milo shot past.

"Hey," Macy muttered. Milo was not the sort of dog to run. Generally, he was much happier lying in the shade. But when he emerged from between the tables, she saw that he had a grungy rope toy in his mouth. Out from beneath another table shot a beagle in hot pursuit.

"Hey!" Macy shouted as Milo headed for the river. "Milo, *no!*" she cried. But Milo dove heedlessly into the river, paddled around, then climbed up on the bank, taunted the beagle with his toy, and dashed up to the tables, where he paused to shake the water off his coat.

"No!" Macy cried again.

The beagle barked, and Milo was off again.

"Macy Clark?"

Startled by the sound of a male voice, Macy whirled around and came face-to-face with an army officer in full dress uniform. Her heart skipped a beat. What was he doing here? Finn was dead. Dead for three long, miserable years. Three years in which Macy woke up every morning to face the heartache of his absence all over again, missing her sun and moon, realizing that it wasn't a bad dream, that he wasn't going to come through the door with his tanned arms and his straw hat pulled low over his eyes, grinning like he wanted her with syrup for breakfast.

"Beg your pardon, ma'am—I am Lieutenant Colonel Dan Freeman with the United States Army," he said. The bags under his eyes made him look like a sad old hound dog. "I need to speak with you, please."

"Me?" she asked as Milo and the beagle dashed in

between them. "Is it the fund-raiser?" she said, thinking wildly that perhaps the army didn't approve. "It's the fund-raiser, isn't it?"

"The fund-raiser?"

"Project Lifeline," she said. "My friend Samantha and I—we wanted to help the families of fallen soldiers because they really need more than just the death gratuity. Not that the gratuity isn't generous. It is! But there is all this . . . this emotional stuff that money can't fix. So we started Project Lifeline. That's okay, isn't it? Surely *that's* okay."

What was she saying? She didn't need the army's permission! Macy was rambling, which wasn't like her at all, but there was something about the officer's demeanor, his blank look, that made her anxious. "You've never heard of us, have you?"

He shook his head. "No, ma'am."

Macy swallowed down a very bad feeling.

A barking dog and the sound of a car's wheels crunching on the gravel drive in front filtered into her consciousness. Someone shouted, "Bad dog!"

"What is it?" Macy asked softly. "What has happened?"

"Would you like to sit down?" he asked.

Now Macy's belly swooned. "Sir . . . I am about to host a fund-raiser."

"It can't wait, ma'am," he said, and smiled. "Maybe we can sit at one of those tables."

"How did you find me?" she asked, ignoring his gesture toward her tables.

"Your neighbor told me you were here and was kind enough to give me directions."

"Okay," she said resolutely, despite the rubbery feeling in her legs. "Okay, Lieutenant Colonel Freeman, you can't tell me anything worse than what the army has already told me, right? So please, whatever it is, just say it."

"Yes, ma'am," Lieutenant Colonel Freeman said. He kept his hound-dog eyes steady on her as he reached into his coat pocket, took out an envelope, and held it out to her.

Her heart pounding, Macy stared at it. She didn't want to touch that envelope. It was impossible that it could contain anything that had to do with her— *Finn is dead! He's dead, he's dead!* The officer shifted slightly, moving the envelope closer to her, and Macy reluctantly took it. Her hands were shaking so badly she could hardly open it; the envelope fluttered to the ground as she unfolded the letter.

"Ma'am, if I may," the officer said. "The secretary of defense regrets to inform you that we have made a gross error in concluding Sergeant Finn Lockhart was killed in action because he has indeed been found alive. On June eighteen, at oh two hundred hours . . ."

Macy never heard the rest of what he said. She couldn't breathe, she couldn't speak, and everything began to swirl around her. The last thing Macy saw was Lt. Colonel Dan Freeman lurching forward to catch her as she melted.

2

Everything after that was a chaotic blur. There were colorful hats bobbing around her, ladies tittering at the news—*Macy Clark's husband is alive!*

Macy clung to Laru. In the chaos, she couldn't seem to grasp that it was real. *They'd said he was dead.* The army had rolled right up to her house in their official car, with their official officers, with their official news, and their official death gratuity, as if they were tipping her for having given her husband's life to the war. They'd told her he was dead while Finn's horses grazed in the pasture beside them, while Milo sniffed at the officers' shoes. They'd said he was dead. It was so final; he was dead, dead, dead, dead, dead.

And now, three years later, this man was telling her Finn was alive. *Alive.* The love of her life, alive! Not dead. Not in heaven as the pastor had assured her. *Alive!*

Macy wanted to know where Finn was; when could she see him; was he hurt; why, if he'd been rescued on the eighteenth, was she only hearing about it four days later; where had he been for three years; *when could she see him, when could she see him, when could she see him?*

It was a dream. It had to be a dream. How could it be real? After three years of mourning, how could it be real?

Someone thrust a glass of sangria into her hand. Macy put it down. Lt. Colonel Dan Freeman explained they waited to contact her until they verified Finn's identity. He said Finn had been held captive by the Taliban (to which there was a loud and collective gasp) and had escaped. He said Finn was on his way to Germany, where he would undergo a complete physical evaluation and intelligence debriefing before returning to the States. He said Macy could speak to Finn as soon as he reached the air force base in Germany.

"Dear God, what will Wyatt Clark say to all this?" Mrs. Corley asked of no one in particular.

Macy had been so absorbed with the news that Finn, *her* Finn, was alive, not dead, not gone, that she'd momentarily forgotten about Wyatt. "Does he know?" she asked Lieutenant Colonel Freeman. "Does Finn know about my husband?"

"Ma'am, we think those matters are best left to the family, but we have trained personnel if you'd like for the army to tell him—"

"No," she said quickly. "No, no, I'll tell him."

"There are some things you should know, Mrs. Clark," Lieutenant Colonel Freeman said. "Some laws you should be aware of."

Some laws. What laws? Why did she need laws? She didn't need anything but to see Finn. *When could she see him?*

There were laws, her mother told her later; she'd already looked into it.

It was just like her mother to take charge right away. Jillian Harper, Esquire, was the toughest civil litigator in the county, and if you didn't know that, she'd be sure to fill you in. She was tough, all right, and had even proven to be too tough for Macy's dad.

Jillian and Bobby had met in high school—Jillian was in drama club and on the student council, and Bobby was on the basketball team. Macy and her sister Emma often wondered what Jillian and Bobby had seen in each other, because it was all gone by the time they came along. Their parents fought and bickered their way through their children's early years. Bobby Harper was a land developer. He had some good years and some bad years. In the bad years, Jillian told him how she'd seen this coming and how he was going to have to do things differently. In the good years, Bobby believed money should be spent and he didn't see anything wrong with rewarding himself with a new car, or a family trip to Spain. He argued there was plenty of time to save for college.

There was never any peace in the Harper house and the Harpers divorced when Macy was twelve and Emma was ten. Macy and Emma didn't see much of their father after that except at birthdays and the holiday visitations spelled out in the divorce papers. Their father always seemed to have more important things to do than spend time with them. Their mother told them he was too selfish. Their father told them she was too hard.

Bobby had moved to Dallas a few years ago and Macy didn't hear from him much, except when he came back to Cedar Springs to see friends and family. Even then, their meetings were brief and superficial. He usually dragged them along to some dinner or party . . . someplace he didn't have to really talk to them.

In his absence, Macy's mother tried to run her and Emma's lives.

It seemed like her mother had hardly absorbed the news that Finn was alive before she'd called a friend who specialized in family law. Then she'd come to Laru's, fearing that Macy would not be able to drive after hearing such stunning news.

"You need to understand what this all means," her mother said as she drove Macy home.

"Mom," Macy said, closing her eyes, "can we . . . can we just celebrate the fact that Finn is alive? That's the only thing I care about at the moment. Can you believe it? After all this time, he's alive!"

"Yes, it's . . . it's unreal," Jillian said. "But the moment Wyatt gets wind of it, he'll want to know what his legal rights are. It comes down to this, Macy. You have what is called a putative marriage, which means essentially that you entered your marriage believing the first one was dissolved by death. Now, as your first marriage was *not* dissolved by death or appropriate legal action, your second marriage is essentially void. Practically speaking, that means you must file suit to declare your current marriage void. However, if you want to stay with Wyatt, then you must file suit to divorce Finn. When the divorce is granted, your marriage to Wyatt is automatically validated as long as you continue to live as man and wife and represent yourself as such."

"*What?*" Macy said, her mind reeling. Divorce? Voided marriages?

"I am saying it is up to you," Jillian said. "You need to understand that, Macy. Ultimately, *you* have to decide which marriage you want to keep and act accordingly. Do you want my advice?"

Macy didn't. She looked out the car window, still trying to absorb the fact that Finn was alive. Lieutenant Colonel Freeman had left Laru's to drive out to Finn's parents' ranch and tell them the stunning news. She could imagine Finn's mother on the floor right about now. "I should call Rick and Karen," she said, ignoring her mother's question.

"Don't you do anything until you have thought this through!" Jillian said sharply. "You know the first thing Karen is going to ask is if you are still married to Finn."

Finn. Her Finn, her heart's greatest love.

They turned onto a county road and flew past the old Rooster Dance Hall. It was one of the oldest surviving dance halls in Texas, and it was packed every Thursday, Friday, and Saturday night. For the last three years, Macy had avoided driving on this road, but today, her heart skipped at the sight of the Rooster.

It was where Finn had proposed to Macy.

She'd never forget that night. It was late July, and

the air had been so hot and sticky that her blue cotton dress had clung to her. She'd worn cowboy boots and a red cowboy hat, which Finn had teased her about. "You need a little red wagon and a six-shooter," he'd said. Finn had worn jeans, a white shirt, and his good black cowboy hat. Macy smiled dreamily at the memory. There was nothing quite as sexy as a cowboy.

The dance floor was partially covered and partially exposed to the elements. Outdoor lights were strung through the trees, and little lanterns hung every six feet. Finn and Macy had danced outside with the hope they'd be cooled by a breeze that never came until Macy had begged for a beer.

But before they'd walked off the dance floor, the band had struck up a slow waltz. "One more," Finn had said, and had taken her in his arms, had begun to move languidly, humming in her ear. He'd whispered, "You know I love you."

"Mmm . . . I love you, too," Macy had said, and dropped her head back to look at the lights as Finn spun her around.

Finn had pressed his mouth to the hollow of her throat and said, "Macy . . . come to the ranch with me."

"Tonight?"

"Tonight and every night. Come to the ranch and be my wife."

Macy had jerked her head up, surprised he'd said it, fearful he was teasing her. "What did you say?"

He'd grinned in that charmingly lopsided way he had. "I said, marry me, baby."

Macy was speechless. She hadn't expected it. They'd dated eight months, and he'd never given her any hint . . . but this was the one thing she'd hoped for, the one thing she wanted above all else. She loved him so much, more than she'd ever loved anything or anyone.

Her silence caused Finn to stop in the middle of the dance floor. "I don't have all the right words," he'd said, his smile fading. "But I love you. I want to be with you now and forever, and I hope like hell you want the same thing. Macy Harper . . ." He'd stepped back, bent down on one knee, and put his hand in his pocket. "Will you marry me?" he'd asked, and produced a ring.

As they sped past the Rooster, Macy closed her eyes. *He was alive.* That beautiful, sexy cowboy who had proposed to her right in the middle of the dance floor was *alive*, and her heart soared with jubilation.

"Macy, did you hear what I said?" her mother asked, poking her and nudging her back to the present.

"What?"

"We'll need to review this with Wyatt."

Macy closed her eyes again. *Wyatt. Oh God, poor Wyatt.* Wyatt was her husband, her rock. He was the one who had lifted her up from the darkness after Finn was gone. She'd been drifting aimlessly for over a year when she met Wyatt, and he'd infused light into her life again. She loved him.

She loved *two* men. She loved two husbands.

3

Macy had always wanted to go to Washington, D.C., but she didn't even notice the Washington monument as they descended to Ronald Reagan Airport three days later. Her sister Emma had to remind her twice to look out the window.

She and her family were greeted by a pair of servicemen who put them into cars and escorted them to a hotel in Washington, via Constitution Avenue. They drove past a monument. The Lincoln Memorial, Macy thought, but she was too scattered to really look. She couldn't stop thinking about Finn, about what he'd endured.

The next morning, they were driven out to Andrews Air Force Base to greet Finn's plane.

The room in which they were asked to wait was the color of putty—the walls, the floor, the caulking around the three windows that overlooked a parking lot. It seemed to Macy to be too drab for an occasion as glorious and stupendous as this. It was the only thought that seemed to register in her fogged brain. That, and the panicky sensation of not being able to breathe.

Can't breathe. Can't breathe.

She and her family sat at a long, highly polished table in faux-leather chairs. Macy focused on the portraits on the wall. There was the president in the middle, flanked by military personnel she did not recognize. She shifted her gaze to the window, wishing someone would open it, but no one else seemed to notice the lack of air. They were all too excited, too happy, too nervous. None of them could contain their impatience.

Finn's parents, Rick and Karen Lockhart, sat on Macy's right. Karen clutched the small gold cross she'd worn since Finn had joined the army, and her new dress and matching jacket rustled with her fidgeting. Macy looked down at her clothing—a new print skirt and sweater set, courtesy of Laru. She also wore a necklace of tiny seed pearls that Finn had given her for her twenty-second birthday the first year they were married. On Macy's left were her mother and Emma. There had been quite a discussion at home about who would come with Macy, and they had collectively decided that given the circumstances, the fewer companions, the better.

Jillian smiled at her now and rubbed her shoulder. *"Relax,"* she said.

Macy wished Laru had come instead of her mother. Her mom meant well, and Macy envied her ability to take traumatic surprises in stride. But her mother kept watching Macy expectantly, as if she believed Macy would collapse at any moment.

What really annoyed Macy was that she did indeed feel on the verge of collapsing.

Don't crumble.

She twisted her wedding ring around her finger and bounced one leg nervously. The army said Finn had been a war prisoner, a true hero who'd managed to stay alive and escape by sheer will and cunning. He was coming home today. *He was coming back to her.*

Breathe in. Breathe out.

"I just keep trying to imagine what he's been through," Karen said.

Macy did, too.

"I think of my baby over there by himself with those awful people, scared and . . . and *alone*." She shook her head and squeezed her eyes shut.

"I don't understand how the goddam army could have screwed this up," Finn's father said gruffly. He sat with his legs stretched long beneath the table, his beefy arms folded over his chest and exposed from the elbows down by his short-sleeved western shirt. After years of working the Lockhart ranch, his arms looked like tanned leather.

The Lockharts had been ranching in the Hill Country for more than one hundred years. There were three pieces in all: Finn's ranch, bought from his brothers Luke and Brodie after their grandfather had left it to the three of them; the Lockhart homestead, on which Rick still ran cattle; and Uncle Braden's piece, the largest of the three, about an hour away, south of Austin.

"They were so sure he was dead," Rick continued angrily. "Did they even *look* for him?" He made a sound of disgust. "Well, I guess it hardly matters now, because my boy is coming home," he said, his voice catching.

They'd originally been told that the armored vehicle Finn had been riding in had been hit head-on by a suicide bomber. The fire had been so intense that the only thing they were able to recover was a charred dog tag. They'd confirmed Finn's death with DNA and had given that single tag to Macy. It was so badly burned that she couldn't make out anything but FINN R. Not even the LOCKHART.

Macy had buried that piece of tag. What else was she supposed to do with it? Hang it on her rearview mirror as a reminder of his brutal death?

"Have you heard from Brodie?" Jillian asked Karen, referring to Finn's brother, who'd flown to Ramstein Air Force Base in Germany, where they'd taken Finn to be debriefed and evaluated. Macy had talked to Finn several times, but their conversations had been short and filled with disbelief and wonder at hearing each other's voices.

"Not since yesterday," Karen said. "But he said Finn looks good and his spirits are great."

"Of course!" Jillian exclaimed. "He's coming home!"

"I *know*," Karen said, beaming. "I tell you, I can't believe it. But then again, I always had a feeling he was alive. I never told anyone because it just made me sound plum crazy, but I just had this *feeling*, you know?" she asked, pressing her fist to her heart. She looked heavenward. "Thank you, Jesus!"

"Did Brodie talk to Finn about . . . about all that's happened since he's been gone?" Macy's mother could not let it go, couldn't just let things unfold.

"No," Karen said, her eyes going cold. "He said there were too many things going on." Her gaze skimmed over Macy, then shifted to the window. Conversation over.

Breathe in. Breathe out.

The door opened softly; all of them turned expectantly to the officer who stepped inside. He was a thin young man wearing a neatly pressed uniform. His shirt was tucked as smoothly into a pair of pants as Macy had ever seen. He'd said his name, but Macy couldn't recall it now.

"The transport is on approach," he said. "We can move to the tarmac to greet Sergeant Lockhart. Will you follow me, please?"

He's here! Macy's palms were suddenly damp, and again, she had that awful feeling that she couldn't draw enough air into her lungs.

"I tell you, I am so excited I don't know if these old legs will hold me," Karen said with a nervous laugh.

Macy's legs felt like jelly, too. Emma caught her by the elbow and hauled her up, then straightened Macy's new skirt. She smiled happily. "You look pretty, Macy," she whispered. "Really pretty. He's going to die when he sees you." She paused. "You know what I mean."

Macy nodded. She wondered what Finn looked like. She'd seen a picture of him taken shortly after Coalition forces had brought him in. His hair was long and wavy, his face covered with a heavy beard. Another photo was taken in a hospital bed in Germany. In that one, he was smiling, his hair cut stylishly, the beard gone. His face was darker than when he'd left, like he'd been off on vacation, sunning himself. But there was a scar just below his eye that ran up and disappeared into his hairline, a reminder that he wasn't the same as when he'd left.

"Rick, you're going to have to help me," Karen said breathlessly. "My heart is racing."

They walked single file onto the tarmac, to an area that had been cordoned off. For dignitaries, the neatly dressed officer said. There were a half dozen men standing there, all of them with ribbons and medals on their chests. They each smiled and clasped Macy's hand in theirs. "This a joyous day," one said. "We are honored to be able to bring you such good news," another said. They didn't seem to realize that they'd ruined her life by giving her the wrong news three years ago.

A plane appeared in the far distance, and the neatly dressed officer held up his hands. "Excuse me!" he said briskly to everyone. "Let's have Sergeant Lockhart's wife and parents up front, please."

Another distant memory—on the day they'd buried a box in the ground containing Finn's charred dog tag, his favorite saddle, the tiled paw print of a dog who had been his faithful companion for sixteen years, and a Texas Longhorns baseball hat, someone had said the same thing. *Let's have the wife and the parents up front,*

like they were little chess pieces that should be properly
arranged.

Karen was the first to reach the thick red rope that
held them back from the tarmac. Rick put his arm
around Macy and pulled her up to stand with them.
Someone pointed up; Macy's eyes were riveted on the
plane as it slowly drifted down to touch the runway.

Breathe. Breathe.

It seemed to take an eternity for the plane to land
and to turn around and taxi back to where they stood. It
seemed to take another eternity for them to wheel the
stairs to the door, for the door to open. An eternity in
which Macy's breath was coming in painful gasps. This
was real. This was happening. Finn was coming home.

Two soldiers were the first off the plane, followed by
Brodie. Macy held her breath; her stomach clenched
and her fingernails, curled into tight fists, cut into her
palm. Another eternity, the second longest moment
of her life, and Finn appeared, dipping his head as he
stepped through the portal. He paused on the top step
of the Jetway and looked directly at her.

It was Finn. It was really, truly, Finn. He looked
leaner, more muscular than when he'd left for Afghanistan. He was wearing a dark blue coat and light blue
trousers, the army's full dress uniform, but Macy could
see the golden-brown hair beneath his cap, the strong
chin, his large hands, the palms callused from years of
training cutting horses. But mostly, she could see the familiar squint of his copper-brown eyes beneath the polished brim of his dress hat, and the slight hint of a smile.

Macy heard Karen burst into sobs, heard the rumble of a keening cry of relief in Rick's chest. Something snapped; something raw and primal rose up in her, choking the little bit of air she'd been able to hold in her lungs since the news of Finn's survival had snatched the breath from her. Macy didn't realize she had ducked beneath the velvet rope until the neatly dressed officer shouted for her to wait. But there was nothing that would stop her from reaching Finn now. She was running, her skirt flying around her knees.

Finn moved, too, pushing past Brodie and flying down the steps to the tarmac. He didn't look at the brass who had gathered at the bottom of the steps to welcome him home. He didn't look anywhere but at Macy.

She leapt at the very moment he opened his arms. She threw her arms around him and buried her face in his neck. "Finn! Finn, Finn, I missed you! Oh my God, I love you, I love you so much, I've missed you so much!"

"God, Macy," Finn breathed, cradling her head, his face in her hair, inhaling deeply. "I thought I'd never see you again," he said, his voice breaking. "I can't believe I'm holding you. You kept me going, baby. I kept thinking of you; you're the only thing that kept me going. I'll never let you go; I'll never leave you again."

The tears that had been lost inside Macy for the last few days suddenly erupted—they began to stream down her face and she sobbed into his collar, clinging to him. "They told me you were dead! They said you were dead, Finn, you're supposed to be dead!"

"I know, I know," he said, trying to soothe her. "But I'm not dead, Macy. I'm very much alive and I've come home to you, just like I promised you I would."

She clung to him, savoring the feel of his body against hers, the strength of his arms around her. How many sleepless nights had she lain awake, aching to feel this once more?

"Don't cry, baby," he said. "Don't cry. It's all okay. We're going to be fine; we're going to pick up where we left off."

That only made her cry harder.

4

When a soldier is held captive by enemy forces for nearly three years, he thinks a lot about death. In the beginning, during those excruciatingly long and uncertain days, he thinks, *I can't die this way*. He thinks of his wife and his family, of how frantic they must be that he's been lost. He thinks of his buddies, who are looking for him. He thinks of his future, of the things he wants to do with his life, of the kids he hasn't had, and he thinks, *I can't die this way. I can't die this way.*

He remembers his training—*survive, evade, resist, escape*. He uses whatever means he can to assess his situation, to remain calm, to give up nothing, no matter how much it hurts.

But when the soldier begins to understand that no one is looking for him, that they must believe he is dead because they'd never leave him behind, he prays for death. *Please, God, let me die*. He might even refuse to eat in the hope that he will die, but he will discover that hunger is a powerful beast, and eventually, he will eat.

At some point after that, the soldier begins to believe that he *must* live, that God must have a reason for this hell on earth, that there must be a higher purpose. Why else would he still be alive? Why would the enemy hold him day in and day out, moving him from one hovel to the next? There has to be a reason, and if he just hangs on, he'll discover it.

He eats; he tries to build his strength when and where he can. He is constantly looking for an opportunity to escape. It is his only hope.

He hangs by a thread connecting him to the memory of who he is, and to his wife, his one and only love, the one thing in this hell that keeps the desire to live burning in him. He thinks about her often: what she is wearing, her smile, how her gold hair swings around her shoulders. He thinks about what she is doing, and imagines her unconsciously fluttering her fingers in that way she does when she's engrossed in something. He thinks about the intimate moments, how her skin glistens, soft and fragrant, and how her body feels when she wraps her legs around him and her fingers scrape down his back.

He dreams of her through endless days and nights spent on an earthen floor, shivering in bitter cold or sweltering in brutal heat, chained like a dog. There are times, when he is lying on the woven mat staring out the bleak window at a bleaker sky, that he imagines touching her hair and thinks he can feel it on his fingers. He can smell her scent. He can hear her voice whispering in his ear.

And he thinks, *I can't die this way.*

The reunion with Macy and his family was happening so fast, too fast—the next thing Finn knew, he was in a room, waiting to meet more television and print reporters. He didn't give a damn about the press or military brass or anything else but being with Macy. She was sitting beside him, her hand in his, the warmth of it penetrating the fog around him. Finn wanted nothing more than to make love to her, right now, to connect with her in a way he desperately needed to connect . . .

But he was trapped by ceremony and duty and expectations that felt overwhelming, making him feel heavy and fatigued and numb.

The army had tried to prepare Finn for his homecoming, but he was not prepared for all the emotions that had begun to stew in him like a bowl of bad *shorwa*. He was glad to see his family, of course he was, but they all watched him so closely, like they thought he might disappear if they blinked. And his mother hadn't stopped crying.

Finn needed a little bit of space to decompress. He needed time alone with Macy, just an hour or two. Just enough time to find his bearings, to put his face in her hair again, to feel her body next to his.

So far, all they'd done was parade him in front of the press corps where Finn had answered a few questions precisely as he'd been told to answer them. *I am so glad to be home. My first meal is going to be a steak. I was lucky to escape and find the Coalition forces.*

Now he waited in this room, feeling like he was going to crawl out of his skin, surrounded by people who couldn't possibly comprehend all he'd been through. They were laughing and smiling and talking of home, of people he couldn't remember, of a town that seemed a universe away from where he was. But when Finn tried to ask about his ranch and his horses, no one really answered him. They asked questions about what had happened to him in Afghanistan.

That was not something Finn wanted to discuss. That was not something he *could* discuss. He'd been in hell for three years and he'd escaped, and once he'd understood he was truly free, he did not want to look back or think of Afghanistan ever again.

He'd given his family only a terse account of his life in Afghanistan. He didn't know about the bombing other than what he'd been told, for he didn't remember anything but riding in the armored Scout vehicle and horsing around with Danny Ortega, singing a stupid country song. The next thing Finn remembered was waking up in a hospital with a dirty sheet over his naked body and realizing his wounds had been tended to. Danny was gone—no one had to tell Finn that, he just knew. No one—including him—should have survived that blast.

After several hours—maybe days—of lying in that room, of being questioned endlessly by a man whose English made no sense, Finn was taken to a dirt hovel and, for all he knew, left to die.

There was more, so much more that he couldn't bring himself to tell anyone in this sterile room.

"I bet you want some good ol' American food, huh?" his father said, his eyes a little misty. That was all Rick Lockhart had to say to the few details Finn had related, but that was his dad. He hadn't changed a hair on his head since Finn last saw him. He wasn't one to show his emotions, and he'd raised Finn and his brothers Brodie and Luke to be the same way. "I'm gonna get you the biggest, juiciest steak I can find. What do you think about that?" he asked Finn.

What Finn thought was that there had come a point when he'd stopped thinking about the kind of food he missed and thought of nothing but freedom. Honestly, he'd eat dirt as long as it was American dirt. "That would be great, Dad," he said. "How are the horses?" he asked, trying to change the subject.

His father hesitated. "They're horses. They're fine," he said with a shrug.

"How many calves did we have this year?"

Now his father looked at him blankly. "Didn't count. Not many. We had a pretty good drought that didn't break 'til fall and I ended up selling about twenty head.

Brodie says you only got a few scars from the bombing."

"Yeah, a few." Finn guessed that the army had given his family the same song and dance they'd given him about post-traumatic stress. He'd figured it out when Brodie wouldn't say much about home, and he'd seen the pamphlet on Post Traumatic Stress Disorder sticking out of Brodie's bag. *Go easy; don't say anything to set him off*, they probably warned him. That's why they were treating him with kid gloves—they were afraid to say or do anything that might upset his apple cart.

They couldn't be more wrong about that—he was too grateful to be free to have PTSD. There was nothing wrong with him, other than a voracious need to be with his wife. There was nothing that was going to set him off.

Except maybe Macy's cell phone.

It seemed to buzz every five minutes. She'd glance at the number and toss it back in her bag, and then smile so warmly, so gratefully, that he would feel a little more human. She'd answered the phone only once, when they were waiting to meet the press corps. She'd let go of his hand—pried her fingers free, really—and had taken the call out in the hall. When she returned, she smiled at him, took his hand again, and said, "Everyone in Cedar Springs is anxious to know when you're coming home."

Just when Finn was thinking he couldn't take the waiting any longer and was idly contemplating putting his chair through the window, Major Sanderson, Finn's handler, suddenly bustled into the room. "All right then, the bus is en route. We'll be on our way in half an hour," he crisply informed them, as if he were conducting a tour. He passed around a sheet of paper to everyone. "Please review this sheet and let me know if you have any questions." He briskly went out.

Finn glanced at the paper. *The Return: Handling the Media.*

Macy gently squeezed his hand, and Finn smiled at her. God, but she was pretty. Texas pretty. The kind of pretty that wasn't afraid of life. A whole lot prettier than he'd remembered, in all honesty, with big blue eyes the color of a summer sky, hair the color of raw honey. Jesus, he wanted to touch her, to kiss her, to feel her beneath him.

The door swung open and Sanderson swept in again, this time carrying a clipboard. "If everyone could turn his or her attention to the paper I handed out? Let's review . . ."

Every word the major said seemed to float down some long tunnel away from Finn. He was aware of only Macy beside him, of her hand in his, of the tension in her body. He didn't know if he should be thankful he still knew her body almost as well as his own, or apprehensive that she was so tense.

"Any questions?" Sanderson asked.

"Yes," said Rick. "When can we feed this boy?"

Everyone laughed except Finn.

"Sergeant Lockhart has a round of interviews tomorrow, a list of which you will find at the bottom of this sheet of paper. I would like to remind you all that we want to keep these interviews as positive as possible."

"A *round* of interviews?" Macy asked uncertainly.

"Yes. We'll start with *Good Morning America*, and then the *Today* show. After that, we have a *Nightline* taping, and then *Dateline*." Major Sanderson smiled. "We have to keep all the networks happy. There is some talk of an interview with CNN and Larry King, but the details have not been worked out."

Finn blanched. What about his life? His ranch, his horses, his dogs? When did he get back to *that*?

"Wait," Macy said, holding up a slender hand. A diamond tennis bracelet twinkled on her wrist. "You said he was going home after the press briefing. You said he was going home right away."

"We have just a few more press obligations. The current administration puts a high value on our openness with the media. I know you're all anxious to get Sergeant Lockhart home just as soon as possible, but we need to spend a day or two here. Trust me, if we handle it here, chances are you won't be swarmed in Texas. All right then, everyone, if you are ready? The bus is outside, if you will follow Corporal James," he said, indicating a soldier over his right shoulder.

"All of us?" Jillian asked, looking at Macy. "Finn, too?"

"Yes, Sergeant Lockhart, too."

That was the best news Finn had heard all day. He stood up. His mom did, too, and linked her arm through his, pulling him away from Macy. Finn glanced back at Macy and saw anxiety in her eyes. He wondered if this is what Dr. Albright, the shrink who'd talked to him in Germany, had meant when she'd said things would seem strange at first, because Finn was starting to feel like something was a little off. Maybe he was just tired. It had been a long flight home, a long time with the press. He just wanted this day to end, to get out of here and try to get back some of the time he'd lost with Macy.

On the bus, Emma produced a bottle of champagne and some plastic cups. Strange, Finn thought as they toasted his survival, he would have killed for a sip of champagne only a month ago. Now, he didn't want it. He smiled as they toasted him and sipped from the cup. Macy, he noticed, was clutching her cup. She was smiling and laughing along with everyone else, but there was something not quite right in her eyes.

At the hotel, they all stood awkwardly in the lobby for a few minutes until Brodie announced he would get them all a dinner reservation somewhere. Corporal James offered to assist and the two of them went off to speak with the concierge. The rest of them stood looking expectantly at Finn until Macy put her hand in his. "Well! If everyone will excuse us, Finn and I have a lot of catching up to do."

Finn's mother pressed her lips together.

"Come on, Finn," Macy said with a bright smile as she tugged his hand. "Let's go."

Finn grinned at the rest of them. "Later," he said with a wink. This was the moment he'd been waiting for, the moment he would be reunited with his wife.

They rode up the elevator to the fifteenth floor. Macy marched down the corridor, pulling him along. She opened the door to room 1513; Finn held the door open so she could enter first, then locked the door behind them.

Neither of them spoke for a moment. Finn put his palm against her cheek. "I would have sworn you couldn't be any prettier than you were in my mind, but damn it if you're not."

Her lashes flickered. "God, Finn . . ." She put her hands on him, sliding them over his arms, his torso, her gaze following her hands.

Every stroke of her hands brought Finn a little more back to life. This is what he'd lived for. "Listen," he said softly, and reached for her hair, stroking it, letting it slide through his fingers, "there is so much to say and I don't know where to begin. This must seem as surreal to you as it does to me, and I'm sure they probably gave you the speech about not knowing what to expect. I don't either, baby. I just know that I'm home, and I've missed you more than I can ever put into words. I've been gone a whole lot longer than I ever thought I'd be, but I'm still the same old Finn, and I still love you more than life."

Macy gazed up at him with wide blue eyes. She slipped her arm around his waist and pressed her cheek to his chest. "I still can't believe you're here."

She felt so good, so right in his arms. He caressed her face, pushed a strand of hair behind her ear. For so long, he'd woken up believing every morning was his last. But then the woman in the *chadari* veil would appear with his breakfast of flat bread, and he'd figure they wouldn't feed a dead man, and he'd start another day of waiting to see if he would stay alive.

When he thought of all those days, he couldn't seem to catch his breath. He'd made it. He was home. He'd survived. "I can't believe I'm here, either," he said breathlessly. His hands stroked the familiar curves of her body, stirring memories of their lovemaking.

"Why did it take so long?" Macy moaned. "Why didn't they find you? Why did they let me believe you were dead?"

"I'm not dead," he assured her. "I want to show you just how alive I am. God, how I've dreamed of this moment. I've dreamed of touching your skin," he said, his knuckles skimming her chest. "Of tasting you." He put his mouth to her neck. "Of making love to you," he murmured against her skin. Macy sighed and bent her head to one side to give him access.

Without lifting his head, he unbuttoned his coat and shrugged out of it, then took her hand and pressed it to his heart, just like he used to do. He'd crawl into bed when she was sleeping and put her hand against his heart. "*Finn?*" she'd say, and open her eyes and smile at him.

"Feel it beating? I'm here, Macy. I'm really here."

"Thank God," she whispered, and went up on her toes to kiss him.

Finn melted into that kiss and into his wife. She was just as he remembered her—the taste of her mouth, the feel of her lips on his, her body soft and slender against his. He held her tight and kissed her like the first time they'd ever kissed—deep and long.

The sensation flared through his body, lighting him up like a firebomb. He suddenly twirled Macy around and up against the wall. He pressed his mouth against her neck again and caught the scent of her perfume. He moved to the hollow of her throat, bit the pearls she was wearing, and moved again, to the swell of her breasts. He cupped one in his hand, the weight and size so familiar to him, and pushed against it with his palm.

"Jesus, Finn . . ." Macy's voice was shaking as he kneaded her breast through her clothing. She pushed her hands through his hair. "There is so . . . so much I want to say, but I . . ."

"It's okay," he murmured against her shoulder. He knew something wasn't quite right—something with the ranch, he guessed, since no one would talk about it. Before he'd joined the army, he was barely breaking even year-to-year. He figured Macy didn't know how to tell him how far in debt she was.

But that was the last thing on his mind; he slipped one arm around her waist and picked her up, holding her against him. She wrapped her arms around his neck and kissed him as he twisted around and bumped up against the bed. Macy's hands slid from his neck to his shoulders and she suddenly reared back, looking at him with the eyes he'd visualized one long month after another. They were glistening with tears. "Listen . . ." She bit her lip. "Finn, I . . . I—"

"Macy, whatever it is, it's okay," he said anxiously, and loosened his grip, letting her slide down his body to her feet. "We can talk about everything later. It's okay." Right now he just needed to be with her. Not talk. Not think.

"How . . . I mean, do you know?" she asked, looking confused.

"I know that a lot of stuff can happen in three years. Whatever it is, I don't care. The important thing is that we have each other." His gaze flicked over the length of her, and he shuddered deep inside. He pushed her sweater from her shoulders. "We'll start over," he said absently.

She squinted as if those words pained her, then made a sound like she was trying to catch her breath.

"*Macy . . .*" Finn gathered her in his arms again, kissing her eyes, the bridge of her nose. Her mouth. "Tell me we can start over," he whispered. "I need to hear you say it. Tell me that we can go back . . ."

With a sob, Macy threw her arms around his neck. A rush of emotion and desire overcame him, and with a groan, he picked her up and put her on her back on the bed. He came over her, pressed his palm against her face, his fingers spanning her jaw and neck. "Baby, you always did take my breath away," he said, his voice breaking, and when he kissed her again, he could feel her breath fill him, feel her body rise up to meet his.

His desire was overwhelming; he tried to hold himself back, but he could not hold her in his arms and not want to be inside her. It was a ravenous need, as strong as any hunger he'd felt in the last three years. Macy had always had the power to stoke him and he needed, with a desperation that surprised him, to feel as much of her as he could, to be as close to her as he could, if for no other reason than to assure himself that he was truly home where he belonged and with the one person on earth who mattered to him.

Finn's hand brushed her knee and slid up beneath the silky fabric of her skirt to the smooth, warm skin of her bare thigh. He deepened his kiss and slid his hand up higher still, his fingers brushing against her smooth panties, sliding over her pelvis and between her legs.

With a soft moan, Macy raked her fingers down his chest. Finn slipped his hand inside her panties. She was wet, and Finn's need was suddenly impossible to control. He started to fumble with his pants, trying to free himself. He lifted his head to look at his wife, his beautiful wife, and the years melted away. He was reminded of one summer night, after they'd been dancing. She'd been a little drunk, a little frisky, and she'd lain on their quilt-covered bed, completely naked, her hand loosely covering one breast. That night, she had looked at him with so much love that Finn honestly felt he could have lifted a mountain or two.

She was looking at him like that again, but there were tears in her eyes. She caught his wrist before he could free himself completely. "I can't," she whispered.

Finn did not move. He slid his hand into hers,

interlocking their fingers. His heart was racing and blood was rushing through him. "What is it, Macy?" he asked, trying to catch his breath. "Is it the ranch? Don't worry, I'm used to starting at the bottom and working my way up. Whatever happened, I've survived a whole lot worse."

"It's not the ranch. It's . . . it's mistakes and . . ." She closed her eyes.

Finn put his finger on her wedding ring. It was always sliding around her finger. He kissed her cheek, nibbled her ear. "What's the matter, baby? Is it the horses? Did you sell them?" he made himself ask. A champion cutting horse was worth tens of thousands of dollars. He hoped she'd gotten the right price. He kissed her neck at the point it curved into her shoulder.

"They told me you were dead."

"It's okay. We'll get more horses."

"It's *not* okay—"

"Macy, it's okay." He lifted his head and put his finger on her ring again, and through the haze of overwhelming desire, felt something odd. "None of that matters."

"They told me you were dead," she repeated softly. "They said they had DNA and everything."

The ring. That's what felt odd. Finn looked at it—

It wasn't his ring.

She was not wearing the ring he'd sold his pickup truck to buy. This ring was bigger, fancier. He suddenly sat up, jerking her hand closer, staring at that ring. "What is this?" he asked. Macy sat up and tried to take his hand, but he held hers tight, staring at that ring, trying to understand it. "Where is your wedding ring?"

"I . . . I thought you were dead, and I thought my heart was dead, and I don't know how I survived it, I really don't." She was speaking frantically now. "I hardly remember a thing after those first few days. Time sort of . . . it slipped away after your funeral. I was in a daze—I just remember trying so hard to think of things, like the way you smile, and the way you'd say my name, and how you cut the arms out of that very nice shirt because it was hot. I tried, Finn, I tried for a really long time to keep you with me, but bit by bit, you began to disappear, and then one day, I couldn't remember what your feet looked like. And then I couldn't remember your hands," she said, grabbing his hand and running her fingers over his knuckles. "And then, I . . . I woke up one day and realized that life had to go on, that I couldn't lie around all day trying to remember your hands, could I? I . . . what I am trying to tell you is that I . . . *shit*," she said helplessly, and lowered her head, choking on a sob. "I got married again."

Finn yanked his hand free of hers.

Her hands were shaking, and she started twisting that goddam ring, around and around.

"You remarried?" he asked, his voice sounding strange to him.

She responded with a sob.

As the realization slowly sank in, Finn felt something

twist painfully very deep within him. This could not be happening. He'd endured three years to come back to her—how in the hell could she not be *his*? "When?" he managed.

"Seven months ago."

Seven months ago, when he'd been shivering with cold that had seeped into his marrow, and was fighting the ever-present gnawing hunger, she'd remarried. "*Who?*" he forced himself to ask.

Macy averted her gaze. "Wyatt Clark," she muttered.

Wyatt Clark, Wyatt Clark. Finn knew the name, but he couldn't remember how.

"He's . . . he's the land broker," Macy said.

It suddenly came back, all in a stomach-churning flood of memories. Wyatt Clark had come around before Finn and Macy had married wanting to know if Finn was interested in selling his ranch. Macy had married *that* guy? She'd believed Finn was dead and had *married* that guy?

Finn reeled away from her, almost falling off the bed in his haste to get away. Three years roiled through him in one long, nauseating wave, making his knees dangerously weak.

Macy married. But not to him.

Strangely, of all the things he'd feared he'd find when he came home, that had never been one of them.

"Finn, listen—"

"I have to get out of here," he said thickly, shoving his shirttails into his pants.

"Finn, I love you—"

"*Don't*, Macy," he said sharply. "*Don't.*" He looked at the door and thought, *Survive, evade, resist, escape.*

He grabbed his coat and walked to the door, throwing open the bolt. Behind him, he heard Macy phoning Brodie.

5

Two days ago, Macy had flown off to Washington, D.C., and Wyatt Clark had come home and found TV crews sitting outside of Arbolago Hills, the gated community where he lived. They were there the next morning, too. So he'd decamped to his folks' place and hid there while they were off trailering.

The media attention infuriated him—he didn't like his life being exposed. He didn't like reporters showing up outside his office or house, shouting at him, asking him how he felt now that his wife's first husband had shown up alive. How did those vultures think he felt?

This morning, Wyatt was on his way to his house to pick up a few things when he spotted a couple of the rat bastards sitting outside the community gates. He quickly turned onto a side street and headed to his office instead.

Wyatt drove his white Dodge Ram down the two-lane road until he hit the main four-lane into town again. On his way, he drove past the guys who came up from the Valley and sold watermelons and cantaloupe out of the backs of sorry old pickups, and past the Cedar Springs water tower painted with a bucking colt, the high school mascot. He skirted through the alley behind Buck's Best Bar-b-que and the tractor supply store as a shortcut to Main Street.

When he emerged onto Main Street, he noticed the lumberyard was adding a whole new section, which he thought was good for Cedar Springs. The town had grown up around ranching and farm markets. But Austin was slowly encroaching on them—there was a Wal-Mart out on Highway 281 now, and a couple of old bait-and-tackle places on the Pedernales had been renovated into swanky tourist shops.

Some folks in town didn't like that Austin was sliding toward them, Wyatt thought as he drove past the Methodist, the Presbyterian, and the Baptist churches. Wyatt wasn't one of them. With the spread of civilization came new opportunities for development and construction. In fact, he had a couple of projects that depended on it.

At the park, Wyatt turned right. School was out for summer, but there was a line of yellow school buses on the northern end of the park and little kids were out playing soccer. Past the park, he entered the old part of town with the stately brick Victorians. He slowed down a little when he passed the Pinwheel House. The old man who lived there kept a dozen pinwheels in his yard. Every day he'd go out and rearrange them. Wyatt knew this because he and Macy had playfully staked him out a couple of times, determined to discover the reason for the pinwheels.

Just beyond Pinwheel House, Wyatt spied Mary Jo Hinckley puttering around her yard. He ducked his truck onto Eighth Street to avoid her. Seemed like Mary Jo won Yard of the Month every month because of her prized azaleas. But Wyatt knew those azaleas were really a cover for Mary Jo's nosiness. She spent all her time in the yard keeping an eye on Cedar Springs and its inhabitants and then wagged her tongue to everyone at church on Sunday.

He could just imagine what the scuttlebutt around church was these days. The return of the missing soldier was on every channel and everyone in town knew Wyatt's business. Wyatt didn't like that any more than his inability to get hold of Macy, which was making him crazy.

He'd tried four times this morning and all four calls had rolled into voice mail. So he'd called Macy's friend, Samantha, to see if she could get through.

"Aaah . . . I really think I need to stay out of it," Sam had said.

Out of what? Wyatt had wondered. He'd thought of whom else he could call. Macy's sister Emma had gone with her. There was Chloe, her cousin. He'd called Chloe. He could hear her twin toddlers shrieking in the background. Chloe had seemed a little put out with him, but said she'd try to call Macy.

Wyatt looked at his watch. That had been an hour ago. He picked up his cell phone and punched in her number again. When Chloe answered, he said, "Chloe, did you get through?"

"I just got off the phone this minute, Wyatt," Chloe said. "Yes, I got her. She said everything is fine and you shouldn't worry; they will all be home in a couple of days."

"That's it?" Wyatt asked, more than a little exasperated. "Everything is fine and they'll be home in a couple of days? Did she happen to mention why she won't answer her damn phone?"

"Wyatt, come on," Chloe said with a sigh. "You know they're doing all those TV shows. She's exhausted. She said she doesn't even have time to find a ladies' room. Just give her a little space. She said she would call you as soon as she can, but they are all coming home soon. I have to go. Chase and Caden are digging in my flower bed again."

All of them. That meant the soldier, too. Of course—where else would he go? Hollywood? Maybe someone would want to make a movie of his captivity and have him star in it.

Wyatt gritted his teeth and waved as he passed Dotty Givens out walking her dogs. He honestly didn't have anything against Lockhart, but he could not seem to shake the feeling of having been kicked in the teeth. A week ago, on a breezy summer night, he and Macy had made love on board their boat and he'd been the happiest man in all of Texas. Afterward, they'd lain looking up at the stars, her head pillowed on his arm, her leg draped over his, and Wyatt had tried to sing. *The stars at night are big and bright deep in the heart of Texas.*

Macy had squealed with laughter. "You sound like a coyote howling at the moon!"

"Is that your compassionate social worker training talking?" he'd asked.

"I haven't been a social worker in a long time. I'm rusty."

"Well, now you hurt my feelings. You better start working to make it up," he'd warned her.

She'd laughed. "Or what?"

"Or this," he'd said, tickling her as he sang.

They'd made love again, and Wyatt remembered thinking he'd never believed he could be so crazy in love as he was with Macy.

The very next day, his world had exploded into tiny little bits and had scattered between Amarillo and Mexico. He couldn't seem to find his bearings. And it didn't help that he couldn't talk to his wife.

Wyatt pulled up to the front of his office. He was glad to see the reporters had finally given up and gone away. He strode to the glass front door with CLARK RANCH PROPERTIES emblazoned across it and shoved it open so hard that it hit the stack of boxes behind it. His one and indispensable employee, Linda Gail Graeber, cried out with surprise, then gave him a withering look. She was on the phone, which was how she spent about ninety-five percent of her day.

"Sorry, Sandi," she said pertly. "Wyatt just kicked the

door down. As I was saying, I said to the guy, it says three nights and the fourth one is free. Nowhere on that sign, or in this store, does it say those nights must be consecutive."

Wyatt stalked to her desk. "Linda Gail."

Linda Gail glared at Wyatt. "Sandi, will you hold on a minute? Apparently Wyatt needs to speak to me right this very minute." She turned the receiver to her ample bosom and pressed it there at the same moment she picked up the mail. "I am on the phone, Wyatt," she said, thrusting the mail at him. "Here's what you need. The mail is in the same place I leave it every single day."

Wyatt glanced at the mail she'd just shoved into his hand. "No personal phone calls," he warned her, which earned him a dismissive roll of her eyes.

He walked into his office, clutching the mail he would not read, *could* not read since everything had come undone. He heard a sound and turned his head to the right—the little television he kept in the office to watch an occasional professional golf match was on, even though it was only a little past nine in the morning.

He scowled at the screen.

It was tuned to one of the morning news shows. The journalist—a national face whose name Wyatt could not recall at that moment—was talking to Finn Lockhart, the nation's newest and brightest hero.

Finn was in uniform, sitting with his big hands on his knees. Frankly, he didn't look too bad for a guy held by the Taliban for three years. He looked strong. Finn was a couple of inches taller than Wyatt, but those ranch boys were always tall and broad-shouldered.

Finn's hair was more gold than brown. Wyatt's hair was black. Finn had light brown eyes, while Wyatt's were blue. There was nothing similar between him and Finn, and Wyatt couldn't help but wonder what Macy thought when she looked at the two of them. Did she find him as attractive as the farm boy in uniform?

Macy suddenly entered the screen and sat on Finn's right. She slipped her hand into his. Wyatt grabbed the remote and turned up the volume.

The journalist was asking Finn about his escape. He told her in a flat way, like he'd said it one hundred times already, that after years of being chained, he was allowed an hour for exercise, and a careless mistake had given him the opportunity to escape: they forgot to lock the gate. He'd heard Coalition forces were nearby and had started running in that direction. He said he didn't expect to make it, that he expected to die.

The journalist then asked if there was a certain food he wanted to eat now that he was home. "Nah, I don't care," Finn said in a charming drawl. "Just as long as it's made in America," he added, and Macy smiled adoringly at him.

Wyatt felt sick. He held up the remote with the intention of turning it off when the journalist said, "I know that there must be many difficulties in reintegrating with your old life now, but can you tell us what you were feeling when you learned Macy had remarried?"

Wyatt's heart stopped. Macy's smile faded, and she looked at Finn. "Shocked," he said simply, looking at Macy.

"That must have been awful to learn after all that

time in captivity. Were you angry?" the journalist asked softly.

"*Jackass*," Wyatt muttered.

Finn shrugged a little. "Not angry. Just shocked. A lot can happen in three years."

"So where do you go from here, Macy?" the journalist asked, shifting his attention.

"She goes back to her husband, you jackass!" Wyatt shouted at the TV.

"Well, we'll . . . we'll just take it a day at a time," Macy said, looking at Finn. "Right now, we're all just celebrating the fact that Finn is alive and safe at home, where he belongs." She smiled. Finn did not.

"She has to say that, you know," Linda Gail said.

Wyatt jumped—he hadn't even heard her come in.

"If you think this stuff isn't scripted, then you don't know your government," she added as she tossed a couple of files into his inbox.

Wyatt turned off the TV. "I don't want to listen to that garbage in here," he said. "It's a waste of your valuable time."

"Oh, I can spare a few minutes to keep up with what's going on in the world," Linda Gail drawled, "especially when that world is calling here several times a day." She put her hands on her wide hips and watched Wyatt take his seat. "How are you holding up?"

"Me?" He did not look at her. "I'm fine. Just fine. Did the environmental report come in on the Bleecher property?"

"Fine." Linda Gail snorted. "You're so fine you

forgot that you looked at the Bleecher report yesterday. Well the offer still stands, Wyatt. Davis and I would love to have you over for dinner while Macy is away. I can't stand to think of you in that big house alone watching all this news coverage."

Wyatt knew all of Cedar Springs was buzzing about this. The local Austin TV stations and several national stations had been out to film their picturesque downtown. Wyatt's friend Randy Hawkins had told him that the new mayor, Nancy Keller, saw this as an opportunity to spruce the town up. She'd run on a platform of revitalization, and with all the national attention their little town was receiving, she'd managed to convince the city council to do a bit of landscaping around the square.

"That's the difference between you and me. I don't watch it," Wyatt lied. "I've got work to do, Linda Gail."

He opened one of the files she'd left for him.

"God forbid you actually accept a helping hand," Linda Gail sighed, and went out, shutting the door behind her and leaving him blessedly alone.

Wyatt tossed the file aside and removed his cell phone from his belt and glanced at it, hoping he'd missed a call. Maybe Macy had called before she'd gone on that program, but the truck had been so loud he hadn't heard it.

No missed calls.

He was trying to stay sane about this, but he was beginning to get a really bad feeling in his gut. He didn't even know how to *think* about any of this. He'd tried so hard to think straight that he hadn't slept at all since

Laru had called him that fateful afternoon and told him to get home. He'd raced back from San Antonio to find Macy on the deck of their house, her eyes as wide as moon pies and weird mud splatters on her pink dress. She'd looked like she'd seen a ghost. And then she'd told him.

How did a man go about handling that sort of news? He was a newlywed; he was building their life. He was embarking on a very large deal to build a destination resort and spa that would make them wealthy beyond their wildest dreams. He didn't need this. He needed Macy, and now he didn't even know what to expect when she came back from D.C. He couldn't talk about it to anyone—he hadn't even told his folks and hoped to heaven they hadn't seen it on the news while they were motoring across the country. He gathered they hadn't, as they hadn't called him. Wyatt knew he'd have to tell them sooner or later, but right now . . . right now he had this silly, childish hope that somehow, this would all go away. Macy would come home, and they'd go on just as they'd been before.

The one person he did vent to was his lawyer, Jack Zarkowski. He'd done that the moment he heard Lockhart was alive. When he'd explained the situation, Jack had said he needed to read the law. It had taken a couple of days before Jack got back to him, and when Wyatt asked him if his marriage was valid, Jack said, "Yes and no." He explained that Wyatt's marriage was considered void if there was an existing marriage that wasn't terminated by death or legal action, but that the onus was on Finn or even Macy to file a suit to declare her marriage to Wyatt void.

"She's not going to do that," Wyatt said angrily. "So what do we do about him?"

"She needs to file for a divorce from Lockhart. When the divorce is granted, your marriage is automatically made valid. Basically, it's up to her."

"What about property?" Wyatt asked.

"If the property belonged to her before your marriage, it's hers. If the property was Lockhart's, and she inherited it because of his death, it's still his. If she sold it, he's still entitled to the value of it. If I were you, I wouldn't buy or sell any personal property until this is worked out."

The news left Wyatt reeling. This was a nightmare — not only was his business buying and selling land, including land he bought and then flipped for a profit, he was counting on the sale of the Lockhart land to help fund his resort. Not to mention a portion of the Lockhart land was to be used in the resort footprint — they were going to put condos up on the southern end of the ranchland.

Macy. He flipped his phone open and dialed Macy's number, expecting it to roll to voice mail. He tossed the papers on his desk as he waited for the phone to connect.

"Hello?"

Wyatt started at the sound of Macy's voice. "Macy!" he said, relieved and elated and . . . and *relieved.* "Where have you been, sweetheart? I've been trying to get in touch with you for two days."

"I know, Wyatt, I'm sorry. I just haven't had a moment." She sounded exhausted. Her voice was flat, the life gone out of it.

"Are you okay?"

"Me?" She sounded surprised. "I'm fine. I'm just . . . I'm tired. We've had to do this round of interviews and press briefings, and it's been really hard. The whole world is looking at us through a microscope."

"Yeah, it's all over the news," he said. "How . . ." He wanted to ask, he desperately wanted to ask, but he couldn't seem to make himself say the words.

Macy knew him too well, apparently, because she said softly, "He's fine. He's tired, too. And he's overwhelmed. We all are."

"How did he take the news?" Wyatt asked.

There was a pause so long he could have driven cattle through it. Wyatt heard the catch in her voice and the little gasp for air and realized she was crying. "Not well. I'm sure he's confused and hurt, but he'll hardly talk at all. He keeps looking at me like I stabbed him in the heart," she said through a rush of tears. "I feel awful, Wyatt! I *did* stab him in the heart! I might as well have picked up a knife! That's what kept him going—he thought he was coming home to . . . to *us*. I don't know what to do!"

Wyatt anxiously shoved a hand through his hair. If he could, he would have reached through that phone to hold her. "This is why I wanted to come with you, sweetheart. I knew this would be too hard for you."

"What was I supposed to do, show up to greet my

long-lost husband with my new husband? How could
I do that to him, Wyatt? Or *you*, for that matter? No, I
definitely had to do this on my own."

"Come home," he said, his pulse starting to thump
in his neck. "Come home now, don't wait. His folks are
there, right? And his brother? Maybe they can—"

"No, no, the army won't let us," she cut him off.
"They are concerned about how everything looks, and
there are all these people and officials who want to welcome him home. He's a *hero*."

"I'm coming to Washington, then. I am not going to
let you go through this alone."

"You can't come to Washington!" she cried. "That
would make everything so much worse!"

"*Worse?*" he responded angrily. "I'm your husband,
Macy!"

"Think about it, Wyatt! The press would be all over
it. It's not a good idea. Please stay there."

"How am I supposed to—look, Macy, Finn's got
a lot of issues he's going to have to face. You can't be
held prisoner for three years and not bring back some
problems. But you don't need to face them for him. *He*
needs to face them. You . . . you need to come home
and you and I will face whatever the fallout is from this
together. That's what husbands and wives do, they face
hardship together."

"Are you kidding?" she asked with uncharacteristic
ire. "I'm not going to let him twist in the wind after all he's
been through! Can you imagine being held by the Taliban all this time? Do you know they kept him chained?"

Yes, he knew; he'd heard it all just like the rest of the free world. "Macy, darlin', listen to me," Wyatt said, feeling control slip through his fingers, feeling his heart dangling on a very thin string. "I know he's been through a rough time—I can't even begin to imagine how rough it has been for him, and he's a stronger man than I am for having survived it. But the fact remains that you are married to *me* now, and he's going to have to accept that."

"Am I?" she asked tearfully. "Honestly, Wyatt, I don't know that I am married to you. Not legally, anyway. And there are all these questions."

"What questions? Who is asking the questions?" he demanded angrily. If Jillian was stirring the pot—after Jillian's initial legal assessment, which she had freely shared with anyone who would listen, Wyatt had told her to please leave it to him, that he'd handle it, and had immediately called Jack.

"No one," Macy said. "I mean, I guess it's me. I have questions."

Wyatt's heart was beating as if he'd just run through fire. "I told you I'd handle it, Macy. It's not anything you need to worry about now. You need to come home *now*. When you get home, we will straighten out whatever needs to be straightened out. But you need to come home."

"Wyatt, please try to understand. We—oh, wait a minute, I'm getting another call."

"Macy!" Wyatt shouted into the phone. "Macy, wait—do you know how much I love you?" he asked in a desperate bid to keep her on the line a moment longer, to make her understand him. "Do you understand how much you mean to me?"

"Yes, yes, of course!" she responded impatiently. "And I love you, too, Wyatt, you know I do, but I can't talk about this right now!"

"Mac—"

"I have to go! I'll call you later," she said.

The line went dead. Wyatt reared back and gaped at his cell phone. He glanced up, stared blankly out the window at the cows gathered around the little pond, then hurled his cell phone at the wall.

6

Daisy's Saddle-brew Coffee Shop was at the north end of the town square, just a few blocks from Wyatt's office. It was a cute little place with a store for knickknacks and objets d'art up front, and coffee and pastries in back. Linda Gail went there every day promptly at half past eleven on her bank run to meet her posse, all of whom worked nearby.

They were engaged in a lively debate when she

walked in. Reena worked for a CPA. She was a free spirit and had styled her hair into dreadlocks. She was pointing her finger at Anne, a fifty-something grandmother and receptionist, who routinely talked as if she had perhaps ten years left on this earth. That annoyed Linda Gail, but she had learned to tune out Anne's litany of health complaints. The third woman, Cathy, a mother of four and a dental hygienist, always looked exhausted, but she was the most cheerful person Linda Gail had ever known. Linda Gail had three kids, and that was plenty. If Davis hadn't had the snip done after their daughter was born, Linda Gail would have killed him. She really would have.

Samantha Delaney was working the counter when Linda Gail ordered her usual caramel frappuccino with extra whipped cream. Linda Gail had always felt a little sorry for Samantha. She'd moved to Texas shortly before her husband was deployed to Iraq, and not quite two months later he was killed in action. Samantha had stayed on in Cedar Springs—something about her mother having a new boyfriend back in Indiana, and Samantha feeling more comfortable here. Linda Gail couldn't imagine being without a mother to lean on, but at least Samantha had Macy. The two young women had met in a survivors support group and had become thick as thieves . . . until Macy married Wyatt. Samantha seemed to have been a little lost since then.

"Did the news crews move out?" Linda Gail asked Samantha.

"Yes. One of them said they'd probably be back when the hero came home."

"Oh great," Linda Gail said with a roll of her eyes.

"They're good for business," Sam said with a shrug.

"I suppose they are," Linda Gail agreed for the sake of being agreeable. She picked up her coffee and sauntered over to the table. "I could hear you old hens outside," she said to her friends as she fit herself onto a chair. "What's got you all worked up?"

"We're debating who your boss's wife is going to end up with," Anne said. "Or *should* end up with."

"So?" Cathy asked excitedly as Linda Gail sipped from her drink. "Who is she going to choose, do you know?"

"How would I know?" Linda Gail asked, and licked the cream from her straw. "It's not like I've talked to her."

"She has to choose her original husband," Reena said. "There is no other answer."

"Why is there no other answer?" Anne demanded. "They buried him and she fell in love with another man. Who is to say the second one is not the right one for her? Everyone assumed the first one was her only true love, but I happen to believe a woman can have many true loves."

"Why, because you've had three?" Reena asked with a snort.

"So what if I have?" Anne said defensively.

"Whether Linda Gail's boss is the right one or not, Macy married him, and she can't just toss him out like an old pair of tennis shoes," Cathy said with an affirmative nod.

"What about the soldier?" Reena asked. "He was a *prisoner* of *war* for three years. Doesn't he deserve to come back to the life he had?"

"What about her life?" Anne said. "It's not like we're talking about a dog."

"There's a dog, too," Linda Gail said. "Milo. It was Finn's, but now it belongs to Macy and Wyatt."

"How's Wyatt doing, anyway?" Cathy asked, trying to seem sympathetic instead of completely titillated by what had become the biggest scandal in town since the ex-mayor's affair.

Linda Gail drank thirstily before speaking. She liked drawing out the drama. She lowered her cup and looked around at her three friends. "This is not to leave this table, understood?"

They all nodded eagerly.

"He's a basket case."

"*Really?*" Cathy asked, and the three of them leaned forward, anxious to hear the details.

"He's not sleeping, he's not eating. Yesterday, he almost forgot a closing. He never forgets a closing. And today, he forgot that he read an environmental report just yesterday."

"Wow," Reena said.

"Has he said anything?" Anne asked.

"Not a damn word," Linda Gail said. "But I know this—he loves her. I've known Wyatt for a long time, and Lord, he has been through some women. But he's never loved anyone like he loves Macy Clark."

"He's a good-looking man," Anne said, as if that

excused the way he used to cat around town. "Love that black hair and blue eyes combination."

"Yes, but did you see *Finn*?" Cathy whispered. "Oh my *God*," she said, putting a hand over her heart.

"Stop it, you guys," Reena said. "This is heartbreaking, and Wyatt is going to get the short end of this stick, I just know it."

"Well, if he does, I know who will be waiting in the wings," Linda Gail said casually.

"Who?" Reena demanded.

"Caroline Spalding."

The other women gasped in perfect unison. Linda Gail nodded. Caroline Spalding was Cedar Springs's most notorious divorcée. She was very regal, blonde, and wealthy, and like a lot of rich folks, lived in the Hill Country. It was a short drive to Austin, but close to home, and the views were beautiful.

As if that weren't enough, Caroline was a true barracuda. She was dangerous because she didn't come across as one—she quietly pursued men, married or not. "It's true," Linda Gail said. "She's called twice since the news broke because she suddenly needs help with a land deal."

"She's barking up the wrong tree," Anne said irritably. "Wyatt and Macy love each other. He's not going anywhere."

"But she loved Finn Lockhart first," Reena reminded them all. "And you should have seen the way Finn looked at her on the *Today* show. It's obvious that he loves her something awful."

"Imagine, having two handsome men want you," Cathy said with a sigh. "I'd be happy if Jerry just wanted me on Saturday night."

They laughed. But as the talk moved to just how hot Matt Lauer was on a scale of one to ten, Linda Gail couldn't help but worry about Wyatt. In spite of his gruffness, Linda Gail was fond of him. He was like a little brother to her, and she knew that he loved Macy more than the air he breathed. Wyatt wasn't the easiest guy to get to know, and he didn't have a lot of close friends. He was gruff to the point of being rude sometimes, and God, he was a driven man. But there was something about Macy that softened him.

If this deal didn't go his way, Linda Gail worried what it would do to him.

If one more person asked Macy what she was going to do, she could not be responsible for their safety.

The last person—a perky, tiny little Tinkerbell from CBS—had asked with an affected smile, and it had taken all of Macy's strength to keep from telling the woman to mind her own business. Why couldn't people just rejoice in Finn's being alive and coming home? Why couldn't the big news story be his miraculous survival? That was all Macy could think about when she looked at him. The reality of it was sinking in a little deeper each moment. It was incredible he was *here*.

She started each interview grinning with glee, hardly able to contain her joy. But then some journalist would deflate her with intrusive questions about her second marriage. How could anyone think the decision she faced was one that could be made with the glare of TV lights in her face? Didn't everyone understand that she was teetering on the edge of a chasm that had just opened up in her life, and there was nothing to guide her away from the edge?

She just wanted to celebrate Finn. She would deal with the rest of it later.

Macy hoped the scrutiny would end when they left D.C., and it did for the few hours it took to fly back to Austin. The army had supplied them with a plane and everyone sought a little space after so much time in close company; they'd scattered. Finn was the last to board. He walked past Macy to the back of the plane and sat with his brother Brodie for the flight home.

Macy was expecting that. Since the moment she'd told him she'd remarried, he hadn't really spoken to her except on camera. He'd been so stunned and angry that she'd called Brodie and retreated to Emma's room, waiting for Brodie to call her back.

Only Brodie didn't call her back. Finn didn't

want to see her. Macy had hoped that once he'd had time to relax, she could talk to him. But that hadn't happened.

When they arrived in Austin, they were greeted by the local media, more of Finn's family, including his older brother Luke; Nancy Keller, the mayor of Cedar Springs; and other government officials. They were ushered into a reception hosted by the Friends of Fort Hood, all arranged by Major Sanderson.

Exhausted, Macy stood to one side, listening to Finn's garrison leader, Colonel Deavers, tell Finn that he should get an agent to field the requests for interviews and book and movie deals. "It's a miraculous story," the colonel said.

"Yes, sir," Finn said.

Colonel Deavers looked at Macy. "It must have come as quite a shock to you, Mrs. Lockhart."

"It was an answer to my prayers," she said, and smiled at Finn. He looked down.

"There will be a lot to sort out," the colonel opined.

Macy smiled and nodded that yes, there would be things to sort out, more than the colonel could possibly know. Life was moving at lightning speed, and Macy was no closer to knowing what to do than she had been the afternoon she'd been reunited with Finn. Oh, but her heart had swelled at the sight of him, her body had responded instantly to his touch. She had believed, in those few feverish moments in the hotel room, that her path was clear, and the path led to Finn.

But then Wyatt's anguish had crept into her

consciousness, and she recalled his devastation when she told him Finn was alive and the heartache in his voice over the phone, and Macy had realized that there was no clear path.

She loved two men. She loved them differently, but she loved them both nonetheless, and it left her incapable of making a decision. Or eating or sleeping, for that matter. She was paralyzed.

"I suspect they will want your story, too, Mrs. Lockhart," Colonel Deavers added with a smile.

Clark. Her last name was Clark.

"We'll talk about it," Finn said, and put his hand possessively on the small of Macy's back. "Will you excuse us, sir? I need to get Macy something to eat."

"Of course," the colonel said, and gestured toward the buffet.

Macy didn't want food—the scent of something on the buffet was making her nauseous as it was. "I'm not hungry," she said as Finn led her away from the officer.

"Me either," he said.

He led her off to the side, to a dark corner near the buffet. He gave her a faint, sad smile, and Macy felt a tug of deep longing. "Just think, a few more minutes of this and you can finally go home."

"Yes, but not exactly the home I was hoping for," he said. "I'd like to talk a minute, Macy. We haven't had much of a chance."

"No, we haven't. And there is so much I want to say." That she was sorry, so very sorry. That she still loved him, had never stopped loving him.

Finn put his back to the crowd and wearily ran a hand over his hair. It was lighter now, a sandy brown with streaks of blond. He was leaner, and harder, too. The shadow of a beard covered his chin and jaw. Tiny lines fanned out from the corners of his copper-brown eyes that hadn't been there before, and Macy realized he'd aged more than the three years he'd been held captive.

Three years. Three years and nine months since he'd left Texas, to be exact. Macy had heard the tale of his capture, his captivity and his daring escape along with everyone else. Yet she wanted to hear more, to hear all of it, to know exactly what he'd endured in those three years and nine months. But remarkably, those questions seemed small when compared to the big question that sat like an elephant between them: Where did they go from here?

Finn touched her hand. "You okay?"

That was so like Finn to worry about her when he was the one who was being dragged through the wringer. She smiled. "I feel like I've won the lottery. How about you?"

"I'm glad it's almost over." He glanced back at the people gathered in the room, then looked at her again. His gaze moved over her face and flicked to her chest. There was a distant sort of hunger in his eyes, and it stirred a familiar fever in her. "I want to thank you. You've been great the last couple of days," he said. "I couldn't have done this without you."

"Liar," she said, smiling sheepishly. "I've barely

strung a coherent sentence together. You are the one who's been great." He'd been charming when he needed to be and at ease throughout, squeezing her hand when he felt the small tremors in her and pulling her up when she wanted to sink. On those occasions when he was interviewed alone, she marveled at how strong and how relaxed he looked, whereas she'd found the attention excruciatingly painful.

"I'm serious," he said, and casually freed a strand of her hair from her collar. "It's not so tough for me. All I had to do was say it was great to be home. They were putting the hard questions to you."

"Impossible questions," she muttered, and averted her gaze a moment, her mind full of complicated thoughts. "It was hard to find the right words to respond with. It's even harder finding the right words to say all I want to say to you."

Finn's jaw flinched. "You seemed to find the right words."

"No, I mean . . . I didn't tell you how sorry I am for everything, for what you've been through, for what you came home to. And how indescribably happy I am that this is real, that you are really here. Who would have dreamed this could happen?"

"I did. I dreamed something like this could happen every day."

He said it in a way that suggested he thought she should have, too, and guilt stabbed Macy—she hadn't dreamed hard enough or long enough. "I wish I could have dreamed it," she said softly, "but I never could seem to stop having nightmares about how you must have suffered when you died."

Pain skimmed his features, but Finn's expression quickly shuttered again. Macy suddenly realized that was what she had been seeing these last two days—he'd been hiding behind a mask.

"I wanted to let you know that I am going to stay at Mom and Dad's for a few days," he said. "Brodie says there's not much at the ranch to go back to. He says the house is empty and the cattle and horses are gone. Dogs, too."

His voice was cool, and Macy couldn't blame him. It was just something else he'd thought he'd be coming home to. The horses had not only been his business, they'd been part of his family. He loved them; he had a gift for connecting with animals, especially horses.

When Macy had first met Finn, he'd lived alone with the stray dogs he took in on the three hundred acres of the Two Wishes Ranch. He and a grizzled Mexican named José Banda trained cutting horses. Cutting horses had once been used to cull sick cows from herds of cattle, but now they were used mostly in competitions to separate calves from herds. Macy hadn't known any of this, of course, until Finn had taught her. And she'd learned that a good cutting horse could sell for thousands of dollars.

José had taught Finn everything he knew about training horses, and the two of them became known as some of the best trainers in the southwest, their services in high demand. They'd kept about three dozen cattle on the ranch for training purposes, and two high school kids had worked half days with them, learning the business.

But training a horse took time, and money was slow to come in. When they'd first married, Macy had just graduated from college and had secured a position as a social worker with a nonprofit agency that mentored kids in the foster care system. Her salary was laughably low, but she loved the work. She'd been good at it, and her caseload grew. It eventually got so big that she spent more time driving around central Texas than she did mentoring. It seemed like the only thing she managed was a quick check on the welfare of the kids on her list—there was no time for anything else. She didn't feel like she was helping anyone but the oil companies.

Finn convinced Macy he needed her at home. She had a better head for numbers and bookkeeping than he did, so Macy quit her job and stayed home to keep the books. Unfortunately, that didn't take very long. She ended up spending a lot of time hanging around Finn, watching him work.

Finn had acquired three cutters of his own, which he entered in competitions for a little extra money. Those horses had been with Finn longer than Macy had, longer than any of the stray dogs he'd taken in. It had killed Macy to sell the cutters, but there was nothing to be done for it. Even if she could have afforded their upkeep, she couldn't care for them by herself.

When he'd left her to join the army, Finn had told Macy the ranch would take care of itself. For a few months, it had. But then the officers had come and told her Finn had been killed. And then the cattle got sick. The veterinary bills were high, even with Finn's brother Luke providing the service and Macy paying only for the medicine. A big chunk of the death gratuity provided by the army had gone to pay bills and taxes. Macy had also received life insurance for Finn from the government, but her mother had been frantic that she would spend it all on the ranch and had made her put a chunk of it in mutual funds for her future. That was a great idea, but the market had taken a nosedive since then, and she'd lost about thirty percent of it. The two high school kids graduated, and then it was just Macy and José, and . . . and she couldn't do it.

One day, under a hard Texas sun, Macy told José of her decision to shut down the cutting horse business. She'd given him six months pay as severance. She never knew if it was the heat or the news that made his eyes water, but José had said little more than "*Gracias*," and had packed up his beat-up, boxy, old red pickup. She'd heard he'd gone on to a *vaquero* job south of Dallas-Fort Worth.

Macy looked at Finn now with all of that running through her mind and said, "I am so sorry."

"I understand," Finn said, but his jaw was clenched. "It was too much for you."

"It *was* hard, Finn. It was a lot harder than I ever thought it could be. The cattle had to be fed in winter, and that year we had a drought, so we had to buy a whole lot more feed than usual, and the horses needed to be watered, and then the cattle got a respiratory disease . . ." Her voice trailed off. It had all started one night when she'd heard an awful howling outside. She went out and discovered one of the dogs—a big dog they called Tank, who easily weighed one hundred pounds. He'd eaten something or been bit, she didn't know, but he was in distress. He was too heavy for her to lift, and Macy had cried and cried waiting for Luke to come. The dog had died with his head in Macy's lap before Luke could get there.

A few weeks later when the first calf got sick, she'd felt completely helpless.

"Your dad and Brodie and Luke tried to help out when they could," she said quietly. "But they have their own lives and Luke was opening the clinic, and Brodie had started a new job, and they couldn't come around as often as I needed them, and then some of the cows got sick and we had to destroy some. The ranch was bleeding money and I couldn't seem to stop it."

"No need to explain," Finn said.

"No, I *need* to explain," she insisted, desperate to justify a decision that had seemed so right at the time. "I know better than anyone how much the cutters meant to you. It killed me to do it, you have no idea. I felt like I was abandoning a part of *you.*"

He snorted and glanced impatiently over his shoulder. "You mean the part of me you could remember?"

"What?"

Finn looked up; his eyes were flashing with . . .

anger? Disappointment? "Just going back to what you said, Macy. You said I started to disappear from your memory. My hands, my feet . . . So when did I disappear completely? When you sold my horses?"

"That . . . that is so not fair," Macy said, her voice low. "You are misconstruing what I said. You never disappeared, Finn, not for a moment. You were always in my thoughts and in my heart," she said, pressing her hand against his heart.

He covered her hand with his, squeezed it. "Until Wyatt Clark showed up, anyway," he said.

She pulled her hand from beneath his. "Please don't do that. You cannot begin to understand how deeply I mourned you and how ecstatically happy I am that you are alive." But as the words left her mouth, she realized how hollow they must sound. "Losing you hurt worse than anything I have ever felt. People would ask, How are you coping, Macy? and I'd say fine. But I wasn't fine. I wasn't coping. And I didn't tell anyone because words couldn't describe the pain I was feeling."

Finn nodded. "You know the thing I keep wondering? I wonder when you decided to move on. How long did you mourn me—mourn us—before you were ready for someone else? You've been married seven months, so somewhere between three years ago when you thought I died and seven months ago when you remarried, you said, okay, I'm ready," he said, gesturing between those two invisible dates.

"You're being unfair."

"Macy." He sighed and raked a hand through his

hair. A chunk of it fell back over his eye. "I'm only try-ing to understand how long you gave it before you let me go and let him in. It's a fair question."

"Finn, *stop*—"

"I can't help but ask! You helped me get out of there! I had this fantasy of you, and all the things we'd do when I was free. I'd imagine how many dogs and horses and cows we could fit on the ranch." He laughed wryly and looked down. "I had this fantasy that we'd travel, and we'd have this great life with lots of kids, and I imagined Christmas mornings with them, or teach-ing them to ride, or watching them play football or act in one of those little kid plays they do in elementary school."

He looked up again, his expression sad and angry. "But then I came home and found you married to someone else, and I'm still trying to wrap my mind around that. Sorry if I ask some hard questions, but I think I'm entitled to know."

Macy's belly began to roil.

"Did he come around looking for a grieving widow?" Finn asked curiously.

"No," Macy said. Wyatt wasn't like that. "Dad intro-duced us."

Finn snorted at that. "So the old man just showed up one day and introduced you to your next husband?"

"Finn, please," Macy said, pressing a hand against her abdomen. "We had *buried* you."

"Just tell me how long you waited after you thought I'd died before you hooked up with Clark."

As if she'd just turned him off and Wyatt on one day, could name the exact moment she'd let go the memory of him and allowed herself to love Wyatt. "Roughly two years," she said tightly. "I spent two years thinking of you every moment of every day. Mourning you. Wishing I had died with you. And then . . . then one day I didn't want to worry or die anymore. I don't know how it happened—it just happened."

"Wow," Finn said, his gaze sliding over her. "Two years."

His indignation suddenly angered her. "You act as if I should have assumed you were alive in spite of all the evidence to the contrary! I am sorry if I can't describe the loss and the despair I felt to your satisfaction, Finn, but believe me, there were days I never got out of bed. I spent many, *many* long nights surfing the Web, putting your picture up at every fallen soldier Web site I could find along with a personal tribute because that was the only thing I knew to do to soothe my grief, and that didn't even *touch* it. There were days I didn't eat. There were very long days that I didn't do a damn thing but wander around the house, looking for you. Cows were outside calling for food, and I didn't care. There were entire days when I did nothing but worry that I hadn't said good-bye to you the right way. I'd said good-bye like you were coming back, not good-bye like I'd never see you again, and I couldn't do anything but worry about it."

"Jesus—"

"I got the black boxes with your stuff from the army and I thought I would have something that had your scent, something I could touch and hold on to, but you know what? They *washed* it all! I couldn't smell anything but detergent! And you know what else? I was very angry, especially with *you* for joining the army to begin with. What the hell, Finn? Why did *you* have to go? Why did you have to risk everything that we had?"

Finn didn't speak.

"All that sorrow and anger almost buried me," Macy heatedly continued. "Ask anyone here. So forgive me if one day I decided my life was still worth living, even without you. That's right, I tried to find a way to live my life without you. What else was I supposed to do?"

He looked stunned. *Let him be stunned,* Macy thought bitterly. "I'm sorry if I didn't grieve correctly, but no one gave me a manual for that, any more than they gave me a manual for how to put everything back the way it was when my lost husband turned up blessedly alive."

She moved to pass him, but Finn stopped her by taking her arm. "Before you flounce off, I want to tell you something."

Macy tried to remove her arm, but his grip tightened.

"I didn't get a rule book either," Finn said quietly. "I never even thought of the possibility you might have remarried, can you believe it? Maybe that was dumb, but I didn't, and now I don't really know what I'm supposed to do with you. Am I supposed to accept that you moved on? I've tried, Macy, but it's not that easy for me."

Macy glanced down. Her hands were shaking. "Me either," she admitted in a whisper.

He caressed her arm with his thumb. "I'm not trying to upset you. But I'm a plainspoken man, and I'm just going to tell you straight up. I can't stop thinking about you. Hell, I haven't been able to stop thinking about you since the moment we met, but now I can't stop thinking of you with him. It makes me feel sick. I love you, Macy, and I didn't come this far to lose you. You need to know that. You need to know that I want you, and I'm not going to give up on us until you tell me to, and even then, I'm not sure I can. Beyond that, I don't know what else to say."

There was a time those words would have melted her right into his arms. This evening, they stirred an unbearable yearning for something that was bigger than desire. Those words went right to her heart and warmed it, hurt it, made it beat like it hadn't beat in years. They were almost too intense after the emotional swirl of the last week; another wave of nausea came over Macy. She pulled her arm free of his grip, gulping for air. "Excuse me," she said, and hurried past him to the bathroom.

Inside the small bathroom, Macy gripped the edge of the sink, her eyes closed, her belly churning. She was a horrible person. He was home, alive, and he still loved her, and she felt wobbly. It reminded her of the physical pain she'd felt when she'd lost Finn—too great to endure.

When the nausea passed and she emerged, Brodie was standing outside the door, his arms folded over his chest. "Did you tell him about Two Wishes?" he asked quietly.

The ranch—oh God, the ranch. "No," she said, and when Brodie looked accusingly at her, she added, "I don't need to tell him anything, Brodie. I am going to fix everything. He doesn't need to know. What's the point?"

"You're making a mistake, Macy," Brodie said. "He should hear it from you."

"Just trust me, will you?" Macy asked with exasperation, and ducked around him. "Everything is under control," she said as she passed, and ignored Brodie's dubious expression.

8

Finn's head and heart were racing, giving him an excruciating headache. He lost sight of Macy after their talk; Brodie said she'd left with her mom.

He wanted out of there, away from all the peering eyes, the smiles, all the hugs and pats on the back, proclaiming him a hero. He was starting to feel claustrophobic. Antsy.

At last, Finn said good-bye to all the military

personnel and Friends of Fort Hood, the reporters, his
extended family, and God knew who else, and piled
into his father's Chevy Suburban with his entourage,
headed for home.

He rode in the front passenger seat, a seat of honor,
apparently, as his mother had insisted he take it. But as
the Suburban pulled onto Highway 71, they were met
with an onslaught of lights rushing by in the opposite
direction. The lights were blurring into each other and
Finn blinked, trying to focus. He instinctively braced
his arm against the frame of the car. He didn't like riding in the front, sitting up high with nothing but glass
around him. He felt dangerously exposed and defenseless. He tried to tell himself this was Austin, not Kabul,
but it didn't help his anxiety.

He was so tense he could scarcely respond to the
many questions his brother Luke put to him, could
not concentrate when Mom talked about the family
reunion she wanted to have as soon as possible. Finn
could feel the trickle of perspiration running down his
back as cars darted around his father's lumbering machine. His heart lurched every time a dirty little white
car swept past them—they reminded him of the car
that drove into Danny and him, and there seemed to be
an inordinate number of them in Austin.

By the time they reached the old home place, his
nerves were frayed. He spilled out of the Suburban
and quickly walked away from it, pretending to get a
good look at the house where he'd grown up, but gulping for air before anyone could notice. The house, a

fifties-style ranch, was surrounded by scrubland and flanked to the south by a barn bigger than the house. A windmill that didn't pump water anymore stood on the north side. The place looked exactly as it had the day Finn left, as if time had stood still on this little ranch.

Someone put a hand on his shoulder; Finn flinched and whirled around.

"Hey," Luke said, quickly lifting his hand. "I didn't mean to scare you, man. Are you all right?"

"I'm fine," Finn said. "I was just wondering—you think Dad has any whiskey?"

Luke grinned. "Are you kidding? It's still under the oil cans in the garage. I'll get it and meet you on the back porch."

Finn grabbed his rucksack from the back of the Suburban and walked inside the house.

"Finn, you'll be in your old room," his mother called from the kitchen. I'm going to fix us some sweet tea."

Inside, the house looked the same as it always had. It was built of limestone with a beamed ceiling in the living room and a linoleum floor in the kitchen his father had been promising to replace for ten years. One long corridor led to all the bedrooms.

Finn walked into the one he'd shared with Brodie until Luke had gone off to college. He dropped his ruck on the bed and looked around. It was the same as the day he'd left it ten years ago. His rodeo trophies were lined up on a shelf above his bed. There was a pair of cleats on the dresser. Brodie's, he figured, as Brodie had been the one to play baseball. A poster of

Pamela Anderson dressed in a string bikini—complete with the obligatory mustache and glasses drawn on by his best friend Mike—was still tacked to the wall.

Mike was the reason Finn had joined the army. Not the only reason, but the one that got him thinking about enlisting. Mike had come from a working-class family who didn't put much store in college. Mike did, though, and the most realistic way for him to get there was through the G.I. Bill. He'd joined up after high school, did his time, and was just about to get out and go to college when 9/11 happened. Mike re-upped. And he died in Iraq.

Several months after he died, Finn had seen his pickup on a dirt lot next to Highway 281 with a sign that said, FOR SALE, GOOD CONDITION. That was all that was left of Mike. He'd been reduced to a pickup on the side of the road, and Finn . . . Finn couldn't let that happen. So he'd signed up for Mike. In memory of. Because Mike had the balls to die for his country.

But it was more than that, really. It was for all of the soldiers who were dying over there. Guys like Finn, guys who supported the war, who were doing the best and only thing they could to avenge 9/11. Finn was young and strong and good with a gun. He felt like he had a responsibility to himself and to his country.

He'd been married to Macy almost three years when he told her. She laughed at first, but when she saw he was serious, she was furious. She didn't believe in this war or any other. "It's a dead-end war! There will never be peace there!"

"It's not any more dead-end than social work," he'd argued. "And you'd still be doing that if we didn't live so far out."

Macy had gasped. "But those are *children* you're talking about!"

"Exactly," he'd said. "You do what you can to protect innocent kids. Here or there, it doesn't matter."

"Okay, what about *our* kids?" she'd demanded. "We'll never have them if you get yourself killed!"

"But, baby, if I don't get myself killed, just think of how much better we'll be for it. Think of what better parents we'd be."

In the end, she'd given in. But she hadn't liked it.

Finn had set up everything so that it would be easy for Macy. José was there, and Finn had assumed everything would be okay . . .

He looked away from Pamela and Mike's scribbling.

Yes, his room was just as he'd left it with one notable exception: There was a computer atop a small desk, shoved up against the wall beneath the window. On the right of the monitor was a mouse pad and mouse; on the left, a stack of correspondence and a jar to hold pens and pencils.

His mother walked in with a glass of sweet tea and noticed him looking at it. "We made this into the computer room," she said apologetically. "I hope you don't mind."

"Not at all."

"Is this going to be okay?" she asked, gesturing to a stack of fresh towels at the foot of the single twin bed.

"It's great, Mom." Finn ran a hand through his hair. He was feeling a little closed in.

"Tea?" she asked, holding the glass up.

"No. But thanks."

She put the glass down. "Finn?"

He was surprised to see tears in her eyes. She'd cried so much since he'd come home; how many tears did she have left? "Mom, stop," he said softly, and pulled her into a hug. "Come on, now. Everything is good."

"I'm sorry," she said tearfully. "But you can't imagine how grateful I am to have you home. I look at you and I get down on my knees and thank God for giving my child back to me. It's a miracle. I just wish *everyone* understood what a miracle it is."

"What do you mean?" he asked.

"Oh, nothing, really," she said, shaking her head. She patted his chest and stepped away to the dresser, where she anxiously rearranged a half dozen pictures of him. "I just want you to know that your father and your brothers and I understand how blessed we are to have you back."

By process of elimination, Finn deduced that his mother meant Macy wasn't as thankful for his survival as they were. "What, Mom . . . you don't think Macy is feeling quite as blessed?" he asked with a laugh.

His mom rearranged two more pictures. "I don't know if she is or she isn't, she hasn't said. But if I were in her shoes, I wouldn't have remarried so quickly."

This was the last conversation Finn wanted to have

with anyone, much less his mother. He wondered if Luke had found the whiskey yet. "I wouldn't expect Macy to give up her life just because mine was lost," he said.

His mother attempted to shrug indifferently, but her pinched expression at the mention of Macy's name said it all.

"I'm tired, Mom. I'm going to have a drink with Brodie and Luke." He moved toward the door, but his mother had tears in her eyes again.

"Ma," he said, embracing her once more. "Come on, now. I'm home. It's all behind us," he said, even as a trickle of doubt ran down his spine.

9

About ten miles north of the old Lockhart place, Wyatt stood on the deck attached to the back of his house, staring at the lake that looked black as ink now that the sun was going down.

Milo was sprawled in the open doorway, his head between his paws, his eyes following Wyatt's every move. Just beyond Milo was a pristine house scented with fresh flowers—Wyatt had filled the vases and even a couple of buckets with the armload he'd bought at Austin Flowers. In the kitchen, in a warming oven, was a meal of sea bass and asparagus. Wyatt had picked it up from Twin Sisters Catering after calling one of the sisters and pleading for a special meal. When he said the name Finn Lockhart, they had jumped at the chance to cook something for "The Hero." Wyatt had tried to explain that it wasn't for Finn, but he wasn't certain they'd understood him. He was beginning to think that if he uttered Finn Lockhart's name, he could get the keys to any bank vault in town.

Wyatt checked his watch again. Two minutes had passed since the last time he'd looked. "Damn," he muttered, and glanced at Milo. "How long does it take to drive from the airport?"

Wyatt wasn't exactly the type to feel anxious about a woman. He'd always had a lot of feminine company; he dated his way through college, dated more when he graduated and got into the development business. For a long time, he'd believed he wasn't the marrying type—he liked his work, liked having time to play golf on weekends. He was the guy who could get in a round or two, then clean up, go to Austin, and hit the clubs.

But then he'd met Macy at a country club event. He knew of Macy—everyone knew of everyone in a town like Cedar Springs—but he'd never been formally introduced to her. That night, her dad, Bob Harper, was in town from Dallas and was trying to sell Wyatt some land he needed to unload. Bob had

introduced Wyatt to his daughter, and Wyatt had
thought Macy looked sad and vulnerable. But he also
thought she was really pretty in a down-home way.
There was something about her, something he wanted
to hold and protect.

That night, he'd coaxed her number out of her and
called her. He'd long suspected that they went out the
first time because Bob Harper pressured her to do so for
the sake of the deal.

If that was true, it worked. Macy had charmed the
socks right off of Wyatt. She talked about being a social
worker, a line of work she'd recently returned to after
her husband was killed in action. She was so exuberant
about it, so funny with her anecdotes about some of the
children she'd mentored.

After a few weeks, Macy felt comfortable enough
to ask Wyatt along to a Harper family picnic. At that
picnic, Wyatt watched Macy with her cousin Chloe's
twin boys. Macy was jubilant with those children. She
chased them around a tree, jumping out from behind
it to scare them into uncontrollable laughter. She held
their hands and walked them down to the lake so they
could feed the ducks. She took turns swinging one up
in the air, and then the other. All afternoon, her expression was one of pure joy.

Wyatt knew that day he wanted her and he wanted
children with her. That desire had only gotten stronger
with time.

At last he spotted car lights on the road below, wend-
ing their way up. He walked into the house and to the

windows that overlooked the drive, saw Macy's mother's car, and felt a surge of elation and relief—and a twinge of foreboding.

He walked out onto the drive to meet them. Macy looked exhausted when she climbed out of the backseat of Jillian's BMW and walked straight into his arms. At the same time, Jillian got out and pulled Macy's suitcase from her trunk. Wyatt let Macy go to help his mother-in-law. "Jillian, Emma, do you want to come in?" he asked, bending over to wave at Emma in the car.

"No, thank you, Wyatt. It's late and I've got to go to work in the morning," Jillian said. She patted his cheek. "Anyway, you need some time with Macy."

"Bye, Mom. Thanks for everything," Macy said wearily.

"I'll call you tomorrow, honey."

Wyatt waited until Jillian and Emma had backed out of the drive before following Macy inside. She was still in the foyer, fending off an exuberant Milo, who was thrilled to see her. He butted her with his head and rubbed against her leg until she leaned down and scratched him behind the ears. Then she stepped into Wyatt's open arms again.

"Macy," he said, and kissed her, wrapping her in a tight embrace and resting his chin on the top of her head. "My God, I have never been happier to see anyone in my life." He reared back and looked at her; exhaustion shadowed her eyes. "You're worn out. Let me pour you a glass of wine."

"Wyatt—"

"I've got supper waiting. Have you eaten?"

"No, but I—"

"You are going to love this, then," he said, as he pushed her bag out of the way and removed her purse from her shoulder. "I actually convinced Twin Sisters Catering to make a meal especially for us. It took some doing, but it's in the oven. Sea bass and asparagus and a polenta that made my mouth water. Oh, and they even threw in a couple of slices of their flourless chocolate cake."

"Thanks, I appreciate it, but I'm . . . I'm not really hungry," Macy said.

Wyatt put her purse down. She was looking at him strangely, almost as if she was trying to work out where she'd seen him before. Or maybe that was Wyatt's fear talking, fear that had held him by the damn throat the last couple of days.

He reached for her again, slipping his arm around her waist. "Come and have a drink and unwind a little, sweetheart." He ushered her into the sunken living room. He'd paid a premium for this lot, high on the cliff, just so he could build a house like this with a stunning view. He'd just started building it when he met Macy. Before too long, he knew the house was for her. "How was the flight?" he asked.

She sighed and shook her head. "Long." She slipped out of his embrace and walked to the door that led onto the enormous deck, Milo on her heels.

At the bar, Wyatt quickly poured her a glass of wine, grabbed a beer for himself, and followed her outside.

A breeze had cooled the evening; it wasn't quite as sultry as it had been earlier. Wyatt handed the wine to Macy, who was staring out over the moonlit lake.

Wyatt put his arm around her middle and pulled her back against his chest. He could feel some of the tension leave her body; she leaned into him, resting her head against his shoulder. "Can you imagine," she said wearily, "what it must have been like for him, chained to a wall for three years?"

Wyatt closed his eyes. He didn't want to talk about Finn. He didn't want *her* to talk about Finn. He kissed her temple and asked softly, "Don't you want to take a break from all that imagining?"

"I wish I could." She took a sip of wine and stepped out of his embrace. "Wyatt, I . . . I . . ."

She looked as if she was in physical pain. Wyatt reached for her hand, but Macy shifted slightly, just out of his reach. "Jesus, Macy, what is it? Are you all right?"

"Yeah," she said, nodding, then abruptly shook her head. "No. No, I'm not all right. I am so confused."

A tic of panic shot through him. "There's nothing to be confused about. I know how hard this has been for you, but you're home now, and I—"

"I think I should go stay with Laru for a few days."

He was too stunned to respond at first.

Macy pressed her lips together as if she were steeling herself for his reaction and put the wine glass down. "Please listen to—"

"*What?*" he demanded. "You're going to *stay* with Laru? What does that mean?"

"I just think that given the circumstances, I need to go someplace where I can be alone and . . ." She glanced down at Milo, who was lying at her feet, panting. "And think."

"Why can't you think here? This is your home," Wyatt said, his pulse ratcheting up with his alarm. "And it's a big damn house. There are plenty of places to think here. What is it you need to think about that requires you to be at Laru's?"

"Isn't it obvious?"

"No," Wyatt said emphatically. "No, it sure as hell isn't obvious, Macy. Why in God's name would you go stay with Laru?"

"Because I don't know what to do!" she cried, throwing her arms wide and startling Milo to his feet. The dog raced to the railing and barked. "I can't *think*. I don't know which way to turn. If I turn left," she said, jabbing her left hand in the air, "there is the man who was the love of my life, the man that I married seven years ago. But they said he died, and I believed them, and now, if I turn right," she continued, jabbing her right hand in the air, "there is the man that I fell in love with, the man who *saved* me. So there are *two* men who I love more than I can say, and I am desperately confused." She dropped her hands. "I don't know what to do!"

"There's only one thing you can do, Macy," Wyatt said sternly. "I am not going to let you go because the army got this all so goddam wrong."

"You can't blame the army!"

"The hell I can't!" he shouted. "You are married to me, and I love you. You can do your thinking here."

"Actually, I don't think I *am* married to you."

"It's not so clear-cut," he said, working to stay calm. "I know your mother thinks she's got this all figured out, but *my* lawyer thinks the law is open to interpretation," he lied. "As it stands, you are married to me until declared otherwise by a court."

Macy started to turn away from him, but Wyatt put down his beer and caught her shoulders, forcing her to look at him. "I know you loved him, Macy, I've always known that. But I know that you love me, too. We've shared some extraordinary moments, haven't we? You have to face what is and deal with it."

Macy's blue eyes suddenly flashed. "I have to *deal* with it? What exactly do you think I've been doing? I am dealing with it the best way I know how, Wyatt. Only I can work through it, but I have to be alone to do it, away from *both* of you. I am going to leave so you don't have to."

She was serious. She was going to walk out the door. Wyatt's pulse jumped another notch. "You can't do this. You can't walk out on our marriage."

"I'm not walking—*Wyatt.*" She abruptly caught his face between her hands and her eyes roamed over it as if she were memorizing it. "You are right—I love you so much. But I loved—*love*—Finn, too, and I have to think how this is all going to work. I have to figure out how to live with two of you in my heart. Can't you see that?"

"Do you want to be with me?" he asked gruffly, appalled by how much he needed her to say yes.

"Yes," she said. "*Yes.*" She went up on her toes and kissed him sweetly before sliding down again and dropping her hands from his face. "Just give me some time, will you? That's all I am asking. I am going to get some things together—"

"You're going *tonight*?"

"I think I should."

"Jesus, Macy," he said, and dragged his fingers over his neatly cut hair. "Look," he said, "I'll sleep on the boat." He could see that she was about to argue. "Just tonight," he added quickly. "Tomorrow . . ." He didn't say anything else. Tomorrow, in the light of day, he'd convince her to stay.

Her smile was far too grateful. She laced her fingers through his and kissed his knuckles. "Thank you for being so understanding."

He wasn't understanding. He didn't understand at all.

"Will you excuse me? I'm wiped out and want to take a bath." She started inside, Milo on her heels. She paused at the door. "Oh, I almost forgot—the closing date for the sale of Two Wishes Ranch? We need to cancel that, obviously."

"I don't know about that." He snorted. "The property issue is a whole other mess."

"What do you mean?"

"You can't just turn back the clock," he scoffed.

Macy blinked. "Maybe not, but we can give Finn

his land back. We *have* to give it back. Will you please cancel the closing?"

"Then what do I do?" he asked irritably. "That land is part of the resort deal."

"Wyatt . . . you'll have to find the money someplace else."

"It's not just the money, Macy. It's the land. You know that part of Two Wishes is also part of the resort footprint."

She frowned. "You own land on the other side of the footprint. Can't you use that for the resort?"

Wyatt rolled his eyes. "It's not that easy. There are easements and ingress-egress considerations."

"But it's the right thing to do," she said firmly.

Wyatt clamped his jaw shut. Macy apparently took his silence as agreement, because she walked into the house.

10

Macy awoke from a dead sleep and looked straight into the eyes of Milo, who had laid his head on the edge of the bed and was making little whimpering noises.

When she opened her eyes, the dog began to writhe with excitement.

She pushed herself up on her elbows, shoved the hair from her eyes, and looked at the clock next to the bed. It was almost eight o'clock. "Ohmigod," she said, and fell back onto the pillow, covering her face with her hands. Last night, when she was sitting cross-legged on her bed and drinking wine from the bottle, she knew that she was going to pay for it, but she hardly cared. She'd needed desperately to dull her senses, to numb her thoughts.

This morning, her head was killing her.

Milo's eager tail thrashed the drapes behind him with such ferocity that Macy had to roll over, grab his collar, and tell him to sit. "Are you hungry?" she asked, and Milo gave her a high-pitched wail as he leapt over her and onto the bed, hovering over her and trying to lick her face.

"All right, all right," Macy said, and pushed his snout away from her face as she worked to untangle herself from the sheets. She wondered where Wyatt was. It was unlike him to sleep late. But he'd spent the night on the boat and maybe he'd had a few last night, too.

Macy stumbled into the bathroom, washed her face, brushed her teeth, and took a long, hard look at herself in the mirror.

Pathetic.

Her eyes were bloodshot. Her hair looked like turkey buzzards had nested in it. There were dark circles under her eyes, the result of a lack of sleep and water for what felt like days. "You look like hell, Macy Lynn," she announced to herself.

She felt like hell, too.

She looked down and saw that she was wearing one of Wyatt's old T-shirts. She'd always loved this T-shirt—it was one he'd worn when he'd played baseball at the University of Texas. Many washings had softened it and his scent was embedded in the weave.

Milo barked at her.

"All right, all right, already," Macy said, patting his head, and staggered along to the kitchen with Milo on her heels. There was a note on the counter from Wyatt: *Went to get some coffee. Back in a few.* Wyatt had never learned how to operate the coffeemaker. He was funny that way, so capable, so smart, but couldn't operate a coffeemaker. And he never remembered to take his blood pressure medicine. Or refill it, for that matter.

Macy took three aspirin, filled the dog's food bowl, refreshed his water, and left him in the utility room, munching contentedly.

The thought of getting dressed filtered into her brain, but she was feeling too sluggish to attempt it. So she dragged herself through the house, wandering aimlessly. Her gaze landed on a delicate handblown glass cow on a shelf in the den.

That blasted cow. Her mom had brought it back from Italy after she'd traveled there to celebrate a birthday with friends. At the time, Macy had been annoyed that with all the shoes and handbags and clothes in Italy, her mother had brought her a Venetian glass cow. But her mother was so pleased with it. She said it reminded her of Macy's new life as a cowgirl with Finn.

Jillian Harper had never really warmed to Finn. She didn't like his background. He hadn't been to college like Macy. Hadn't traveled like Macy. And being a rancher's wife was not what she'd envisioned for Macy, oh no.

Then again, her mother had never had any reservations about Wyatt—she'd loved him from the moment she met him.

When Macy told her mother she was going to marry Finn, her mother had shaken her head. "Ranching is such a hard life."

"How do you know, Mom?" Macy had asked, wondering when, between college and law school and raising a family right in the middle of suburbia, her mother had lived on a ranch. "It can't be harder than my job as a social worker," she'd added. In Macy's job, she'd seen some of the worst of humanity. How could Finn's good, honest labor be harder than seeing a kid passed from foster home to relative and back again, unloved and unwanted?

"Cows smell, they bellow when they are hungry, and they require a lot of work. Your husband will never be home, you know. He'll always be out working cattle or training horses."

"You make it sound like one of those huge cattle ranches, Mom," Macy had chided her. "It's not that at all. It's small, and he only keeps cows to train cutting horses."

"It's not *you*, Macy," her mother had insisted.

"Maybe you don't know me as well as you think," Macy had said, ending that conversation.

But in a way, her mother was right. Macy was hardly a cowgirl. She had had pizza delivered out to Two Wishes, and had lounged in a bikini by the stock tank when she should have been doing something useful, like planting a kitchen garden or canning preserves. And Finn's parents were right, too. When she and Finn had married, they'd warned Finn that Macy wasn't cut out for that kind of work.

It wasn't that Macy didn't want to work. She *did* work. She kept her job as a social worker until she and Finn had agreed that all the driving and the hard, emotionally exhausting work was wearing her down. Plus, she and Finn wanted children, as soon as they could have them. So Macy had quit her job and had tried to help around the ranch.

She was good at cleaning out the horse stalls, but José didn't like her doing that. She was great at keeping the books. But she wasn't very good at doing the ranch-wife things, as defined by Karen Lockhart. Once, when one of the calves got sick, Karen showed up and told Macy, "He's got sick cows. You need to get out there and help him."

"Help him do what?" Macy had asked.

"Feed the calf!" she'd cried, and had marched Macy out there to show her how to stick a huge syringe down a calf's throat and get some milk and medicine down her. It was awful—the calf struggled, spewing medicine and milk all over her.

When Finn—dirty and wearing stained chaps, and generally looking so hot he could melt a girl's heart—found her trying to medicate the calf again later that afternoon, he grinned. "What are you doing, baby?"

"Trying to doctor this damn cow."

Finn squatted down next to her, grabbed the calf's head in a bear hug, opened the calf's mouth with one hand and squirted the stuff in, then let the calf go. It jumped to its feet and, bleating, loped away.

Wide-eyed, Macy stared at the calf, then at Finn. "That's it?" she cried. "That's all you have to do?"

He smiled and opened his arms. "C'mere," he said, and wrapped his arms around her. Macy remembered his incredibly arousing scent—who knew leather and sweat could be so sexy?

"Let's agree," Finn had said. "I'll do the doctoring."

"I want to help you," she'd said earnestly, and she did, more than anything.

"Just you being here helps me," he said, and pushed her hair from her eyes.

"Finn—"

"Hey, you do help. You drive the truck when I'm putting down hay. You keep the house and the books, and you keep me warm at night. I couldn't ask for more."

Macy could. She longed to be more useful, but couldn't even ride a horse very well.

Yet in spite of her inability to assume the role of cowgirl very effectively, Macy had been happy on the ranch. *Very* happy. Happier than she'd ever thought she could be.

Macy picked up the glass cow and continued on to
the master bedroom. It occurred to her that it wasn't
fair to take something that had a sentimental value associated with Finn and not something associated with
Wyatt. Wyatt was her husband now, and she loved him
in spite of this sea change in her life. So she turned
around and walked to Wyatt's home office. There was
a picture of the two of them at a black-tie gala. Wyatt
was looking adoringly at her, and Macy was smiling at
whoever had taken the picture. Macy remembered that
night. Wyatt was on the board of a children's hospital
foundation, and the event was a big Christmas ball the
foundation held each year.

They'd gone with David and Aurora Bernard, a couple who had been friends with Wyatt before Macy had
met him. She'd never really befriended them quite like
Wyatt wanted. She never felt like she belonged among
the country club set, and David and Aurora did not go
out of their way to make her feel welcome. Wyatt dis-
missed her concerns as insecurity on her part.

The night of that event, Macy had worn a designer
gown she'd found at Davenport Village in Austin. It was
outrageously expensive, but Wyatt had insisted she buy
it. "I want you to shine," he'd said, and in that dress,
Macy had felt like she was shining. It had been a lovely
evening, with dancing and haute cuisine. Then Wyatt
had surprised her with a stay at the Driskill, an elegant
old hotel in Austin. They'd had breakfast in bed after
they'd made love. And then Wyatt had handed her a
Tiffany box.

"What's this?" Macy had asked, surprised.

"It's for you," he'd said, beaming.

"Why?"

"Why not?" he'd asked. "Open it."

Inside was a diamond tennis bracelet. He'd given it to her just because he loved her.

There was another picture of Macy, the day she'd competed in the Danskin Triathlon. She'd come in the bottom third of her age group. Wyatt had taken the picture of her just after she crossed the finish line, when she was still wondering what she was doing out there in hundred-degree heat. With her hair in two ponytails, she'd stood with her hands on the small of her back and her legs planted wide apart, gasping for air while Wyatt snapped his pictures.

Why he'd framed it, she'd never know.

Macy picked up the picture. And a paperweight that looked like a miniature golf bag. And a few other things.

In fact, Macy wandered from room to room in something of a fog, picking up things that reminded her of Finn or Wyatt, filling her arms until she was forced to dig a gym bag out of the hall closet to hold all the mementos she wanted to take with her. When Finn had supposedly been killed, people had told her to get rid of his stuff if she wanted to move on from her grief. It had taken her a long time to do it, but she'd finally given in, only to discover that even though the things were gone, the memories were still there.

She should never have gotten rid of so much.

Wyatt came in, carrying two coffees, and found her wandering about like a madwoman. "What's the matter, kid?" he asked gently.

"Just picking up a few things before I go," she said with an insouciant shrug. She gave the gym bag a yank; it slid across the polished wood floor and the threshold of the master bedroom behind her.

"You're still determined to leave?" he asked, his gaze flicking over her bare legs.

"Yep."

"Are you certain?" He lifted his gaze and took a tentative step toward her, putting the coffees down in an art nook built into the wall. "I've been thinking . . . you don't really need to go, sweetheart. We can work through this. If you want space, I'll give you space, but you don't need to go to find it."

"No," Macy said, shaking her head.

"We've always been able to work through things," Wyatt said, and abruptly reached up to stroke her cheek with his knuckle. That small touch of his finger sent a shiver through her, and Macy closed her eyes.

"You know that whatever you need, I will give you. Everything will be all right, Macy, because I will walk to the ends of the earth for you if I have to."

Wyatt was her savior. *Everything will be all right.* He'd told her that on their first date, when she'd felt so awkward and uncertain about dating. He'd said it the first time they'd made love. She hadn't been with anyone for so long. *Everything will be all right.* He'd said it on the anniversary of Finn's death, and other occasions when she hadn't been able to face the world. He had saved her, had lifted her up from the depths of despair.

Macy opened her eyes and looked up into the face of the man she'd married. With his blue eyes, his thick black hair, and his easy smile, Wyatt was a handsome man. Everyone in town thought so—she'd heard it a million times. And he was a good provider, a hard worker, a good lover. Macy knew how much he loved her, and he . . . he was the sort of man any woman would want as a husband.

But he wasn't Finn. She could not seem to rid herself of that traitorous thought. *He wasn't Finn.*

"Everything will be all right," he said again.

She was *married* to this man, and he looked so earnest, so hurt. She didn't want to hurt him; that was the very last thing she wanted. Tears began to blur her vision. She nodded and glanced at the floor.

His hand moved from her face to her shoulder. "Don't go. Please don't go."

Macy didn't know what to say. Confusion paralyzed her.

Wyatt stepped closer, bent his head, and touched his lips to hers. His kiss was so soft, so full of devotion, that Macy felt a familiar longing in her groin. "Don't go," he whispered, his lips now against her temple. "Don't go."

Macy tried to breathe; she tried to make her body move, but instead she just stood there, her arms hanging limply at her sides, her body wanting his touch, her mind wanting distance from the intimacy. It seemed strangely wrong, as if she were being unfaithful to Finn.

Wyatt cradled her face; his finger stroked her brow, her temple, and fluttered to her neck. The reverence with which he touched her made her feel even weaker, and Macy gripped his wrist, holding herself upright as his hands and mouth moved over her skin.

"Wyatt," she said, but it was all she could manage. There was a familiar comfort in his touch, and it was something she desperately needed after the week she'd had.

She didn't know how they came to be inside the master bedroom, and she didn't protest when he put her on the unmade bed and came over her to kiss her, his hand on her bare knee, then her bare thigh, then sliding up beneath the T-shirt and brushing against her panties.

Warmth spread through Macy's body, making her feel sluggish. Her hands floated up around Wyatt's neck and her lips moved on his, her tongue against his, but she felt as if she were an observer. When his finger slipped inside her panties and dipped into her cleft, Macy was surprised by how damp she was. Her body was responding to her husband's touch, but her mind was somewhere else. She slid her hands over his muscular arms, digging her fingers into them as she pressed against him and his erection.

"I don't want you to go, sweetheart. I don't want to be without you. I love you too much to lose you." He was sliding his body down hers in one excruciatingly slow movement.

The fog that clouded Macy's brain seemed to thicken. One of Wyatt's hands tangled in her hair while he stroked the wet heat between her legs with the other. Purely sexual instincts took hold—she didn't need to think, she only had to react.

Wyatt paused to remove his pants, then rolled onto his back, pulling Macy on top to straddle him. Macy pulled the T-shirt over her head and watched Wyatt's eyes rake over her body. He sighed with longing as he sat up and took her hand in his and kissed her throat. "I love you."

Macy could hear him through her fog, could see the sincerity in his gaze. She pressed her hand to his cheek and smiled, and felt the single tear that drifted down her cheek.

"No, no, no," he murmured, and kissed her cheek. "Don't cry." He enveloped her in a tight embrace and pressed his mouth against her shoulder, and then lower, to her breasts.

Macy dropped her head back and allowed herself to be swept away. Wyatt rolled her onto her back and explored her body with his hands, his fingers trailing over hot skin, his eyes devouring her. He cupped her breasts, squeezed her nipples, then took her breast in his mouth as his hand drifted down the plane of her belly, slipping between her legs and into her body, sliding in and out.

"God, but you drive me crazy—you always have," he said breathlessly, and settled in between her legs.

"Mmm," she said, and brushed her fingers through his hair.

With his gaze on hers, Wyatt slowly pushed inside her, catching his breath as he did.

Macy closed her eyes and allowed him to push her farther out into that ocean of sensation. She heard her sigh of pleasure as he moved inside her. She laced her fingers with his, caressed his back and his buttocks, moved with him. He was so hard, so hot, so thick inside her; she drifted along.

It had never been like this.

Wyatt knew her well—he sensed her climax and thrust powerfully and quickly into her as she fell away from him and the world.

It had never been like this, because Finn had never been in bed with them before today. But he was here now, on the edges of her consciousness, trying to make his way in.

Wyatt shuddered into her and collapsed to her side, his heart beating hard and his breathing labored. "*God,*" he said with breathless appreciation. "That was . . . unreal."

Macy blinked up at the ceiling. He was still inside her.

He lifted up on his elbow and kissed her. "I have to say, you really had me worried." He gently dislodged himself, then rolled over on his back and closed his eyes, a contented smile on his face.

Macy inched toward the edge of the bed.

"What's the rush?" he asked, and put a hand on her belly.

"I have to go," Macy said, scooting out from beneath his hand.

Wyatt opened his eyes. "Where?"

"Laru's. I told you."

A frown darkened his face and Wyatt abruptly sat up. "What the hell, Macy?" he asked angrily. "You're still going after what just happened here?" he asked, gesturing to the bed.

She had to go, *especially* after what had happened. She swung her legs over the edge of the bed and glanced back over her shoulder at Wyatt. "I don't know how to make it easier. If I could, I would, believe me." She stood up.

"Macy, dammit! Don't go!"

"I'm sorry," she said, and padded into the bathroom, shutting the door behind her.

11

Finn dreamed he was under heavy enemy fire. He was running through the confusing maze of streets in Kabul, ducking into doorways when he could. The fire was drawing closer; he ran again, finding himself in a blind alley, a dead end.

There was a woman in a blue *chadari* standing at the end of the alley. No one could be trusted; Finn cautiously approached her, his rifle raised, the woman in his sights. He heard the *rap rap rap* of gunshots nearby. He drew closer, but as he did, he noticed the woman's wide blue eyes, the only part of her he could see. He blinked, quickly rubbed his eyes, and looked again. "*Macy?*" he whispered.

The woman quickly raised a rifle she'd been hiding in the voluminous folds of her *chadari*. *Rap rap rap*.

Finn woke with a start, groping for a gun, frantic to find it until he remembered where he was. He sucked a calming breath into his lungs and sat up.

He heard the *rap rap rap* again—someone was at the door of his room. Finn stumbled to his feet and opened it. "Dad," Finn said roughly, rubbing one eye. "What are you doing?"

"Just checking on you, son." His father looked strange standing there. Finn was still expecting to see turbans and *chadaris*. "You're sleeping. I'll leave you be," he said.

"No, no," Finn said. "What time is it?"

"Ten."

Ten. He'd been awakened at seven every morning for the last three years by the slide of a tray of food across the dirt floor, or the heel of a boot in his back. For a long time, the first real human contact he would have each day was with the boy, Nasir, who had big green eyes, almost too big for his face. He would stare at Finn through a gate as Finn tried to rouse himself, day after day.

Once he was awake, he'd begin his day of alternately

sitting and pacing, save the one hour at midday they allowed him into the courtyard to walk around. Nasir would follow him then, watching Finn feed scraps of food from his bowl to the stray dog in the compound, and then, as Nasir grew older, helping Finn feed the stray.

"Your mom made pancakes," his father said.

"It's good to be home," Finn replied. "I'll be there in a minute."

With his father gone, Finn sat on the edge of the bed in his parents' house and stared at the wall. *Ten o'clock.* He hardly knew what to do with himself. The army handouts suggested that he engage in routine behaviors, but hell if Finn knew what was routine anymore. There were a few things he wanted to do, like see his land. His dogs. Maybe catch up with a couple of friends, if he could find them. But beyond that, he had no idea what he would do.

He got cleaned up and dressed. The smell of pancakes lured Finn down the hall. As he passed the utility room, something in a box on top of the dryer caught his eye. He backed up a step.

Sticking up out of the box was a folded corner of an American flag. Finn stepped into the utility room and looked at the box, but instantly recoiled, his gut taking a nauseating dip. He took a tentative step forward, peered into the box again, and removed a tri-folded flag. And a Purple Heart.

His breathing grew shallow as he put those two things aside and removed a large frame. It was a collage—a picture of him in full dress uniform in the center, to the right of his head the image of an American flag flying at half-mast. Below that was a gold star, the symbol of the U.S. Army. To the left was a print of his rank insignia and a copy of the bulletin from his funeral. *Finneus Theodore Lockhart*, it said. *Sunrise: March 10, 1979. Sunset: August 18, 2006.* On the front was a picture of a green forest with purple flowers—nothing like anything he'd ever seen and damn sure no place you'd find in Texas. *I will dwell in the house of the Lord forever* was written in script across the page.

Inside the bulletin, the date of his birth and death were printed again, above words that blurred as Finn stared at the date of his death. *August 18.* He felt a bit of perspiration on his scalp, and put the bulletin down.

There were more things in the box, little mementos from his life. A scratched and faded toy car he did not recall or recognize. A picture of him wearing a cowboy hat, boots, and chaps, grinning like a fool as he stood beside the first cutter he'd sold for top dollar as part of the local 4-H program. There were some medals from high school track—Brodie had been the jock, but Finn had done okay in track. A baby picture of him when he'd had a mess of long, blond curls, and more pictures from Little League, cub scouts, a prom. At the bottom of the box, turned upside down, was one of his wedding pictures—Macy and him with his parents.

She'd looked beautiful that day. Finn remembered how he'd felt when she'd put her hand in his for the first time as his wife.

He felt clammy and hot as he put the items back in the box. The last thing he picked up was the tri-folded flag. They usually gave that to the wife, he thought, and wondered if Macy had given it to his mother and father.

"Hey."

Luke's voice startled Finn. Having determined, at three in the morning when they'd finally drunk all the whiskey, that they shouldn't be behind a wheel, Luke and Brodie had crashed at the house. Luke frowned at the box. "Come on, man, don't look at that stuff. You want some pancakes?"

"So what's up with this?" Finn asked. "Did she have . . . a shrine?"

"What?"

His mother popped her short-bobbed head around Luke. She'd put on a little weight since Finn had left, and the curls on her head were grayer, but she was still Mom. She was wearing a pair of beige pants that hit her about mid-calf, tennis shoes, and a T-shirt that had a little bouquet of flowers painted on it. She also wore some new rectangle-shaped glasses instead of the big circular frames she used to wear. "What are you boys talking about?" she asked cheerfully.

"Mom, I told you to put that stuff in the attic," Luke said, clearly irritated.

She looked at the box. "Oh!" She looked at Finn. "People said such nice things. We had the memorial at the high school, and all the seats were filled."

"*Mom!*" Luke exclaimed. "Finn, come on," he said impatiently. "Let's eat some pancakes."

"I made them just for you, Finneus," his mother said, beaming. "Are they still your favorite?"

Were pancakes still his favorite? Finn didn't know. He only knew there was a gulf beginning to widen within him, between the man he'd been when he'd left Texas and the man he was now. His pulse was racing again, and he felt irrationally angry with his mother for even asking.

"Dude . . . are you all right?" Luke asked.

Besides feeling that the walls were closing in and about to crush him? "Just hungry, I guess." He stepped past Luke and his mother and headed for the kitchen.

In the kitchen, his mother buzzed happily around the stove, sent Luke to wake Brodie, and flipped pancakes and eggs and sausages as she rattled on about cousins Finn could scarcely remember.

Finn looked around the kitchen as she talked. They still had the blue wallpaper with the tiny pink roses and matching curtains over the sink. There were pots and pans stacked on top of the cabinets and the countertops were covered with small appliances and a black-and-white TV that was on, tuned to some talk show. Nothing had changed while he'd lived four or five lifetimes.

His mother scraped sausage from an iron skillet onto a platter and put it on the breakfast bar. "How'd you sleep, hon?" she asked Finn.

"Good," he lied.

"It must be a real relief to sleep in an honest bed, huh? Brenda Todd asked if you were going to be here later because her son Greg wanted to stop by."

Greg Todd? Finn had gone to high school with him, but they'd never been friends. "Why?"

"Why?" She laughed as Luke returned from his mission. "Honey, you are a local hero. Greg works for the *Cedar Standard*. He wants an interview. Oh, that reminds me. A nice young woman from the *Austin American-Statesman* called, too. Major Sanderson said he would be in touch about television and radio interviews—oh, I almost forgot! The *mayor* would like you to be in the Fourth of July parade," she said proudly.

Finn wasn't planning on doing any interviews anywhere and he damn sure wasn't going to be in a parade.

His mother put a short stack, scrambled eggs, and a glass of milk in front of him. The sight of all that food made him a little queasy. His stomach hadn't been the same since the bomb, and the crap he'd had to eat the last three years had done a number on his system. But his mother was watching him, so he took a healthy bite.

She stood with her arms crossed, her smile full of satisfaction. "Well?" she asked.

"Fantastic," Finn said through a second mouthful.

"Oh my Lord," she cried happily to the ceiling. "I am so blessed to have all my boys home!" Her eyes were tearing up again. "My heart just nearly bursts every time I look at you, Finn."

"Mom—"

"So what would you like to do today?" she asked, changing the subject.

"Not sure," Finn said, putting his fork down. "Thought I'd see Macy. Where does she live?" He had no idea where that had come from—he hadn't planned to see her.

His mother's smile instantly faded. "Why?"

"Why?"

She suddenly turned away from Finn to the stove. "Well, I don't think you need to see her right off," she said a little testily. "Seems like you'd want to settle in and get reacquainted with your family before you tackle that mess. There are a *lot* of people wanting to welcome you home."

"Mom," Luke sighed.

"I want to see my dogs, Mom," Finn said. "She's got my dogs, right?"

"*Dog.* She has one. She gave the rest away." She said it with a look that suggested Macy should be tried and hanged for it.

"Luke, where does she live?" Finn asked evenly.

"Arbolago Hills."

Surprised, Finn looked at his brother. Arbolago Hills was a gated community with million-dollar homes. It was built up on the banks of the Pedernales River and Lake Del Lago. "Wow," he said. "Nice."

"What's nice?" Brodie strolled into the kitchen bare-chested, scratching his belly. His hair—brown like Luke's—was sticking straight up.

"Arbolago Hills," Luke said.

"She did well for herself," Finn said, for lack of anything better to say.

"Sure she did," his mom said. "She's a pretty girl. She knew what she was doing."

"Oh Jesus." Brodie sighed and sat down at the bar next to his brothers. When they were kids, they'd called Brodie the runt. He was three years younger than Finn, four years younger than Luke, and he'd been small with a bad stutter. He'd outgrown both afflictions and was now a big guy and a real charmer. He winked at Finn. "Mom has some definite opinions."

"I think we all do, but I am the only one willing to say what I think," their mother snapped, and shoveled pancakes onto a plate, which she placed in front of Brodie. "And I don't think he oughta go around there, that's all."

"I just want to get out," Finn said, pushing his plate away. "Just get out and breathe a little." His belly was roiling; he couldn't eat another bite. "I want to see my place. I probably won't even go by Macy's." Like hell he wouldn't—Arbolago Hills? Something about that made him crazy. "Just out of curiosity, when did she leave Two Wishes?" he asked.

"Ah . . ." Brodie looked at Finn. "A couple of years ago?"

"So who looks after it?"

Brodie shrugged. "Not much to look after." He took a bite of pancake.

Finn looked from Brodie to Luke, who was likewise focused on his breakfast. "She said it was more than she could handle."

"It was a big job," Luke agreed. "She needed help."

"She could have gotten help," his mother said with a sharp tone.

"Lord," Luke muttered.

His mother shrugged and turned back to her skillet.

There was something they weren't telling him, Finn could feel it. "Well, she's got help now. And I'd like to have a look at it." He looked at Brodie. "Borrow your truck?"

"You bet," Brodie said. "Just drop me in town."

12

Samantha Delaney worked at Daisy's Saddle-brew Coffee Shop. It was the first job she'd managed to hold after emerging from the nightmare of losing her husband, Tyler, in Iraq. She'd meant for it only to be a temporary job until she could get back into teaching, but she'd come to like it and she'd been there two years now.

She was working behind the coffee bar at lunchtime when Linda Gail Graeber and her husband Davis came in. There was obviously trouble in paradise, because Linda Gail came in first with a dark look and slapped her purse onto the counter. Davis wandered in behind her and the two of them stood side by side, glaring at the menu above Samantha's head.

"How are you guys?" Samantha asked.

"*I'm* fine," Linda Gail said. "Give me one of those mackey-otos, or whatever you call 'em."

"I'm fine, too, but I am going to ask you how you are today, Sam, before I go barking a drink order," Davis said evenly.

"He thinks he's such a gentleman, but you ought to hear the way he was talking to me not ten steps from your door. Give him a vanilla latte."

"I can order for myself," Davis said to his wife, and fished out a wad of bills from his pocket. "My wife thinks if you disagree with her, you're automatically a jerk. All I said was, there's something wrong with Macy Clark if she doesn't go back to her first husband. There's no other answer, don't you think, Sam?"

No. No, there was no other answer to Samantha's way of thinking, but she kept her mouth shut.

"There certainly is," Linda Gail snapped. "She is married to Wyatt Clark now. What is he, just a bag of trash for her to throw out? Sam, will you please ask my husband what he wants so we can get this order going?"

Samantha looked at Davis.

"I'll have the vanilla latte and I'll apologize for Linda Gail's surliness."

"I don't need him to apologize for me. We're all grown-ups here. Sam, you probably wanted to know what he's going to drink sometime today just so you could get on with your life. As for me, I'll have to listen to his black-and-white opinions for the rest of my blessed life."

"Large or small?" Samantha asked.

"Large," Davis said. "You tell me, Sam—didn't Macy promise to love Lockhart *first*? Doesn't that promise trump the second promise to Clark? You can't have two bites at the apple. You have to dance with the one that brung ya, am I right?"

"Oh, I'm sorry," Linda Gail said snidely. "I didn't realize I was at a barn dance."

"What would *you* do, Sam?" Davis demanded.

"*Davis!*" Linda Gail hissed.

"What?" Davis snapped, and looked at Linda Gail. Whatever he read in her expression made him color slightly. He looked down, threw some bills on the counter, and averted his gaze. "I'm sorry, Sam. I forgot."

Everyone forgot eventually, but Samantha would never forget. Not for a day, not for a minute. The wound of losing Tyler felt as raw today as it had on July 28, 2006, when the officers had come to her school to tell her Tyler had been killed in action in Baghdad.

"That will be eight seventeen," Samantha said, forcing a smile.

"Good Lord," Linda Gail muttered. "Did they deliver the beans from Bolivia in a gold chest?"

"If she didn't order those Italian coffees, we might be able to afford our mortgage," Davis said to Samantha. The bell on the door clinked behind him as someone entered the store. Samantha picked up the bills Davis had thrown down and opened the register.

"If he didn't think he had some divine right to play golf every dang weekend, we might be able to afford a mortgage, a coffee, *and* a new car," Linda Gail said, crossing her arms across her bosom.

"I'll be right back with those drinks," Samantha said, and handed Davis his change.

She turned away and gulped for a bit of air as Linda Gail turned to face Davis and asked, "What have you got against—oh, excuse me," she said, as whoever had come into the store had obviously stepped up to the counter.

"Be right with you!" Samantha called out as she made the macchiato.

As she steamed the milk, she thought about Macy with her golden hair and blue eyes. Samantha, with her unruly black hair and dark brown eyes, had always envied Macy's prettiness.

Samantha had been fairly new to Texas when Tyler was killed. She didn't have any friends, and her family was all in Indiana. It had taken her a few months to get up the nerve to join a survivors group, but it was there that she met Macy, and the two had hit it off immediately. Macy had taken Samantha under her wing, and for that, Samantha had been truly grateful. They started having coffee a couple of times a week.

They'd eventually realized they were the only two widows in the group without children. The rest of the members had families and needed so much more than the death gratuity and the life insurance Uncle Sam provided. Many of them blew through the money, almost as if they were buying their way out of their grief. Families like that needed more financial support, and college funds, and help planning their futures without their loved ones. But they also needed counseling, a mentoring program for the kids, and for many of the widows, something like a handyman service to help with those chores around the house their husbands had done. Soon after, Macy and Samantha began to learn that families of gravely wounded soldiers, who were often in even deeper financial straits, also needed those services.

They decided to start an organization to raise money for those services. They both had some related work experience, Macy with her social work and Samantha with her involvement with mentoring programs when she'd taught school, so they'd formed Project Lifeline.

Working on Project Lifeline had pulled Samantha from her fog. She'd found it fulfilling, and more important, it had given her something to think about other than Tyler.

They were currently planning a big fundraiser for the end of the summer. "Life Under the Texas Stars" would be a nighttime festival with all proceeds going to Project Lifeline. It was a huge undertaking, and Samantha had to hand it to Macy—she had lined up some fantastic entertainment and vendors. Samantha had done her part, too, but Macy had a real knack for it. It wouldn't be the big event it was shaping up to be without her. Everyone loved Macy. She was personable and cheerful and had a way of explaining things so that no one could refuse her.

Samantha remembered one afternoon when Macy had been babysitting her cousin's toddlers, Chase and Caden. She'd brought them along when she and Samantha paid a visit to Fox Service Company, hoping to persuade the company to donate five free home cooling unit inspections to their cause. The manager of the company was a friend of Wyatt's and was happy to invite the four of them into his office. While they were talking, Chase got his hands on a marker and drew a big black line on Macy's expensive leather purse. Both the manager and Samantha had stared, wide-eyed, as Macy laughed. She took the marker from Chase, then excused herself to clean him up.

Samantha was horrified, and said so when they left the office with the five free inspections. It was a beautiful purse.

"Yeah, but it's just a purse," Macy had said cheerfully.

That was Macy—easy and cheerful and persuasive.

Project Lifeline meant a lot to Samantha and Macy. Samantha had assumed they would run the organization until the war was a distant memory, but all that changed when Macy had called her in shock to tell her Finn was alive. Stunned, Samantha had listened to Macy crying with relief and joy. *Alive!* How was that possible? Why wasn't Tyler alive? *Why wasn't it Tyler?*

Samantha had tried to absorb the shock while Macy

babbled about what that meant. She loved Wyatt, she said. But she loved Finn, too.

If someone told Samantha that she could have as much as a single moment with Tyler, she would give up everything and everyone for it. *Everything.* That Macy could even hesitate for the space of a breath had turned something sour inside Samantha. She resented Macy for that moment of indecision. And that resentment was festering into anger. Samantha had seen Macy on TV with Finn looking so happy, but Samantha knew what was in Macy's heart.

She had no idea how she'd manage to face Macy the next time she saw her. Honestly, she didn't know if she could face Macy at all without letting on how much she envied her for being so incredibly lucky to be able to choose between *two* men she loved.

Samantha shook her head and turned around to the counter with the drinks. "Here you are," she said, but it wasn't Linda Gail and Davis standing there; it was Brodie Lockhart. Linda Gail and Davis had taken a pair of armchairs near the periodicals, both of them staring out the window. Samantha followed their gaze and saw what had captured their attention.

"Hey, Sam," Brodie said with a charming smile. If there was one thing the Lockhart men had in abundance, it was good looks.

"Hi, Brodie," Samantha said, set the Graebers' coffees on the counter, and nervously ran her palms down the sides of her apron. "What can I get you?"

"A couple of plain ol' coffees, please." He reached

in the back pocket of his very tight jeans for his wallet. "What's that going to set me back?"

Samantha had to think a moment. "Five twenty-five."

Brodie withdrew a ten from his wallet and handed it to her.

Samantha quickly rang up the coffees and gave him change. "You want those for here?"

"No thanks," Brodie said, still smiling. "Gotta run."

Samantha looked over Brodie's shoulder at his brother, Finn Lockhart. There he was, in the flesh, Macy's husband. *Alive.* It was so unfair. Everyone's soldier should come home, not just hers.

Finn was waiting outside, leaning back against the fin of the pickup, his hands shoved in his pockets. His hair was lighter than Brodie's, more of a golden brown, but just as thick. He was squinting at something down the street, and he reminded Samantha of the painting that hung in city hall, of an Old West cowboy leaning up against a split rail fence. He had that hard, lean look of strength to him. It was sexy, frankly, and it made Samantha resent Macy even more.

"Have those right out," she muttered as an image of Tyler danced in her head. She wondered what he would look like if he came back.

Samantha had just finished pouring the coffee when she heard Brodie say, "Hey!" She glanced over her shoulder; he was running out the door.

He was too late—Finn had driven off in Brodie's truck.

13

Macy pulled her Jeep into the Shell station to get gas and some water for herself. When she got out of the Jeep, Milo, who was hanging halfway out the back window, tried to lick her face, but Macy dodged his tongue and scratched him behind the ears instead.

Wyatt would be angry when he discovered she'd taken Milo—he loved that dog. Macy hadn't decided until the last minute, but Milo was *her* dog.

Now, as Macy leaned into the Jeep and across the gearshift to reach her purse, Milo began to whimper.

"I gave you love, buddy," Macy said, distracted. "Where is my billfold? Please don't tell me I left it at home." She climbed into the driver's seat to shake out the contents of her purse onto the passenger seat. Milo whimpered again, then barked, his tail beating against the driver's seat. "Milo, *wait*," she said, finding her small billfold.

Milo slammed his whole body into her seat. Macy backed out of the Jeep, but as she did, Milo barked again, startling her, and she banged her head against the doorframe. "Ouch!" she cried, and with her hand on the top of her head she whipped around, her gaze landing on Finn, who was standing behind her with a look of amusement on his face.

Macy's heart leapt at the sight of him. Lord, but he'd always had that effect on her. He wore civilian clothes—a pair of jeans that fit him like a glove, a chambray shirt that made the copper in his eyes shine. His hair was brushed back and over his collar. He looked amazing. The scar on his temple was the only thing that indicated he'd been through the hell of war.

"Hey," he said, his eyes moving up to her hair.

"Hey," she replied, grinning like a fool. She'd probably never get over being completely overjoyed to see him alive and well. But Macy was suddenly aware that she did *not* look amazing. She was wearing a pair of knee-length, cutoff sweats and a camisole. After this morning's events, she hadn't found the energy to dress appropriately, but then again, it never occurred to her she'd run into Finn. "Oh," she said, putting a hand to her hair. "Oh, man."

"How are you?" he asked.

"Me?" She self-consciously dragged her fingers through her hair. "I'm good."

Milo barked again. He'd managed to get one paw out the window and swiped at Finn. Finn smiled as broadly as Macy had ever seen him smile, and Milo was exuberant. This was Finn, the man who had saved Milo from certain death when he'd been dumped in the country. Macy knew the story by heart—Milo had wandered to Finn's door, close to death, covered in ticks and a bad case of mange. Finn and Luke had brought him back to life.

"I didn't mean to startle you, but I saw you drive by with Milo and I wanted to see my dog," he said.

His dog. Not her dog, not Wyatt's dog.

"Hey, sport," Finn said, and put his hand to the dog, his expression full of unguarded affection.

Macy pushed Milo's head into the Jeep so she could open the door. The dog made a keening sound of joy as he leapt from the Jeep and lunged for Finn, planting his paws on Finn's shoulders with such force that Finn had to catch himself with a step backward. Tears wet Finn's eyes, and he went down on his haunches with Milo, burrowing his face in the fur of Milo's neck.

"Oh, Finn," Macy whispered, kneeling down beside him.

He looked embarrassed and quickly dragged his sleeve across his eyes. "I'm okay," he said with a sheepish laugh. "But I have missed my dogs." He scratched Milo's ears again. "Mom said you got rid of Lucky and Bruno."

Karen Lockhart could really grate on Macy's nerves. "Your mother," she sighed. "I didn't get rid of them, Finn. But I couldn't take them all to town when I left the ranch."

"Yeah, about that . . . why did you leave it?" he asked. "I understand selling the stock, but why did *you* need to leave Two Wishes?"

That was simple. She was lonely, despondent, miserable. Every place she looked reminded her of Finn and her loss. "Well . . . I thought you were gone." It was amazing how she could still tear up at that. "And I found it pretty awful there without you."

He looked at her a long moment. "I think I'd find it pretty awful there without you, too. So you left?"

She nodded. "I got a small apartment in town, but there wasn't enough room for all the dogs." Macy thought of that day, how small and empty she'd felt. She was beginning a new life she hadn't asked for or wanted. "I asked everyone in the family if they could take them, but no one had the space or the time to give them. Your mom was perfectly happy with me giving the dogs to Ed Boudine at the time, and he took really good care of them."

"Took?"

There would be no end to the bad news, it seemed. "Lucky got sick and he had to put him down. Bruno's still with him, and Milo . . . I could never have given Milo away." Finn swallowed and shifted his gaze to the dog.

"Cancer," Macy added softly, her voice breaking a little. "Lucky had cancer. But Bruno is still out there chasing squirrels."

Finn nodded again. "That's the only thing Bruno could ever do that was worth a damn."

Macy smiled.

"So you just left the ranch sitting there?"

She hadn't exactly left it sitting there. She should tell him, Macy knew she should tell him that it had all but been sold, but she was going to fix that. And Finn had endured so much bad news as it was. "Something like that," she admitted.

Finn seemed to accept that. "Hey, buddy," he said, sending Milo into another fit of apoplectic wiggling as he scratched the dog's throat. "Maybe I'll drop by and check on Bruno," he said absently. He gave Milo another hug and stood up. Milo was instantly at attention, his head cocked back, panting eagerly, watching Finn's every move.

Milo had been the one constant in Macy's life, the one thing that kept her connected to Finn all this time. "Do you . . . do you want Milo?"

Finn looked startled by the question. "What—you mean now?"

"No, I . . . I mean, he's been with me a long time, and I'd . . . I'd hate to lose him." It would devastate her. "But he's your dog, Finn."

"That sounds a little final, Macy. Like we're dividing the sheets."

She didn't want to think of dividing the sheets—that was the furthest thing from her mind. "I'm going to stay with Laru," Macy blurted.

Finn cocked a brow.

"Yep. Laru," she said to his unspoken question.

"Does that mean—"

"It means I need some space to think," she said, and opened the Jeep's door. "Are you taking Milo?"

Milo answered that by jumping into the back seat of the Jeep. Someone honked as they drove by, but Finn didn't seem to notice. He squinted at Macy and shifted closer. "What's going on, Macy?" he asked in a low, soothing voice.

Macy stepped back, afraid of what she might do if he got too close. She might throw her arms around him, might press her face into his neck, might put her hands in his hair, might crumble, just crumble, crumble, crumble.

"If you want out of your marriage to Wyatt, you know no one is going to fault you. Least of all, me."

Macy shook her head. "It's not that simple."

"You wouldn't be alone," he said, and took another step closer. "I'd be there to help you."

Macy's heart began to pound. What sort of hell was this? She wanted Finn; she wanted him as badly as she'd ever wanted him, yet she could still feel Wyatt's body on hers from their lovemaking earlier. "I honestly don't know what I want," she said. "Everything is so different now."

"The only difference is that I've been gone awhile. Everything else is the same."

"It's not. You know it's not," she said softly. "Lucky is dead. You were held by the Taliban for three years. Your horses are gone. I am remarried. *Nothing* is the same."

He tangled his fingers with hers. "We can make it the same—"

"Wishing won't change what is. In all honesty, I don't know how well I even know you any longer, Finn. I mean, you've been through so much, and I guess so have I, and in some respects, it feels like we're strangers. Don't you feel that?"

"Can't say that I do. But baby, if you think we're strangers, then we need to keep talking and holding onto each other 'til we're not strangers anymore."

Oh God, how she wanted to do just that, to hold onto him until the last three years faded away.

Someone passed by and honked the horn. She heard the word *hero* as the car sped by.

Finn heard it, too. He glanced up the street a moment. "You take Milo," he said, and reached in through the window to pet the dog one last time. "We'll talk about him when I've gotten settled in."

"Okay," Macy murmured.

"Laru's, huh?" Finn said.

Macy nodded.

He smiled a little and touched her hair, twisting an end loosely around his finger. "Don't worry yourself so, Macy," he said. "Trust me—we're gonna figure this out." With that, he shoved his hands in his pockets and turned away from her, ambling back to Brodie's pickup. He climbed in, started it up, and pulled out onto the road, where he flipped a U-turn.

It wasn't until his truck had disappeared down the road that Macy realized the man behind her was yelling at her to get the gas or move the Jeep.

14

Finn should never have chased after Macy like that, but he'd seen Milo as she'd gone by and he'd reacted without thinking . . . and then he'd seen her climbing out of the Jeep, her legs slender and tan, and he couldn't help himself.

Damn it to hell, she was pretty, as pretty as the first time Finn had laid eyes on her in the parking lot of the University of Texas football stadium. Mike had scored tickets to a Longhorn game and they'd joined some of Mike's friends. Macy showed up with the girlfriend of one of the guys. She wore a Longhorn tank with little shoulder straps and a UT baseball hat. And she had a pair of tiny orange longhorns painted on her cheeks.

She was pretty, Finn remembered thinking at the time—just pretty, but not astoundingly so. Yet there was something about those big blue eyes—kindness, genuine warmth—that had drawn him in and held him from the first moment they met. He hardly said a pair of sentences to her that night. He asked her if she was into football.

"Not really," she'd said with a smile. "But I'm graduating next May, so I'm being supportive." She held up her little finger and forefinger. "Hook 'em Horns."

Finn had smiled. "What are you studying?"

"Social work," she'd said proudly, to which he'd said nothing. He didn't know what *to* say to that. "I know, I know," she said, still smiling. "Bleeding heart liberal and all that, hard job with no money. My parents were really hoping for law school, and I was really hoping to win the lottery." She'd laughed at her joke. "Well, I didn't win the lottery, so I guess this is the next best thing."

Finn remained silent. College wasn't exactly his thing, and he didn't want to sound ignorant.

"I'm kidding," she said, touching his hand. "Not about law school, because I *really* didn't want to do that. About the lottery. I mean, don't get me wrong, that would be great, but I really like social work. I guess I'm just a sucker for kids. So what about you? What are you studying?"

"I'm not," he said. "I train cutting horses."

"Cutting horses!" she exclaimed, her eyes lighting up, and for a moment, Finn thought there was a connection. "That sounds really cool. What do they cut?"

It should have ended there. She knew nothing about ranching or horses, and he knew nothing about college or social work. But Finn could think of little else for days afterward. He'd never been a very good dater, but somehow he'd screwed up the courage, got Mike to track down her number, and called her.

Now, he thought, she was the most beautiful woman on the face of the earth, at least to him. It was true what they said—beauty was more than skin-deep.

It was that long line of memories of Macy and the

hope of holding her again in his arms that made Finn run his mouth today and try to talk her into leaving the man she'd married after him. Honestly? He'd seen a crack in her veneer.

Laru's. Finn remembered where Laru lived. Nice place. Great place to get away.

He pulled into the parking lot of the Saddle-brew Coffee Shop and parked the truck. He'd just shut the door of the pickup when Brodie stepped outside. So did two others—a large woman and an even larger man rushed toward him, startling Finn. He instinctively put his back against the truck and looked around for an escape.

"Sir, I just want to shake your hand," the man said, extending a beefy hand. "It's not every day that a person gets to meet an actual hero."

"I—"

"My husband ought to at least introduce himself," the woman said, crowding in beside her husband. "His name is Davis Graeber, and I am Linda Gail Graeber," she said eagerly. "I went to school with your Uncle Braden."

"We've heard an awful lot about you, sir," Davis Graeber said, thrusting his hand forward again in such a manner that Finn felt compelled to take it. "What you endured must have been hell."

"Yes, sir," Finn said and looked over the top of Mrs. Graeber's head to Brodie, who was coming toward him with two more people in tow. What had he done, called for backup? Who *were* these people? As they crowded around him, he began to feel the big blue Texas sky press down on him.

"So what are your plans now that you're home?" Mrs. Graeber asked as two women and Brodie formed a half-circle around Finn. "Are you staying with your mama? I know she's so happy to have you home."

Finn couldn't seem to find his voice; his tongue suddenly felt thick in his dry mouth.

"Do you have a job, Finn? Because if you need a job, my family will give you one," another woman said. "We've got a brickyard, and we could always use a good man like you. We'd be awful proud to hire you on."

"I heard you were going to be on the big float in the Fourth of July parade," Mr. Graeber said to the obvious delight of the others.

Finn didn't want this; he didn't want any attention. He'd always been the guy to hang back—he was shy that way. All he wanted was his old life back; he didn't want any part of a parade, or the adoring smiles of these people. An overwhelming image of dismembered bodies flashed across his mind's eye, and Finn looked anxiously at his brother.

Brodie understood him, because he said to the small assembly, "He just got home, folks. We're hoping he can just breathe for a few days." He gave Finn a bit of a friendly shove away from the driver's door and opened it. "I'll drive," he said, and gestured to the passenger seat.

Finn flashed a smile at the enthusiastic little crowd. *If only they knew*, he thought. If they knew some of the dark thoughts that went through his head, were going through his head right at this moment, they wouldn't think he was such a hero. He waved and climbed into the passenger seat. Brodie rolled down his window and put the truck in reverse. "Thanks for welcoming my brother home," he said. "I'm sure you'll be seeing Finn around town." Then he backed the truck out of the lot and pointed it toward town.

He sighed irritably and glanced at Finn. "You took off in my truck, dude."

"Yeah," Finn said, and looked out the window. "Sorry about that."

"Where'd you go?"

"Nowhere." It was hard to explain that for a few minutes at a gas station, he'd tried to be the man he'd been before Afghanistan. "Just took a little ride."

"Next time, don't leave me behind with the blue hairs," Brodie said gruffly. "So, are we heading to Macy's?"

Finn looked out the window. "I ran into her."

"You did? Where?"

"In town. Look, do me a favor and take me out to my place. I want to see it."

Brodie didn't speak; when Finn looked at him, his brother's eyes were on the road, his jaw clenched. "What?" Finn asked.

"She didn't tell you?"

"Tell me what?" Finn asked.

"Dude . . . there is something you need to know," Brodie said tightly.

Finn snorted. "Don't tell me—the house and barn burned down and there is nothing left but charred earth."

But Brodie didn't laugh. He kept staring ahead.

Finn's gut tightened. "What is it?" he demanded.

Brodie sighed. "Finn, listen. I didn't want to be the one to tell you this—"

"*Say* it."

"They sold it. Or if it's not sold, it's damn close to being sold."

Finn's gut clenched. He could feel the blood drain from his face. "Why didn't she tell me?" he snapped. They'd just talked about it. She could have told him.

Brodie didn't answer.

A rush of hot anger surged through Finn. The combination of seeing Macy and wanting her so badly, the crowd, the whole ordeal of coming home, and now the news that the ranch had been sold, was more than Finn could handle. He slammed his fist into the dash. "*Jesus!*" he shouted. "Didn't anyone try to stop her? You just let her sell land that's been in the family for more than one hundred years?"

"Calm down!" Brodie said. "We couldn't have stopped her if we wanted to, Finn. None of us could take it over, and Uncle Braden said to let it go—"

"God *damn* it!" Finn bellowed. He glared out the window, trying to make sense of it. His horses and cattle, Two Wishes Ranch, his dogs, his wife—all gone. He felt betrayed, completely and utterly betrayed.

"Okay, look," Brodie said, sounding nervous. "Uncle

Braden thinks the city will annex a good piece of it anyway—"

"Turn in here," Finn said, pointing at Rawhide, an old cowboy watering hole on the fringe of town.

"Where, the *Rawhide?*" Brodie said disbelievingly, squinting at it.

"Turn *in*," Finn demanded, pounding the dash.

He had the door open before Brodie could even bring the truck to a halt.

At that moment, Finn didn't care why Macy had sold it and had failed to tell him. At that precise moment, he realized that the life he'd once lived in the Hill Country of Texas was truly dead and buried and the only thing that mattered to him was tequila. How much, where, and how soon he could get it.

15

Macy bounced down the gravel drive to Laru's house, parked in her big circular drive, and let Milo out of the backseat. The damn dog raced for the river, and she heard the splash as he dove in. Macy didn't bother trying to call him back; she was emotionally spent. She slung her purse over her shoulder and dragged herself and all her confusion to Laru's front door and rang the bell.

She expected Ernesto or Consuelo, Laru's part-time hired help, to answer the door, not Jesse Wheeler. Jesse was about four years older than Macy and was known around Cedar Springs for riding rodeo, which he did with fearless élan. He was a good-looking man, too, with dark, wavy hair and striking green eyes. Macy knew him because he'd shown Finn's cutting horses a couple of times. One summer, when he'd broken his arm in a particularly fierce bronco ride, he'd been the dream of every woman in Cedar Springs.

Jesse planted one arm against the jamb above his head, then grinned as he casually scratched his bare belly, which, Macy couldn't help but notice, was as hard as the rock on the house. "Macy-cake Clark," he drawled. "I haven't seen you around in a while."

Confused, Macy looked past him. "Is Laru here?"

"Macy, hon, is that you?" Laru appeared from behind Jesse, ducking beneath his arm to stand in front of him. She was wearing a very short silk robe and her hair was mussed. There was no mistaking what had happened here this afternoon, and Macy was stunned. Jesse had to be at least fifteen years younger than Laru.

"Girl, what are you doing out here?" Laru asked, peering past her to the Jeep. "Is Wyatt with you? I thought you'd be tied up with everything for at least a week."

"No. I . . ." Macy hesitated.

"Is something wrong?" Laru asked, her eyes narrowing with concern. "Did something happen?"

"No, no! I just . . . need to talk to you, Laru." She glanced sheepishly at Jesse.

"Ah," Laru said and turned around, putting her hand on Jesse's bare waist. "Do you mind giving us a minute?" she asked, and went up on her tiptoes—and probably kissed him but Macy couldn't be entirely certain, because she ducked her head at the last moment.

"Sure," Jesse said.

When Macy heard him shuffle away, she looked up at Laru. "*Jesse Wheeler?*"

"What?" Laru responded with a shrug. "He's cute!"

"He's practically young enough to be your son!"

"He is not!" Laru protested as she grabbed Macy's arm and drew her inside. "He's in his late thirties."

"He's thirty-two."

"Okay, thirty-two!" Laru conceded. "What is age but a number? Anyway, I am sure you didn't come out here to lecture me about my love life, kiddo." She linked her arm with Macy's, and led her into the enormous great room with the big picture windows and stunning view of the river.

Laru had a gorgeous, sprawling house. A massive limestone fireplace on one end and a high-end gourmet kitchen and beautiful limestone-and-granite bar on the other flanked the great room, with its high, box-beamed ceiling and recessed lighting. On one side off the great room were the master suite, library, and office. On the other side, behind the kitchen, were the guest rooms.

"So how long has this been going on?" Macy asked, looking around for signs of Jesse.

"Well, *Mom*, for a bit," Laru said with a laugh. "Come on, now, what about *you*? How are you, honey? How is Finn? Jilly said he looks good."

Jillian, Macy's mother and Laru's sister, despised being called Jilly, and Laru was the only one who was allowed to use that childhood name. "He looks . . . he looks amazing," Macy said with a smile. "A scar on his temple is the only visible sign of his ordeal."

"Poor guy," Laru said. "I always had a soft spot for Finn Lockhart. Jilly said you were trying to work out what you're going to do."

"I was," Macy said. "I mean, I *am*. Oh God, it is so hard, Laru. I don't know what to do. I love Wyatt, but it's *Finn*. *My* Finn."

Laru smiled sadly at Macy.

"I can't stay home. I can't think straight there. Laru, I need a place to stay."

Laru blinked. "What does Wyatt say about that?"

"He doesn't like it," Macy said as tears welled in her eyes. Lord, she was sick of tears. She'd cried buckets and buckets when she'd been told Finn had died, buckets and buckets when he'd come back to life. It seemed impossible she had another tear inside her, but here they came. "I still love Finn!" she blurted. "Heaven help me, I never stopped loving him, and I *still* love him. But I love Wyatt, too! He saved me from myself, Laru. He brought me back to life again, and he didn't ask for this and he doesn't deserve this. I don't know what to do!" She angrily swiped at the tears that began to slide down her cheeks.

Laru opened her arms and wrapped them around Macy. "Of course you can stay here, sweetie," she said. "As long as you need."

Macy sincerely hoped Laru meant that.

Wyatt couldn't get any work done, not with the events of the morning still weighing heavily on his mind. A woman didn't make love like Macy had that morning and then get up and walk out. But trying to figure out what was in Macy's head was just making him crazy. His powers of reasoning had been seriously depleted; frankly, he felt as if he'd been kicked in the head.

He was thinking of leaving, of getting out of the office for the afternoon, when he heard Linda Gail say, "He's on the phone."

But Wyatt wasn't on the phone and hadn't been on the phone for a while. He got up to see who Linda Gail was talking to and saw Caroline Spalding. She was a couple of years older than him. She had a pretty smile. Rumor had it that Caroline got around, but she'd always reminded Wyatt of a preacher's wife.

"Hello, Wyatt," she said.

"Hello, Caroline."

"Wyatt, are you off the phone already?" Linda Gail said, popping up between them. "Here, you need to return these calls. Caroline, maybe you can come back when Wyatt's got a little more time."

"I just need a minute," Caroline said.

Wyatt had no idea why Linda Gail was acting so batty. "Come on back, Caroline," he said. With her back to

Caroline, Linda Gail scowled something fierce—if looks could kill, he'd be a dead man right now.

Caroline walked into Wyatt's office stepping daintily over the plat maps and rolled-up blueprints and the basketball he never used anymore. Wyatt perched on the edge of his desk. "What's up, Caroline?"

"Well, for one thing, I am thinking of selling some land and need a broker. I need the *best* broker, and that is you."

"Thanks," he said with a smile. "What land?"

"A chunk my dad left to me. He passed away last year, and it's been sitting there unused. It's out near the resort you're building."

That bit of information certainly perked him up. The more alternatives he had to the Lockhart piece, the better. He'd planned to use a portion of the Lockhart land in the footprint of the resort, and the profit from the sale of the rest of the land to help fund the resort. He could work around the footprint problem if he had to, but it was the profit that he really needed. Without the sale of the Lockhart ranch, he was short, and investors were expecting it to be funded and underway by the end of the month. "You've got my attention."

"I'd like to show it to you and see what you think."

"Maybe we can take a look at it this week," he suggested.

"I would like that." She smiled again, shifted closer. "How are you holding up, Wyatt?"

"Fine," he said. "Why do you ask?"

"It must be so hard."

"I don't know what you mean. Everything is good."

She smiled wryly. "I don't blame you for not wanting to talk about it. But if you ever want to, maybe we could have a drink. I think you'll find that I am a good listener," she said, looking directly into his eyes.

Wyatt smiled. "I don't think so, Caroline. I'm married, remember?"

"I remember. I'm just offering a shoulder, Wyatt. Call me if you need it."

"Thanks. But the only thing I'm going to call you about is that land." He stood up and walked to the door. "I'll have Linda Gail get in touch."

"I'll look forward to it," Caroline said with a smile. In the front office, she said, "Good-bye, Linda Gail. I'm sure we'll speak again soon."

Linda Gail smiled thinly. When Caroline stepped outside, Linda Gail swung around in her chair and leveled a dark look on Wyatt.

"Linda Gail, I don't need a hall monitor," he said before she could start in. "Set something up with Caroline so I can go look at her land." He grabbed up the mail. "I won't be back. Lock up, will you?"

"Don't I always?" Linda Gail said pertly.

Outside, Wyatt sat in his truck, trying to decide where to go. He didn't want to go home—it *wasn't* home right now; it was nothing but a heap of limestone and brick with a tile roof. All that he'd put into that place for Macy seemed like a big cosmic joke now. So he put his truck in gear and drove aimlessly, until he found himself at Daisy's Saddle-brew.

As he walked into the Saddle-brew, he overheard a couple talking about the Fourth of July parade and "The Hero." He looked at them blankly for a moment, then shifted his gaze to Samantha Delaney behind the counter.

She smiled sweetly at him. "Hey, Wyatt. You look like you could use a large, black, really plain coffee."

Wyatt chuckled. "How'd you know?"

"You're sort of predictable," she said with an easy smile.

"Wyatt, you old dog!"

It was Randy Hawkins. Randy was richer than anyone in Cedar County—oil money—and he liked dabbling in ranch deals. He sauntered up beside Wyatt. "Coffee, black, sweetheart," he said to Sam, and Wyatt wondered if Randy was also predictable. "Glad I ran into you, Clark. Are you still trying to find a buyer for that land east of Fredericksburg?"

Trying? Wyatt was desperate. "Sure am," he said.

"I've been thinking about it. Have Linda Gail call and I'll find a time we can go have a look," Randy said. "So how's everything else? I hear the hero's home, huh?" he asked congenially, as if Wyatt had brought Finn Lockhart home himself.

"Seems like," Wyatt responded, and took the cup of coffee Sam put before him.

"Yeah, I saw him up on Guadalupe Street earlier today talking to your wife."

Wyatt's heart suddenly stopped pumping. He hid his shock behind a sip of coffee.

"That must bite," Randy said with a sympathetic smile. "Come home after all that time and find your wife has moved on." He shook his head.

Sam slammed Randy's coffee down and it splashed. "Whoa!" said Randy, jumping back and looking down at his shirt. "Careful, sweetheart!"

"Samantha," she said. "My name is Samantha."

Randy's brows rose. He picked up his coffee as Sam walked away. "PMS, anyone?"

"I'll have Linda Gail get in touch," Wyatt said. He looked at Sam. "See you, Sam."

"Bye, Wyatt. I'll see you tomorrow."

Wyatt turned and walked out, gripping the coffee cup so tightly that it was bending inward, liquid spilling out the little hole in the top. He walked outside and tossed the cup into the trash on his way to his truck.

He was fumbling for his keys when a blue truck pulled up. Wyatt didn't pay much attention to it until he heard the driver say, "I'm not taking you home like this, Finn. Mom would string us both up and invite the coyotes to feast on our hides."

Wyatt kept his head down as the driver walked past him and into the coffee shop. He lifted his head then and looked at the passenger in the blue truck, and his gaze locked with Finn Lockhart's. Wyatt didn't know if he or Lockhart moved first, but Lockhart was out of the truck amazingly fast for someone as unsteady on his feet as he seemed to be.

"Hey, don't run off on my account," Lockhart said as he moved around the front of the truck.

"You're drunk," Wyatt said.

Lockhart laughed derisively. "No shit. You would be, too, if you found out your land was gone."

Okay, Wyatt saw where this was heading. He decided to be the sober guy here and get in his truck and drive off. He turned away.

"Hey, don't run off. Let me ask you something, there, sport," Lockhart said.

Against his better judgment, Wyatt paused and glanced back.

"Do you make a habit of hitting on women whose husbands are fighting a war?" Lockhart asked, bracing himself against the hood of the truck. "Or did you just single out my wife?"

"I didn't hit on her," Wyatt said evenly.

"Yeah, they warned us about guys like you," Lockhart said with a sneer. "Predators who move in on vulnerable women and charm the land right out from under them."

"Look, pal, you were dead. And she—"

"She *what*?" Lockhart said, his expression turning dark.

That was enough for Wyatt. He took several steps toward the drunk. "Don't come at me like I stole your wife in some ugly affair. She was a widow. It was legit."

"But she's *not* a widow," Lockhart said, swaying a little. "So you should be a man about it and back off. Like all the way to Oklahoma, some place where I can't see you or smell you."

"Maybe *you* ought to be the man here," Wyatt snapped.

Lockhart lunged for Wyatt at the same moment Randy opened the shop's door, holding it for Lockhart's brother, who was carrying two coffees. "Hey!" the younger Lockhart shouted when he saw what was happening. He dropped the two coffees and grabbed his brother, wrestling him into his truck as Lockhart shouted, "You think you can take what's mine? I'll make your life hell, Clark!"

Randy watched the brouhaha, shaking his head as the blue truck sped away. "You hear about stuff like that," he said. "Soldiers see things over there that makes them so nutty they start going 'round like a blind dog in a meat market."

Wyatt was so angry he was trembling. He didn't want Macy anywhere near that blind dog.

16

About a week after her soldier son arrived home, back from the dead, Karen Lockhart had her husband pull a cardboard box down from the attic. Rick grumbled about it—the box was behind the Christmas decorations, he hit his head on a beam, and he noted that the insulation needed to be redone, which upset him because he didn't like paying for things like that and he didn't need any more chores—but he brought the box down and dropped it on the kitchen bar.

"Thanks, sweetie," Karen said. She hadn't called him sweetie in a while, but their relationship had been infused with a new vitality since Finn had come home.

Karen opened the box and withdrew her collection of crosses and praying hands. She'd put them away after they'd been told Finn had died in combat, convinced there was no God in her life. But then God had shown her a miracle, had brought her dead son back to her, and Karen's faith was fervently renewed.

Reverend Duffy was very happy to see her return to the fold. He was disappointed Rick hadn't returned with her, but Rick had promised Karen he would think about it, and she assured Reverend Duffy that he would be back very soon.

Karen had also rejoined the Women's Circle of Caring, a group of churchwomen devoted to worship and charity work. She thought it would be a great place to reconnect with her old friends at church—until she learned they were working to help the Project Lifeline gala fund-raiser. Karen was all for the cause of helping the families of fallen and wounded soldiers, but she didn't care much for Macy, not since she'd up and married Wyatt Clark. Not that Macy had just up and married him without *some* discussion, for she had come out to the house and told Karen and Rick she was considering marrying him.

They'd told her to go ahead, they sure had, because Karen was certain Finn would have wanted that. But *she* didn't want that. She thought Macy ought to have mourned her son a little longer, thought she owed Finn that much.

And then Macy and Samantha Delaney had started Project Lifeline, a dumb name to Karen's way of thinking. She would have come up with a good acronym and worked backwards. Something like . . . *Wishes. Women In Search of Happy EndingS.* This fund-raiser, "Life Under the Texas Stars" or something, sounded like a cheesy prom night to Karen, but it sure had the whole town talking. Seemed like folks were almost as excited about it as they were about the new Hill Country Resort and Spa. There were even rumors that Lyle Lovett was going to perform.

Karen had smiled through her first Circle of Caring meeting and tried to be enthusiastic about the fund-raiser. God had given her son back to her, and if that is what He wanted her to do, then she was going to do it.

As for her son . . . Karen wished Finn was a little happier. Oh, he was happy—he laughed and carried on with his brothers, watched baseball, rode Rick's old horse. He said he just wanted to hang out and be with his family right now. He said he wasn't comfortable talking to other people about his time in Afghanistan. That was like Finn. He'd always been the quiet one, the shy one. But there was something in his eyes Karen didn't like, a veil over them that kept her from seeing the son she knew. It wasn't that Karen was naïve and didn't realize there would be a period of adjustment after what he'd been through, but she still expected him to be . . . different.

Really, he'd done nothing but drink since coming home, and it worried her. She'd told Major Sanderson that Finn wasn't up to interviews just now. And a man from New York kept calling about a book and said he could wait until Finn was ready to talk. She'd finally made excuses to the mayor about the Fourth of July parade and had gone alone to watch it. Her boys wouldn't go with her and stayed with Rick while he barbecued. So Karen went, and she imagined her son Finn riding the big float and got big tears in her eyes.

Oh, and Macy called that week.

Rick told Karen to be patient. Karen wanted to be patient, but Finn needed a guiding hand, and she was his mother. She had a responsibility to help him adjust to civilian life. She tried to talk to him about any issues he was having, or urge him to think about what sort of job he might want to get when he was ready. She tried to impress on him the importance of looking to God and Jesus for guidance.

But Finn rebuffed her; he would roll his eyes impatiently and go out with Brodie and Luke again. Last night, she hadn't even heard him come in.

Karen picked up a decorative cross she'd bought the year the family had vacationed in Taos, New Mexico. It was made of clay and hand-painted in the colors of the desert. Finn really loved the mountains and the Indian culture around Taos, and Karen thought the cross would be a reminder of good times and God. Holding the cross, she walked down the narrow hall to his room.

She knocked, but there was no answer, so she opened the door just a bit. She could see Finn lying on his bed, one arm slung over his eyes. The covers came up to his waist and he was bare-chested. The room was dark—he'd pulled the shade down and closed the curtains.

It was one o'clock in the afternoon. With a frown, Karen made her way to the windows and drew back the drapes. When she lifted the shade, she heard him grunt. She pasted a bright smile on her face and turned around, still holding the cross. He'd rolled onto his side, his back to her, and her smile rapidly disappeared—his back was marked with purple welts and puckers of skin. Shrapnel wounds.

Karen instinctively touched one of the scars; Finn flinched and moved closer to the edge of the bed. "Stop, Mom. What do you want?"

Karen withdrew her hand. "Look what I found," she said. When Finn didn't roll over, she thumped her finger against his shoulder. "*Look.*"

With another groan, Finn rolled onto his back and blinked up at the cross she held aloft. "What about it?"

"Finn! Don't you remember? We got this in Taos. I was thinking, wouldn't it be nice if maybe you took a little trip to Taos? Just a couple of weeks. The weather is so good this time of year, and you could camp out the way you like. You know, rejuvenate."

Finn looked at her like she'd lost her mind. "Mom. I've had enough living in the wilderness to last me a lifetime. The last thing I want to do is go sleep on the ground somewhere."

"Oh." She hadn't thought of it that way. He started to roll over again, but Karen said, "What are your plans for tonight? I thought I'd make a roast."

"Mom, just let me sleep, okay?"

"It's one o'clock, Finn."

"So?" he asked sharply.

Karen bit her lip. She turned around and put the cross up on the dresser, balancing it against the wall. "Macy called again. She wants you to call her. I don't know why she can't let you settle in first."

Finn grunted.

"Major Sanderson sure wants to talk to you. So does that book publisher. He thinks your story would make a great book. Think of that, Finn! Your story in a *book*!"

"Mom, please leave me alone. *Please*," he implored her.

Karen knew she was irritating him, but in one last desperate attempt to engage her son, she asked, "Have you given any more thought about going to church with me?"

"Jesus *Christ*," he said angrily, and suddenly threw back the covers and swung his legs off the bed.

"Finn!" Karen said sternly. "Don't speak His name like that! I don't understand you! You are a miracle, and you owe God your worship!"

Finn turned his head and looked at her with those darkly veiled eyes. "A *miracle*? Are you kidding me?"

Karen gasped. "Don't you have any faith?" she demanded.

"I have faith, Mom. I have faith that I'm no damn miracle."

"How can you say that?" she cried. "You came back from the *dead*, Finneus!"

"Do you honestly believe that, Mom?" he exclaimed incredulously as he pulled a green army T-shirt over his head. "Because if you do, let me assure you that I feel exactly like I did every day of the last three years sitting in a hellhole in Afghanistan. That's no miracle."

"But you escaped!"

"Yeah, I escaped," he said angrily and stood up, towering over her. "But I don't think God singled me out from a bunch of other men and women and said, *Okay, Finn, you are My chosen one. Go now and find your wife and your land and your animals scattered to the winds.* No, Mom! I was lucky. *Lucky!* Not blessed! The only reason I am alive today is because I—" He suddenly stopped and shoved both hands through his hair. "Jesus, I don't need this right now," he muttered.

"Because you what?" she pressed him.

"Nothing," he said, and grabbed a towel that was hanging on the door of the closet. "I'm going to take a shower."

"What about a prayer group?" Karen called after him. "Would you at least go to prayer group with me?"

Her answer was the sound of the hall bathroom door being firmly shut. With a sigh, Karen sank onto the end of the twin bed. There had to be a way to reach her son. God hadn't brought him back so she could watch him wallow in his bed like an old drunk.

17

Finn knew he was causing his mother grief, but that wasn't his intent. He'd never been much of a drinker, and he was privately a little surprised at how easily he'd taken to it, how much he seemed to need it. He supposed it had something to do with the stupid sense of despair that was weighing him down. It seemed odd to feel despair, because he was beyond thrilled to be free and home with his family. But disappointment about Macy and his ranch kept eating at him, like an infection growing from the inside out, and nothing seemed to take away that inflammation but booze. Not sleep, not food. Just booze.

The bitter disappointment had kept him from Macy, too. His anger at her for putting the ranch up for sale had been so strong he was afraid to go near her. But then the anger had subsided and hurt steamrolled in to take its place. And now? Now he supposed curiosity had him by the throat. He needed to know a few things.

Late that afternoon, he slipped out of the house when his mother went down to the barn to talk to his dad and took one of the old pickups they kept around for fieldwork. Finn would hear about it tomorrow, but Brodie and Luke were growing tired of carting him around from bar to bar. They didn't drink like Finn found himself drinking, and moreover, Finn knew he was sorry company. His brothers wanted to talk, to know more of how he'd lived in Afghanistan. Finn didn't want to talk. He didn't want to relive a moment of it. He didn't want anything but to stay numb, to keep from feeling alone and lost, to keep from remembering that everything he'd clung to, everything that had kept him afloat the last three years, was gone.

Since Brodie had told Finn that Macy had sold the ranch, he hadn't been able to drag himself out to the ranch to have a look. He didn't think he could bear to see it. But that afternoon, he tried. He got as far as Cedar Creek Road, but in the end, he couldn't turn onto the road to his place, and kept driving west until he ended up outside the gates of Laru Friedenberg's house.

Finn parked outside Laru's overdone wrought-iron gate and stared down the gravel road that led to the house. He'd stopped for a six-pack on the way over, and pulled out a beer and twisted off the cap. He sipped slowly as he considered his options. He could walk down there, knock on the door, and ask Macy why she'd decided to sell the family ranch he'd worked so hard to buy and to keep. What was the harm in her keeping it? Maybe Luke and Brodie could have come up with the money to buy it eventually. Whatever she had to say for herself, he'd listen quietly to her answer, and then he'd walk away, because nothing she could say could justify her actions.

Or, he could demand that she make everything right again, put back together the pieces of the life he'd entrusted her with when he'd left.

Better yet, he could climb up on the cliff behind Laru's house with his beer and think about it some more, because he could feel his anger bubbling up inside him like heartburn.

The sound of a car coming down the road decided him. He put the truck in gear and ambled on to a public boat slip parking lot. Finn got out of the truck with his six-pack and went for a little walk.

Macy did not find the peace and thought-inspiring quiet at Laru's as she'd hoped. She'd spent her week at Laru's in front of the television, mindlessly flipping through channels, her mind skating haphazardly through memories and random thoughts.

No matter what she did, she couldn't seem to think coherently. Just when she believed she knew what she had to do, something would remind her of Wyatt or Finn and she'd get confused all over again.

Fortunately, Laru didn't push her. The first day, she'd sat cross-legged on the bed of the guest room while Macy unpacked, examining the things Macy had stuffed into the gym bag.

Laru had picked up a pinecone. "What is this?" she'd asked, squinting at it.

Macy had hardly spared it a glance. "A pinecone."

"I can *see* it is a pinecone, but why did you bring it?"

"It's a memento from my honeymoon with Finn in Lake Tahoe." She remembered almost every moment of it. They'd stayed at a resort on the northern end of the lake and spent their afternoons sitting in big Adirondack chairs on the beach, talking about their future.

"How many kids should we have?" she'd asked him one afternoon while they sipped lattes.

"At least nine," he'd said instantly.

"*Nine?* Do you want to kill me?"

"No, I need you! You're part of the softball team I want to field. Picture it—the Lockharts take on every church league in Cedar County."

Macy had laughed. It was so much fun, imagining their future together. And it had been a cleaver through her heart when she'd believed that future had been blown away by a suicide bomber.

Laru had gingerly put the pinecone down.

Macy frowned. "There's a golf ball in there, too, from my honeymoon with Wyatt in Hawaii." At Laru's curious look, she'd shrugged indifferently. "It was all I could find."

Somewhere, she had a lei from that honeymoon, too. She and Wyatt had stayed at a big, fancy, expensive resort. Wyatt had taken his golf clubs along on the trip and had managed to get in a round every morning. "Here," he'd said one morning, handing her a credit card. "Go and shop."

It was very generous, but Macy was not much of a shopper. She didn't buy anything but a bathing suit cover-up. She'd been very surprised when a few nights later, Wyatt had presented her with a gold necklace, the pendant shaped like a tropical bird.

"What's this for?"

"You didn't buy much for yourself," he'd said with a shrug.

"So what is up with these honeymoon mementos and this other stuff?" Laru had asked, stretching out on the bed and propping her arms behind her head.

Macy glanced at the pile of memories she'd so hastily gathered. "I don't know. Just some stuff to help me think," she'd said, and turned around, biting her lip to hold back the tears that suddenly seemed so quick to fall.

"Tell me what's going on, sweetie."

"If I knew, I'd tell you."

"Can you maybe sketch it out somehow?"

"Sketch *what* out?" Macy had asked as she hung some things in the closet.

"You know. Pros and cons, that sort of thing. Something to help you make a decision."

"If only it were that easy." Nothing could be more complicated. "This is too hard and too important, and too . . . it's too hard," she repeated dumbly.

"I know it is, sweetie." Laru stood up and kissed

Macy's cheek. "I'm here if you need me," she'd said, and had left Macy alone the last week.

There were a couple of things that hampered Macy's progress in divining her way through the mess of her life that week. First, the sights and sounds of Laru's hale-and-hearty love affair were everywhere. "Don't you ever leave?" Macy had demanded of Jesse just this morning, when he'd startled her by strolling out of the guest bath wearing a towel around his waist.

"Not if I can help it," he'd said with a wink, grabbed an extra towel, and disappeared again.

And, naturally, there was Macy's family, who could never leave anything well enough alone. Her sister Emma, who was trying to find a job in finance and having no luck, had made it her personal responsibility to visit Macy and report the town gossip. Wyatt was working long hours, which Macy knew, as he had called her every day. Caroline Spalding had been hanging out at his office, supposedly working on some land deal. Finn was drinking a lot; Emma said everyone in Cedar Springs had seen the Lockhart brothers out on the town night after night.

Perhaps that was why Finn hadn't called her. She'd called him three times now, but never got farther than Karen, who would only say tersely, "He's out." Macy left messages, but Finn never called.

On the Fourth, Laru and Jesse went to town to watch the parade, and Emma came out to the house to keep Macy company. Wyatt had called, wanting Macy to come out on the boat.

"I can't—I don't feel very well," she'd said, which was true. Nothing in particular; just a general malaise.

"Macy, it's all going to be all right," Wyatt had assured her. "Don't get too worked up."

That was easier said than done. She'd tried several times to speak to Finn, and had tried again the afternoon of the Fourth, but got Rick instead. "Sorry, Macy, he's out with his brothers shooting at cans."

"Shooting at cans? That's what he's doing instead of riding in the parade?"

"Guess he wasn't up to the parade," Rick said.

Emma seemed concerned about Finn's drinking. "That's not good," she said. "You know what happens to a lot of these servicemen, Macy. They get post-traumatic stress and they never get over it."

"Do you think Finn has PTSD?" Macy had asked, alarmed.

"I don't know, but it seems worth a mention. I read this article in the *New York Times* about it—basically, the person who goes off to war is not the person who comes back from war."

"The person left behind is not the same, either," Macy had muttered, and helped herself to more tortilla chips.

And so it had gone.

Macy didn't do as much work on the fund-raiser as she would have liked. She was aware that things were falling through the cracks, but she couldn't seem to get motivated to do anything about it. One day, she remembered something that couldn't wait and called Samantha.

"I just remembered something!" Macy said when she'd gotten Sam on the phone. "Hey Cupcake! is going to donate—"

"I know," Sam said, cutting her off. "I've already talked to them."

"Oh." Macy had been taken aback by Sam's abrupt manner, but figured she had it coming—she'd let things slide. "So how's everything?" she'd asked brightly.

"Fine, Macy. Everything is under control."

She detected a tone. "Great," Macy had said. "Listen, Sam . . . I know I haven't been much help lately. I really, really appreciate all that you're doing. I'm just so messed up right now, it's hard to think."

"Yeah," Sam said.

Sam was miffed. Macy vowed to do better. "You know what? I am going to get right back into the swing of things this week. First, I am going to get these envelopes stuffed so we can get them out the door. And then maybe we could have lunch and talk about what all needs to be done," she suggested.

"Yeah, maybe. It would be great if you could get the envelopes stuffed."

"I will—"

"I'm sorry, Macy, I have to go," Sam said. "I'm at work." She said good-bye and hung up.

Bewildered, Macy had hung up, too, and had gone in search of the envelopes and flyers.

Later that afternoon, as she was mindlessly stuffing envelopes with her thoughts a million miles away, Laru startled her with a bright "Hey!" as she walked into the dining room where Macy was working.

"Hey," Macy said listlessly.

Laru paused and eyed her critically. "Weren't you wearing that yesterday? And Friday?" Macy looked down; she hadn't even noticed that she was still wearing the same shorts. Laru didn't wait for an answer. "So when are you going to venture out into the world, kiddo?" she asked cheerfully as she pulled open the fridge and studied the contents.

"Why? Am I overstaying my welcome?" Macy asked anxiously, aware she'd been at Laru's for a week now and had given no indication that she was leaving soon.

"Of course not!" Laru exclaimed as she pulled a yogurt from the fridge. "I just know you'll want to get on with your life eventually, and I think you would figure that out sooner rather than later if you, you know . . . got out. Maybe you could clean up and go see how Finn is doing."

Macy wanted to go, but she was a little scared and a little confused that he hadn't returned her calls. "I'm not sure what's going on with him," she said. "I've called, and he doesn't call back."

"Well, I'd say of the three of you, Finn is probably having the hardest time adjusting. I bet he could use a friendly face. And think about it . . . What if *you* were stuck out on some spread with Karen Lockhart?"

Macy gave her aunt a lopsided grin. "Excellent point."

"In the meantime, Wyatt called," Laru said, patting

Macy's shoulder before moving on. She paused at the arched entry leading to the hall and licked her spoon. "He asked if he could come out. I told him to be here at six."

"No!" Macy cried, her hands going to her hair. It was already a quarter past five.

Laru smiled and sauntered on. "You've got to deal, sweetie."

If Macy had had the energy, she would have tackled Laru and given her what for. But she'd need all her energy to feed Milo and jump in the shower. She got up, filled the dog's bowl, and put it out on the porch.

But Milo wasn't on the porch where he usually lay waiting for Macy. She looked down to the river, figuring the dog had gone in for the umpteenth swim of the day. She stepped out onto the grass, walking down to the river to find her dog.

18

How Milo had found him, Finn didn't know, but the dog had been happy to see him, loping up the slip to the picnic table Finn was sitting on.

Finn roughhoused with him, but then he couldn't get the dog to leave. As hard as he tried, Milo wouldn't go home, and Finn had ended up throwing sticks into the river for him to fetch, which Milo did gleefully, over and over again, as Finn slowly moved him downstream to Laru's.

Just as he knew eventually she would, Macy appeared on the back porch. She didn't notice him as she walked down to the river's edge. She moved stiffly, her eyes on the ground before her. Her appearance surprised Finn; she looked like her hair hadn't seen a brush in days, and as she came closer, he saw a curious stain on the hem of the cropped Dallas Cowboys T-shirt she wore. She was also wearing some very short shorts, and Finn had a moment to admire her legs before she looked up and noticed him.

"Finn!" she cried.

"Hi, Macy," he said, moving closer.

She stared at him wide-eyed, as if she were seeing a ghost. But then Milo emerged from the river and trotted to where she stood, dropped the stick, and shook the water from his coat. Macy squealed and did a funny little hop that Finn would have found endearing at one time. He realized he was too angry to be charmed.

She'd *sold* his *ranch*.

Finn continued toward her, uncertain of what he would do or say, but wanting an explanation.

As he neared her, Macy dragged her hands through her hair. He could see the dark smudges under her eyes that indicated a lack of sleep. "What are you doing out here?" she asked, stepping closer to him. "You should have come to the house. Laru would love to see you, and I— You look great, Finn. Karen must be taking good care of you. I'm so happy to see you! I've been calling—did Karen tell you?"

"Yes." He looked at the house, then at her. "I didn't plan to stop," he said. "I was out for a drive and thought I'd go see what was left of the ranch, but then I remembered—you *sold* it."

The color drained from her face. "Did Brodie tell you that? It's not sold! I asked Brodie not to tell you that!"

"A better question is why didn't *you* tell me?"

"Why? Because it felt like piling on! Jesus, Finn, you've been through so much, and I knew the closing would be canceled so I didn't see the point in even bringing it up. It's still your ranch."

"It was set to close?" he asked. "So you had it sold for all intents and purposes."

Macy didn't answer right away. "Well . . . yeah," she admitted. "But I stopped the closing when we found out you were alive." She smiled, as if that resolved everything. "That's *good* news," she added hopefully.

"How, Macy? You know better than anyone else how hard I worked to own that piece of land. You know the dreams I had for it."

"Of course I do! But Finn . . . I didn't think you were coming back. Don't you see?"

"I get that. But you know what is sticking in my craw? You didn't think I was dead very long before you began to shed me from your life."

"That is *not* true!"

But Finn's anger had been building the last few days, and it suddenly sparked. He grabbed Macy's arm, forcing her up against the wide trunk of an old live oak tree. "You have no idea what it's like to live day-to-day when the only thing keeping you alive is a dream of your wife, your land, your work. You have no idea what it's like to come home and discover that even the *memory* of you has been left behind."

"Do you think you're the only one who knows what it's like to be left behind?" she exclaimed. "I know what it's like to be left behind. I know what it's like to have your husband enlist, to beg him not to go, to plead with him to stay—for *our* sake—and then watch him march off to a war you don't believe in and stand there and pretend to be a patriot when your heart is breaking and crying out for him to come back, to let someone else fight the damn war, to let someone else *die*! And I *know*," she said, angrily shoving his chest with both hands and causing him to step back, "what it's like to be left behind and try to keep a working ranch together that was supposed to run itself and have everything go wrong! I know what it's like to have some guy in an army uniform show up and say, *We regret to inform you that your husband died on August eighteenth at fourteen hundred hours*, and when you wake up from the shock of that, you realize that he was so sure he'd come back, he never told you what to do with the life he left behind!"

A tear appeared and slipped out of the corner of her eye. "I don't blame you for being angry," she said, her voice softer. "I can't begin to imagine the pain you've suffered. But I didn't *shed* you. I didn't even know who I was without you. I did the best I knew how to do, I swear to you I did. You have to stop punishing me. *Please* stop punishing me. *Please*."

Something in her earnest voice wrapped around Finn's heart. His soul had hardened to a big block of ice in three years. But his feelings for Macy had a way of breaking on that ice and melting it. He suddenly didn't feel so furious; he felt numb.

"I can't keep defending myself to everyone," she said, her voice breaking. "I didn't do anything maliciously. I couldn't have prepared for this. And I don't know what the answers are, even though God knows I have tried to figure it out. Do you remember when you told me why your ranch was named Two Wishes? That your grandfather said there was no such thing as one wish, because when one wish was spent, another one popped up to take its place? And when he wished for a ranch, another wish for horses popped up—"

"What does that have to do with us now?" Finn asked.

"I have two wishes," she said tearfully. "I wish I could make you happy." She touched his face. "But then I wish I could make Wyatt happy. He's been good to me, Finn, and I want to make him happy, too. I love two men, but I can't make them both happy. It's impossible." She lowered her head and pressed her fingers to her eyes.

Finn narrowed his gaze on her. "What about what is best for *you*, Macy? Have you thought of that?"

Macy opened her mouth to respond, but quickly shut it.

It was possible, Finn knew better than anyone, that she hadn't even thought about what was best for her. He impulsively touched her cheek. "What would make you happy in all of this, baby?" he asked softly. "What do *you* want?"

"Don't do that," she muttered and tried to look away, but Finn caught her chin and forced her to look at him. "Let me help you out here," he said low. "I think I know what you want, but I think you don't know how to get there, or you're afraid to admit it. Do you remember the first time we made love?"

She blushed. "Come on, Finn."

"I remember it," he said, ignoring her. "I remember it so often that sometimes, I can close my eyes and feel your skin against my cheek," he said, letting his gaze roam her face, her curiously arousing mess of hair. "I think about it all the time," he said, touching his finger to her lips. "It was incredible."

Macy's chest rose with her breath. Her eyes locked on his and she slowly leaned back against the tree.

"But you wouldn't admit you wanted to make love, remember? You were afraid to want that for yourself," he said, laying his hand against her collarbone and slowly sliding his fingers to her bare skin in the vee of her T-shirt.

"Stop," she whispered, but Finn moved his hand to the smooth column of her neck and rested his thumb in the hollow of her throat. He felt her pulse leap at his touch and flutter rapidly.

Macy drew another rough breath.

"You were shy at first, but then you relaxed," he continued quietly. "And your skin started to burn." His hand slipped into her shirt, his fingers brushing against the swell of her breast. "When I pushed inside you, you were warm and wet." He stepped closer, straddling her legs with his, delving deeper into her shirt, his fingers feeling the lace of her bra. "Your eyes were so blue, I could see the light in them. I could see how much you liked the way I was touching you."

She drew her breath in a soft gasp. Her lips, wet and plump and enticing, parted. He bent his head, his mouth brushing across the corner of hers. "You were tight," he whispered, "but you opened for me, Macy, because it was what you wanted. It made you happy."

Macy closed her eyes.

Finn brushed his lips against hers again, sliding over them, touching the tip of his tongue to them. "Do you remember?" he whispered. "Do you remember riding that crest together?"

She began to quiver—from fear or restraint, he didn't know, but he put his arm around her back and pulled her against him. Macy didn't move, but when Finn slipped his tongue between her lips, she kissed him back.

She wanted him. She nipped at his lips, her chest filling with his breath, her breast pressing into him. Finn caressed her body, her breast, her face and ears, her arm, her hip.

He tried not to demand too much of her, tried to stay gentle, but it was almost impossible. His body was raging with need, his heart racing with hope he'd not felt in a very long time. That kiss, beneath the twisted boughs of an old live oak, took him back to a better, simpler time, when they'd been one. He could feel her body resonating against his. He could taste the salty path of tears that slid to the corner of her mouth, and the warmth of her breath.

And just as he began to believe that he could go home again, he heard someone call her name. It took Finn a moment to process the intrusion; it took Macy even longer. It sounded like Laru, and Finn felt a bit of apprehension.

"Macy, are you out there?" Laru called from somewhere on the back porch.

"Oh God," Macy murmured.

"Wyatt's here!" Laru called.

Macy looked at Finn. "Laru invited him over." She put her hand against his face, ran her thumb over his lip.

Tension had built in Finn to the point he thought he was going to explode—he didn't need any intrusions now. "You never said what would make you happy," he said, ignoring Laru.

Her gaze flicked over his face; her hand slid to his chest. "*You*, Finn," she said, her voice breaking with emotion. "It's always been you."

His heart skipped a beat. "What does that mean?"

She shook her head. "I don't know."

"Don't go inside."

"I have to," she said. "I don't want to disrespect him."

"You can't leave me hanging, baby."

"I know, I know," she said, squeezing her eyes shut a moment. "But I can't leave him like this. Finn, I don't have all the answers, but I know this with all my heart—I have never loved anyone the way I love you."

"Macy, are you coming?" Laru shouted.

Macy peeked around the tree and looked up at the house, then at Finn.

She was going. Finn took her hand and kissed it, then stepped back. Neither of them spoke, but he felt a current of emotion and desire flowing between them.

"I love you," she whispered, and stepped away.

Milo jumped up and followed Macy as she began the slow walk to the house.

Finn watched her until she stepped onto the covered porch and he couldn't see her any longer, his heart beating hard with hope.

19

Wyatt was standing in the living room, a huge bouquet of flowers in his hand. "Hey," he said, taking in Macy's dishevelment when she came in through the back door. "Are you okay?"

"Fine!" She stuffed her hands in the pockets of her shorts. "Oh, you mean . . . you mean *this*?" she said, looking down at herself. "Yeah . . . I wasn't expecting anyone today, and I was working, and I . . . I guess I didn't get around to a shower."

He didn't say anything to that. "Hey, buddy!" he said happily, going down on his haunches to rub the coat of an ecstatically happy Milo, who Macy hadn't realized had come in behind her. Wyatt was dressed nicely in black slacks and a turquoise polo shirt. He looked handsome, Macy thought. Strong and capable. He'd always appeared that way to her, as if he could hold the world on his shoulders if necessary, and honestly, there was a part of Macy that still wanted to melt into those capable arms. *Everything will be all right.* She'd melted so many times before when he'd said that.

He looked good. But then she thought of Finn on the back lawn. *Do you remember the first time we made love?*

Wyatt looked up from the dog and smiled. "Milo!" Macy said. "You're not supposed to be in here. Come on, out in the yard." To Wyatt, she said, "Sorry, but I can't keep him out of the river and Laru keeps threatening to make dog burgers."

"Maybe y'all should come home with me," Wyatt suggested with a wry smile.

Macy tried to smile, but she couldn't manage it. She opened the door and shooed Milo out, then looked at the flowers Wyatt held. "Are those for me?"

"Actually, these are for Laru," he said, holding them

out to Macy. "For taking my phone calls. I forgot to give them to her when she let me in."

Macy moved forward to take the flowers from him. But Wyatt misunderstood her intention and surprised her by kissing her. It was an awkward, clumsy kiss. She quickly took the flowers and put them between her and Wyatt. "I'll put these in water."

She walked into the kitchen to put some space between them, but Wyatt followed her. "So . . ." Wyatt said as she looked for a vase. "I've really missed you, sweetheart. I was thinking maybe we could grab a bite to eat and catch up. I can put those in water if you want to jump in the shower."

No, no, she didn't want to go out, she didn't want to catch up. She wanted to crawl under bedcovers and hide from him. She couldn't bear the thought of hurting him any more than she already had, so she methodically continued with the task of putting the flowers in water.

"Aren't you going to say something?" Wyatt asked. "I'll be right with you, or no, I'll order a pizza, or . . . or, hey, how about this one? Wyatt, it is *so good* to see you."

"I'm sorry," she said instantly. "It *is* good to see you." She put the vase down and smiled sheepishly. "But I don't think I should go out."

He blinked. His smile faded. "Look, Macy, I'm not going to pressure you. I'm not going to ask you how long this is going to go on, or what we're doing, even though I am dying to know. I came out here because you are my wife and I miss you. Let's go and get a bite to eat and talk about . . . about the big Project Lifeline fund-raiser. That's not off-limits, is it? I saw Sam this afternoon and she filled me in on some of the stuff that's been going on."

He looked so hopeful. What could it hurt, really? In truth, Macy could use a break from Laru's house. "Nothing fancy, okay?" she warned him. "Just a burger or something like that."

"Whatever you want," Wyatt said, his relief evident. He'd always said that to her, too—*whatever you want*. Wyatt Clark was a good guy. No matter what secret desires lay in her heart of hearts, he'd been really good to her and deserved her kindness and respect at such a difficult juncture in their lives. *Everything will be all right.*

Macy smiled affectionately. "Give me thirty minutes. There's beer in the fridge." She walked past him and touched her fingers to his hand as she went.

A quick shower was all it took to transform Macy into a goddess. She looked fantastic in a summer dress and sandals. She'd tamed her hair; it was bouncing around her shoulders. Wyatt hoped he'd never taken her for granted, because that would have made him a fool. Dammit, he had a very pretty wife.

The sun was sliding toward the horizon in a sea of burnt orange. It was a gorgeous evening, the sort of evening that reminded Wyatt why he loved Texas. At least he'd won the battle for some decent food, and frankly, Macy looked a little wan. For the sake of keeping the evening relaxed and pleasant, he kept the conversation confined to work.

He asked her about the fund-raiser she'd been planning the past three months. She'd been stuffing envelopes, she said, and there was a big committee meeting late this week where they would approve the program. The event, to be held at the Salt Lick Barbeque outdoor venue, would have music and dancing, casino tables and a cash bar. For the kids there would be a petting zoo and big jumpers and artists to paint their faces and draw their pictures. Macy was going to be the evening's host and preside over the silent auction for which they were collecting an array of great stuff.

Wyatt could imagine Macy hosting the event. She was charming and funny and everyone loved her. He was really proud of the work she'd done. When she'd first told him about the organization she and Sam wanted to create, he'd thought it was a huge undertaking and privately wondered if Macy really understood what she was getting into. But Macy and Sam were naturals at it. They'd gotten Project Lifeline off the ground fairly quickly and had gone straight to work lining up volunteer services. For the gala, they'd promised that one hundred percent of the proceeds would go to the families of the men and women who had given their lives in the war or were critically wounded.

Wyatt had given five grand to the effort, but with all the turmoil in their personal lives he'd lost track of the progress of the gala. He'd had coffee with Sam one night when she was closing up shop and she'd told him what was going on with the fund-raiser. But what Wyatt remembered most about that night was when he'd stood up to leave, Sam had said, "Sorry, Wyatt. I know how hard it is to feel like you're losing someone."

The remark had made him flinch. "I'm not losing anyone," he'd said.

Sam had shrugged a little. "Look, if you ever need to talk . . . I'm here."

Wyatt looked at Macy now. Was he losing her? He remembered their first date. She'd just gone back into social work, some really awful job with Child Protective Services that involved taking children from their homes. He thought it sounded dreary and depressing, but Macy had been passionate about it. She'd told him about a little girl who'd been neglected, and how smart she was, how she deserved everything the world could give her. Macy had truly believed she could make a difference.

That sentiment had astounded Wyatt. And it had moved him. He remembered thinking even then that he had to have this woman.

"Hey, are you remembering to take your blood pressure medicine?" Macy asked him. Wyatt had to think about it, which made Macy sigh and smile. "What am I going to do with you?" she asked with some affection.

"I don't know . . . come home?"

She smiled. "What about your work? How's it going?"

"Pretty good," Wyatt said. The truth was that he didn't know. Thank God for Linda Gail—she was keeping things on track for him, because Wyatt hadn't been able to think about what he was doing. Funding

for the Hill Country Resort and Spa was constantly
on his mind. He didn't have it cobbled together just
yet, especially since he couldn't rely on the sale of the
Lockhart land, and his investors were getting antsy. He
hoped Caroline would really sell and wasn't just trying
to get in his pants, and that Randy would really buy and
wasn't looking for some sweetheart deal. Frankly, he
didn't trust either one of them.

"Did you make the call?" Macy asked.

"The call?"

"You know . . . to cancel the closing on Finn's
ranch."

He'd managed to survive the dinner by just enjoying Macy's company and not hearing her say that man's
name. But just a mention of him was enough to bring
the truth about Wyatt's life crashing down on an otherwise pleasant evening, and he had to work to keep from
popping off and saying something he'd regret. "Yeah,"
he said, although it was a lie. It was the last thing on his
mind, and he didn't want to hear about it from Macy now.

Macy smiled with gratitude. "Thanks, Wyatt. I know
how hard this must be for you. I really appreciate what
you're doing for Finn."

That was enough to ruin what was left of the evening. Wyatt pulled out his wallet. "Let's get out of
here," he said. He turned to signal the waiter and found
David and Aurora Bernard walking toward them.

"Look who's here!" David called out. "Good to
see you two together. After all that news coverage, I
thought you'd flown the coop, Macy," he said jovially.

"Ah . . ." She looked at Wyatt.

Wyatt stood up. "Great to see you guys. We were just finishing up."

"Don't run off! I hear you've got some prime real estate you're hoping to flip. And I'm not talking about the land," David said with a wink.

At Wyatt's puzzled look Aurora said, "I think he means Caroline Spalding?" She shifted her cool gaze to Macy. "Macy, you look so pretty tonight," Aurora purred. "David, I think we interrupted a date."

"No," Macy said at the same moment Wyatt said, "Yes." They looked at each other.

"Come on, won't you have one drink?" David asked.

"Not tonight," Wyatt said, and put his hand under Macy's elbow, helping her to her feet.

David laughed as Aurora studied Macy from head to foot. "All right. I know when I'm not wanted. Tee time tomorrow morning at eight, Wyatt. Are you going to come?"

"Wouldn't miss it," Wyatt said. "Good night, David. Aurora."

Aurora waved her fingers at them as Wyatt escorted Macy out of the restaurant.

Neither one of them said much on the ride back to Laru's for a while. But then Macy said, "Caroline Spalding?"

"What of it?" he asked.

"Nothing," Macy said. "I think she's after you."

"How can she be after me? I'm married," he said irritably.

Macy snorted. "That never stopped Caroline. And Aurora would like nothing better."

"Personally, I don't give a damn what Aurora thinks, but if you do, living away from me isn't helping matters."

"What?" she said, turning in her seat a little to stare at him. "What is that supposed to mean?"

"It means, get off the damn dime," he said angrily as he pulled up to Laru's door.

"Wyatt—"

"No."

"No?"

"I tried to do it, Macy," he said. "From the moment you told me Finn was alive, I've tried to be supportive. I've stayed calm, I have given you the space you claim to need, but you know what? It's been almost a week since you left, and in that week, I've had to struggle to get you on the phone, I haven't seen you, and dammit, you even took my dog. So I came to you. And you balked at going out with me, and now you act like you can't wait to get out of the car. Now, if we were just dating, I'd take the hint and you wouldn't hear from me again. But we're not dating, we are *married*. We need to file your divorce papers from Lockhart and get back to being a married couple."

"Do I have a say?" she asked tightly.

He groaned with exasperation. "Look, how long is this going to go on? Because I'll tell you right now, I don't intend to live away from my wife and I want it straightened out."

"I just asked for a little time. I'm sorry I couldn't wrap up one of the greatest traumas of my life in a matter of days, Wyatt, but I couldn't."

"What the hell is there to wrap up? Either you file the divorce papers or the suit to declare our marriage void. One or the other, Macy."

She didn't say anything. He studied her a moment. Her expression was inscrutable—too inscrutable, too calm. "Have you seen him?" Wyatt asked bluntly.

There was a slight shift in her expression and she instantly shook her head. "No." But Wyatt knew Macy, and his gaze narrowed slightly. She said again, "No," but guiltily averted her gaze. "I've run into him a couple of times, but it's not like I am *seeing* him."

"What do you mean, you've run into him a couple of times?" Wyatt demanded. "I thought you were out here *thinking* and trying to decide what to do."

"I *am*," she said, glancing up at him again. "But he saw me at the gas station on the way out and stopped to say hello to Milo. It was just a few minutes."

Wyatt waited, but Macy said nothing more. "You said a couple of times. When was the other time?"

She suddenly glared at him. "You know what, Wyatt? I don't have to tell you or anyone else who I see or when or where." She reached for the door handle.

He leaned across her and put his hand over hers. "I am your husband. Don't I have a right to know?"

She sighed irritably and stared out the front window.

"You've left me, Macy. I'd be stupid not to ask if you are seeing him."

Macy turned her head and looked at him, her eyes flicking over his face. "I am not *seeing* him. I have *seen* him, but I didn't seek him out. Nevertheless, I . . . I don't know that I want to divorce him, Wyatt."

Stunned, Wyatt reared back. "You're serious," he said.

"I love you, Wyatt. But I love him, too. I always have."

Those words cleaved him in two. Wyatt moved his hand to the nape of her neck, beneath her silky hair. "Listen, Macy. I am not going to beg you. If you want to be with Farmer Finn, then go." He let go, reached across her, and opened the car door.

"Wyatt, let's not end the night like this."

"Go on, Macy. Do what you've got to do. But go." He expected her to argue, to beg him for more time. But Macy got out of the car. Wyatt suddenly felt like he was going to hyperventilate.

Macy leaned down and looked inside the car. "Will you please try to understand, Wyatt? This is difficult for all of us."

He was starting to wonder if he'd done something to piss God off. One day everything was great and the next, his whole world had exploded. "You've made your decision for now, I guess. I need to go. Shut the door, would you?"

"Wyatt . . . I am so sorry—"

He reached across the car and pulled the passenger door shut. He had to get out of there before he did or said something he would regret.

Sorry. The word clanged like a death knell in his head. He revved the engine and spun his tires on the gravel drive. As he barreled up to the main road, he got out his cell phone and flipped it open, dialed a number. His pulse was pounding.

The phone rang. "Caroline?" he said when she answered. "How about that drink?"

20

Macy went from feeling awful to feeling as helpless as a pig in quicksand, as her father used to say.

She'd never seen Wyatt look so angry, so distraught, so hurt, and she couldn't bear that she was the cause of it. Her guilt—a new and faithful companion to rival Milo, who was sprawled on the end of her bed—made for a sleepless night. She was awake at six, lying on her back, staring blankly at the ceiling. Wyatt . . . he'd given her so much, had adored her so completely. Was she being too hasty, rushing toward a decision? Had she really thought everything through? Could she imagine life without Wyatt?

About three months ago, Wyatt had seen Macy at

the daycare where her cousin Chloe took her toddlers, which was just around the corner from his office. Macy liked to stop there from time to time when she saw them outside playing. Wyatt had come into the yard and sat on a bench, watching as Macy helped the boys swing, then down the slide, catching them when they came down.

Finally, exhausted from chasing two eighteen-month-olds, she'd fallen onto the bench beside Wyatt and put her hand on her knee.

"It might be a good thing you lost your job," he'd said.

Macy didn't think so. A statewide shortfall had led to cutting the staff back to bare bones. The last ones in were the first ones out, and Macy had gotten her pink slip on a Friday afternoon with instructions to hand over her caseload. She'd been trying to get on with a nonprofit since then. "Why?" she asked.

"Because I think we need to have our own kids," he'd said, covering her hand with his.

She must have looked uncertain because he twisted toward her and said, "Macy, let's have babies. Let's do a nursery and all of that. Let's bring little Macys and Wyatts into this world."

"I can still work and have kids."

"It's a thankless job. And being a mother is a full-time job."

He'd talked her into it, maybe because Finn had said essentially the same things at one time. "Can't save them all, baby," he'd said.

So Macy had stopped looking for work and started thinking about having babies.

And now, she had to stop thinking of the past and get her life moving again.

She made herself get up. She'd missed the last two or three weekly weaving classes. Not today. She showered and put on a silky floral skirt, a linen top, and a little bit of makeup. She had just slipped on her sandals when her cell phone rang.

"Hello, Macy?" a woman's voice asked pleasantly when Macy answered it. "It's Lucy Simms."

Uncomfortable with her mother's legal advice or that of any of her mother's friends, Macy had contacted Lucy Simms about her unique marital situation. "Hi, Lucy," she said. "How are you?"

"I'm great! Sorry to call so early, but I've been doing some research and found something I thought I should pass on. Have you decided which paperwork you want to file?"

"I, ah . . . I'm still weighing things."

"Sure, sure," Lucy said, sounding like she was in a rush. "Here's a little wrinkle for you to think about. Your first husband's estate must be restored to him, and I remember you said it was on the block. Have you sold it?"

"No," Macy said. "It was scheduled to close, but my hus—Wyatt has cancelled the sale."

"Good! Because if it had sold, you'd have to pay your first husband the value of the real property, but unfortunately, he'd not get the real property returned to him.

I remember you said you wanted him to have the land. This all has to do with the buyer being held harmless. Following?"

"Yes," Macy said.

"That's it. Just let me know which way you want to go at your earliest convenience and we'll get it going."

"I'll call you soon," Macy said, hoping that much was true.

She hung up and stared at the wall. If Finn had escaped just two weeks later, there wouldn't have been a ranch for him to come home to. He would have lost it all. That was too close for comfort.

Macy shook her head and called Sam. "I was thinking, maybe we could have lunch before weaving class? I could really use someone to talk to. It's been complete craziness since Finn came home," she said.

"Craziness. Why?" Sam asked.

"Why? Well it goes like this: I have to divorce Finn to make my marriage to Wyatt legal, or declare my marriage to Wyatt void so that my first marriage stands."

"Uh-huh?" Sam said.

Uh-huh? What was up with Sam? "Okay, well, this decision is sort of a life-altering event, and I could use a friendly ear."

That was met with silence. Macy waited. "Hello?" she said softly.

"I really can't, Macy. It's my only day off this week and I have a ton of errands to run."

Macy blinked. "Okay," she said carefully. "But I'll see you in class?"

"Sure," Sam said. "See you." She hung up, leaving Macy feeling confused and wondering what was wrong with her friend.

Samantha was already seated at their table when Macy walked into the Hill Country Weavers in Austin. Samantha thought Macy looked very fresh and put together with her cute skirt and top and sandals for a woman with two husbands.

It was a rude thought, and that bothered Samantha, because she'd had several of them lately. Macy was her best friend. Maybe her *only* friend. Samantha hadn't been very social since Tyler died.

But since the news about Finn broke, Samantha hadn't been able to look at Macy the same way. She kept finding things wrong with Macy, and that bothered her, too, because she really wasn't a fault-finding person. Samantha liked to believe she was a good and loyal friend. And Macy had been so kind to her the first time she met her at the survivors group. Samantha had not wanted to go, really, because it seemed impossible to share that kind of grief. But at the same time, she felt like she was drowning in it.

Macy seemed to sense just how dejected Samantha was feeling that day—she'd walked up to her at the break and said, "Do you like bagels?"

Samantha had shaken her head.

"Me either," Macy said. "I wish people would be less health conscious and bring some good old Round Rock doughnuts. Seriously—a *doughnut*. We lost our husbands! We don't need bagels, we need dough-nuts!"

It was the first time Samantha had heard someone joke about it. She must have looked at Macy strangely, because Macy said, "Hey, you can't cry *all* the time." She smiled. "I'm Macy Lockhart, widow."

Samantha remembered how odd it had felt when she'd tried to smile back. "Samantha Delaney, widow."

"What was his name?" Macy asked.

"Tyler," Samantha had responded, almost choking on the word.

"Do you have any pictures?"

Samantha had pictures and stories—and Macy had listened to every single one of them.

It was Macy's idea to take art classes together to get their minds off their losses. They'd begun with photography, but that hadn't worked—they were only reminded of how many photos would be taken without Finn and Tyler. They'd gone on to ceramics, which had been a little better, except that the instructor, Pat, had two sons in Iraq and loved to talk about the phone calls and letters she got from them. She acted like they were on vacation over there, just chilling in Basra. Neither Macy nor Samantha could focus on working with clay, and they'd ended the class with a pair of mis-shapen wine goblets.

After ceramics, Macy had met Wyatt, and Macy and Samantha's foray into art had taken a small detour. Macy suggested boot camp. "We need something to kick our butts and get us back into life, right?" she'd said, and had pulled a reluctant Samantha along. Macy was right about one thing—it kicked their butts. After they'd finished boot camp, Macy's relationship with Wyatt had turned serious, and Samantha didn't see her as often. But Macy had called her at the beginning of the year to see if she wanted to take the weaving class, and Samantha . . . Samantha had been so desperate for something to do and for a true friend that she'd leapt at the chance.

When they'd seen the looms, they'd both agreed—their projects would be something easy. Samantha wanted to make a wall hanging for her mother. Macy had done a lot of research on the Lockhart family name and wanted to a weave a lap rug of the Lockhart clan plaid. Both projects were basic squares with some color in them, and that seemed doable to the two of them.

Unfortunately, Samantha had done something wrong, and her perfect square of a project was beginning to resemble a triangle. It seemed to be a symbol of her life, going off in a direction she did not want.

"Hey," Macy said as she took up her seat next to Samantha. "Wow, I love that shade of red on you, Sam."

Self-conscious, Samantha looked down at her blouse. No one ever complimented her. "Thanks. So how goes it?"

Macy sighed. "Let's just say I've had better weeks." She put her purse down, looked at Samantha, and tried to smile. "It's good to see you, Sam. I've missed you. What have you been up to?"

"The usual," Samantha said, meaning absolutely nothing. "Work. Project Lifeline."

"Yeah, thanks for covering for me," Macy said. "I'm sorry I didn't get much done. Just too much on my mind," she said, making a fluttering motion at her head. "But at least I got the envelopes stuffed."

"Great," Samantha said, and began to fidget with her weaving frame.

"Wyatt said you and he had coffee," Macy said.

Samantha concentrated on her frame. "He showed up when I was closing." When he'd come in, Samantha had been reminded of how she and Macy would meet at the end of the day and Wyatt would come in to get Macy.

"So tell me the truth, Sam. How did he seem to you?" Macy asked.

Samantha's hand stilled on the frame. Was she kidding? "He was upset," Samantha said coolly, shifting her gaze to Macy. "He really needed a friend."

Macy's face fell and she looked down. "Yeah." She suddenly sagged, braced her elbows on the table, and covered her face with her hands for a moment. "Honestly, Sam—I feel like I am drowning." She lowered her hands and looked at Samantha.

Samantha could see that Macy was tortured, but instead of feeling empathy, she was annoyed.

"It is the cruelest, hardest thing to make this choice," Macy said.

"Personally, I don't see the problem," Samantha said bluntly. "There is only one answer."

Macy looked at Samantha. "Only one answer? There are two men involved, remember?"

"How could I forget? Not everyone seems to think your situation is as big a drama as you do."

Macy gasped. "Hey! I'm talking to you because you are my best friend!"

"And I thought you were mine, Macy," Samantha said curtly, feeling the simmering anger begin to boil. "But you seem to have forgotten that I've lost my husband and he's not coming back!"

"Are you *kidding*?" Macy said hotly. "You're going to make this about Tyler, just like you make everything about him?"

"Ladies, excuse me."

The voice startled Samantha and Macy both. They looked up into the smiling face of their instructor, Eliza. "We're going to be reviewing fibers today before you get started on your projects. We'll be starting in about five minutes."

"Thanks," Macy said, and waited until Eliza had moved to the next table before turning to look at Samantha again.

She seemed almost sorry for Samantha, and that made Samantha even angrier. "Look, I'm sorry, Sam," she said, putting her hand on Samantha's arm. "I didn't mean that. I would give anything if you could have Tyler back—"

"No, don't do that," Samantha said, jerking her arm free of Macy's touch. "Don't you become one of those people who tells me *sorry, sorry for your loss*, because you know sorry doesn't cut it. *Sorry* is a stupid, empty word!"

"Yes, I know, I know, but it's true—"

"Oh for God's sake, would you stop?" Samantha snapped.

Macy's eyes narrowed. "What's going on with you?" she whispered hotly. "Why are you talking to me like this, like I'm your enemy? Do you think you're the only one who needs a friend?"

The anger inside Samantha surged to a new and dangerous height. "What's going on, *Macy*, is that I can't sit here and listen to you whine about your dilemma. You *have* no dilemma! Finn came home, end of story! You ought to be on your knees thanking God that he's alive, and welcome him home and never let him out of your sight again! *That's* the only right answer!"

Macy blanched. "I *do* thank God he's alive! But what about Wyatt?"

"What about Wyatt? Yes, I feel sorry for him because you are putting him through hell. But here's the big difference between you and me—I wouldn't have a second husband to worry about. I would have *never*," she said, her voice shaking, "let go of Tyler like you let go of Finn. Haven't you noticed? I never go out. I never date; I haven't thrown out any of his stuff or even packed it away. I don't because I still love Tyler and I still miss him so much that I don't even want to get up every morning." Tears were running down her face now, and Samantha swiped at them.

But instead of humbling Macy as she'd fully intended to do, Macy's eyes shone with fury. "So I guess you think you're honoring Tyler's memory by living in your own little hell, huh? How dare you judge me like that, Sam, just because I didn't grieve the way you did. Excuse me if I chose to live my life for *me* instead of Finn."

"You never should have married Wyatt," Samantha said in a low voice.

"Yes, Sam, you've made your opinion of that perfectly clear at every opportunity. But I'm not *you*."

"Oh, come on, Macy. You can't tell me you ever loved Wyatt like you loved Finn," Samantha challenged her.

Macy gaped at her. "No, I never did. But that doesn't mean I didn't love Wyatt; I still do. And I can't deny it just to satisfy the rules you've created in your sad little world." She angrily grabbed her purse. "I'm suddenly starting to wonder why I ever told you anything at all," she said, and stood up, slung her bag over her shoulder, and headed for the door.

"Macy?" Eliza called after her. "We're about to start."

"Sorry, Eliza," Macy said coolly. "Suddenly I don't feel very well." She walked out, letting the door slam shut behind her.

Wide-eyed, Eliza looked to Samantha, but Samantha shrugged and pretended to focus on her frame. But she was seething, her heart beating so rapidly she felt short of breath.

In the parking lot, Macy turned the ignition of her Jeep. Then she sat, sickened and shocked by her harsh words with Sam, trying to catch her breath, her forehead pressed to the steering wheel. This situation was impossible, it was absolutely impossible, and there was no one in the world who could understand how difficult this was, not even, as Macy had wrongly believed, her friend Samantha.

She lifted her head and put the car into gear, pulling out onto Congress Avenue. She was headed for Cedar Springs.

She made one quick stop at a convenience store. While she was inside her cell phone rang. Macy looked at the caller ID—it was Emma.

"Hey, what are you doing?" Emma asked when Macy answered.

Macy put her things down on the counter and pulled out her wallet. "Actually, nothing," she said.

"Great! Come over to Mom's. She's in Austin all day. I had a great interview this morning and now Chloe and the boys are here. And hey, Ruthie's Bar finally reopened. I'm free, Chloe's got a babysitter, and we want to check it out tonight. Can you go?"

"On a Monday night?" Macy asked uncertainly.

"Yes! On a Monday! What better day? And besides, the place is packed every night."

The guy behind the counter bagged her items and took her twenty-dollar bill.

"Yes," Macy said. "Yes. I am so there," she said.

Emma laughed. "You sound like a woman who

could use a couple of stiff ones. We'll be out back when you get here."

Macy hung up. She'd put the world on hold for a couple of weeks. What was one more day?

21

Emboldened by Macy's promise that the land was still his, Finn drove out to Two Wishes.

He thought he'd get a boost from it, but it only depressed him more. For a man who had seen some very black days, that was saying a lot.

It was nothing like the way he'd left it. The old ranch house, built in the late nineteenth century out of hand-struck limestone, sat in empty disrepair. Judging by the broken windows, the graffiti painted on the living room walls, and the butts of different types of smokes lying around, kids had been hanging out there, smoking pot and drinking beer. The toilets were a disaster, as was the kitchen. Someone had ripped out and stolen all the copper tubing, a common problem on new construction sites because of the high price copper would bring. Apparently, that extended to old houses now.

The barn, which Finn and Brodie had built over a mild winter, was untouched, but it was perhaps even more devastating to see it standing empty. It was the most vivid reminder that his prize cutting horses were gone, as were his cattle, his dogs, and even the pair of ducks who'd made the old stock pond home—all gone. The place he'd built with his blood and sweat and sheer determination had been abandoned to thugs and thieves, and a huge, commercial FOR SALE sign sat at his front gate.

To add insult to injury, when Finn drove around the acreage on the old two-track roads, he discovered that someone had started to clear the mesquite and cedar on the south end of his property which backed up to a strip of land abutting Cedar Creek Road. Finn had always suspected it would become prime commercial real estate one day, but he thought it might take twenty or thirty years. Apparently, he'd been wrong about that; the growth in and around Austin since he'd left to join the army was incredible. Yet he didn't understand the clearing of his land. If the ranch hadn't been sold, who was clearing the mesquite and cedar?

As Finn circled back around to the entrance, he grew even more dispirited. It would take a lot of time and money to bring his ranch back to where it had been—hell, a good cutting horse cost at least ten thousand dollars; a great one, fifteen thousand and up. That didn't include the equipment and the cattle he'd need in order to train new horses. The house needed repair, and while he could do a lot of the work himself, it would take time and money.

The thought of starting from scratch was over-whelming to Finn.

He'd ended up at Ruthie's Bar. How, he didn't really know, as he recalled nothing of the drive into Cedar Springs. He remembered Ruthie's as being a hole in the wall, but now it seemed trendy. The old wooden bar, marked by time and cowboys that worked the Tri-ple Z Ranch west of town, had been replaced with glass and chrome. The pine dance floor had been replaced with a big circular dance track with a bar in the middle.

Finn sat at another bar near the entrance nursing a few beers, his thoughts scattered between his ranch and Afghanistan. He felt like he didn't really belong in this town anymore. He wasn't sure where he belonged. His life had been at a standstill for three years while the rest of the world had moved ahead. He'd been left behind. The more he drank, the more he felt like he didn't even belong in his scarred body. Finn Lockhart, as he remem-bered himself, *thought* of himself, had ceased to exist, and now he was the guy everyone kept calling a hero.

He wasn't a hero. He was the farthest thing from a hero.

But someone calling him a hero bought him a whiskey. Maybe two. Finn was beginning to lose track. He nodded and answered as politely as he could when someone would ask after him, but he kept it short, avoiding eye contact. He didn't want any friends right now, save the one that was in the glass before him.

He must have had a few, because he didn't no-tice when Erin—or Kristen—whoever, slid onto the barstool next to him. When he became aware of her, he pushed his hair out of his eyes and smiled. He was feeling no pain.

"I was going to ride on your float," she said.

Finn wondered if the float she was going to ride was the same thing he had in mind, but then she ruined it by saying, "You know, in the Fourth of July parade."

Ah, the parade, the damn parade, the hero's welcome. Finn smiled. "Is that right?" he said, and instead of thinking about that damn parade that had gone on without him, he imagined her breasts in his hands and ordered a drink for her and one for himself.

He became so preoccupied with the idea of asking Kristen if there was some place they might go and have mindless—and for him, increasingly necessary—sex, that he failed to see Macy come into the bar.

When Kristen left him to go to the ladies' room, Finn was hanging on to the bar so he wouldn't slide off his little pinhead of a barstool. It was then that he spotted Macy and it threw him even more off balance. He'd managed to put her and Afghanistan out of his thoughts for a while, but in his current inebriated state he felt foolish for not realizing she was there, and a moment or two of boyish uncertainty passed.

Not that it mattered. Macy hadn't seen him, either, apparently. She'd cleaned up since he'd last seen her. Her hair was brushed and pulled back in a silky, golden tail. She had on a sleeveless blouse that fit tightly across her breasts and something dangling at her ears that gave off little sparks of fractured light.

Macy was sitting in a booth next to her sister Emma and across from her cousin Chloe, laughing at something one of them had said. That laugh swept over Finn like the Texas heat, making him testy and uncomfortable. How the hell could she sit there laughing? Was her life so carefree that she could *laugh*?

Finn pivoted around on his stool so that he was facing her. It was only a moment or two before Macy looked up and noticed him. He could see the surprise flicker across her face, could see her smile falter.

"Do you want another drink?" Kristen had returned but Finn hardly spared her a glance from the corner of his eye. "Why not?" he said dispassionately. Kristen settled on the barstool. Finn put his arm around her waist and pulled her to his side.

"Hey, I think I like this," she purred, and picked up what was left of her drink, sipping daintily. "Hey, Rory, could we have another round?" She settled against Finn.

Finn's eyes never left his wife's. Macy, however, averted her gaze and looked down when Kristen leaned in to whisper something Finn didn't really hear and didn't really care to hear. When he didn't respond, she put her hand high on his thigh. "What are you thinking about?"

Finn nodded in Macy's direction. "See that woman over there? The one with the honey-colored hair?"

Kristen looked around. Her smile suddenly faded.

"That's my wife. Wait—*was* my wife," he said with a derisive chuckle, and thought of yesterday, of kissing

Macy on Laru's lawn, of the way she made him feel almost whole again. "See," he said, turning a bit toward Kristin and pulling her even closer, "she used to be Mrs. Lockhart. But she thought I was killed in combat, just like everyone else in this town. Macy didn't let that get her down, no sir. She got married just as soon as she could and she's *still* married, even though I'm not dead! Now does that make any sense to you, Christie?"

"Kristen," she said, and tried to push away from him. "I didn't know she was here," she added, and pushed again, this time managing to dislodge Finn's hold.

"Ah, don't run off," Finn said loudly as she picked up her purse. "You're not bothering Macy. Hell, *I'm* not bothering Macy." He laughed loudly. Several people turned to look at him.

"Look, I don't want to get in the middle—"

"Girl, you aren't in the middle!" he scoffed, and caught her arm. "There's not a damn thing to be in the middle *of*," he insisted, and in the process lost his balance and half-slid off his stool. He caught himself with his elbow and righted himself.

"Hey, pal," the bartender said sternly as more people turned to look. "Keep your voice down and be nice to the lady."

"You talking to me?" Finn asked, squinting at the bartender. "Aren't I your hero anymore?"

"Look, I'm all for giving a soldier a break," the bartender said, and picked up the two whiskey neats he'd put down on the bar. "But I'm gonna have to cut you off. You've had too much."

"Says who?" Finn demanded, suddenly very angry, the force of it surprising him. "I don't give a damn what you think. I want that whiskey."

"You're not getting it," the bartender said evenly. "You need to go on now."

"You think you're man enough to make me?" Finn snarled.

The bartender sighed. "Come on, Sergeant Lockhart. Don't embarrass yourself. Why don't you get up and go home, huh? Is there someone you want me to call?"

Finn laughed and turned his head to say something to Kristen, but she was gone. Macy was watching him, as were half the people in the bar. Finn turned back to the bartender. "What are you waiting on?" he demanded. "Give me the damn drink!"

The bartender shook his head and started to turn away, but Finn was drunk and angry enough to be stupid. He lunged across the bar and caught the bartender's shirt with his fingers, startling the man. "I'm not kidding around here, *dude*. Give a hero a damn *drink*."

The bartender threw him off and from somewhere— Finn never saw them or sensed them—a couple of guys grabbed him. Finn snapped. The rage that had been simmering just beneath the surface seemed to break, and he swung wildly with it. He connected with a chin, he thought, and swung again, and people started shouting.

Whoever Finn hit swung back, and the force of the punch sent Finn and the other guy who'd attacked him tumbling over a table.

Finn kicked and swung his arms, but he was too

drunk to fight well and was quickly thrown up against the door of the bar. He saw his attackers then—a couple of bouncers—and wanted to throw himself on them and let them beat the piss out of him. That would make him feel better than he'd felt the last several days.

But he was stopped by Macy's sudden appearance. "Finn!" she cried, grabbing his head and forcing his gaze down so he would look at her. "What are you doing? Are you insane?"

He was. He was insane with crazy anger and despair. He couldn't even find the words to answer her. He sucked in air, felt a jolt of pain through his jaw. He had no idea what he was doing; he just wanted to feel human again, to feel something other than disappointment.

"If you don't get him out of here, I'm calling the cops," the bartender threatened from somewhere behind Macy. "I don't want to do that because he's obviously been through a lot, but I'm not going to have him coming in here wrecking my place."

"We're leaving," Macy said, her eyes never leaving Finn's. "Right now."

"Macy, you can't go with him! He's acting crazy!"

Finn recognized Emma's voice. She sounded afraid of him. "Emmie," he said thickly. *Emmie, Emmie, it's me, it's Finn!*

"He's fine," Macy said resolutely. "He just needs to regroup."

"He needs to sober up," someone said. "He probably learned to drink like that over there."

Oh yeah, right, as if alcohol was easy to find in a

Muslim country and the Taliban were kind enough to let him drink even if it was.

"He knows he needs to sober up," Macy said coolly. She draped Finn's listless arm over her shoulders. She dabbed at his nose with a cocktail napkin, which was surprisingly painful. He glanced down and noticed blood all over his shirt.

"Macy, please don't leave with him," Emma said again. "He could go off."

Finn saw the flash of anger in Macy's eyes. She turned away from him. "For God's sake, Emma! This is *Finn*! He's not going to go off, and even if he does, he would never lift a finger to me. You *know* that. Stop making him sound like a monster," she said heatedly as she dug through her purse. "Here are my keys," she said, shoving them at Emma.

"Wait!" Emma cried. "What are you going to do? How will you get back to Laru's?"

"I am going to take *his* truck," she said. "And he is going to sleep this off!"

The door abruptly opened at his back and Finn stumbled through, Macy at his side. Her strength was surprising—she kept him from falling flat on his ass and somehow managed to move him down the street, away from the bar.

The night was warm and the air heavy, weighing down on him and the various parts of his body that were beginning to ache from the fight. The fog in his brain was beginning to lift a little, thanks to the dose of adrenaline that had pumped through his veins.

"Of all the dumbass things you've done, this has to take the cake," Macy snapped as she marched him down the sidewalk. "Are you insane?"

"Is that a rhetorical question?"

"You could be in *jail* right now," she chided him as she looked back toward the bar.

"How could you laugh?" he asked thickly.

"What? I'm not laughing! Do you see me laughing?"

"In the bar," he tried to clarify. "You were laughing," he said, and in a lame attempt to demonstrate, he leaned back, did his best *ha ha ha*, and almost fell over.

"Do you mean with Emma and Chloe? God, Finn, I wasn't laughing. I was being polite! I can't even tell you what they were saying. Jesus, how did you get so damn drunk?"

Finn couldn't help but grin at that. "Kind of surprised me, too, to be honest."

Macy sighed irritably and looked around. "Where is your truck? There it is," she said, and grabbed his arm, pulling him along.

"Wait—where are we going?"

"To your mom's."

"God, no, Macy, *no*," Finn said, shaking his head enough to make himself dizzy. "Have a heart. Anywhere but there."

She sighed and peered at him curiously. Her gaze softened; she pushed the hair from his eyes. "I should kick your ass, you know that?"

"Someone beat you to it," he said with a wince.

She held up her hand, palm up. "Keys."

"Baby, you know I'm not going to let you drive my truck—"

She suddenly thrust her hand in his jeans pocket, and when she didn't find them there, she thrust her hand into the other pocket. Swaying a little, Finn held out his arms and let her. Macy pulled the keys from his pocket and dangled them in front of his face. "Get in," she said. "And if you even *think* about arguing, I will pick up where the bouncers left off and finish you, Lockhart. You are in no condition to drive." When Finn didn't move immediately, she shoved him toward the passenger door.

Macy had never been as mad at Finn as she was driving that old truck down Cedar Creek Road. Drunk and fighting? What next, a night in jail? She glared at him.

Finn winced a little. "I know that look," he said, and slid further down in his seat. "Where are we going?"

"Someplace where you can sober up," she said curtly, and turned onto a gravel-packed road.

He looked up and saw the direction they were

heading. "No," he said, shaking his head. "I don't want to go to Two Wishes. Turn around, Macy. Go someplace else, I don't care where—just not there."

She ignored him.

"Turn the damn truck around!" he shouted.

"Hush," she said. "I can't take you home with me and I can't take you home to your mother, although that would serve you right, having to listen to Karen go on about you being drunk and disorderly. But even as mad as I am, I won't do that to you. So there is only one place I know to take you."

"Just take me home then. I'll deal with Mom. I'm fine, anyway," he said petulantly. "Nothing can knock a good drunk out of a man like a couple of fists."

"You're not fine, you're a mess!" She punched the gas; the truck bounced over another bump in the road and Finn groaned. She careened around the corner, coming to an abrupt halt outside the gate of the Two Wishes Ranch, the headlights pointing directly at the huge FOR SALE sign on the fence. Macy was out of the truck before Finn could even reach for the handle. She wrestled with the heavy chain that attached the metal gate to the fence post, and when she'd unlashed the gate, she pushed it back against the fence, cursing that the dirt was ruining her sandals.

She returned to the truck in the glare of headlights, climbed into the driver's seat, put the truck in gear, and started down the gravel road to the old house. The road was pitted from early summer rains, and the truck dipped and bounced over it. By the time they reached the house, Macy felt exhausted. She killed the motor and the lights and sagged back in the seat, looking out the front windshield at the summer night.

It was lit by a full moon and sprinkled with stars, and it was one of the many things about the ranch that Macy missed. Out here, the stars were so big and clear that a person could almost believe she could reach up and touch them. It was a spectacular summer view, particularly on a night like tonight with the smell of honeysuckle and roses filling the air. Finn had planted a pair of rosebushes on either side of the front door when they'd first married, and those bushes had grown wild, both sagging under the weight of so many pink blooms.

"Now what?" Finn asked.

Macy's answer was to get out of the truck. She walked around to the front bumper and leaned against it. There was no electricity out here now, but the full moon bathed everything in a soft, silver light. She hadn't been out here in months. It was too painful; this place held her best and worst memories, and in the last few months, the worst overshadowed the best. When she looked at the house, she thought of the officers driving up, of those endless days after she'd been told that Finn had been killed.

Finn appeared on her right and leaned up against the grill alongside her, propping one boot on the bumper. "Next time I take to drinking whiskey, shoot me, will you?" he said, and rubbed his forehead a moment. He looked up, sighed, and shoved his hands into his jeans. "Nice night."

"Beautiful night," she agreed.

"Know what's funny? There aren't nights like this in Afghanistan."

"Really? What sort of nights are there in Afghanistan?" she asked cautiously. The army had said not to push his memories of the war or captivity, but to allow Finn to come to them naturally.

He didn't answer straightaway. "Long," he said at last. "And cold as hell."

She looked at him. He had sobered, although he was standing a little crooked. He glanced down at her, his brown eyes black in the moonlight. There was something else in them, too, a painful distance, and Macy suddenly needed to know what had happened to him, how he'd managed to survive, to come back to her. "What was it like?"

He snorted and looked up at the sky. His body tensed; he folded his arms tightly across his body. "Nothing I'd want you to know," he said quietly.

"I want to know," she said. "I *need* to know."

"Why?" Finn asked, looking at her curiously.

"Because I love you. That's why."

He smiled wryly. "You know, I used to dream I'd hear you say those words to me. The first time, I was lying on a gurney and I heard you whisper in my ear that you loved me. It woke me up. Weird, huh?"

"Not at all," she said, and touched her fingers to his waist. "I used to hear your voice, too. Once, when I was riding Fannie," she said, referring to his best cutting horse, "I heard you say, *Ease up, Macy, before you snap the poor girl's neck.* I actually thought I heard you say it and I turned around, expecting to find you behind me, surprising me with an unscheduled visit home." She laughed at her own wishful thinking. Finn had taught her how to ride. Or had tried. Macy was a horrible rider. She would cling to the pommel while he trotted in circles around her. "It's okay, she's not going to hurt you," he'd say.

"She might throw me," Macy would insist.

"Not unless you choke up on the reins or hit her flank too hard. Ease up, Macy. Pretend she's one of those little kids you help."

Macy would laugh at that. "Not exactly easy to make that leap."

"Try," he'd urge her.

She looked at him now. "I guess you told me to ease up so many times that my mind heard it as clear as if you were standing there."

Finn gave her a fond smile. "Did you ease up?"

Macy laughed. "I think so."

"I bet you didn't," he said. "I bet you thought you were giving her some slack, but you were clinging to her as tight as a new pair of jeans." He chuckled softly. "You are so good at most everything you do, but when it came to riding, you were just about the worst I ever saw."

"Hey!" Macy cried, laughing.

"It's true, baby." He smiled, folded one arm over his chest, and looked down. "I heard your voice clear as a bell that day. I woke up in a gray room on a gurney. I looked down and saw dirty sheets and a lot of blood, and an IV hooked up to my arm. Then I looked to my right—and right into the barrel of an assault rifle."

"Oh my God!" Macy exclaimed.

"I guess I knew that I'd been operated on, but I didn't know if it was to kill me or to heal me, and I remember being so . . ." He paused and looked away a minute. "So *scared*," he said, his voice breaking.

Macy's heart began to ache. She slipped her hand into his. "That must have been so frightening. Thank God they kept you alive."

"Only because they thought they'd get something out of it. They had a little guy named Tariq who spoke some English. He'd say, *Please, Mister America, you know where the enemy goes, please*," Finn said, mimicking him. "But I wouldn't tell them anything. And though they tried, there was nothing they could do to me that made me hurt any worse than I was already hurting."

Those words made Macy feel ill.

"It didn't go on forever," he said reassuringly. "After a few days passed, even they knew whatever they thought they could get out of me had gone stale." He spoke so casually.

"What . . . what happened then?"

"Then? I don't think they'd intended for me to live. But I can be kind of ornery, and I wasn't going down that easy."

Macy squeezed his hand. It seemed a ridiculous gesture, but the only thing she knew to do.

He told her about living in hovels and rooms carved into the sides of hills in and around Kabul as he was moved around to avoid detection. He said that for weeks, he was certain the army was coming for him, because they would never leave one of their own behind. But he finally realized, as time passed, that they had to believe he was dead. His dog tags were gone, he sensed no urgency from the warlords who tossed him between each other like a hacky sack, and time was passing. Finn knew, he said, because he counted every moment.

Macy tried to imagine the fear once that gut-wrenching realization set in, but she couldn't fathom it.

"Once I realized they weren't coming for me, I was a maniac," he said with a lopsided smile. "I tried everything I could think of to get out of that hellhole." He described escape attempts that inevitably ended in beatings, or worse. He was heavily guarded and routinely beaten and Tariq, the little guy who had spoken to him the first day, told him in broken English that there was a debate among the warlords whether or not to kill him. "I figured I was in the middle of some power struggle," he said, shoving one hand through his hair. "But I knew I was near Kabul, and if I could manage to escape, I had a reasonable chance of making it to safety."

"You were right," Macy said.

Finn shrugged. "Sort of. I've never told anyone this, Macy. I had a duty to escape. And I had an opportunity about a year ago, and I choked."

"Choked? What do you mean?"

He avoided her gaze. "Just that—I choked. I couldn't do it, I couldn't run. I'm no hero. I had a duty to escape and I couldn't do it."

Macy listened, spellbound, as he told her that the warlord who usually held him ignored him, but his young son was fascinated by Finn. "Nasir was his name. I think he was about three or so when I first saw him. They'd leave me in a bare room with an open door most days, but with one leg chained to the wall. Nasir started coming around with the woman in the *chadari* who brought my meals. When the weather warmed, the kid would play in the central courtyard and I'd watch him. About the same time, a stray dog showed up. The old mutt was starving and I would feed him some of the food I'd hidden away."

Macy could believe that, given his extraordinary affinity for animals. He'd talked a little about that stray while they were in Washington.

"That boy saw the dog, and that was it," Finn said with a small smile. He said the boy began to venture closer to the dog and Finn. It wasn't long before Finn had befriended Nasir and began to teach him words in English. Doggie, of course. Foot, because Finn said he was barefoot for much of his captivity.

"I'm glad you had something," Macy said. "I know that sounds stupid, but at least you had a dog and a boy—"

"Yeah, well, Nasir is the reason I couldn't escape," he said, almost bitterly. He told Macy that a couple of times, he would hear gunfighting nearby and assumed it was Coalition forces closing in on the Taliban. He'd been in the same place about ten months when the gunfighting was on top of them. The woman in the

chadari hurried out one morning to unlock his chains;
Finn supposed it was because they meant to move him
quickly. "I had my chance," he said. "A missile hit and
took the door and wall from the courtyard and started a
fire in half of the house. So I took off. But when I was
crossing that courtyard, I saw Nasir. His mother was in
that fire, and he was trying to run inside to get her." He
swallowed. "He was terrified, Macy. He was screaming
for her and wailing like you have never heard a child
wail. The fight was moving closer, and I . . . I had a
choice. I could run and save my life and know that
Nasir would probably lose his, or I could save his life
and lose my chance to escape, maybe even my life. I
only had a moment to decide, but I . . . I just couldn't
let that boy die."

"Oh my God, Finn," Macy said, her heart swelling
with pride and awe and sorrow. She stroked his arm.
"My God, I don't know what to say."

"I couldn't save the dog," he said morosely. "Dumb
thing wouldn't come when I whistled and was hit by
gunfire."

Macy wrapped her arms around his waist and
pressed her cheek against his chest. "I am so sorry,
Finn. I can't imagine how horrifying that must have
been."

"Nah, don't be sorry," he said, but his body was stiff,
his arms lifeless at his sides. "I thought I'd die saving
Nasir, but the truth is, things changed for me that day."

He told Macy that only moments later, Taliban soldiers had burst into the burning house and had found

the boy in Finn's arms, clinging to him. They'd ripped Nasir out of Finn's arms and shoved Finn out the door, moving him to some other house.

But after that day, he was moved less often and was rarely beaten. "I think even the food got a little better, which isn't saying much," he said. The best news of all was that he was allowed out of his chains once a day to stretch his legs in the courtyard under the dark watch of Taliban militia. Twice more they would drag him off his pallet in the dead of night and make him kneel down and hold some sign while masked gunmen hovered over him and another guy taped them with a camcorder, but he didn't fear it as he once had. "Seemed almost for show," he said. "I'd resigned myself to the idea that that was going to be my life, living on a pallet on a dirt floor, getting an hour a day to stretch."

"But then you escaped?"

"I was handed a gift from Nasir's father, I think," he said.

"A *gift*?"

"Yeah. I never saw Nasir again after the fire, but one day, out of the blue, Tariq came in and said Coalition forces were sitting two kilometers directly south. That was all he said. The next morning, when the woman brought me food and unlocked my chains for exercise, she left the courtyard door open. It wasn't the routine, and I saw my chance. I took off, ran two kilometers south and right into the hands of Coalition forces that just happened to be Americans. Maybe it was an incredible coincidence, but between you and me, I think that was my payback for saving Nasir's life."

"Finn . . . that is an *amazing* story. Why haven't you told anyone about Nasir?"

He sighed. "I'm a soldier, baby. I should have run. They wanted to make me a hero, and I . . ." He put his arm around her waist. "It's a story better left dead and buried. I don't want to talk about that anymore if it's all the same to you."

Macy smiled into his shirt. He was warm and smelled just like she remembered, a little spicy.

"God, I've missed this place," Finn said, letting her go and walking away from the truck. He put his hands on his waist and looked around. "I have so many plans for it. I want to build a bigger barn," he said, gesturing in the direction of the current barn. "Maybe bring in more cattle than I had before. It's going to take some major scratch and a lot of rebuilding." He looked at Macy, his expression hopeful. "But we could really make this work, baby."

Macy drew a breath.

"We were good together," he said, moving toward her.

"The best," she agreed.

"Remember that afternoon in the barn?"

Macy smiled. They'd made love on the hay one blustery January day under a horse blanket. There hadn't been anyone around for miles, but it had felt decadent and oh, it had been fabulous. "You know I do." She closed her eyes, recalling other familiar scenes from their life together. Riding horses at sunset in the fall. Planting a garden one spring. Lazy Sundays spent entwined in each other's arms, watching the Cowboys play football.

The best days of her life were here at Two Wishes Ranch.

"Hold on," Finn said, and walked around to the driver's side of the truck, opened the door, and rolled down the window. He turned on the radio, cranking it up. The music of a country station wafted through the open window as he walked back around to the front of the truck, pushed back the swath of hair that had fallen in his eyes, and planted his hands on his hips. "Remember dancing down at the pond?"

She laughed. "I would hardly call it dancing. Dodging cow pies was more like it." One summer evening, she'd planned an evening picnic at the stock pond. Finn had rigged a boom box. But the cows, thinking that where there were humans there must also be food, had gathered around, crowding them onto a little grassy strip. Finn and Macy had danced on the grassy spot at the edge of the pond, surrounded by cows standing on the bank or chest-deep in water.

Finn dipped his head a little and held out his hand, palm up. "Mrs. Lockhart?"

Macy didn't hesitate—she put her hand into his. She laughed with delight when he yanked her into his chest, dramatically bent her backward like a ballroom dancer, then straightened her up and locked his arm around her waist while holding her hand aloft. "I don't guess you found any rhythm while I was gone, did you?"

"Just because I didn't grow up in a dance hall like you is no reason to disparage my dancing skill."

"I'm not disparaging your dancing skill, Macy. You don't *have* any dancing skill," he said, and as she laughed he twirled her around, leading her into a country waltz while Carrie Underwood serenaded them from inside the truck. "Lucky was the day a beautiful woman came into my life, perfect in every way save her two left feet," he said.

"Charmer."

"Gorgeous." He twirled her again.

Finn was a natural, smooth dancer. He could make her feel light as air when he moved her around a dance floor—or an uneven gravel drive. With Finn guiding her, Macy could dance very well. Under that starry sky, he pressed her into his body and held her close like he was afraid of losing her, and she danced like a ballerina.

Finn playfully moved her around the drive, dipping her and spinning her while he hummed along with Carrie Underwood. Macy pressed her cheek to his shoulder. How many times had she cried herself into a stupor listening to a song like this, remembering a moment like this? How many times had she dreamed of being in his arms one last time, her heart hoping such a miracle could be true while her mind was telling her that she'd never feel this way again?

Just the memory of those awful, black days brought tears to Macy's eyes, and she turned her face to Finn's shoulder. He dropped her hand, wrapping both his arms around her, holding her tight. "It's okay, baby," he murmured in her ear. "It's over. I'm home."

He knew her so well, knew what was bothering her. His effort to soothe her made the tears well faster. After what he'd endured, she should be comforting him, but he was holding her and she could hear the steady, solid, reassuring rhythm of his heart.

It was several moments before she realized they weren't dancing, but swaying softly in the night breeze. Carrie's song had ended; Patty Griffith was now sending a soft folk ballad out the window to them. Macy kept her eyes closed, reliving the life she'd thought lost to her forever. All those lonely nights she'd lain in bed, her hand on his pillow, wishing him back, willing him back.

And here he was, walking out of a dream and into her arms.

When Finn bent his head and kissed her temple, she knew she'd never divorce him. She'd really known it all along—she could not be on this earth and not be with Finn. When he moved lower, kissing her neck, she was lost.

The effect was electrifying, sending a thousand little jolts of longing through her. If only she could peel back the years, return to the moment she'd met this man, to the days and weeks that had followed, those glorious moments of falling in love with him, of *being* in love. If only she could relive what they'd had together, could stand at the crossroads when Mike had died and Finn had decided to go to war and convince him to make a different decision, to turn down a different path, to still be *here*, together, just like they were now.

She didn't realize Finn was moving her slowly backward until she bumped up against the tail of the truck. Finn stopped moving then and cupped her head in his hands. "This is where we belong, Macy," he said. "We've had some stuff happen, but we can fill a few holes and patch a few cracks and get back to where we were. You know that, don't you?"

"Yes. This is where we belong. My heart never left you, Finn. My life did, but not my heart, not ever." It was the only truth Macy was entirely certain of.

Finn kissed her possessively. His hands slid up her ribs and under her arms, and he lifted her up, setting her on the tailgate. "I'm going to do what I should have done the moment I got home and show you just how much I missed you, how much you mean to me."

Her blood raced the moment he uttered those words, making her weak with longing for him. How could she have questioned this?

Finn grabbed her hands, pushed them around behind her back, and held them in his grip. "Look at me," he quietly commanded her. "I don't have much that means anything to me anymore. Only you, baby, and you mean the world to me. I know it's not easy, but the fact is, you were mine when I left here and you're still mine, and I am going to prove it to you. So I am going to unbutton your blouse," he said, his dark eyes sweeping over her. "And then I am going to take it off of you." He let go of her hands and slowly, deliberately, unbuttoned her blouse and pushed it off her shoulders.

He made a sound of longing when he cupped her breasts, drew another hard breath, and slowly released it. "You are as sexy as I remembered," he said, and leaned down, nibbling her through the fabric of her bra as he unhooked it with his hand. He slipped his hand beneath the loose bra and filled it with her breast, filling his mouth with the other.

Macy leaned back and braced her hands against the truck. She closed her eyes, letting the night and the pleasure wash over her.

Finn lifted his head and kissed her hard and possessively, his tongue tangling deeply with hers. When he broke the kiss, he roughly caressed the side of her head. "The day we married I told you it would be forever. Do you remember that?"

"Every word," she said breathlessly.

He stepped between her legs, pushing her short skirt up her thigh, then sliding his hand between her legs. "It's still forever." She was wet, her body aching in a way she hadn't experienced in years, aching for his touch. He stroked her through her panties, and Macy gasped with pleasure. "Lie down and close your eyes," he ordered her.

Macy didn't hesitate. She lowered herself into the bed of the truck. Finn came over her, kissing her, then moving further down her neck to her breasts, lavishing his attention on each one, then moving further down her body. Her eyes closed, her body submerged in the sensations he was giving her, she relished every touch.

Finn slid one palm down her leg to her ankle and lifted her leg up, draping it over his shoulder as he sank between her legs. His tongue lashed across her clitoris and Macy groaned.

"You want to know what I imagined every single day?" he asked roughly as he slipped two fingers into her body, causing Macy's back to arch. He dipped down between her legs and touched his tongue to her again. "This. Tasting you. Making you come."

Pleasure exploded within her as he began to lick her.

Macy slowly slid her arms out wide, opened her eyes, and looked at the stars above her head. There was nothing in the world right now but those stars, and her and Finn. There was nothing but the familiar and deep abiding love she'd always felt for him, the incredible shifting sand of pleasure running through her.

The urgency with which his mouth and tongue moved on her began to increase; she could feel the staggering moment of release pressing down on her as he slid his tongue inside her, matching a rhythm the two of them had known before. It was more pleasure than Macy could bear. She gasped for air, clawed at the truck, and just when she thought she was lost to the sensation, Finn surged up, ripped her panties with his hands, and slid into her at the same moment she found her release.

Wave after staggering wave of pleasure shook through her as he moved inside her. She cried out, groping for him, clinging to his body. The muscles of his arms and shoulders were taut as he held himself above her and moved furiously, his eyes closed and only one word on his lips: *Macy*.

This wasn't just wild sex; this was something deeper, and Macy understood that this was, unequivocally, where she belonged: to Finn, with Finn. It had always been so and always would be so.

Finn thrust into her with a strangled cry of release, then collapsed onto her, his hands tangling in her hair, stroking her skin. His cheek was pressed against her shoulder, his face turned away, but Macy felt the damp warmth of his tear on her skin. He'd felt this moment just as deeply as she had.

A moment later he shifted and braced himself on his arms on either side of her, stroking her hair. "How soon can you come home?"

Tears filled her eyes, and Macy lifted herself up, wrapped her arms around his neck, and buried her face in his shoulder. "Just as soon as I tell him."

She had no idea how long it was before she finally pulled away from Finn. She sat up, tilted her head back to look at the stars once more. "I have to go," she said softly, and groped for her bra. Finn had one arm behind his head, stretched out long and naked beside her. She saw the scars on his body and winced. "Laru will be wondering where I am and I don't want her calling around and alarming everyone," she said, touching her fingers to his scars.

With a sigh, Finn reluctantly sat up. "I'll drive you." He slid off the back of the truck, found his jeans, and

pulled them up over his hips. He offered his hand to
help her down. With his arm around her shoulders,
he walked her to the passenger side of the truck and
helped her in, but before he shut the door, he asked,
"When will you tell him?"

"As soon as I can," she promised, but even as the
words fell from her mouth, Macy could not silence a
nagging question in her head.

23

Linda Gail had had to work late again. Wyatt had been
throwing work at her like the apocalypse was coming
and he had to sell every last ranch in Texas before
that happened. Davis said he would fix dinner for the
family and Linda Gail was expecting to come home
to a nice hot meal, a relatively tidy house, and a wine
cooler.

She walked into the kitchen, saw the mess, and
dropped her purse on the floor out of sheer exhaustion
and frustration.

"Hey, hon," Davis said, appearing from the living
room, still munching on something.

"I thought you said you'd make dinner," Linda Gail said peevishly.

Davis looked surprised. "I did!"

"Ramen noodles and Cheetos, Davis?" she said, marching to the kitchen island and swiping up the empty Cheetos bag.

"That's what the kids wanted!"

"Just because they *want* junk doesn't mean you *give* them junk."

Fortunately for Davis, the phone rang just as Linda Gail was gearing up. She grabbed the phone as she stuffed the Cheetos bag into the trash. "Hello?"

"Hey, it's Reena," her friend chirped. "What are you doing?"

"I just got home from work and now I am picking up after Davis and the kids." Bowls and empty ramen packages littered the counter, and spilled packets of flavoring trailed all the way to the sink. Harvey, a pound mutt, heard Linda Gail's voice and bounded into the kitchen to shadow her, his tail banging against the cabinets and kitchen barstools as she moved around. "And then I am going to decide the best way to kill Davis. Hanging is too kind," Linda Gail added, and tossed a biscuit to Harvey.

"So get a load of this," Reena said, glossing over Davis's demise. "My daughter was at Ruthie's tonight— you know that place?"

"That old bar at the end of town?"

"Right, but they completely renovated it, and now it's real popular among the twenty-somethings, including, unfortunately, my daughter Taylor, who is down there every night. I told her, if you put as much effort into finding a job as you do partying, you'd be mayor of Cedar Springs."

"Reena, no offense, but I've got a hungry dog and a mess in the kitchen and laundry that's been piling up for a week."

"Oh, I know, I know! I just wanted to tell you that The Hero was there tonight and so was your boss's wife."

And *why* did Reena think she cared? Linda Gail wondered. "Oh-kay," she said.

"Well, Hero had a little too much to drink and got into a fight, and guess who left with him?"

"I can't guess."

"Macy Clark. From what Taylor said, he got drunk as a cedar chopper at a rooster fight, then got mad about something and was going to take on the whole bar. But they have those guys from Lonnie's Gym that work there and even Finn Lockhart couldn't take them on—well, anyway, the only one who could get through to him was Macy. Taylor said it was quite the show."

"So what happened?"

"Macy actually inserted herself in the middle of the fight and got him to look at her. Taylor said it was like magic; he suddenly calmed down and focused on her, and she was focused on him, and, well, you know . . . it looked like there was a connection there. And then they left."

"Where'd they go?" Linda Gail asked as she swatted

at the dog when he started nosing around for another biscuit.

"Who knows? But they didn't come back, and everyone who saw it is buzzing. I just thought you ought to know, because I know how Wyatt can get when he's in a bad mood."

"Yeah, thanks for letting me know," Linda Gail said, knowing better than anyone how Wyatt could get when he was in a bad mood.

Wyatt heard about the incident at Ruthie's on his way into work Wednesday morning. After his spectacularly awful date with his wife, and then an even worse outing with Caroline Spalding for a drink—what was he thinking?—Wyatt had made the decision to go out of town for a couple of days, leaving right after his golf date with David Bernard. At the empty hunting cabin of a friend, he'd gone through some paperwork and made some phone calls. Lots of them, really. The more he worked, the less he thought about the chaos that was suddenly his life. And he needed some time to think about how he was going to get Macy off the idea that she was going back to Lockhart.

She wasn't thinking clearly. She was being emotional, feeling bad for Finn. That was Macy, always caught up with the downtrodden. When Wyatt had calmed down, he'd realized that she wasn't thinking past her nose. He would have to help her make a decision. So he called her. He got her voice mail and left a message that they needed to talk.

By Tuesday evening, his fear of losing Macy was about to bring him out of his skin. He'd left three separate messages for her and hadn't heard a word in return.

Wyatt had a very bad feeling. Again.

He drove back to town that night, arriving a little after eleven. It wasn't easy, but he resisted the urge to drive out to Laru's again. On the one hand, he felt like he was owed an explanation, something other than *sorry, Wyatt*. On the other hand, he had his pride, and he wasn't going to sniff around Macy like a whipped dog.

Wednesday morning, he was up before dawn, wandering around the house, noticing that some of Macy's things were missing—her shoes, which she left everywhere, and the stack of books she intended to read that stayed on the desk in the kitchen. It felt as if she were already gone.

Already gone.

Wyatt couldn't believe he was thinking that.

She wasn't leaving him, she was confused! Who wouldn't be? He had to be patient, be the logical, reasonable one in this.

On his way to work, Wyatt stopped in at the Saddlebrew for a cup of joe and ran into Bob Franklin.

"Hey!" Bob said. "You're up early."

"Yep," Wyatt said. "Got a lot of work." He turned to Sam, who looked a little bleary-eyed. "Hi, Sam."

She smiled. "Hi, Wyatt. Predictable black coffee?"

"Please," he said.

"Yessir, it's good to be working," Bob said. "The way

this economy keeps sliding, it's nice to know people still have that opportunity."

"Yep," Wyatt said. He wasn't much of a morning person, and even less so in his current frame of mind. He was moving to pass Bob and say his farewells when Bob said, "It's none of my business, Wyatt, but I just wanted you to know that Debbie and I are real sorry about what you and Macy are going through."

Wyatt paused. "Thanks," he said uncertainly. "But I think everything will be fine once her . . . once Lockhart gets his bearings."

"Once Lockhart gets his bearings?" Bob asked, seemingly confused.

"Yes. Why?" Wyatt asked, peering curiously at him. "What's the matter?"

Bob shook his head. "That's what I get for listening to Debbie. She heard about the thing that happened at Ruthie's, and I—"·

"*What* thing?" Wyatt interrupted.

Bob reared back a little. "Nothing worth repeating. I don't know what I'm talking about, and you know Debbie, she can talk until she's blue. I just misunderstood whatever it is she thinks she heard. Never mind me—you have a good day now," he said, and turned away, walking briskly out of the store before Wyatt could question him.

"What thing?" Wyatt asked Sam.

"I have no idea," Sam said as she handed him his coffee. "Don't worry about it. You know how this town is—they love to feed on gossip."

"You're right," he said, but he had a funny feeling.

Wyatt was mildly surprised to find Linda Gail already in the office when he arrived. She usually eased in around nine or so.

"Good morning!" she said cheerfully as Wyatt walked through the door.

"You're here early," he said gruffly.

"Why, I'm fine, Wyatt. Thank you for asking."

Wyatt sighed. "Sorry. Good morning, Linda Gail. You're here early."

"Yes, I am," she said, beaming a smile. "I have a lot of work to do. You worked hard these last two days, which means I've got even more to do than usual, so I came in early to get caught up."

"I won't get in your way." Wyatt started toward his office, but he paused at the door and looked back at Linda Gail, who was standing at the copy machine. "Hey," he said.

Linda Gail turned partially toward him, a stack of papers in her hand.

"Did you . . . did you hear anything about, ah . . ." Wyatt choked. Was he insane, or was he about to ask Linda Gail if she knew anything about his wife?

"Yes," Linda Gail said, sparing him the agony of finishing his sentence. "Do you want to know what I heard?"

He was relieved by her no-nonsense response. "I'd be grateful if you'd tell me so I don't look like an idiot when the next person mentions it."

Something flickered over Linda Gail's brown eyes, something like pity, which made him want to turn and

walk away. But he just stood there, because he had to
know what was going on.

"You know Ruthie's Bar?" Linda Gail asked. Wyatt
nodded.

She told him what had happened there Monday
night. He was so angry and alarmed that he couldn't
move, couldn't do much of anything but stand there
and grip the door handle. He was so stupid, thinking he could just be patient and Macy would come
around.

"Wyatt?" Linda Gail said, now looking alarmed.

"Thanks," Wyatt said, and dropped his hand from
the office door and started back to the entrance.

"Wait—where are you going?" Linda Gail asked,
turning a full circle in order to follow his path.

"There's something I need to do," he said brusquely.
Like get his wife back.

"No, wait, wait," Linda Gail said, hurrying to the
door and putting herself between Wyatt and the exit.
"Don't go doing something rash, Wyatt Clark, because
you'll regret it. And besides, Randy Hawkins is on his
way here!"

"Randy?" he asked, trying to shake off his anger.

"Randy Hawkins is meeting you at nine, remember?
To drive out and look at that piece you've got? You've
been chomping at the bit like a racehorse to show
Randy that land so you can sell it."

That was true. Wyatt needed a deal—he had a Hill
Country Resort and Spa investors meeting next week
and he needed to show them he had a plan. Wyatt

glanced at his watch—it was ten until nine, and if there
was one thing you could count on, it was that Randy
was always on time.

"Right," he said to his watch. "I'll wait for him outside. Call Caroline and set up a meeting."

"Caroline Spalding?"

He didn't have time to coax Linda Gail along. If Caroline was going to list with him, she needed to do it. "Just
do it, Linda Gail," he said, and started to walk out.

"What may or may not have happened at Ruthie's
doesn't mean anything," Linda Gail tried. But Wyatt
gave her a cold expression that relayed his opinion of
that theory, and walked out the door.

24

While Wyatt was waiting for Randy, Macy was lying
facedown on her bed, her hair covering her face. In
the hand that dangled off the edge of the bed she held
a picture of her and Finn taken at an Independence
Day lake party several years ago. She was wearing long,
tropical-print surfboard shorts, a bathing suit top, and
a big floppy hat. Finn had on his straw cowboy hat, a

muscle T-shirt that said *Lucchese Boots* across his chest, and plain brown board shorts. Macy was laughing at something the person taking the photo had said—one of those big, openmouthed laughs, which she thought was odd now, since she couldn't remember the joke any longer.

But what struck her about the photo was Finn. He was smiling in that lone cowboy way he had, like he knew something no one else knew, or saw something no one else saw.

In her other hand, which was balled up beneath her pillow, Macy held a picture of her and Wyatt on a cruise along the Pacific coast they'd taken last summer. It had been one of many surprises from Wyatt, just because he'd wanted to surprise her.

In the picture, they were standing in the ship's casino. Macy was wearing the dress Wyatt had bought her—a shimmering peach silk that she'd loved—and holding a stack of chips. He was wearing the Hawaiian shirt she hated, but never had the heart to tell him. He loved that shirt. They looked picture perfect, a happy couple very much in love. They'd *been* that perfect couple. They'd talked about children, both of them wanting several, and they'd started trying this summer, and now . . . *now.* . . .

Everything will be all right.

Milo whimpered to be let out of her room. Macy got up, pulled a shirt on over her shorts, and opened the door. Milo scampered down the hall.

"Macy-cakes Clark, is that you?" Jesse called.

Macy stuck her head out the door and saw Jesse down the hall. "Who wants to know?"

"Just making sure you're alive," he said, strolling down the hall toward her. "You never miss having a couple of bowls of Froot Loops and when we didn't see you this morning, I worried something was wrong."

"Nothing's wrong," she said, realizing that she sounded defensive as hell. "Where's Laru?"

"Out telling Ernesto how to do his job," Jesse said with a grin, and paused outside her door. "What you got there?" he asked, nodding at her hand.

Macy looked down. She was still clutching the picture of Wyatt. "Nothing," she said, and moved back into her room. A brush. She needed a hairbrush.

"Lot of nothings in this room," Jesse observed, propping his shoulder against the jamb.

"Okay, Jesse, you've seen me, I'm alive," Macy said, and pushed a handful of her hair from her face. Where was her hairbrush?

"You coming? I'll put out some Cap'n Crunch for you."

"Thanks. I'll be there in a minute," she said, and looked away.

Still, Jesse didn't move. Macy glanced back to see why he was loitering and noticed he was looking at something at the foot of her bed. Macy followed his gaze and saw the pregnancy test stick that she'd thrown to the end of the bed and left there. With a cry of alarm, she lunged for the stick, but it was too late. Jesse was staring at her, eyes widened with shock, as if she'd done something criminal.

"That is none of your business!" she cried, shoving the stick under her pillow.

"I'll take it from that reaction that it came up positive," he said dryly. "Jesus, girl, you're a *mess*. Now what are you going to do?"

"I don't know what I am going to do, but if you breathe a word of this to *anyone*, Jesse Wheeler, I will personally wring your neck!"

He looked slightly offended. "I wouldn't give you up."

"Not even Laru," Macy cried, pointing her finger at him.

"*Especially* Laru. You think I'm crazy? If she knew this, she'd be all over you like spines on a cactus, and just about that prickly."

"Tell me about it," Macy muttered.

"Is there anything I can do to help?" Jesse asked. Macy instantly looked up, suspicious. But Jesse shrugged. "I like you, kid. If I can help you, I'll do it."

"I don't know," she said uncertainly. The pregnancy test changed everything. She still wasn't sure she believed it. The two tests she'd taken hadn't turned as blue as the picture on the box. She and Finn had tried for two years to have a baby, and she and Wyatt had just started trying. It had taken two weeks!

"Would it be rude to ask who is the father?" Jesse asked.

"Are you kidding? It's Wyatt's, Jesse!"

"Hey, okay," Jesse said, throwing up a hand. "I know you're in a tough spot. When I heard about the scene at Ruthie's—"

"What?" Macy cried. "You *heard* about that?"

Jesse was beginning to look a little uncomfortable. "Macy, have you *been* to Cedar Springs? Because in case you didn't notice during the twenty-eight years you've lived here, it's a small town and everyone knows everyone else's business. I think the only person who hasn't heard about what happened is the guy who owns that hubcap place out on 71, and only because he's deaf."

"Ohmigod," Macy moaned.

"Look, don't freak out," Jesse said. "That test could be wrong."

"It could?" Macy asked hopefully. "See, that's what I was thinking!"

"Oh, yeah. I had a girlfriend once who thought she was pregnant. That thing came up so blue you'd think the sky was in her bathroom. But it was wrong. Turns out she had too much stress or something like it."

Stress! Macy was under an incredible amount of stress. She looked at the stick.

"But if it turns out to be right, you let me know if you need something," Jesse said. He walked out, leaving Macy with hope that it was false.

Randy pulled up in his black Dodge one-ton Hemi pickup at precisely nine o'clock. He gestured for Wyatt to get in his truck. Wyatt preferred to drive, but he never argued with a prospective buyer.

They drove out west of town and deep into the Hill Country to have a look at the prime ranchland Wyatt was hoping to sell Randy. They got out and walked a good ways into six hundred unspoiled acres so Randy could size it up for grazing suitability.

In the middle of a grassy patch, Randy swept off his trucker hat and looked at Wyatt. "You're right, Wyatt—this is good land."

"I thought you'd like it."

"Let's go on back to town and talk," Randy said.

A wave of relief rushed through Wyatt—Randy was going to buy, he could feel it. "All right," he said dispassionately.

As they started back to the truck, Randy asked, "So how are you these days, Wyatt? That soldier still in town?"

"Yep," Wyatt said curtly. He really didn't want to talk about it.

"So what's up with that?" Randy asked unabashedly, squinting at him. "Must be strange for your wife, man, and you've gotta be in a strange place."

So strange he couldn't see a foot in front of him. Wyatt needed this deal too much to risk offending Randy by telling him to keep his mouth shut. "Yeah, she's got to make some decisions, I guess." He said it with a laugh that sounded more like a bark to him than anything else.

"Hey, man, I didn't mean to pry. I just figured—"

"It's complicated," Wyatt said.

"Okay," Randy muttered as they trudged up the hill. "So how's the resort and spa coming?" he asked jovially, changing the subject.

Wyatt glanced at Randy. "Truth is, the idea for that project was developed on the land Lockhart owned before he was given up for dead. It was part of the package I put together and I was about to close the deal on behalf of my wife, and then Lockhart drops out of the sky and wants it back."

"Oh man," Randy said sympathetically. "How much land are we talking?"

"Three hundred acres of prime ranchland."

"What did he run on it?"

"A few dozen head of cattle. His real business was training working cutting horses."

"Yeah, I seem to remember that," Randy said, nodding. "Pretty good at it, too, wasn't he?"

To hear Macy tell it, he was God's gift to horses. "I gather he was one of the best in the southwest."

"That sucks," Randy said.

"Yep. Yeah, this whole thing really sucks," Wyatt admitted, letting his guard down for a rare moment. "We were using the southern end of the property for a condo development, and we'd even begun a little of the excavation on the southern end of his ranch. I mean, I represent the seller and the buyer—I couldn't see the harm in it, but then wham, the bottom falls out when this guy turns up alive."

"No kidding. When was it supposed to close?"

"Tomorrow afternoon," Wyatt said. He had yet to

cancel the closing. Couldn't remember, didn't want to remember, something like that.

"You've got the legal authority to sell?"

"Yes. My wife couldn't face selling it but knew it had to be sold, so she gave me power of attorney." He explained the legal situation to Randy as his lawyer Jack had explained it to him: If Wyatt sold the land, he would have to return the value to Finn, but they wouldn't take the land from the new owner. At least in that scenario, Wyatt would be out the money, but he'd have the land.

Randy stopped walking, put his hands on his hips, and looked at Wyatt. "Look, Wyatt, I don't want to get in your business, but I get the idea you don't want this guy around."

Wyatt snorted. "Would you?"

"You haven't met my wife," Randy said. "But I'm serious about this. If you want the soldier to move on, the best way to make that happen is to sell that land. If he doesn't have a way to make his living, then what's he going to do? He's going to go somewhere he can have the kind of space he needs to run cattle and train cutters. West Texas, most like."

Wyatt stared at Randy. What he was suggesting was so unethical, so outrageous, so abhorrent that Wyatt couldn't believe Randy had even *said* it.

But Randy merely shrugged. "I'm just saying, if you want that guy gone, the best way to do it is to go ahead and sell his livelihood."

"Okay, a, that is not exactly legal at this point, and b,

all he'd have to do is take it to a judge and get it back," Wyatt said incredulously.

"That's right. But think about it. They've done the title search, right? A big title company in Austin isn't going to connect Lockhart to that land at this point. They're just shoving papers under your hand to sign. Legal or not, you know as well as I do that stuff gets through these closings that shouldn't all the time. So it happens. Then Lockhart will be going up against a conglomerate that's already begun excavation on a multimillion-dollar project. You think he's got the kind of money he'd need to fight it?"

"He'd have the proceeds from the sale of the land," Wyatt pointed out.

"That money will be sitting in your account. How's he going to get it unless you give it to him? Furthermore, what if you just wrote him a check? He's still going to want his land back, and he'll run through all his money and them some trying to get it back. Then he'd have nothing. No, he'd take the money and run."

"No," Wyatt said, shaking his head. "I'm not going to do anything that underhanded. It's not right, Randy." He meant it. He would do whatever it took to save his marriage, short of stealing the land right out from under Lockhart as Randy was suggesting.

"Suit yourself," Randy said, and started walking again.

25

Finn's nightmares kept getting longer and more vivid instead of fading away as he'd hoped, terrifying him in the middle of the night and waking him with a pounding heart and sweat-drenched body.

He'd gotten into the habit of drinking a couple of beers to get back to sleep.

That particular morning, he couldn't get back to sleep because his mind was on Macy, on his ranch, on where he went from here. He should never have let her out of the truck two days ago without something more than a vague promise to call it off with Wyatt. He'd expected to hear from her by now.

Why hadn't she called him? After that explosive night at Two Wishes, he'd thought that was it; situation resolved, nothing left to do but tell Wyatt and tidy it up with whatever legal action was required.

The anxiety was making him crazy. He could call her, but Finn felt like he'd laid it out there more than once. He needed Macy to make the next move.

He tried to keep his mind from blowing up by working around the folks' place. He repaired a fence and hauled out some salt licks, dropping them around for the cattle. He helped his dad work on an old tractor. When he finished that, he drove down to Two Wishes and took down the FOR SALE sign. But then he wandered aimlessly about. There was so much work to be done, work that required money. Finn couldn't ask his folks for it. The only other option he had was to get a job and work on the ranch in his spare time. That idea only added to his anxiety, which felt like it could pick him up and carry him off at any moment.

Finn returned to his folks' house and helped himself to a beer. He guzzled it and was contemplating another one when he felt someone else in the kitchen. He glanced over his shoulder.

His mother was standing there, staring disapprovingly at the beer in his hand.

"What?" he snapped.

"I worry about you."

God, he didn't want to have this conversation again. "Don't worry about me, Mom. I'm fine."

"You're fine, huh? Is that why you don't sleep? Why you won't talk with the man from New York? Why you won't let anyone help you?"

"The only help I need is getting my life back on track," he said irritably, and decided to have another beer after all. He grabbed it out of the fridge and opened it.

"Finneus, you drink around the clock! Don't you see that is not normal?"

"I'm not exactly normal anymore, Mom. It's not like

I'm home from college." He opened the cabinet and pulled down a bag of tortilla chips.

"Oh Finn," his mother said with disgust. "At least let me make you some lunch."

"Nah, I'm good," he said.

His mother snatched the bag of chips from his hand. "You're *not* good. Now listen to me," she said sternly as she put the chips back in the cabinet. "You have got to get some help. I was talking to Reverend Duffy and he said—"

"Mom, don't," Finn warned her. "Don't start preaching at me. I can't take that."

"I am not preaching at you! I am trying to get you to see that you need help! Finn, please, for my sake, talk to someone!"

"I don't need to talk to anyone!" he exploded. "Why is that so hard for you to understand? I need my life back! I need to get out of this house, to buy a couple of horses and get Macy, and I need to start *living*! I haven't lived in three years, Mom! I haven't—"

He suddenly couldn't speak. There was a pain in his chest—a stifling sort of pain—and he winced, clutching his chest.

"Finn!" his mother cried, and put her hand over his, the other on his forehead. "Oh dear God! I'm calling 911—"

"No, no," he said, and gripped her hand. The pain passed. "It's nothing. Indigestion. Too many beers." He had to get out of his parents' house. He patted his mother's hand. "Really, I'm fine."

He put the beer down, squeezed his mother's shoulder, and moved past her. He didn't look at her—he wasn't so far gone that he liked seeing the fear in her eyes.

"Where are you going?"

"I'm going to grab a shower," he said.

"What about lunch?"

"No, thanks, Mom!" he said over his shoulder, and walked down the hallway, past the new shrine she had put up on the wall—all the various clippings about his survival, framed and arranged around his Purple Heart.

Either he got out of here, or he would lose his freaking mind.

Macy never ate her cereal—she'd gotten sick again. As she was preparing to leave for an afternoon meeting about the gala, Jesse handed her a cheese sandwich and some crackers. "Try to eat the sandwich and put these crackers in your purse. Eat them if you get nauseated."

Macy gave him a quick, appraising look. "How do you know this stuff?"

"I'm a multitalented kind of guy," Jesse said with a wink. "And I was the oldest. My mom had four more after me, so I learned a couple of things."

"Thanks, Jesse."

"Thank you for what?" Laru called, padding out into the entry in bare feet and the extremely short bathrobe she favored. She rose up on her tiptoes and kissed Jesse. "Thank you for what?" she asked.

"For cleaning up the kitchen. She's running late," Jesse said. He ruffled Laru's hair and started toward the kitchen.

"God, Macy, you are so pale," Laru said, folding her arms and studying Macy's face. Behind her, Jesse whirled around and made a slashing motion across his throat. He pointed to her Jeep, indicating Macy should go. "Are you feeling okay?"

"Just tired," Macy said. "I better run—"

"This is craziness," Laru said. "You've got to come to some conclusion, Macy—for *your* sake. You're going to ruin your health if you don't. Look at you, you're so bloated!"

"Bloated!" Macy cried, her hand going to her belly.

"You devour carbs—what do you expect?"

"Okay," Macy said, working hard to remain even, "I really have to run."

"Why are you in such a hurry?" Laru asked, her brow furrowing with suspicion. "I know that frantic look. What's going on?"

"I'm late." *In more ways than one.* "I've really got to go." She waved her fingers as she hurried out the front door and down the flagstone walk to her Jeep. As she got into the driver's seat, she glanced back and saw Laru standing there, still frowning.

"Lord," she muttered, and started her car. But she'd barely reached the end of the drive when her cell phone rang.

"Macy, I've been hoping you'd call," Finn said when she answered. His low voice was like a salve to an open wound, and tears welled in Macy. She was on a hormonal roller coaster and felt like she was about to plummet again. "I need to see you, too," she said tearfully.

"Are you crying?"

"No! *Yes*," she said, pulling over to wipe the tears from her eyes.

"What's wrong—has something happened?" he demanded.

"Nothing's happened. It's . . . it's *everything*," she said. "Everything! It should be so simple, Finn, but it just gets harder—"

"I'm coming to get you—"

"No, no," Macy said, and shook her head, clearing it. "No, really, I'm all right. I'm just tired. I'm on my way to a meeting about the fund-raiser. I missed the last one, so I can't miss this one, and there is so much work to do, and honestly, I've been useless—I can't let them down."

"When can I see you?"

"I'll call you—"

"I'm not waiting for you to call me—"

"Finn, please. I'll call you, just as soon as I get out of this meeting. I have to think of a place we can meet—"

"What do you mean?"

"Austin," Macy said, her mind rushing ahead. "People won't recognize us in Austin."

There was silence on the other end. "Am I understanding you? You want to meet in Austin like . . . like we're having an affair?"

That was precisely what she meant, but when he

said it like that, it sounded so base, so strange. "No, I don't mean that," Macy said. "I just don't . . ." She didn't know what she was doing.

"When are you going to tell him?" Finn asked quietly.

Her head was throbbing now. "I . . . I'm going to, but it's very hard. I mean—" She had no idea what to say. She could scarcely think.

"Okay, Macy," Finn said. "Okay. But I need to see you."

"All right, yes. I'll call you just as soon as I can."

He didn't answer right away. "Listen . . . I'm sorry, baby," he said softly. "I'm sorry this is so hard on you."

"I'm sorry for us all," she said.

The "Life Under the Texas Stars" fund-raiser meeting was in full swing when Macy entered. She was at least fifteen minutes late, maybe more, and she waved as she hurried to her seat. But as she took her seat, she detected uneasiness in the room. Macy looked around the table; there were Mr. and Mrs. Francis, who had lost a son in Iraq and had donated quite a lot of energy and money to Project Lifeline. And Misty Fitzgerald, whose sister had served three tours in Iraq before she was discharged. Misty's sister had committed suicide about three weeks after that, a victim of PTSD. There was Jasper Adams, whose son was at Brook Army Medical Center in San Antonio, his legs gone, his torso and arms badly burned. And Brian Cahill, whose father had been killed by friendly fire.

And last but not least, Samantha Delaney, who was sitting at the head of the table, staring at the paper in front of her.

"I'm sorry I'm late," Macy said, feeling conspicuous. "I know I've been a slacker, but I finished stuffing the mailers. They're in my car, ready to go."

No one said anything.

"Please don't stop on my account," she said. "I'll catch up."

"Macy, we've been talking," Sam said, still looking at her notes. "And we've come to a difficult decision." She glanced up then, her eyes dark and surprisingly cold.

"We have?" Macy asked, looking around the room.

"We think we need to substitute someone else to host the event. Brian knows Rick Barnes from the local NBC station and thinks he can get him to be the emcee."

Macy blinked. *She* was supposed to be the emcee, to run the silent auction. They'd been over it already and everyone had agreed she'd be the best person for the job. But there was something in Sam's expression that caused Macy's heart to slide. "But why?"

"We . . ." Sam glanced around the table. "We don't think it's a good idea because your husband came home, and . . . and you haven't decided what to do with him."

"I haven't decided what to *do* with him?" Macy echoed incredulously. "What has that got to do with being the emcee of a silent auction? I've worked as hard as anyone sitting at this table," she reminded them.

"Macy," Mrs. Francis said kindly, "this isn't a knock against your hard work, or abilities, and Lord knows you've poured your heart and soul into this. But Sam's right—your situation has changed and we don't want this important event to be overshadowed by your circumstances. I'm sure you don't want that either. Everyone in this town is talking about it."

"Talking about what?" she asked uneasily.

Mrs. Francis looked uncomfortably at the others. "Who . . . who you're going to choose."

Shocked, Macy gaped at them. "It's not a lottery," she said quietly.

"Of course not," Mrs. Francis said. "But the local media wants to know if you're going to be at the fundraiser and the mayor thought it would be a great opportunity to give Mr. Lockhart the key to the city, but we thought, what about Mr. Clark? He's a generous donor and has been a great supporter. Do you see our dilemma?"

Macy couldn't believe it. She looked around the room. "Is this a joke?" she asked hopefully.

"We wouldn't joke about something like this," Sam said quietly. "We know how much it means to you."

Sam knew better than anyone else. They'd sat up like schoolgirls the night they'd conceived the idea, talking about the possibility, excitedly planning it. "You're right, it does mean quite a lot to me," Macy said. "We came up with the idea together, Sam. We've worked a long time to organize it. I've booked some of the best music acts in the area and convinced people to donate services and activities they wouldn't have otherwise donated. And now, because my husband is alive, you are going to remove me from the event?"

"We're not removing you," Jasper said uneasily. "There's plenty of work to be done besides standing out front."

"Right. Stuffing envelopes," Macy said. "I've done that. I am ready to raise quite a bit of money in the auction."

"But the thing is, Macy, you've got *two* husbands," Sam said, as if she were explaining this to a child. "We don't want your two husbands getting all the press for this fund-raiser. Surely you can understand that we want to keep all the attention on the work we are doing, can't you?"

Macy felt ill. "Samantha, come on. Don't do this."

The color drained from Sam's face and she looked down. Macy looked around the room. Everyone was staring at her, unable to answer.

"Okay," she said, getting to her feet. "I understand. I've got all the mailers in my car. I'll leave them on the hood of yours, Sam." She picked up her purse.

"Macy! Don't leave!" Mrs. Francis pleaded with her. "There's a lot we need to talk about!"

"You guys seem to doing fine without me." She glanced at Sam on the way out, but Sam was looking at her notes again, her jaw clenched resolutely.

26

Macy sat in her car, staring blindly at the gray VFW hall. She had no idea where to go from here. Her life was almost completely unraveled now.

She glanced at the clock on the dash. It was half past two. She could go back to Laru's and cry some more. Or, she could go home and grab the mail and a few clothes while Wyatt was at work. "Right," she muttered under her breath. "Choose the path of least resistance. That's helpful."

Or she could face Wyatt and tell him the truth.

Macy called his office. "Hi, Linda Gail," she said. "Is Wyatt in?"

"Macy, how nice to hear your voice. No, Wyatt's not here. He went out to see some land and was going to work from home after that instead of driving all the way back into town. How are you getting on?"

Macy chatted with Linda Gail for a moment, then put her Jeep in drive and headed for Arbolago Hills.

She hadn't been home since the day she'd left after returning from D.C. She looked up at the house from the drive. It was a beautiful home, and there were plenty of people out in the world who would think

she was insane to give this up. Like her mother. She'd
called again last night to grill Macy about what she was
doing with her life and then had told her what to do.
"I'm so worried about you, Macy," she'd said. "I haven't
heard from you, and that's not like you. Laru says you're
sleeping too much, too."

"Are you kidding?" Macy had said, disgruntled.

"I think you should take up running again. Emma
runs in those five- and ten-K races to keep herself fit."

"Mom!"

"All right, honey," her mother had said. "But I just
want to say one more thing, and then I'll stop. You
need to be careful. You don't want to lose Wyatt."

That was the last thing Macy had been able to toler-
ate, and she'd abruptly ended the conversation. As if
she could possibly alienate her current husband any
more than she'd already done.

Wyatt's truck was not in the drive of the house. He
hadn't made it home yet, she supposed, and decided
to grab a few things while she waited. Macy walked
into the house through the garage door and dropped
her purse on the kitchen counter. Out of habit, she
picked up a dirty glass from the countertop and put it in
the dishwasher before she even realized what she was
doing. She paused and looked around her. Mail was
haphazardly stacked at the end of the bar, unopened.
The sink was full of dirty glasses and bowls, and from
all outward appearances, it looked as if Wyatt was existing on chips and hot sauce. The trash was overflowing
with empty jars of salsa, beer cans, and a couple of fast

food bags. And his blood pressure medicine was by the sink, the bottle empty.

Macy dried her hands and walked into the great room. It felt odd being in here now—almost like she was intruding on Wyatt's private space. She looked out the picture windows, across the deck and to the lake. On summer evenings, they would sit out there to catch a breeze while they watched the boats go by. Or, if Wyatt got home from work early enough, they'd take the boat out for a sunset cruise. He'd bought the boat for her. She could take it or leave it, but of course, she'd never told Wyatt that.

Macy turned away from the windows and walked on, to the master bedroom. She paused in the doorway and looked at the unmade bed. She remembered very clearly the last time she was in this bed, the earnest way Wyatt had made love to her. The memory made her ashamed and she sagged against the doorjamb. Her husband had tried to love her, and all the while she was thinking of Finn.

Poor Wyatt. Try as he might with the house and the trips and the gifts and the love—Macy knew how much he loved her—he couldn't make her love him the way she loved Finn. She couldn't really say why that was. It wasn't anything about Wyatt—he was a wonderful, caring man. There was just something about Finn that touched her like no other.

Macy walked into the room and picked up two shirts that Wyatt had tossed on the floor. He was incapable of finding and using a clothes hamper. She sat down on the end of the bed, looking at the shirt, trying to remember the moment she fell in love with Wyatt.

Twenty-two months had passed since Finn's death when her dad introduced her to Wyatt. Macy once told Emma that might have been the best thing their father had ever done for her. Macy had been taken by Wyatt—he was handsome and kind, a true gentleman. He was a land broker, her dad said, and had a track record of turning large ranches over for huge profits.

"He's trying to put together a big resort deal," her dad had said. "You know, a family vacation destination, complete with water sports, a horse track, shopping, fine dining, and luxury condo rentals." Macy had been mildly intrigued.

Apparently, Wyatt had seen something in her, too, because he began to call her. She didn't want to date, but Wyatt wouldn't take no for an answer. He'd cheerfully worn her down until she went out with him a time or two. Macy was impressed that he seemed to understand her loss as well as anyone could who had not been through something similar.

On their fourth date, Wyatt had kissed her. It was nothing to write home about—just a small kiss good night—but after that, he began to pursue her like she was a land deal. And Macy . . . well, she supposed she needed the attention, because she didn't try to dissuade him.

But when did love walk in? At what moment, what event, what day did she know she loved Wyatt? She could remember the precise moment she knew she loved Finn. It was a blustery winter day, when they'd gone horseback riding and he'd made her a picnic of sandwiches. When they reached their destination, they discovered the water he'd packed had leaked, ruining the sandwiches.

Finn was not the least daunted. He built a fire out of dead mesquite, picked some cactus, peeled it, then roasted it over the fire. It was perhaps the most delicious food Macy had ever eaten. They'd sat huddled together, eating cactus, admitting their dreams and hopes, and Macy had fallen hopelessly in love with him.

As for Wyatt, she guessed she knew on the anniversary of the night Finn had proposed to her. She was at a movie with Wyatt, thinking about that night at the Rooster with Finn. The theater was dark, and Macy tried to hide her silent tears. Honestly, she never really understood how Wyatt knew, but he put his arm around her and held her, and whispered, "I promise you, Macy, everything will be all right."

She had believed him. She had fallen in love with him.

"Macy?"

Wyatt's voice startled her; she gasped like a guilty cookie thief. "Wyatt! You scared me!" She tried to smile. She thought she was ready to talk to him, but she suddenly didn't feel so ready. "I didn't hear you come in."

He looked at her strangely, as if she didn't fit into this setting. "What are you doing here?" he asked, and Macy could hear the hope in his voice, that brief moment of belief that perhaps she had come home for him.

Seeing his hope made her feel queasy. "Linda Gail said you'd be here." She shifted her gaze to the bedroom floor.

"I'm going to straighten this up," he said quickly.

Macy couldn't help a small smile. "We both know you're not."

He relaxed then and squatted down to pick up a pair of discarded jeans. He stayed there a moment, looking at the jeans, then lifted his gaze to hers. "Am I a fool to think you being here is a sign that life is going to get back to normal sometime soon?"

When she hesitated, he clenched his jaw and rose up, still holding the jeans.

"Hey," she said softly, "do you remember the moment you fell in love?"

"Wow," he said, and glanced at the jeans. "I wasn't expecting that."

"Sorry," she said instantly, regretting the question.

He carelessly tossed the jeans onto a chair with other jeans. "Yeah, I know," he said, and looked at her. "I know it was the night I first met you."

Macy laughed. "You did not think you loved me when we first met!"

"What's the matter? Don't you believe in love at first sight?"

"Well, yeah. But not when one of us was a basket case when we first met—and it wasn't you."

"I didn't think you were a basket case. I saw a pretty woman with a self-deprecating sense of humor, a bright smile, and the warmest blue eyes I've ever seen."

"I hardly said a word!" she exclaimed laughingly.

"You said enough," he said, his demeanor quite sober. "I remember you were wearing black slacks and heels and that silky pink thing," he said, gesturing to his torso. "It was perfect. I'd always been a love 'em and leave 'em kind of guy, and I remember thinking *whoa*, someone just knocked me off my feet."

"Wow," Macy said incredulously. "I never knew that."

"You did," he said. "But I think you've forgotten it in the last few weeks. So . . . do you remember when you knew?"

"Yes." She smiled. "It wasn't anything in particular, but one night when we were at the movies, sitting together in the dark, you had your arm around me, and I just knew."

Wyatt smiled, then suddenly caught her hand. "Come on. There is something I want to show you." He pulled her off the edge of the bed and hurried her down the hallway.

"Where are we going?" she asked.

"You'll see."

He led her outside, onto the deck, then down the steps to the boat dock. They walked all the way to the end of the dock and stood beneath the little arbor Wyatt had built there last fall. He'd strung outdoor lights through the slats and had brought in some massive clay pots, into which he'd planted bougainvillea and hydrangeas. The crowning touch was the two chaise lounges with cushioned seats and built-in cup holders. They'd both been absurdly pleased with the cup holders. They'd spent many evenings down here, just hanging out on the water's edge, nibbling on cold suppers, drinking wine or beer, and watching boats go by.

Wyatt pointed down the lake. "See that radio tower?" he asked.

Macy looked at the far end of the lake. The radio tower was several miles away; she could see the top of it. "Yes."

"I made a deal to sell some land this morning," he said, and turned around to Macy. "It was the last piece of the puzzle. Do you know what that means?"

She shook her head.

"It means that radio tower is on what will be the eastern tip of the Hill Country Resort and Spa. It means that in spite of Lockhart, I've put together the funding I need to build and develop it. And that means I can give you whatever you want, Macy. It means we can send our kids to any college they want. It means you'll never have to worry about a thing. Everything I ever promised you is about to come true, sweetheart. This is all for you, for *us*, for our future together. I've never been shy about letting you know that I would do anything for you."

"I am so proud of you," Macy said.

"I don't want you to be proud. I want you to love me. I want you to be with me, to have our kids, to do everything we set out to do."

Her pulse began to climb uncomfortably. What if she was carrying his baby? Wyatt had a right to that life, didn't he? He had as much right to his dream as she had to hers. But she couldn't tell him—what if she *wasn't* pregnant? What if Jesse was right and stress had resulted in a false positive? "I am proud of you and I love you . . . but it's not that simple anymore," she said.

Wyatt suddenly turned away and stood with his back to her a moment, staring at the water, his hands on his waist. And then he abruptly faced her. "Why is this so damn hard for you, Macy?" he bit out. "What am I missing? What is so lacking about our relationship that it's even a *question* to you?"

Resentment was coming off him in waves. Macy took a step back. "It's a whole lot more than just a question. There is one other person—"

"Can he offer you this?" Wyatt exploded, gesturing wildly to the house. "Can he offer you a life of security?"

She felt a wave of nausea.

"I know what happened Monday," Wyatt snapped. "I know you rescued the poor, broken G.I. Joe from the bar and left with him. I know he's gotten a hell of a lot more of your attention than I have. If you're going to declare this marriage void, then just do it and stop stringing me along!"

She was going to be sick. Macy put a hand to her stomach. She opened her mouth to speak, but whirled around, leaned over the railing, and vomited into the lake.

"Jesus!" Wyatt cried. He was instantly at her side, his hand on her back. "God, Macy, are you all right?" he asked fearfully.

"I know you are unhappy with the situation," she said hoarsely, and dragged the back of her hand across her mouth. Wyatt dabbed at her perspiring forehead

with his shirtsleeve, but Macy pushed his arm away.
"You have to trust that I will do the right thing, Wyatt."

Wyatt blinked.

"Please trust that I will do the right thing for all of
us!"

"Ohmigod," he muttered, his gaze raking over her,
the color draining out of his face. "Ohmigod, you've
been with him—"

The nausea was swelling in her again. She pushed
past him and ran up the dock and the steps to the
house. She could not stand there in the summer sun
and tell Wyatt that she loved Finn more, or better, or
differently, but that she was carrying the child Wyatt
had wanted. Or that a baby didn't figure into it all
somehow, because it did. She would have to tell him
soon—but not today, not like this. Not when she was
about to be sick again.

27

Karen Lockhart watched Finn get in the old farm truck
and drive away much too fast up the gravel road. She
looked at her husband, who was hunkered down over

a late lunch, and demanded, "Did you see how he left out of here?"

"Aw, leave him alone, Karen. He's got a lot on his mind."

"I don't intend to go to his funeral a second time, Rick," she said sharply.

Rick rolled his eyes and reached for another slice of white bread. "You're being overly dramatic," he said. "The boy just escaped Afghanistan a few weeks ago. Give him some time—he'll work things out."

Karen looked out the window again. *Dear Jesus, please help my miracle son,* she prayed. *I can't lose him again. I won't lose him again.*

Reverend Duffy said she should give this one to God to handle, but Karen couldn't do that. How could she? Finn was her son. "He could get on his feet and get on with his life if he'd quit pining over Macy Harper," she remarked bitterly.

"Her name is Macy Clark and you don't need to go meddling in his business," Rick warned her.

"I never cared for that one."

"For God's sake, Karen! You were the first one on the Macy Harper bandwagon when he met her!"

"I was blinded by his devotion to her, that's all. I've never liked the Harpers. They don't have the same morals we do."

"What is *that* supposed to mean?" Rick demanded.

"Bobby Harper cheated on Jillian for three years before they split up."

"That's the dumbest thing I ever heard," Rick said,

his brow furrowing. "Jillian Harper is a fine-looking woman."

"Oh!" Karen exclaimed angrily.

"I'm just saying," Rick said with a shrug. "Now you lay off Macy and Finn and let them find their own way in this, do you hear me?"

Karen frowned and pressed her lips tightly together.

"Why can't you just let it be, Karen?"

"I'll say it once more, Rick—I'm not losing him again." She picked up the phone and punched in Brodie's number.

Finn drove mindlessly into town, his mind foggy from the beer he'd drunk, his thoughts as scattered as the trash lodged against the barbed-wire fence on that lonely stretch of road. Finn had never been the sort of guy to give in to feelings of despair. He was generally pretty positive and upbeat. But he could not seem to rid his head of the thought that seemed to beat like a drum—he had nothing. No place to call home, a house that needed to be gutted, a ranch that had no stock. He had no one to turn to who understood the dark thoughts that would pop up out of the blue, or his need to drink. He had nothing substantial to occupy his hands, much less his thoughts.

Things were beginning to feel a little out of control.

I can't live this way. I can't live like this, like a madman, like a crazy vet.

In town, he drove around the town square twice, wincing at the billboard outside the courthouse that

read WELCOME HOME FINN LOCKHART. AN AMERICAN
HERO. He didn't like the attention, the notion that he
was somehow a hero for having survived. He didn't do
anything heroic. Heroic would have been figuring out
a way to kill those bastards and himself with them. Not
sit around chained to a wall feeding a stray.

Finn had no particular destination, but he'd seen all
he wanted to see of Cedar Springs. He had the urge to
drive out to Laru's, but something told him that was a
bad idea. He decided instead to drive out to Arbolago
Hills and see where Macy lived.

He would wish for a long time to come that he
hadn't done that.

It was a gated community, but Finn slid in behind
another car, waving at the gateman like he knew him.
If the gateman thought he shouldn't be in the community, he sure was slow picking up the phone to call
the cops.

Finn had a general idea where the house was,
based on what Brodie had told him, and drove down
to the end of Arbolago Boulevard. He found the house
easy enough—there were only a half dozen built out
over the cliff. It was a big house, one of those that
looked like it belonged in a magazine. But it wasn't
the size of the house or the spectacular view that
caught Finn's attention. It was the fact that Macy's
Jeep was parked in the drive, right next to a white
pickup truck that had CLARK RANCH PROPERTIES emblazoned on the sides.

His head began to hurt. He supposed he could

assume the best, but something about it didn't sit right with him, and as Finn drove on, intense anger began to build in him. He decided to head to Brodie's little house on Holly Street before he did something wrong, like bash in the windows of Wyatt's truck. Finn gripped the steering wheel until his fingers ached in a struggle to keep himself from turning around and doing just that.

He was going to have to face up to it—life had changed since he'd gone off to war. Maybe Macy had changed, and maybe what he thought he knew of her didn't fit anymore. He wouldn't be the first soldier to believe there was something so strong between them that even time and distance couldn't touch it and be proven wrong.

Brodie lived in a neat little tract house with rose-bushes planted along the front porch. Lucas put himself through veterinary school and Finn started the horse ranch, but Brodie had never had such entrepreneurial aspirations—he liked sports and the outdoors and work at a lumberyard was just fine for him.

Finn pulled into the drive and got out of the truck. Brodie had bought this house with the money Finn had paid him for his share of the land their grandfather had left them. It was perfect for a bachelor, an old-fashioned house with a detached garage, a kitchen entrance, and sun awnings on the windows. As Finn walked up the drive to the kitchen entrance, he heard a dog bark. He leaned over a chain-link fence and smiled at the mutt that came bounding toward him. He scratched the dog's neck before looking for the key that Brodie used to leave under a pot by the door. The key was still there—it was nice to know that at least some things never changed.

Inside, the house was surprisingly neat. "Tidy boy," Finn said to himself, nodding with approval as he looked around. He let the dog in the house and watched as he raced to the front door, then down the hall to one of three bedrooms. While the dog searched for Brodie, Finn opened the fridge. "Dude . . . where's the beer?" Finn said out loud and squatted down to have a better look. There wasn't a single bottle of beer, but in the freezer, Finn found a bottle of Schnapps. That had never been his thing, but in the absence of anything else, and with his head pounding mercilessly, he poured some into a glass and downed it.

A few minutes later, he was on the couch in Brodie's living room, a bag of Fritos by his side, the bottle of Schnapps on the table, and the dog lying next to him. Finn absently petted the dog as he stared at an episode of *SpongeBob SquarePants*.

The last thing he remembered was Squidward doing an interpretive dance. The next thing he knew, someone was kicking him. Finn reacted as if he were still in Afghanistan—he surged up, caught the offending foot in one hand, and jerked backward. He heard a cry of pain as he and the enemy went down, crashing onto and breaking the cheap coffee table.

"Goddammit, Finn!" Brodie roared, and shoved him

off his body. He hopped to his feet and looked at the coffee table. "That's just great," he said, and kicked at a broken leg.

Reality came cascading back, and Finn rolled onto his back and looked up at the ceiling. The dog licked his face.

"Scout!" Brodie barked. "Come on!"

Finn heard the sliding glass door open and the dog trot out. The door slid closed again. Finn pushed himself up and draped his arms on his knees as he watched Brodie picking up Fritos and the spilled bottle of Schnapps. "Sorry, bro."

"Sorry?" Brodie said irritably. "You come into my house uninvited, drink my Schnapps, sleep on my couch, and then attack me?"

"I'm really sorry about that—it's a habit I need to break." He looked at Brodie. "Why are you drinking Schnapps, anyway? That stuff is nasty."

Brodie gave him a withering look and walked into the kitchen with the debris. Finn sheepishly followed him. "Let me do it," he said when Brodie got a broom out of the pantry.

Brodie obligingly shoved the broom at him. "What's going on with you, man?" he demanded.

"What do you mean?" Finn asked thickly as he swept up crumbs from the saltillo tile in Brodie's living room.

"Dude, you've been home a couple of weeks, give or take, right? And in that time you've upset Mom, you're drinking like a damn fish, you sleep all day and stay up all night. Everyone is talking about the scene at Ruthie's like you're a psycho, man."

Finn didn't say anything. He didn't tell his brother he was up all night because he couldn't stand to dream of Afghanistan, of bombs falling, of being chained to a goddam wall unable to fend for himself, of people being blown to bits. He didn't tell him he drank because that was the only thing that seemed to numb him sufficiently not to think of his life and of Macy.

"And you're not doing a damn thing to get your life back," Brodie said. He slammed a cabinet door shut and stared pointedly at Finn. "Remember what you said in Germany? You said you couldn't wait to get home and get on with it."

Honestly, Finn could hardly remember Germany any more. Everything but the moment he was living in had begun to fade into nothingness. Frankly, he liked it that way—it kept him numb and blind. He didn't have to think. "I've done some work around the folks' place—"

"You fixed a fence, Finn. And I wasn't talking about that, I was talking about Two Wishes."

"I need money to get that up and running."

"Then get a job! Look, I'm going to be blunt," Brodie said, and took the broom from Finn so he would focus on him. "You've got to get your shit together. I did a little asking around, and I found this guy in Austin who runs a therapy group—"

"Are you out of your mind?" Finn snapped, and walked away from his brother into the kitchen.

"Finn, listen to me—you've got some classic symptoms of post-traumatic stress—"

"Brodie, don't be an idiot—"

"—and this guy is doing some amazing work with guys coming back from the war."

Finn braced himself on the kitchen counter and worked to draw a steadying breath. "I don't have *that*," he snapped. "I'm fine."

"I don't know if you've got it or not, I'm just saying you're not *you* and obviously, you could use some help."

"I don't *need* help," Finn said again, and closed his eyes. His blood was pumping hard in his neck. It felt like his head could blow off his shoulders at any moment.

"So, what, you're going to hang out with Mom and Dad for the rest of your life, drinking beer?"

"Get off my back."

"Mom and Dad aren't in a position to take care of you forever. Dad needs back surgery, did you know that? And what about the ranch, anyway? What about getting some horses? Luke told me just a couple of days ago he's got a pair of rescued horses that have been neglected and could use a place. Whatever it is, just *do* something, and for God's sake, stop moping around about Macy—"

With blood roaring in Finn's ears, something detonated inside him. He angrily swiped at some canisters on the kitchen counter and sent them crashing to the floor. He whirled around and kicked with all his might at the refrigerator, and still the roaring did not stop. Brodie grabbed his shoulders and tried to shove him up against the wall, but Finn was too quick and too strong for his little brother; he managed to twist around, shove Brodie against the wall, and hold him there with his arm across his throat.

"Let me go, Finn," Brodie said angrily.

His green eyes were blazing with anger and pain, and the roaring began to subside in Finn. Appalled by what he'd just done, he jerked away from Brodie. "Brodie, I—"

"Get out of my house before I call the cops." Brodie's face was red with fury.

"I'm sorry," Finn said. "Man, I am so sorry."

Brodie's response was to point at the door.

With his head down, Finn walked out. He opened the door to his truck and was climbing in when Brodie appeared on the back stoop. "Hold up!" he barked, and strode to Finn's truck. He thrust his hand toward Finn; he held a yellow scrap of paper between his fingers. "Take it," he said.

Finn took the paper; Brodie pivoted sharply and strode back to his house, slamming the kitchen door on his way in. Finn opened the paper. In Brodie's scribble it read, *Dr. Ed Rock 442-6944.* Finn shoved the paper in his pocket and got in his truck. He wasn't going to go see some goddam shrink.

He drove out of town and pulled onto the highway in the direction of Dallas, and thought, *Dallas . . . why not?* There sure wasn't anything keeping him here.

28

~

Macy was shaking when she left Arbolago Hills.

Honestly, she wished she could leave Cedar Springs for a time, go some place where Finn and Wyatt didn't exist, where she could be alone with her thoughts and only *her* thoughts. Not her mom's, not Sam's, not Emma's, not Laru's.

"Hey," she muttered, "that's not a bad idea." She was not the sort to run from her problems—at least she didn't think she was—but she'd never had problems quite on this grand scale. Running seemed like the only viable solution. She would leave Cedar Springs, give herself time to recover from the extraordinary events of the last few weeks, get over this stupid morning sickness emotional roller coaster thing, and decide what to do in a calm and rational manner.

Macy was so convinced that was what she must do, in fact, that when she reached Laru's, she ran inside to pack a few things.

In the guest room, she paused only long enough to check the mail she'd picked up at home to make sure she wasn't leaving something behind that needed her attention. She quickly flipped through some bills and then saw an envelope from Hill Country Weavers. "Great. I've probably been axed from the program there, too," she muttered, and ripped open the envelope.

In the envelope was a note from Eliza, the instructor. *Macy*, she wrote, *I admit I've always been a bit of an Anglophile. I've been intrigued by your project and did a little research I thought you might find interesting. We look forward to seeing you back in class. Fondly, Eliza.*

Behind the note were pages printed off the Internet. It was a census of Cedar County conducted in 1848. The census listed three hundred inhabitants, their marital status, their parents' names, and the places of their birth. If they didn't hail from Texas, they most likely hailed from Arkansas or Tennessee. But there, in the middle of the roster, was a pair of Lockharts.

Duncan Lockhart, the entry read, *born 1818 at Eilean Ros, Scotland. Parents, Liam and Ellen Lockhart. Wife, Glenna Lockhart, born 1820, Aberfeldy, Scotland. Property owned: two mules, twenty-four heifers, forty cows, one bull, one section plus two hundred acres.*

Macy tried to imagine how hard the journey from Scotland must have been for them. She wondered why they had come, if they had been running from something or to something. Just seeing their names made her think of Finn and the sacrifice he'd made, of his unflinching, unselfish bravery. The tears—the stupid, blinding tears that seemed to follow her everywhere of late—welled up and her vision began to blur. She gasped for breath at the same moment her knees buckled. Macy grabbed onto the dresser to keep from pitching to the ground and sank down to her knees.

"*Macy!*" she heard Laru cry. "Are you all right?"

She wasn't all right—she was fractured, splitting into a million little pieces of herself and the person she thought she once was. To her horror, Macy began to sob.

She felt Laru's strong arms envelop her. Laru held Macy as she cried, rocking back and forth, her chin on Macy's head. How long Macy cried, she had no idea, but when the well had at last dried, she wiped her nose with the back of her hand and looked at Laru.

"*Ugh,*" Laru said with a grimace at the sight of Macy's face and handed her a box of tissues from the dresser.

"Thanks," Macy said tearfully.

"Should I call Jilly?"

"God, no, please," Macy said wearily.

Laru frowned as she pushed Macy's hair from her face. "I won't, but on one condition. You must see a doctor as soon as possible."

"Yeah," Macy said with a sheepish smile. "I could use some sleeping pills. Or something."

"I'm not talking about sleeping pills, Macy. I'm talking about an OB/GYN. The sooner you see one, the sooner you know when you conceived and when you are due. You can't figure out the rest of your life until you know that."

Macy's eyes widened. "Did Jesse tell you?" she asked

angrily, pausing in the wiping of her nose. "He promised he wouldn't tell you!"

"Excuse me?" Laru shot back. "*Jesse* knows you're
pregnant?"

"Oh God," Macy muttered. "You mean he didn't tell
you? Wait—how do you know?"

"No, he didn't tell me, and I will find out later why
he knew and I didn't. I know because of the morning
sickness and the raging hormones and the fact that you
left the packaging for the pregnancy test on top of the
trash."

"Ohmigod," Macy moaned. "I can't do *anything*
right!"

"Your inability to hide your secrets notwithstanding,
you need to see a doctor," Laru said again. "For the
baby's sake and for the sake of knowing who—"

"It's Wyatt's!" Macy cried.

"You're certain?"

"Beyond a shadow of a doubt, Laru."

"Still—"

"I know, I know," Macy said, throwing up a hand as
she sagged against the dresser. "I'm not prepared for
this. Not six weeks ago, Wyatt and I decided to try, but
my God, I never thought it would happen so easily!
Finn and I tried to have a baby for two whole damn
years and nothing happened. I wish we had—God, I
wish we had. If we'd had a baby, he never would have
left, he never would have died!" The damn tears started
to drip again. She squeezed her eyes shut and put the
tissue to her eyes. "I love Finn more than . . . more

than anything. But I also love Wyatt and I may be carrying his baby. I don't know what to do."

"You'll figure it out," Laru said, shifting to sit beside Macy, propped against the dresser, too. "It may seem impossible now, but it's not. As you get older you'll figure out that life is just one damn thing after another, and you won't even be able to remember if this damn thing happened before or after another damn thing."

"That's hard to imagine," Macy said sullenly.

"I know you'll make the right decision for you and the baby," Laru continued. "But the first thing you have to do is go and see a doctor. I have a friend who is an OB/GYN in Austin. Her name is Debbie Schuler. I will call her today and ask her to get you in as soon as possible."

"Okay," Macy said, grateful that Laru was handling it.

Laru smiled and wiped mascara from Macy's cheek. "One piece of friendly advice. If I were you, I wouldn't breathe a word to anyone until you're sure. That's something else you learn as you get older—adding gasoline to a fire is rarely a good idea."

Wyatt couldn't stay in the house after that argument with Macy—the place still had her vibe, her scent. He headed back to his office, noticing for the first time how many of the yellow ribbons adorned cars in his part of the country. Seemed like everyone was related to a soldier. Not him. He thought it was a sad testament to his life that he had nothing substantial but his work and his wife.

For some reason, that had seemed okay to Wyatt

until now. He'd been raised an only child and was used to making his own way. He felt pathetically lonely right now. He wasn't even that close to his parents. They'd been driving around the country in a massive RV for years and his conversations with them were superficial: How's the weather, how 'bout them Cowboys, etc. Nor did he have any close friends he could call. His buddies were mainly golf buddies, not the sort of friends he would burden with this. The next best thing he had was Linda Gail and her husband, and Wyatt would hardly call them friends, really.

Although it was nearly 4 PM, Wyatt spotted Caroline Spalding's Mercedes parked outside his office. When he walked into the office, she was standing next to Linda Gail's desk. "Well, hello, Wyatt. I was just going to leave you a note."

"Hello, Caroline. How are you?"

"Good! Hey, I had an idea. When I close on the land my dad left me, I thought I might buy something closer to Austin. You know, something I could build on. Do you have anything you could show me?"

Wyatt didn't think today was the best time for him to do so, but Caroline seemed the perfect diversion from a pretty rotten day thus far. "I think I've got something. Can you give me thirty minutes?"

"Absolutely," she said. "I'll just wait outside." She smiled at Linda Gail as she went out.

Wyatt watched her walk out to her car. He turned and saw Linda Gail busily typing something, her back very straight and stiff.

He couldn't help himself. Perhaps it was because he needed a friend right now more than he'd ever needed one in his life, or perhaps it was because he and Linda Gail were closer than he gave them credit for being. Whatever it was, something made him blurt, "I'm losing her."

Linda Gail looked up, surprised. "*Caroline?*" She snorted. "Honey, you're a big fat whale and she is reeling you in like a champion fisherman."

"Not Caroline! I'm losing Macy," he said. "I'm losing her, Linda Gail, I can feel it. And I don't *want* to lose her."

Linda Gail blinked. Slowly, she stood up. "Bless your heart, Wyatt. But you're going to have to fight for her," she said, almost as if she'd been expecting this conversation.

"What do you mean?"

"I mean you are going to have to court her like she's never been courted before."

That was the best advice Linda Gail could offer? "I sent her flowers a couple of times last week."

Linda Gail shook her head. "That's not what I mean, Wyatt. This isn't you trying to dig out of the doghouse. You're in way deeper than that."

Not exactly comforting news.

"Hey, don't get me wrong, that's a good start," Linda Gail hastily added. "But you've got to *court* her. You've got to make her think she's the only woman you would go to the ends of the earth for, and that you are there for her right now, because she's going through the worst crisis of her life. If there is one thing a woman wants in a time of crisis, it's a man who can and will stand up with her. She doesn't need another problem; she needs support and protection."

Wyatt had no idea how to make Macy feel supported and protected. He thought he'd already done that. "She knows that," he said uncertainly.

"I can promise you she doesn't know which way is up right now."

He could believe that much was true. "Tell me what to do, Linda Gail," he said hopelessly. "I don't know what to do."

29

The next morning, when Karen discovered that Finn hadn't come home the night before, she started calling around, looking for him. When she finally got Brodie on the phone, he told her what had happened.

Karen panicked. "Where'd he go?"

"Don't know, Mom. Don't care," Brodie said curtly. "I gave him the name of a doctor in Austin. The rest is up to Finn."

"But we can't just leave him out there somewhere!" Karen cried.

"What are we supposed to do, track him down and haul him in?" Brodie said irritably. "He might as well have stayed in Afghanistan if you're going to keep that tight a rein on him."

Rick said basically the same thing. So did Lucas, her oldest. Even Reverend Duffy told her not to panic.

It was too late for that. Karen called Macy Clark. Of course, she had to try two or three different numbers before she finally tracked her down at Laru Friedenberg's. If Karen's opinion of Macy could be lowered any more, it was then. Karen thought Laru was about as loose as any woman she'd ever heard of. She ought to be living in Austin with the rest of the hippies and leave Cedar Springs to good, decent folk.

And Laru didn't try and warm up to her, that was certain. But she at least gave the phone to Macy.

"Hello, Macy," Karen said primly when Macy answered the phone. "I am trying to find my son. Have you seen him?"

"Finn?"

Granted, Karen had three sons, but she really wouldn't be calling Macy to ask about Brodie or Luke, would she, now? "Yes, *Finn*. He didn't come home last night and I am trying to find him. When is the last time you saw him?" There was a very pregnant pause on the other end of the line. "Macy? What are you hiding?" Karen demanded.

"I'm *thinking*, Karen, I'm not hiding anything!"

"If you'd *thought* a long time ago, we wouldn't be in

this mess, would we?" Karen snapped. Macy gasped. Rick, who was sitting in the other lounger watching baseball on TV, glared at her.

"What do you mean by that?" Macy asked.

"Why don't you just let him go, Macy? It's obvious he's all twisted up over you, but you married Wyatt Clark just as soon as you could, and you aren't doing Finn any favors now by dragging this out. He could get on with his life if you'd let it go."

"For God's sake, Karen," Rick muttered.

"Am I wrong?" Karen asked him. "I don't care if it makes Macy upset! I want what is best for my son!"

"When I married Wyatt, you gave me your blessing," Macy said, her voice shaking. "If I'd thought for one single moment that Finn might be alive, I would never have married Wyatt, and you know that, Karen. You know how much I loved Finn."

"That's what I'm saying! You *loved* him. I am asking you to love him now and just end this so he can get on with his life! And I say that hoping it's not too late!"

"I am going to hang up now," Macy said, her voice even lower.

"If you hear from him, you tell him to call me, Macy!" Karen cried. "You tell him to call me, because I am worried *sick* about him, and I don't want to lose my son again! I will *not* lose my son again, do you hear me? I will fight with everything that I've got to keep from losing my son again!"

The line was dead, she knew. But she didn't realize the tears were streaming down her face until Rick handed her a tissue and put his arm around her. "He's all right, Karen. You've got to stop worrying like this. Finn's all right. You're not going to lose him again."

Easy for Rick to say. He didn't have that dream every night, the one where someone came to her door to tell her Finn was dead again.

When Finn called later that afternoon to let her know he was okay, Karen let him have it.

Finn had realized, as he drove aimlessly yesterday afternoon, that he was near Bill Gaines' place. Bill Gaines had wanted Finn's cutters as long as Finn had been in the business. Finn had not been surprised when Brodie told him Bill had bought the horses, and sure enough, Finn found Fannie, his best mare, just by driving around Bill's spread.

He spotted her in the pasture, trotting around the fence perimeter. He pulled over and got out of the truck, walked up to the metal fence, and propped his arms against it, watching the old girl. He hadn't been there fifteen minutes when a truck pulled up behind his. A man got out, adjusted his cowboy hat, and walked a little crookedly to the fence where Finn was standing.

"Can I help you, sir?" he asked in a neighborly way.

"Just admiring the horseflesh," Finn said.

"Ah yes, we've got a fine stock, don't we, now," the man said, stepping up beside Finn at the fence. "Some of the finest in all of Texas."

"The black one there—any chance she's for sale?" Finn asked, pointing at Fannie.

The man squinted across the pasture and laughed. "Not her. She's our best cutter. Quick as a hiccup and can turn on a biscuit without breaking the crust. Wouldn't know it to look at her, would you? Cutters usually ain't that tall. I bet she's eighteen hands if she's one."

Seventeen, Finn thought. "She's a good one, all right," Finn said. "I trained her."

The man snorted. "Well now, either you've been drinking whiskey from your boot or you're mightily confused," he said congenially, and propped his foot on the lowest rung of the fence. "She come from down around Austin. Used to be a fella down there who trained cutting horses, but he was killed in the war." He glanced at Finn sidelong. "You don't look dead to me, friend."

Finn didn't feel like explaining the whole thing to this guy and nodded, keeping his gaze on Fannie.

"It's easy to get confused in this heat," the man said. "Hotter'n the blazes of hell out here. Yeah, we got her and a couple of others, along with a guy named José who used to work with the man from Austin. Now he's someone who can train a cutter for you. Knows horses just about better than anyone I ever run across."

Finn's heart leapt. He looked at the old cowboy. "Is he still around?"

"Oh sure. Stays up there at the old homestead in the bunkhouse. No one lives up there no more. The place is dilapidated. I'll be honest, this guy's a superstitious old Mexican, meaner than a junkyard dog. But he don't like being away from the horses."

Finn knew that. José had always slept in his

bunkhouse, too. Sent almost every dime he earned back to Old Mexico. "Any chance I can talk to him?"

The man laughed. "You ain't gonna try and steal him away now, are you?"

"Nah," Finn said, and forced a smile.

"Come on around then," the man said, and stuck out his hand. "John McBride. I run this section for a guy named Bill Gaines. And you are?"

"Lockhart," Finn said, taking his hand. "Finn Lockhart."

"Follow me on around, then, Finn," John said, clearly unaware that he was talking to the man from down around Austin who used to train cutters.

Friday afternoon, Macy's suspicions were confirmed.

"Well?" Laru asked, opening the door as Macy trudged up the walk to the house.

"Yes," Macy said solemnly. "I am pregnant with Wyatt's baby. Six weeks along."

"Oh, Macy," Laru said sympathetically.

"I mean, just *days* before I found out that Finn was alive, I conceived a baby with Wyatt! God help me, Laru, I don't want to stay with Wyatt out of a sense of duty or guilt! But then again, it's Wyatt's baby. How can I take a baby from its father?"

Laru hugged her tightly. "Let's go sit down," she said, and led her into the living room.

"I don't know," Macy said once they were seated. "I keep thinking of the kids I worked with. They had parents in different places, siblings from different fathers or mothers. Their lives were a mess. Is that what I am thinking of doing to my baby?"

"You can't compare your situation to those kids."

"Why not?"

"For starters, we are talking about three extremely responsible adults here, not three deadbeats."

"Okay," Macy said, turning to face Laru. "But is it fair to take this child from a father who would love him or her? Its not like Wyatt and I fell out of love. I care very much for him. I *love* him. I can't see how it is right to take his child from him."

"You're not taking the baby from its father."

"Yes, I am. You know it wouldn't be the same as it would be if we were there together, day in and day out," Macy argued.

"No, but look, Macy—families are different now," Laru said. "Sometimes, blood kin isn't as important as surrounding a child with love. It takes a village to raise a child."

Macy couldn't help but smile. "That is the standard refrain in social work."

"Maybe because it's true. The thing you need to remember is that if you are unhappy, that child is going to know it, and it won't be entirely happy, either."

Macy considered that a moment.

"When are you telling Wyatt about this?" Laru asked.

"Today," Macy said with a sigh.

"No time like the present." Laru handed her the phone. Macy frowned but she took the phone and called Wyatt's office.

"I'm sorry, Macy," Linda Gail said when she asked
for Wyatt. "He's not in. He took Caroline Spalding to
lunch, and then he's driving down to San Marcos for
the weekend. He's playing in that big golf tournament
with David Bernard."

"Oh right, right," Macy said, remembering that now.

"And he's got a closing down there on Monday, so
I don't expect to see him until late afternoon on Monday."

Great, Macy thought. This wasn't exactly the sort
of news she could phone in. She needed to tell him
in person. "Thanks, Linda Gail. I'll catch up with him
Monday."

30

It was ten o'clock on a hot, muggy Sunday morning
when Finn knocked on Laru's door. He propped one
arm against the jamb and leaned into it, expecting a
fight. Yeah, he'd taken off for a couple of days, but he'd
called in and let his mom chew on him. He knew Macy
had tried to get hold of him, too, but he'd needed to
take care of a few things.

It was good that he'd gone. He'd cooled off, had a better perspective.

Laru opened the door a moment later. Of all of Macy's relatives, Laru was definitely his favorite. He loved her free spirit and live-and-let-live attitude. She stared at him for a moment, then threw her arms around his neck. "Finn Lockhart! What a sight for sore eyes!" she cried. "Lord, it's good to see you." She suddenly reared back, clutching his arms, and stared into his face, ignoring Milo, who raced out the front door and tried to put his paws around Finn's neck.

"Wait a minute," Laru said, and stepped back. "Did you call first?"

Finn knew what she was going to do and managed to get his boot in the door before she shut it. "Do I need to call?" he asked, holding the door open with one arm, scratching Milo's ears with the other. "Come on, Laru. Let me in. I need to talk to her."

Laru didn't speak. He could almost hear the cogs in her head cranking as she mulled it over. "Come on now, Laru," he said carefully, as if he were coaxing a dog out from under a porch. "We go way back, you and me."

She grinned. "You look great, Finneus Lockhart. You really do."

"You look pretty damn good yourself, Laru. You wouldn't be changing the subject, would you?"

"Finn, stop! Macy's got a lot on her mind and she's a little miffed, to be honest."

"I only want to ask her a couple of things. I'll be

nice, I promise. No trouble." Milo barked. "Now see? That's Milo's vote for me. Come on, Laru—for old times' sake."

She sighed. Milo's tail was banging against a big potted plant. "Let me go tell her—"

"Let me." He smiled. "Sit, boy," he said to Milo, and the dog sat instantly.

"I'm as bad as that damn dog," Laru said, and opened the door. "I never could resist you, you old ranch hand." She threw her arms around his neck again, hugging him tightly.

"Thanks, Laru," he said. "Which way to Macy?"

"In the guest room. You know where it is."

He looked down at Milo and held his hand out, palm facing the dog. "Stay," he said firmly, and the dog stayed.

Someone—Laru, she figured—lifted the comforter off her leg, and Macy, in the fog of sleep, reflexively kicked out.

"Ouch," a male voice said.

Macy's eyes flew open. She pushed herself up on her elbows and stuck her head out of the comforter, looking back at the head of the bed.

"You scared me," Finn said. "A person's head is usually on the pillow."

Macy quickly scrambled to her knees. "Where have you been?" she demanded. "Are you okay?"

Finn smiled. "I'm fine. Mom told you, right?"

"The only thing she would tell me is that you were

alive, basically. What are you doing here? Where have you been?"

"I came here to talk to you." He gestured to the bed. "Do you realize you are sleeping upside down?"

"Laru let you in?" Macy said, her heart still pounding. Maybe next time Laru would allow a marching band in to wake her up—it would be no less startling. She dragged the comforter around her—Laru liked to keep the house at sub-zero temperatures—and looked at Finn again. "Where have you been, Finn? I was so worried."

Finn didn't answer right away. Macy was sleeping in an old camisole and some boy-short panties that barely covered her butt. One of the spaghetti straps of her camisole had slid down her arm and the fabric over her breast was gaping. She realized what Finn was seeing and grabbed up the comforter.

"No," he said quickly, throwing up a hand. "Leave it."

Macy did not let go of the comforter, but neither did she lift it to cover her. "Could you maybe have called?"

"I could have. I'm sorry I didn't. But I needed to do a couple of things on my own." He gave her body a sultry smile. "Mmm-mm," he said with a shake of his head as his gaze skated over her bare legs. "I'll say one thing for you, baby—you sure do make a man want."

Finn looked at her as if he wanted to devour her, and while the effect was terribly sexy, she blushed.

He lifted his gaze to her breasts. "I've got a proposition for you," he said to them before meeting her gaze.

She sincerely hoped it was the sort of proposition he was making with his eyes. "Oh, yeah?"

"Come with me for the day," he said. "I need your help."

Macy unthinkingly dropped the comforter. Anything. Anything he needed. What was it about him that could beckon her at will?

"I hate to tell you to get dressed," he said, taking her in. "I like what I'm seeing. I like it a lot," he added, and shoved his hands in his back pockets, almost as if to keep from touching her. "But we've got something to do, so get dressed. And wear something comfortable."

She stepped toward him, lifted up on her toes, and kissed the corner of his mouth. "I am so happy to see you, Finn. You have no idea."

One corner of Finn's mouth tipped up; he put his hand on her waist. She could see the desire in his eyes, could feel it rising up in her. Finn groaned softly. "Get dressed before I chew that top off you," he said, and bent his head, touching his lips to the small patch of skin at her temple.

The sensation shimmered through Macy. She dropped the comforter as desire thrummed between them. "I ought to have your hide for disappearing like that."

"You can have my hide and more," he murmured, and skimmed her lips with his.

It was a sweet, tender kiss, but it seared her like a branding iron.

She closed her eyes and sighed with pleasure as she sank back onto her heels. Finn's hands cupped her face and tilted it up to his to kiss her. He shifted into her, his body touching hers, and his warmth and her relief that he was all right combined to send Macy's heart falling and tumbling, back to the place they'd been before she'd discovered she was pregnant.

He moved to her neck as his arm slipped around her waist, pulling her closer, so that her breasts were pressed against his chest and his erection pressed against her. She sank into him. She wanted to pull him onto her bed, pull the comforter over them, and sink even deeper into the desire that was filling her up. She wanted as much intimacy with him as she could before she had to tell him the truth. She might have done it, too, had nausea not begun to swirl in her belly. She swallowed it down and said breathlessly, "Bathroom," and put her hands between them, pushing him lightly. "Have to."

Finn lifted his head. His eyes were burning with desire, stark and untapped. But he stroked her temple again, then her hair. "God, I missed you," he said. He dropped his hand. "Wear your hair down. I like it down."

She smiled. Macy had never been able to resist Finn Lockhart, especially when he talked to her like that. Her helplessness where he was concerned allowed her to forget, if only for a few hours, that she was carrying Wyatt's baby.

———

Finn elected to wait outside because he couldn't trust himself not to have his way with Macy on Laru's fancy sheets. He sat on the split rail fence that lined the drive beneath the shade of an old live oak. Milo lay at his feet, acting a little like he was afraid Finn would take off without him. In addition to Milo, Jesse Wheeler was keeping him company. "Dude," Jesse had said when he'd wandered outside and had seen Finn leaning up against the railing. "Welcome back."

They chatted for a bit, Jesse telling him he'd heard some wild stories about his time in Afghanistan and Finn admitting he'd been to hell and back. But it made him uncomfortable, and he turned the conversation back to Jesse. "So what is up with you?" he asked, nodding to Laru's house.

Jesse grinned. "Some folks think I've gone off the reservation here, but I'm having a great time with Laru. It won't last forever, but it's good for both of us now." He began to tell Finn how he'd ended up at Laru's, and while Finn was certain it was an interesting story, he hardly heard a word Jesse said. He was thinking of that kiss in Macy's room. It had lit a furnace in him that was burning out of control. He was finding it damn near impossible to be respectful of the issues they had.

He was never so thankful as he was when she finally came walking out of the house, a tote bag slung over her shoulder. She had on a big sun hat, but she'd left her hair down and it was skimming her bare shoulders. She was wearing a skimpy little top that rode a little high, revealing her belly button, and a pair of shorts that came down to her knees. She also wore a pair of land-to-water sandals. Her legs, slender, shapely, and tanned, were almost as much fun to look at as her backside, a view of which she was giving Finn and Jesse as she leaned over the back of his truck to put the massive tote bag in the bed.

She turned around, put her hands on her hips, and stared at the two of them. "Jesse, what are you going on about now?"

"Just filling him in on what he's missed," Jesse said.

Macy's eyes narrowed.

"About *me*, Macy-cakes," Jesse cheerfully clarified. "I'll let you tell him your own dark secrets." He pushed away from the fence. "You two have fun."

As Jesse strolled back to the house, Finn looked at Macy. She instantly threw her hands up. "Don't ask me," she said. "I was as surprised as anyone to find him here. Now are you going to tell me where you've been?" she demanded, folding her arms.

Finn smiled and walked to the passenger side of his truck and opened the door. "Get in, Fancy Face, and I'll tell you all about it."

Macy grinned at him, adjusted her hat, and climbed into the pickup truck. Milo hopped in, too, eliciting a cry of alarm from Macy when he walked over her and settled into the middle.

It felt just like old times, Finn thought as he walked around the front of the truck to the driver's side.

31

~

Macy said there was something about the smell of an old pickup that made her nostalgic. Finn smiled and nodded like he knew what she meant, but privately, he thought maybe the stress was getting to her—he didn't find anything nostalgic about the scent of leather, animal, and man mixed together.

However, the scent of her perfume was nostalgic and pretty damn arousing.

"So where did you go, Finneus?" she insisted as he pulled onto the highway, and gave him a playful tap on the shoulder.

"Up near Dallas-Fort Worth."

"Dallas-Fort Worth! What for?"

He glanced at her from the corner of his eye. "I wanted to see if I could get my horses back."

Macy gasped and twisted in her seat to look at him. "*Did* you? Please tell me you got them back!"

She looked so hopeful that he wished he could tell her that, but shook his head. "After Bill Gaines bought them from you, he split them up. He sold Fritter to a ranch in Montana. They're entering him in competitions. I'm not sure where Bosco ended up, but I think Oklahoma."

Macy's face fell. "But he said . . . he said he wouldn't split them up," she said, clearly bewildered.

"I'm sure Bill Gaines said whatever he needed to say to get them. He's wanted my horses for a long time."

"What about Fannie?" she asked morosely.

"Well, now, he had the sense to keep Fannie," Finn said with a smile. "The good news is that I found the old girl and I got to see her. But he's not selling."

Macy slumped against the serape-covered seat back.

"It's not all bad news," Finn assured her. "I found something else."

She gave him a wry smile, as if she expected him to say that he'd found a pair of favored boots or something equally insignificant. "What?"

Finn grinned. "José Banda."

Macy squealed with delight. "José! How is he? What is he doing? Is he okay?"

Finn laughed. He reached across Milo and squeezed her shoulder. "He damn near had a heart attack when he saw me, but he's okay now. And he's coming back to work with me as soon as I am on my feet."

"That's fantastic! I can't wait to see him. But Finn . . . just like that, without telling anyone, you decided to go up to Dallas-Fort Worth?"

"I guess a little like that," he admitted, and told Macy about his abrupt departure. He told her about his uncertainty when he didn't hear from her, which made her flinch. He told her about the argument with Brodie, about taking off with no real purpose but then deciding to find his horses. He told her about finding

José, and teared up a little when he related how the old
man had fallen to his knees with a prayer of thanks to
the Virgin Mary for the miracle of Finn's survival.

Finn did not tell Macy about the night he left the
Gaines ranch and stayed in a Motel 8 on the highway,
or the dream of a missile blowing Nasir to bits. He
didn't tell her about drinking well past the point of co-
herence, or how he woke up sick with José leaning over
him, scolding him in Spanish. He didn't tell her how
shamed he'd been, or how frightened he was because
he didn't remember much of anything or even recognize himself anymore.

He didn't tell her that the next day he'd pulled the
mangled piece of paper Brodie had given him from
his pocket and called the number scribbled on it. He'd
come back to Austin and met with Dr. Rock, and after
just one meeting, Finn had felt a little bit of hope.

He was also making new plans about where to go from
here. But he wanted Macy with him. He wanted Macy's
partnership, her love, her smile to start his day, and he
didn't know how to get that across but to show her.

Macy listened with rapt attention as he talked, pushing Milo's snout from her face from time to time when
the dog was feeling affectionate. "Wow," she said when
he'd told her all that he would. She shook her head and
looked out the window a moment. "I'm so sorry," she
said, so low that he almost didn't hear her. "God, Finn,
I wish I could go back. I wish I could take back the decisions I made after you supposedly died."

Finn hoped she meant Wyatt, but it was a pointless

hope. "I guess Granddaddy was right," he said. "No such thing as a single wish, because once you wish it, another one is born. Every wish is really two wishes."

"I guess," she said, and hid her face in Milo's neck. A moment later she looked up and forced a smile. "Where are we going?"

"Almost there," he said.

Finn pulled into a drive that wound around some live oak trees and ended in the parking lot of a very large and very brown corrugated-metal building. Two glass doors marked the entrance and a sign above them read LOCKHART VETERINARY AND ANIMAL HOSPITAL. Macy had heard Luke had moved south to be closer to rural areas that needed veterinary services for large animals. Luke specialized in ranch animals.

Finn got out of the truck; Milo leapt out after him and went racing around the corner. "What's going on?" Macy asked as she stepped out. "Are you going to work with Luke?"

"Nope." He smiled, took her by the elbow, steered her to the entrance, and ushered her into ice-cold refrigerated air. At the counter, a woman in scrubs patterned with playful cartoon dogs took them back to the pens where Luke was working. The clinic was one wide central corridor lined with livestock pens.

They walked past two pigs, which stuck their snouts between the rungs of the gate and sniffed at them. There was a cow, chewing her cud, which hardly seemed to notice them at all. One pen held what looked and sounded like an entire herd of bleating goats. The other pens held horses. The woman pointed to Luke, who was in the last stall with a horse.

A teenager working with Luke held the horse's halter. The horse snorted and tried to jerk his head free of the young man's hold, but Luke quickly injected something into the horse's flank from an enormous syringe. "Steady, now," he said to the horse. "Steady." When he finished, he rubbed the area he'd injected.

The horse, and a smaller horse in an adjacent stall, looked emaciated to Macy. Their ribs were visible, their coats dull, and patches of bare skin could be seen on the smaller one. Finn reached through the gate and stroked the nose of the smaller one.

"Hey!" Luke said, noticing them as he stood up. "You made it." He walked out of the stall and paused to kiss Macy's cheek like he used to do before Finn had gone away, just like nothing had changed.

"Hi, Luke," Macy said warmly. "What a great clinic!"

"Been open a year," he said proudly. He glanced over his shoulder at the young man in the stall. "Okay, J.J., I think we got her done. You want to feed those ornery pigs?"

"Do I have to?" the young man asked as he came out of the stall, but he was grinning. He nodded politely at Macy as he walked past.

Luke was wearing knee-high rubber boots and a rubber apron over jeans. He smiled happily. "Good. Okay, Finneus," he said, looking at his brother. "Are you certain you want to do this?"

"Yep," Finn said, still stroking the smaller horse's nose.

"All right, then. These two are doing a lot better than they look, and they could definitely use the exercise."

What did he mean, they could use the exercise? Macy looked at Finn, then at Luke, but as usual, the two were focused on the horses.

"What's up with the guy who had them?" Finn asked.

"He's in jail," Luke said firmly. "I heard his bail was set at one hundred thousand dollars, so I'm hoping that will keep him there for a while. After that, who knows?"

"What guy?" Macy asked.

"Some jerk from down around Bandera," Luke explained, indicating the horses with his head. "They were neglected by an ass down there who was starving them to death. He'd put them out to pasture in a field that had been grazed down to dirt. No water, no feed. Probably would have succeeded in killing them if a couple hadn't gotten lost looking for their daughter's house and spotted them. I know the sheriff down there, and he brought the horses up here. I've had them a couple of weeks now."

Macy stared at the horses. It was inconceivable to her that someone could deliberately harm an animal. How heartless must one be to starve defenseless horses? "*Why?*" she asked simply.

"I don't know," Luke said. "Ignorance. Cruelty. I wish I knew." He looked at the horses fondly, clearly attached to them. The larger one put his head over the gate and nudged Luke before leaning down to a bucket. "They're doing great now," he said, and held up a pair of apples to the larger horse. "I don't know if they'd make good cutters, but they'd make someone a good horse."

"I can see that," Finn agreed. He took the apple Luke offered and fed it to the smaller horse.

"Don't laugh, but I call them Fred and Barney," Luke said. He glanced at Finn. "I've got all the tack you need right there," he added, nodding to a wall in the back where saddles, bridles, bits, reins, and all necessary accoutrements were kept. "Take it easy and don't run them. They can trot or canter, but it would be best to let them meander. They'll let you know when they're tired and ready to head on in."

"Wait . . . what are we doing here?" Macy asked, looking at Finn.

Luke winked at Macy. "You have a good afternoon, Macy," he said. "I'll see you later." He walked away.

Macy whirled around to Finn. "What is he talking about? Are you going to ride them somewhere?"

"Not me," Finn said. "Us." At that, he started toward the tack wall.

"Oh no," Macy said. "No, no, no, Finn."

Finn ignored her. Macy panicked. She wasn't much of a rider. Granted, Finn had done his best to teach her, and she'd managed to do okay on Fannie and Bosco—but only when Finn was with her. She'd tried to ride Fritter once and he'd thrown her. "He knows you're quaking in your boots, baby," Finn had said unhelpfully that afternoon as he'd helped her up. "Let's get back up and—"

"No!" Macy had cried. "I won't go near that beast!"

"Hey, don't hurt his feelings," Finn had said and had helped her up, then made her get back on the horse.

Just the memory of it sent her into a panic. "Finn—I can't ride these horses."

"Sure you can," he said with cheerful confidence, and hoisted a saddle onto his shoulder, a saddle pad on top of that. "Piece of cake."

"No, it's not a piece of cake, it's more like . . . like bad chili," she pleaded with him as he stepped inside the stall. "I mean, if you want to ride, that's great! I could do something here. Maybe sweep the stall," she said, then looked down at the stall and wrinkled her nose. "Luke could use the help, right?"

"He sure could and that is exactly what we're doing. We're helping Luke."

"Ohmigod," Macy moaned heavenward.

Finn laughed as he stepped into the stall with the smaller horse. "You'll be fine," he said, and stroked the horse's neck a moment before he put the saddle pad on the horse's back. "And I'll be with you." He gave her a reassuring smile as he ducked under Fred or Barney's neck and walked around to the other side to straighten out the pad.

"Finn," she said a little frantically as she hopped up onto the bottom rung of the gate so she could see him. "You know I'm hopeless. On top of that, the last time I was on a horse was a long time ago—"

"Too long."

"Yes, yes, too long! These poor horses have been abused. I don't want to make it worse."

Finn walked around the horse again, pausing at the gate to touch his fingertips to her face and look her square in the eye. "Think of it this way—you're giving Barney the freedom he wants, and nothing tastes sweeter to man or horse than that. He'll be easy for you."

"Wait—how do you know which one is Barney and who decided I get him? I might want Fred. Did you think of that?" she asked petulantly, sensing the argument was a lost cause.

"I don't know," Finn said with a bit of a shrug as he picked up the bit and bridle. He glanced up, a mischievous grin on his face. "You seem like a Barney kind of girl to me."

"I do not!" she cried, pretending to be affronted. They continued to argue whether or not she was a Barney or a Fred girl while Finn saddled up the pair of horses and Macy hung over the top railing of the gate, complaining about her clothing, her footwear, the fact that there was no place to ride around nearby.

She watched Finn as he worked—she'd forgotten just how natural this was for him. Neither horse seemed skittish. He knew how to press back when they questioned him, where to stroke them to soothe them. In only minutes, he had them both ready to ride, and Macy had to admit, both horses looked eager to be out of the stalls and the small adjoining paddock.

Finn led the big one out and tethered him. He then fetched the smaller horse, which he told Macy had to be Barney. "Didn't you ever watch *The Flintstones*?" he asked. "Stay here. I'll be right back." He returned a few minutes later with a backpack.

"What's that?" Macy asked.

"I had forgotten how nosy you are."

"Some people call it nosy, others call it inquisitive."

Finn grinned, a lovely, warm smile that creased his cheeks. "Come on over here, girl," he said, and stroked Barney's neck. "Barney wants out of here before the sun goes down. And I haven't been on the back of a good horse in a long time—Dad's old nag doesn't count. I think I might come out of my skin if I don't get on one soon."

The reminder of his captivity trumped Macy's fear of horses and with a sigh of resignation, she walked to where he stood. Barney turned his head, looking at her with one enormous brown eye, sizing her up. "Man," she said, defeated. "He knows, Finn. He knows I can't ride."

Finn stepped up behind her, put his hands on her waist, and tenderly kissed the back of her neck. "Baby . . . *trust* me."

Finn Lockhart could talk her into anything. She imagined he could talk her into jumping off a cliff if he wanted. Even now, she was the lemming, going along by putting her foot in the stirrup and allowing him to lift her up onto Barney's back. She landed with a cry of surprise. Finn laughed and patted her thigh before he handed her the reins. "Remember the cardinal rule?"

"No crying."

"That's my girl!" he exclaimed and, grinning, walked to the other horse. As Macy watched him fluidly swing himself up, she realized that she'd seen Finn laugh more today than she had in all the time he'd been home. This was his element, the place he belonged. This was what made him happy.

God help her, she would give anything if she hadn't sold his horses.

Sitting a saddle about as well as any man could do, Finn looked competent and sexy as hell as he whistled for Milo, who came charging around the building. "Let's ride, boy," he said to the dog, and the years melted away. Milo ran ahead of them and Finn looked over his shoulder. "Ease up a little, Macy. You don't want to snap her head off," he said with a laugh, and spurred Fred to move.

It hardly mattered if Macy gave Barney some slack or not—he wasn't letting Fred leave him behind, and with a lurch forward, he trotted after the larger horse.

32

The day was beautiful, but hot. Finn liked it that way. His uncle used to say you could tell a native from a transplant because real Texans, he claimed, thrived on heat. Finn had known plenty of native Texans who didn't like the heat, but he did. It felt good seeping into his bones.

If it hadn't been for Dr. Rock, Finn believed he wouldn't be where he was. He was lucky that Dr. Rock had had a last minute cancellation and could fit him in when he'd called. He'd only known the doctor an hour before Dr. Rock suggested Finn attend a group he'd started. All of them were veterans, Dr. Rock had said, all of them having the same sort of troubles Finn had described.

"What—they were presumed dead and came home to find their wives remarried?" Finn had scoffed.

"No—that would be a coincidence of huge proportions," Dr. Rock said with a wry smile. "All of them are having trouble settling back into their old lives. As it happens, they are meeting at four today." He'd said that at a quarter past two on Friday.

Finn didn't want to go to any damn group. Sharing his grief and his confusion with Dr. Rock had been difficult enough, but to share it with a bunch of vets would be tantamount to admitting he was weak, and he had declined.

"Suit yourself," Dr. Rock had said. "You're a man. You can choose to drink yourself to death, and if you find some doctor who will prescribe pills, add that to the mix. It's sure to kill you eventually. And while you're killing yourself, you can alienate everyone who ever cared for you and possibly end up on some street corner begging for coins with a sign that says *hungry veteran* on it. Or maybe you'll take it out on your family, a bitter vet with a big axe to grind. Or, you can take steps to put your life on track. They may be hard steps, but they will get you to where you want to be."

"I'll handle it," Finn had said, and stood to go. "I just wanted something to help me sleep."

"Fine," Dr. Rock had answered congenially. "You'll have to get that someplace else. In the meantime, you might consider if you are any use to Macy right now. Or maybe a better question is, would Macy have any use for you like this? Is she going to take the hard step of coming back to a soldier who has to get his drink on to sleep? Who has some lingering issues from the war and from his return, and blames her for part of it?"

"I don't blame her—"

"Are you sure?" Dr. Rock had asked. "Because you kind of sound like you do."

The conversation had stopped Finn in his tracks. He'd stood there, his back to the doctor, a battle waging inside of him.

In the end, he didn't know what it was that had made him agree to go to the group session, exactly, but he'd known that if he didn't go, he'd end up drinking instead, because he had to fill that emptiness inside him before it grew too big.

When he'd walked into the church where the session was held and had seen the other men sitting around, he'd felt like a fool, like a weak, stupid fool. These guys were soldiers. They'd suffered through months of combat, had watched friends and comrades die. Finn had sat chained to a wall in Afghanistan, rolling a ball back and forth between a boy and a dog. He was a fraud.

When it came time for him to talk, Finn held up his hands. "Sorry for wasting everyone's time," he said. "I don't think I belong here."

"Why not?" asked one of the bigger guys, whose name, Finn would learn later, was Deon. "You think you're better than us?"

"No," Finn said. "Just the opposite. I didn't do a long combat tour. My first months in Afghanistan were mostly securing supply lines. We had some sporadic engagement, but it was a lot of wait and see. I had it pretty easy compared to what you guys probably saw."

"You've probably read about Finn in the paper," Dr. Rock said casually. "He survived three years of captivity among the Taliban in Afghanistan."

All eyes turned to him. "It sounds worse than it was," Finn said.

But Deon gaped at him. "*You* are that guy?"

"Yeah, but—"

"Let me shake your hand," Deon said, getting up and lumbering across the circle to shake his hand. "Dude, you got some *grit*."

Finn didn't think he had so much grit as luck, and said so. Another guy—Jamie—asked how it had happened. It was odd, looking back on that group session now. Strangers asking those questions made Finn uneasy. But he'd wanted to tell those guys his story, and he did.

Finn looked at Macy now. She was holding the reins too tight like she always did, chattering about a rug or something she was making of the Lockhart plaid. He thought about what that group had said to him about

Macy. They'd told him to go for it, to let Macy know exactly what he wanted, how much he loved her. And then they'd told him if she couldn't give him a straight-up answer, to take a straight-up hint and go on with his life.

"You already lost some of your best years, man," Deon had said. "And you gonna lose more of your life waiting for her to figure out if you're her man or not? *She-it.*"

Deon had a point. Finn had been back in Texas a little more than three weeks. He recognized it was not an easy situation for Macy, but she needed to make her decision and stand by it, for all their sakes.

"Ease up, Macy. Give him some slack," Finn said.

She snorted. "Slack or no slack, Barney is not going to change direction or speed," she said laughingly. At that moment, Barney walked under a tree. "Oh!" she cried, bending down to avoid being hit by a limb and grabbing onto her big floppy hat at the same moment. "And I think he is determined to kill me!"

"He smells water."

"I hope so, for his sake," Macy said. "It's really too hot for a beat-up old horse. He's staggering along, it's so hot."

"He's limping because he had a hoof problem. But we're almost to the river."

They crested a small rise, and below it was the abandoned grove of pecan trees that Luke had told him about. "We're almost there," he said to Macy. He'd no sooner had the words out when Fred picked up his pace. He smelled water, too.

Finn let him canter down to the water's edge.

Barney was slower; Finn had already dismounted under the row of old pecans and caught Barney's bridle as the horse crowded in beside Fred. He helped Macy get down—pulled her down, really—before Barney waded into the shallow edge of river. Macy stumbled a little when Finn let her go. "Ouch," she said, grimacing. "Ouch, ouch, *ouch*. My legs feel like jelly."

Finn smiled and tossed the backpack onto a rotting picnic table. Milo, who had disappeared some fifty yards back, reappeared once more, swimming downstream, then going round in a big circle before climbing up on the bank, shaking off, and diving back in again.

"Nice spot," Finn said.

"It's gorgeous!" Macy exclaimed, and removed her hat to wipe her forehead. "It reminds me of the creek that runs through Two Wishes." She smiled brightly. "Do you remember that place?"

"I remember." It was just a small little clearing on the creek's edge, and in the fall, the leaves of the burr oak would fall, blanketing it. Finn loved that little place—he swore some of the best fishing in Cedar County was to be had in that spot.

How many lazy Sunday afternoons had they spent there, Macy reading under a tree, Finn fishing? They didn't talk—they didn't need to. They just existed, as comfortable with one another as they were in their own skin. Finn had never felt that way about another person in his life. He doubted he ever would again.

Macy walked down to the water's edge as he pulled out the things he'd brought along for a picnic lunch.

She scolded Milo when Milo swam out and sprayed her, then scampered back to the cover of the pecan trees.

Finn smiled to himself and glanced at what he'd laid out. He wasn't much of a gourmet. He'd brought some apples for the horses, some ready-made sandwiches he'd picked up at a little deli on the square in Cedar Springs, and, because he knew Macy as well as he did, some bottled water and a couple of gourmet brownies.

"Hungry?" he asked her.

"Starving," she said as she wandered over to survey the spread.

"It's nothing fancy, but it ought to tide us over," he said, and handed her a sandwich.

She grinned at him, her smile as bright and beautiful as a summer morning. She grabbed the offered sandwich out of his hand and settled on top of the picnic table beneath the shade of the pecan tree. A steady breeze made it comfortably warm.

Finn took apples down to Fred and Barney, scattering them on the grass. For Milo, Finn had some jerky. He returned to the picnic table, picked up a sandwich, and opened the wax paper. It was halved; he took one half and munched as he looked out over the scenery.

"This is really a treat, Finn. Thank you," Macy said before taking a bite from the second half of her sandwich. "I needed to get out and just . . . *breathe*," she said with a sigh.

He idly glanced at her. "You weren't kidding when you said you were hungry," he teased her.

"Are you going to eat that?" she asked, pointing to his second half.

Finn laughed. "Doesn't Laru feed you?"

"Yes," Macy said with a smile, "but not enough." She polished off the last of her sandwich and gazed out over the river. "I can't remember the last time I was out in the country," Macy said. "I miss it."

Finn wondered what she and Wyatt did on lazy Sunday afternoons. "What's kept you from being in the country?"

"Nothing," she said with a shrug. "I guess I've been really busy—or was—with Project Lifeline. And, you know. . . ."

"What do you mean *was*?" he asked curiously.

"Oh," she said, flicking her wrist. "The committee seems to think that if I continued to work on the big fund-raiser, any media attention we get would be because of me—well, *us*, really—and it turns the attention from the cause."

Finn frowned. "I thought you founded that organization."

"I did."

"That's not right," he said.

"No, it's okay," she said. "They're probably right. Mom told me that reporters keep calling, wanting my side of the story."

Damn reporters were like dogs with a bone. He put his arm around her shoulders, pulled her into his side, and kissed the top of her head. "I don't want the attention, either."

"I missed you so much, Finn," Macy said softly. "I know I've told you that, but you will never know just how much I missed you."

Surprised, Finn cocked his head to look in her face.

She smiled and pushed her hair aside. "I keep saying it, but I really do wish we could go back in time and start all over."

"There have been many times that I wish I'd never joined up."

"No, I don't mean that," she said. "I wish you hadn't, but you know that. I mean . . . I wish I could go back to the moment Lieutenant Colonel Freeman told me you were alive. I was so shocked, and astounded, and so *happy*. I couldn't really think straight. But now that some time has passed, I think . . ." Her voice trailed off and she looked at the river. "I wish I would have done things differently."

"Yeah, me, too."

"Like what?" she asked, her eyes skating over his face.

"Well, I wouldn't have put so many hopes on two slender shoulders, for one."

Macy colored. "I deserved that, I guess."

"I'm not blaming you, Macy," he said. "It wasn't fair. You're not alone in wishing you'd done things differently. I'm feeling a little better about how things worked out, and I've decided a few things. I wanted to tell you before I told anyone else."

"What's that?"

He took her hand in his. "I can't start up a training

ranch again," he said. "I don't have the money and it would take me years to get a couple of horses trained well enough to turn out to competition or training."

Macy instantly squeezed her eyes shut, as if that news pained her. "I'm so sorry, Finn—"

"I'm not telling you this so you can apologize again, Macy. What's done is done and there's no point in looking back. And I think I've got a better idea."

She opened her eyes and looked at him hopefully.

"See those two horses?" he asked, pointing at Fred and Barney. "They've been treated badly and now they've got no place to go. Their survival depends on some unknown rancher or outfit who doesn't mind that they aren't working horses anymore, just a money drain. They need food, they need care, they need space to roam and graze. That's a lot to ask for nothing in return."

"I don't understand," Macy said, looking at the horses.

"It's an unfortunate fact that there are abused animals in this world. I'd like to turn the ranch into a large-animal rescue operation."

Her eyes widened with surprised. "*Really?* How?"

"It would take some doing," Finn admitted. "I'd have to raise money to get feed and supplies, and then I'd have to let people know there is a place they can bring large animals. Luke said he'd do the veterinary services. I wouldn't be able to pay him much in the beginning, but he's fine with that. I'd need to build a new barn and renovate the house so there's a real office."

"But how would you pay for something like that?"

"Donations and grants. Selling the animals I can rehabilitate. I thought I might be able to get some contracts with local governments who seize animals like Fred and Barney and need a place to put them. They could recoup the costs through court fines."

A smile slowly spread across Macy's face. "Finn . . . that's a *wonderful* idea," she said breathlessly. "It's so noble and so—"

"It's not so noble," he said. "I just want a place misfits can go, myself included."

"You're not a misfit!"

"Yeah, I am, Macy," he said. "I've never been the most outgoing cowboy; you know that. Now, I'm the guy who survived the Taliban. That's all anyone wants from me, but I don't want to talk about it; I want to forget it. I *desperately* want to forget it, and it makes me shy away from people even more than normal. The truth is, I don't know how I fit in anymore, and horses like these two don't fit in anymore, and there are other animals that don't fit in either, like old steers and big cats some of these rich idiots bought when they were cute little cubs and then can't handle when they grow up."

"You're not a misfit, Finn. You're a wonderful, thoughtful man, and this is a perfect idea," Macy said. "I will give you every dime I have left from the death gratuity and life insurance."

"I don't want that money," Finn said.

"Yes! Yes, it's yours, and you have to have it, and—"

"Macy," he said, putting his hand on her knee. "I don't want the money. I want *you*. That's all I want.

I can't do this without you. I need you. I love you as much as I ever did and I'll carry you with me, always. But you have to know that I'm not going to spend any more time trying to convince you that you should be with me. It's time for you to fish or cut bait." He turned toward her, putting his hand to her neck. "So I'm going to ask you once more—will you come build a new life with me on the ranch?"

Macy's eyes filled with tears. She gasped, almost as if the question had caused her physical pain.

Finn's heart sank like a rock. His hand fell from her neck and he stood up.

"Wait!" Macy cried, reaching for his arm. "Can't you see how badly I want to be with you, Finn? To be only yours, to go back to what I believe was a perfect love?" she cried, gesturing grandly. "That's what we had, you know. We had a perfect love. I love you with all my heart, and I haven't been able to think about anything but you."

"Then what is it? Is it Wyatt? Honest to God, Macy, I'll go with you when you tell him. I won't let him touch you or—"

"Wyatt would never hurt me, Finn. And it's not that. Okay it *is* that, because I love Wyatt, too, but I don't want to hurt him, and—"

"We've been through this already, baby. Somebody is going to get hurt. That's just a fact you have to face."

Macy buried her face in her hands. "My God, how did I ever get here?" She abruptly stood up from the picnic table and turned away from him, threw her floppy hat on the table, and stood with her hands on the small of her back. "This is so hard," she said solemnly. "The mud just seems to get thicker and thicker, and I feel like it's pulling me under—"

"Tell me what it is, Macy," Finn demanded. "Tell me whatever the hell it is and I promise you, I will fix it. But you have to tell me, because I am moving on from here, today, and either you're going with me—today—or you're going back to him. You have to decide."

She opened her mouth to speak. Closed it.

"Macy," he said, his voice warning and pleading at the same time, his heart lurching.

"I'm pregnant," she said quietly.

33

Macy hadn't meant to tell Finn precisely that way, but when she finally said it out loud, she realized there was really no good way to tell him.

He was as stunned as she thought he would be, but the one thing she had not anticipated was that he might, for one slender moment, believe it was his. She saw the confusion in his eyes, in that awkward moment that he must have been counting back to the day they'd made love in the back of his pickup truck. "No, Finn— it's Wyatt's," she said softly.

He took an unsteady step backward, as if she'd just punched him. His gaze dropped to her stomach. Macy had never seen such plain heartache on a man before and it made her feel a little unsteady. She sank onto the bench of the picnic table, dismayed by her weakness.

"Have you told him?" Finn asked hoarsely.

Macy shook her head. "I just went to the doctor and I couldn't get hold of him."

"How far along are you?"

Macy heard in that—or perhaps read into it—the question of when she'd last been with Wyatt. "Six weeks." Six weeks, an entire lifetime from where she was now. Six weeks ago, she and Wyatt were trying to conceive a child, talking about names and schools, and what their kid would be when he or she grew up.

"Does anyone know?" Finn asked.

"Laru and Jesse. They guessed, because I've been sick and . . . and hungry," she said.

Finn nodded. Clenched his jaw. Turned toward the river and pushed a hand through his hair. She could see his shoulders rise with a deep breath, then slowly lower again.

"I wouldn't blame you if you never wanted to see me again," she said, her voice breaking. She'd thought a lot about it, had imagined him smiling sadly, agreeing it was probably best they parted ways. She'd imagined him getting in his truck and driving away, but perhaps riding away, as he would surely do at any moment, was more fitting. "It feels like everything is stacked against us," she said sadly. "I don't know what to say, other than I am sorrier than you will ever know," she said, putting her hands on her belly. "Those words must sound so meaningless to you by now, but I am truly sorry."

"I don't care," Finn said, his back still to her.

Macy grimaced with the pain those words caused her. "I don't blame you," she murmured.

"No, you misunderstand." He turned toward her. "I don't care that it's Wyatt's baby. I still want you, Macy, the baby and all."

Stunned, Macy gaped at him. She had imagined every different scenario, but never this one. "You can't mean that."

"I do. I don't care," he said again. "That baby may as well be mine, because it doesn't change the way I feel about you one bit. I love you. I want to be with you, Macy. And if you have a baby, I'll love the baby, too. The only thing that matters to me is that I have you and that we're together—baby and all."

"Do you honestly mean that?" she asked. "Don't you want to think about it?"

"I don't need to think about it. I won't be the first man in America to welcome a child into his life that isn't his. So are you coming with me, Macy?"

"Ohmigod," Macy said. "I never dreamed . . ."

"That's because you didn't spend three years chained to a wall," he said. "If you had, you might have dreamed

about the impossible. That baby is just another part of
you that I will love—"

"*Finn!*" she cried. She threw herself at him, almost
afraid if she didn't, he'd take it all back and this dream
would disappear. She locked her arms around his
shoulders, her face in his neck. Finn held her tightly.
"What about Wyatt?" he asked.

"I know, I *know*. It's so heartless to tell him I'm pregnant but leaving him. But I can't deny what's in my
heart. It would be crueler to remain married when I
want to be with you."

Finn reared back a little to look at her. "Then you're
coming with me?"

"*Yes,*" she said. "Yes, yes, yes . . ." Macy kissed him hard.

"*Macy . . .*"

The whisper of her name riled Macy's blood as Finn
drew her to his mouth, his body.

She was flying and falling at once and clung to his
waist, her leg wedged between his, pressed against
him, wanting to be possessed by him as much as he
wanted to possess her. Finn cupped her face and
stroked her cheek with his thumb while he pressed
back against her. After all the uncertainty and confusion, she was buoyed by his unconditional desire for
her. If she could, she would have disappeared into him
altogether, but Finn lifted his head, gazed into her
eyes, and traced her bottom lip with his thumb. "You
and me, baby. We were destined for each other long
before we knew it."

Macy nodded. "You and me," she whispered.

Finn kissed her again, so thoroughly that she some-how found herself flat on her back on an old, rotting picnic table, beneath a canopy of pecan trees, on the banks of a river, under a summer sky so blue that it almost looked painted. And as Finn showed her just how much he wanted her, Macy fell harder and flew higher than she'd ever done in her life.

When they floated back to earth, they spent the afternoon talking about the changes they'd make to the ranch, dreaming of a new house, a new barn, and the animals they'd have. Macy convinced Finn that the best use of the life insurance money she'd received was to put it toward the rescue ranch. But when Milo was roused from his nap beneath the picnic table and the horses began to snort and neigh at them, they reluctantly returned to Luke's clinic.

Later, when they turned into Laru's drive, Finn parked the truck and looked at the limestone house, then at Macy. "You can't go on living here forever. I can't go on living at Mom's. Let's rent a place in town until we can make Two Wishes inhabitable."

Macy had a fleeting thought of the house in Arbolago Hills and of all the things Wyatt had given her. Right now, those things felt easy to give up.

"But before we do anything, you have to tell Wyatt," Finn said. "I'll come with you."

She was grateful for the offer; he was her rock. "I think that would be adding insult to injury somehow. I need to tell him." *Everything will be all right.*

"You shouldn't do it alone. He's not going to like it when he hears you're leaving him."

"Honestly, I think he knows," she said sadly. "But there's no other way to do it. I owe him this much, at the very least." She owed him so much more.

Finn couldn't argue. "When?" he asked.

"As soon as I can find him."

Macy said good-bye to Finn with another lingering kiss, then slowly climbed out of his pickup truck. She stood at the door of Laru's house, watching his truck pull away.

She didn't realize until he had disappeared from view that Milo had stayed in the truck and had gone with Finn.

34

Wyatt got back from San Marcos later than he intended Monday evening and was encouraged with the message Linda Gail had left him—Macy had called three times while he was gone.

The next morning, Linda Gail told him she'd made reservations for them for that night at Jeffrey's in Austin.

Wyatt was given strict instructions to have an expensive meal, no holds barred, and then move on to music at the Key Bar. "It is very trendy and hip," she'd said. "You could stand to be a little hipper."

Wyatt could honestly say he didn't know how to be hipper, but he was going to try. He had to trust Linda Gail on this one. He was, surprisingly, a little nervous. He wanted the date to be memorable for Macy, for her to understand how much she meant to him. He did not want to screw it up.

Everything was arranged. Now, at noon on Tuesday, all he had to do was call Macy and ask her to join him.

He picked up the phone and called Laru's house.

"Hi, Wyatt. What a coincidence. She's headed into town to your office."

"She's headed for the office?" He really didn't want to ask her with Linda Gail hovering around.

"I believe so."

"Thanks, Laru."

He decided to intercept her. He tried her cell phone, but it rolled to voice mail. He told Linda Gail he was going to grab a bite and got in his truck. As he drove on the road she'd likely take, he spotted her Jeep outside the daycare where Chloe took her kids, and pulled in.

He could hear the shrieks of laughter outside and walked around the corner. Beneath some very old and towering oaks, which provided ample shade, a monstrous playscape had been built. Yellow and red riding cars littered the ground along with a variety of balls and toys.

Wyatt spotted Macy instantly. She was pulling

Chase and Caden in a red wagon around the perimeter of the fence. A little girl was following along behind them. Macy saw Wyatt when they turned the corner. "Wyatt!"

"I, ah . . . I saw your Jeep out front."

"Oh," she said, brushing some hair from her face. "What a coincidence. I was on my way to the office hoping I could grab you a minute and just stopped by to say hello to my two favorite boys," she said, smiling down at the twins.

"Make the wagon go!" Chase cried.

Macy laughed and looked at Wyatt. "Want to walk with us?"

He looked at the kids. "I need to talk to you, Macy."

Her smile faded a little. "Yes. I need to talk to you, too. Give me a minute, will you?"

Wyatt watched her walk around the perimeter of the fence. When they'd made a square, she stopped, picked up each boy and kissed them, then crouched down between them. Wyatt loved the way she looked with those kids, and they clearly adored her. She said something to them and pointed at Wyatt. They both turned to look at him. Macy kissed them once more, waved her fingers good-bye, and joined Wyatt at the fence. "Let's walk down to Daisy's Saddle-brew," he suggested.

The place was deserted at three in the afternoon. Macy took a seat at one of the patio tables beneath the vine-covered arbor while Wyatt went in to get some drinks. Sam was leaning up against the counter, reading a magazine. "Hello, Sam," he said.

"Hey, Wyatt," she said cheerfully. "Black coffee?"

"Actually, today I think I'll walk out on a limb and get something else. What would you suggest?"

"I'd stick your big toe in before going all the way," Sam laughed. "How about a vanilla latte?"

"Sounds great. Make it two, please."

"Two?" she looked up, her expression changing slightly when she spotted Macy sitting outside. "Two it is." She moved to get the drinks.

Macy smiled and thanked him when Wyatt returned with the lattes. As he sat down, he realized he should have gotten an ice tea. It was awfully hot, far too hot for coffee. Macy fidgeted with the cardboard heat band around the cup. "So how are you?" she asked.

Raw. So raw. "I'm good," he said. "I've been really busy. Listen, Macy, I have . . . I have a surprise," he said. "I know it's short notice, but I thought maybe we could go into Austin and have dinner at Jeffrey's tonight."

"Jeffrey's?"

"Jeffrey's. And then, I thought we could hit the Key Bar."

"The Key Bar," she repeated.

"It's live music. Very happening place," he said, realizing he never would say *happening* and *place* together. But these were extraordinary circumstances.

"Ah," she said, and slowly tore the cardboard heat band from the cup.

Wyatt should have trusted his instincts, and he'd be sure to tell Linda Gail that first thing in the morning.

Macy did not want to go—her body language said it all. This was the moment Linda Gail had planned, the moment Wyatt was supposed to sweep her off her feet, seduce her, assure her that he was The One, but the moment felt entirely wrong. It felt awkward, stupid. This was not him, asking his wife for a date. How had he let Linda Gail convince him that it was?

"David and Aurora are big fans of Jeffrey's," he said, aware that he was, already, mentally grasping at straws. "Supposedly the best food in Austin. I think the chef worked in the White House." Linda Gail had said something about the White House, hadn't she? "We could talk. Or not. We could just be together for a change."

"Wyatt, I don't think . . ."

"Or, we could just get some burgers and see a movie if you'd rather," he said, a little too desperately.

Macy looked down and rubbed her forehead a moment.

"It doesn't have to be this hard," he said quietly. "I know we didn't exactly part on the best of terms the last time I saw you and I apologize for that. But let's move past it. Everything will be all right, I promise."

Her shoulders sagged; she looked up at him and Wyatt knew instinctively he did not want to hear whatever she might say. "You haven't touched your coffee. Drink up."

"Wyatt—"

"Let's just enjoy the afternoon, Macy. I'm not asking for anything but company." A breeze filtered through the patio, lifting a bit of her hair. Wyatt had an insane urge to touch her hair, to feel it between his fingers. His longing clouded his vision and a dull fear filled his throat.

"I appreciate the offer," Macy said. "It is obvious you've thought a lot about it."

"Us. I've thought a lot about *us*."

"Us," she repeated. "You have . . . you've always been wonderful to me, Wyatt."

He softened a little bit. "I was pretty rough on you the last time I saw you, and I wanted to make up for it somehow." He glanced sheepishly at her. "I'm really sorry about that. I don't have an excuse for it, other than I've been extremely . . . frustrated."

"I know," she said, and slid her hand across the table and covered his hand.

The small, soothing gesture surprised Wyatt. His heart skipped with a beat of hope. Had he misread her? Had he jumped to conclusions because of his fear of losing her? Could it be possible that the ordeal was coming to an end?

But then Macy drew a breath, and he knew.

"I hope if there is one thing you know above all else, it is that I love you." She lifted her gaze to him, and her blue eyes were swimming in sadness. "You've been a wonderful husband. The best. I am a very lucky woman to have you in my life." She drew another deep breath. "And, I have some news," she said, her voice breaking a little. "I . . . I'm pregnant," she said in a voice so soft that he wasn't sure at first that he'd heard her. But then she smiled a little sheepishly and Wyatt's heart, his battered heart, soared.

"What?" He came out of his seat and impulsively grabbed her up, pulling her to her feet and into a bear hug, twirling around with her. "That is *fantastic*! That's the best news you could have given me!" But even as he was speaking he knew something was wrong. Macy wasn't laughing or exclaiming with him. She was clinging to him to keep herself from falling, not out of shared joy. He loosened his grip and let her slide down to her feet. Macy's hands came up between them.

"No," he said, searching her face. She looked down; Wyatt grabbed her by the shoulders, forcing her to look up at him. "Don't tell me it's *his*!"

"*No!* No, Wyatt, this baby is *yours*."

"Then what is wrong?" he asked. "Why do you look so miserable? Is something wrong with the baby? Is it all this goddam stress we're under?" he asked, his eyes fixing on her stomach.

"The baby is fine—listen to me," she said, and caught his face in her hands, drawing his gaze up. "There is nothing wrong with the baby, and *you* are the father. But Wyatt, I can't . . ." She closed her eyes as if she'd felt a sudden pain. "I can't be with you," she said, opening her eyes. Sad eyes. Eyes that should be bursting with the light of joy were dulled with sadness. "I love you, and I wouldn't hurt you for anything. You have to know that. But I love Finn, too—"

Wyatt suddenly pushed her away.

"I know how hard this must be to hear," she said, her voice shaking, "because it is very hard to say. But I am being as honest with you as I know how to be, and we promised each other we'd always be honest."

"I don't want to hear this," he snapped. "I don't give a damn how honest you think you're being, Macy."

"You *have* to hear it," she said, her voice full of regret. "I can't help how I feel. I have agonized over it, but I keep coming back to—"

"*Shut up*," he said angrily before she said another word. "I don't give a shit how much you have agonized," he spat, and moved away from her, clenching his fist to keep himself from exploding. "I get it, Macy! You are carrying *my* child, you promised *me* the rest of your life, and you want to be with him!" He laughed derisively. "That's about the size of it, isn't it?"

An elderly couple walked by and looked at them. Wyatt forced himself to smile. Macy pressed her lips together as they waited for them to pass, and in that time, Wyatt felt something splinter inside him, the pain giving away to fury. As soon as the couple was out of earshot, Wyatt said, "You can forget it, Macy. I won't give you a divorce."

"But—"

"No buts," he said, cutting her off. "You are carrying my baby. I'm not going to let you take my baby and go live with G.I. Joe! Forget it."

"Wyatt, you're being irrational."

"*I'm* being irrational?" he shouted at her. "How the hell can you say that? You're about to throw away our marriage and *I'm* being irrational! Get a grip, Macy! Come down off your little fantasy cloud! You are married to me whether you like it or not, and I have some say in whether or not this marriage ends!"

"Technically, this marriage doesn't exist," she said evenly.

"Hey!" It was Sam; she'd appeared in their midst, looking alarmed.

"Jesus, Sam, please," Macy said.

"Is everything okay?" Sam asked Wyatt.

"Everything is fine. We're fine," he said, glaring at Macy.

Sam hesitated, but then slowly retreated.

When she'd gone inside, Wyatt said, "You have to file suit to have our marriage dissolved. Do you honestly think a judge is going to sign off on that suit to make this marriage void when you are carrying my baby?"

"I think he has to do what the law says. You can't stop me, Wyatt."

It was true; he knew it was true, and he mentally stumbled, his thoughts and reason collapsing on one another in his panic. He was going to be a father—without his baby or his wife? "Jesus Christ, Macy," he said, bewildered. "How can you do this?"

She swayed a little bit and put her hand to the back of the chair to steady herself. "It's heartbreaking," she admitted.

Fury gave way to fear and Wyatt said, "I've never asked you for much of anything, but I am asking you now—please don't do this. Please, God, don't do this.

That's my baby, Macy. That is *my* baby! Please—" He caught himself, tried to swallow down the angry pain. "Please don't take my life and my baby from me."

Tears welled in her eyes and she suddenly put her arms around Wyatt. "I would never take this baby from you," she said softly. "*Never.* But I have to do what is right for me and for everyone."

"This isn't right for our baby!" he cried, pushing free of her embrace. "And it's damn sure not right for me!"

"This baby will very much be a part of your life. And *I* will still be in your life if you want me. I just can't be your wife."

He made a sound of disgust and flicked his wrist at her.

"Wyatt . . . do you really want me in our house—in our *bed*—knowing that I want to be with another man?"

Of course he didn't want that; he wanted his wife back, he wanted his baby, he wanted the life he thought he and Macy would have. "What about me?" he asked. Macy didn't answer him, but he saw the raw pity in her eyes.

He twisted around, away from her. He couldn't even look at her. He was angry, so angry that he could hardly catch his breath. "As long as we're sharing news," he said in a voice that was barely controlled, "here's some news for you to chew on—whatever it is you and Cowboy Bob think you're going to do, you're going to have to do it someplace other than Cedar Springs, because sold the Two Wishes Ranch." He shifted his gaze to her. "It's all gone, just like the life you had with him, and you can't get it back, any more than you can get your little fairy tale back."

Macy gaped at him, clearly stunned. "You *sold* it?" she said incredulously. "You told me you'd canceled the closing!"

He shrugged indifferently. "I lied."

"How could you do that? It wasn't yours to sell!"

"Like hell it wasn't. You gave me power of attorney. You said, *Please handle it for me, Wyatt, I can't bear to do it,*" he said, mimicking her. "Well, I handled it for you, Macy. I sold it."

"You have no idea what you've done," she said breathlessly.

"Neither do you," he shot back.

She put a hand to her head, her eyes locking on the tabletop. "It's been—what, a little less than a week?"

"The deal is done, Macy. One week, one day—the papers are signed and the money is in the bank."

She glared at him. "You can't do that," she said, her voice shaking with anger now. "By law—"

"By law, if the land sells, he can't get it back. Just the value of it."

"So . . . so what is the point?" she cried.

"The *point* is that he can't set up his little dude ranch here! He'll have to go someplace else. Maybe Mexico. I don't care where the hell he goes, as long as it is someplace other than Cedar Springs!"

"If he goes, I go with him."

"Maybe you do, but my baby won't. I will fight yo
with everything I have."

Macy's jaw dropped. "Where's the money from th
sale?"

"In my account," he said.

"Wyatt . . . that land belongs to *him*."

"Then come and get it," he challenged her, and s;
in his chair and picked up his coffee. He took a carele:
drink; the liquid burned his tongue.

"Oh, my God," she murmured, her eyes widening ;
the implications sank in. "Oh, my *God*."

"Go cry on his shoulder," Wyatt snapped. "I've g(
better things to do with my time than listen to yo
snivel about that goddam ranch."

Macy gaped at him. She abruptly turned away an
walked briskly, one hand pressed against her abdomer
as if she were feeling ill.

Wyatt watched her go. He could feel himself defla
ing, his fury giving way to impotent sorrow.

He didn't know how long he sat there before Sar
came out to pick up the cups. She eyed him closely ;
she wiped down the table. "Are you all right, Wyatt?"

He smiled at her. "Not really."

35

Trembling with regret, anger, and shock, Macy drove straight to Finn's house when she couldn't get him on the phone. She couldn't believe Wyatt had sold Finn's ranch. Wyatt was an ethical man, an honest man, or so she'd always believed. When she thought of Finn's plans, his large-animal rescue ranch—

She came to a halt so abrupt and hard that her wheels slid on the gravel drive. Karen Lockhart came out of the kitchen door, still wiping her hands on a dishtowel. "Macy? Where's the fire?"

"I'm sorry—is Finn here?"

"No," Karen said, eying her suspiciously. "He's out."

"Do you know where?" she asked frantically. Karen frowned. "Please, Karen. I need to speak to him. It's important. Please tell me where he is."

Karen's arms dropped to her sides. She frowned at Macy. "I don't like what's going on here," she said. "He left his phone on the charger and it's been ringing like a tornado bell. Whatever it is you have to tell him, can't it wait 'til morning? I don't want him running off again."

"He's not going to run off," Macy said quickly.

"How do you know?" Karen asked suspiciously.

"Because I know, Karen. I am doing my level best to make this right. Just . . . just please tell me where he is."

She studied her a moment and then sighed. "He's at Brodie's, helping him with some plumbing repairs."

Macy was already climbing in her Jeep before Karen could say more.

She flew back to town and took a shortcut around the elementary school to Brodie's. When she turned into Brodie's drive, she turned off the engine and paused a moment to close her eyes and swallow down another swell of nausea. She hadn't eaten anything since morning and she was suddenly feeling the effects.

When she climbed out of her car, Finn was already walking down the drive to her. He was wearing a pair of faded jeans that were threadbare in all the right places. An old stained straw cowboy hat was on his head, and Macy thought he'd never looked quite as strong to her as he did that moment.

"Macy?"

"I told him," she exclaimed, and started toward him, but her heel caught in one of the bricks that made up the old drive.

Finn caught her.

"I told him, and he . . . he . . ."

"He what?" Finn demanded as he put his arm around her shoulders.

"He didn't take it very well, you know, but then again, who would?" she said, wiping the tears that were flowing again. "I am so sick of crying!"

"What did he do?" Finn asked again.

"Bless his heart, but he was *so* angry. And then he said he had some news of his own, and . . . and I have to sit down," she said, sliding down to the drive as a wave of nausea came over her.

"Baby, are you all right?" Finn asked worriedly, going down on his haunches next to her and stroking her hair back from her face.

"I haven't eaten."

"Everything all right?" Brodie asked as he walked down the drive to them.

"Brodie, you got something she can eat?" Finn asked, his expression full of worry. "Crackers, maybe? Some bread?"

"Yeah," Brodie said. "Come in."

Finn helped Macy up and started to lead her toward the house.

"Wait!" she said, clutching his arm. "I haven't told you everything, Finn. He said he had news of his own, he said . . ." She paused to swallow down another wave of nausea.

"It's okay, Macy. Let's get you something to eat first—"

"*Finn,*" she said, grabbing his arm and making him look at her. "He *sold* it. He sold the ranch! He had my power of attorney and he sold the ranch."

Something flickered in Finn's eyes. His nostrils flared with his intake of breath. "I'll kill him," he said quietly.

"Finn!"

He clenched his jaw and pulled her to his side.

"Sorry, baby, but that bastard picked the wrong fight."
And his jaw remained tightly clenched as he led Macy
into the house.

Macy awoke the next morning on Brodie's couch, a
blanket tucked in around her.

"Morning," Brodie said, standing in the dining room
with a cup of coffee.

"Oh my God . . . what time is it?" Macy asked.

"Eight."

She looked around her—she vaguely remembered
laying her head on Finn's lap last night. She'd been
so exhausted, so nauseated, and so completely spent
from the tears that had fallen when she'd realized she
had made her decision and was safe now. Safe with
Finn. Whatever happened, she was with Finn. So why
couldn't she erase the memory of Wyatt's face and his
devastation from her mind?

"Finn said to tell you he'd call you later, but he had
something he had to do," Brodie said.

"Thanks for letting me crash, Brodie," Macy said.

"No problem." He winked at her and turned toward
the kitchen, but paused and glanced back at Macy.
"I'm glad you're back."

She smiled. "Thanks. You have no idea how much I
appreciate that."

She didn't take Brodie up on his offer to cook breakfast for her, as the thought of eggs made her belly swirl,
and not in a good way.

About an hour later, Macy pulled up at Laru's and

stifled a groan. Her mother's BMW was parked outside. "Great," she muttered.

Her mother was standing in the middle of Laru's great room when Macy entered, dressed in an expensive suit and heels. She folded her arms and glared at Macy. "Where have you been?" she demanded.

"Mom . . . I'm a little too old for that, don't you think?" Macy said.

"I would like to know what is going on."

Macy put down her purse. "I would guess, judging by the way you're going all *Law and Order* on me, that you've heard from Wyatt."

"What are you doing?" her mother cried. "Are you determined to ruin people's lives?"

Emma appeared from the kitchen wearing shorts and jogging shoes. Behind their mother's back, she shrugged helplessly.

"I really don't know what that is supposed to mean, Mom, but no, I am not trying to ruin anyone's life. I am trying to do what is best for me and my baby."

"What? You're *pregnant*?" Emma cried.

"You're doing the right thing by taking that baby from his father?" her mother asked.

"Macy! You're pregnant?" Emma exclaimed again, smiling with delight as she hurried past their mother to hug her. "That's fantastic! When are you due?"

"Late February."

"I am still waiting for an explanation!" her mother snapped. "What do you think you're going to do? Are you really going to give up everything that Wyatt can give you and the baby and go live with some cowboy with nothing to his name?"

Macy's pulse soared with indignation. "That old song again, Mom? Finn's not lofty enough for you? Well here's a newsflash—not that it's any of your business, but yes, that is *exactly* what I intend to do. I love Wyatt, Mom, but my heart and my soul belong to Finn and they always have. You *know* they always have."

"God, that makes me want to cry," Emma said. "I hope I find someone like that someday."

"Emma!" their mother said. "Would you please butt out?"

Emma threw up her hands. She started for the kitchen, but was intercepted by Laru.

"What's going on here?" Laru demanded.

"Laru, for once, don't talk," Jillian said irritably.

"She knows I'm pregnant," Macy said to Laru. "And that I am leaving Wyatt."

"Oh, Macy," Laru said sympathetically. "Good for you!"

"What?" Jillian cried. "Wyatt Clark is a good man!" she snapped at Laru. To Macy, she said, "You have to think of someone other than yourself, Macy. You have to think of that child, and that child deserves to know his or her father. I am disappointed in you, to say the least."

Macy's heart began to pound; an image of Wyatt flashed across her mind.

"Oh for God's sake, Jilly," Laru sighed. "Like she hasn't thought of the consequences of her decision?"

"I *am* thinking of my child, Mom," Macy said,

her voice shaking with anger. "And you don't have to tell me how disappointed you are. You've been disappointed in me for as long as I can remember."

"*What?*"

"It's true! You have always wanted me to be something I'm not. You made me join all those stupid science clubs when I was a kid with the hope that I'd suddenly become good at it and go off to be Madame Curie. But I hated science! You nagged me to go to law school, but I wanted to be a social worker, and that was hugely disappointing to you. And you *never* wanted me to marry Finn! You thought he wasn't good enough for me even then, remember? Now he's everyone's hero and he's *still* not good enough for you! What in the hell does it take?"

"That's ridiculous!" her mother exclaimed. "You're trying to deflect from the real issue here—"

"There *is* no issue here," Macy said sternly. "I have made up my mind. I am going to be with Finn. I cannot live with Wyatt when I don't love him like I love Finn just to please you!" With that, Macy strode to her room, ignoring her mother's cry for her to come back, ignoring the argument that ensued between Laru and Jillian.

Macy shut the bedroom door and leaned against it. Two wishes, she thought. The first, that Wyatt was wrong and she and Finn could go back to the way they were and be happy like they once had been, and the second, that Wyatt would be okay, that he'd find happiness again.

36

Linda Gail could hardly contain her excitement when Wyatt didn't show up at the office as usual at eight o'clock sharp Wednesday morning. She assumed that meant he'd called Macy, they'd had a great night, and now they were sleeping in. Linda Gail felt a little tingly just thinking about it. She'd done something good. She'd helped two people come together who belonged together.

But then Wyatt appeared at half past ten looking a little off, and Linda Gail wished she were anywhere but at work. Wyatt strolled into the office and paused right before her desk, glaring down at her.

"Wyatt? Are you all right?"

"I'm great, Linda Gail."

"That's good," she said, disbelieving. "But I'm sort of afraid to ask how everything went last night."

"How did it go?" He planted his hands on her desk and leaned forward, his eyes boring into hers. "It was a freaking disaster, Linda Gail. We never made it to the restaurant. We never left Cedar Springs. I didn't see the point after she told me she was pregnant with my child but leaving me for Cowboy Bob. *That's* how the evening went."

"Oh, Wyatt," Linda Gail whispered, her heart sinking for him. "I'm so sorry."

"Instead of being sorry, get the city permit office on the phone. I want to get something moving on that development," he snapped, and shoved away from her desk and marched into his office, slamming the door behind him.

That night, when Linda Gail went home, she walked over to where Davis was sitting in his lounger, his Bud Light in hand, and leaned over and kissed him.

"What's that for?" Davis asked, looking pleasantly surprised.

"Just for being you," Linda Gail said, and went on about her business, leaving a smiling husband behind. Until today, she had not fully appreciated her mundane life and her steady husband.

Samantha Delaney burned her hand when she heard Reena and Cathy later that afternoon as they waited for their lattes. "You're kidding," Cathy said flatly when Reena reported that Macy Clark was pregnant with Wyatt's baby but going back to the town hero. "Some hero he turned out to be. They say he drinks like a fish and he's got some real anger issues. He wouldn't even ride in the Fourth of July parade."

"What do you expect?" Reena said. "He's been living in a cave for the last three years and he just came home. And really, what was the point of him being in the parade? Just so everyone could get a good look at him?"

"Everyone has been rooting for him since they found him alive," Cathy said. "You'd think he could show his gratitude a little by going through with the parade."

"Honestly, Cathy, sometimes I wonder what is wrong with you. It's just a stupid parade. He can ride on the big red-white-and-blue float next July and let everyone get a look at him then. He's been through a lot and sacrificed a lot and people like you should get off his back."

Samantha turned around, the lattes in hand.

"Hey, Sam," Reena said brightly. "We're all looking forward to the big to-do next month."

"Thanks," Samantha said, and put the drinks on the counter.

"I just hope Macy knows what she is getting into," Cathy said, picking up her latte. "Some of those vets have real issues. Remember Delores Wynn? Her older brother was one of those Vietnam vets who lived under the I-35 bridge. He was murdered last year by another transient. She said that he was never right after he came home from Vietnam, and lived the last ten years under the bridge."

"They have better mental health services today," Samantha said. "If they can get soldiers to access them."

Reena and Cathy looked at Samantha. "That's good to hear!" Reena said. "So is everything ready for the big fund-raiser?"

More than ready. Sam had worked tirelessly almost around the clock to make sure of it. "Sure is. I think it's going to be a great event."

"Hey! Maybe you can get Macy to bring Finn to that! That way, people like Cathy could get a good look at him."

"Oh, stop, Reena," Cathy said with a laugh, and walked away from the counter.

"He'd be a big draw," Reena said to Samantha as she picked up her coffee.

Samantha nodded. She smiled. She shoved her hands in her back pockets and thought that Finn would have been a great draw, if she could have had him without Macy. Poor Macy Harper Lockhart Clark, with too many husbands. Pregnant with Wyatt's baby and wanting Finn, the man she should have never forsaken. *This mess is just what Macy deserved*, Samantha thought, and turned around to clean the milk steamer.

Jesse was helping Ernesto repair a retaining wall around Laru's rose garden when he saw the big white pickup truck barreling down the drive. He stood up and watched the pickup come to a halt just a little too close to the house. When Wyatt Clark emerged, Jesse smelled trouble and tucked his gloves into his back pocket. He walked out on the drive to greet Wyatt.

"Hey, Wyatt, how are you?"

Wyatt barely glanced at him. He put his hands on his hips and whistled.

"What's going on here, pal?"

"I'm not your pal," Wyatt said. He whistled again.

From inside the house, Milo barked. "Let him out," Wyatt said, leveling a gaze on Jesse.

"Who, Milo?"

"Unless you got another dog in there, yeah, Milo," he said angrily.

This wasn't going to be much fun, Jesse figured. He didn't know where Milo had been, but the old dog had returned with Macy that morning, as happy-go-lucky as he'd ever been. He shook his head. "I can't do that, Wyatt, you know I can't. That's Macy's dog."

"That's *my* damn dog!" Wyatt shouted. "Let him out!"

Jesse didn't have to answer—Laru opened the door and Milo came bounding out, ecstatic to see Wyatt. And Wyatt—he sank down on one knee and wrapped his arms around the squirming dog like Milo was Lassie, finally come home. Laru stood a few feet away, her arms folded, watching him curiously. "Wyatt, what are you doing here?" she asked congenially.

"Nothing to do with you, Laru," Wyatt said, and stood up and opened the door of his truck. "Up," he said to Milo, and Milo leapt into his truck.

"Hey!" Laru cried. "You can't take Milo!"

"Oh, yes I can," Wyatt said. "He's my dog. If Macy wants him back, she can come talk to me about it." He cast a dark look at Jesse, then got into his truck and drove away.

Laru looked frantically at Jesse. "What do we do? Do we call the police?"

"No," Jesse said. He felt bad for Wyatt. He'd really gotten the raw end of the deal. "Let him go," he said.

"If Wyatt needs the dog to move on, let him have the dog."

"But what about Macy?" Laru asked. "She loves Milo."

"She's got Finn," Jesse said.

Wyatt had fully expected Macy to call about Milo. When she didn't, he worried she was plotting a counter abduction, and he took Milo everywhere he went. He wasn't losing Milo to her, too. No way.

He was keenly aware that the news about Macy had spread all over town. He'd made sure of it. He wanted her to be uncomfortable, to have to face the questioning looks everywhere she went. And he wanted Finn Lockhart to know that while he might think he'd won, Wyatt still held the upper hand. At the very least, Finn wouldn't have his little cutting horse ranch around Cedar Springs unless he could put his hands on some major bucks. A lawyer or land out this way was pretty damn expensive, more than a G.I. could afford, more than Finn would have when Wyatt was forced to hand over the profits from the sale of his land. He figured, after closing costs and realty and legal fees, Finn would be about one hundred thousand short. That meant Finn would have to move on, and Macy . . . maybe she'd move with him and maybe not.

To emphasize his feelings on the matter, Wyatt made sure the clearing of Finn's old ranch was under way. Since the sale of the ranch had closed, he'd had a pair of bulldozers out there, grinding up the scrub cedars and mesquite.

Linda Gail, who'd ordered the bulldozers for him, had looked at him askance. "What?" Wyatt had demanded, daring her to challenge him.

"Just doesn't seem right, that's all," she'd muttered. "That's his ranch."

"*Was* his ranch," Wyatt had said. "Just do it, Linda Gail."

She had given him a look much like his mother used to give him when he was a boy and she was ashamed of something he'd done. Not that Wyatt cared. His heart was as hard as the limestone that filled the earth around here.

The nights were the worst for Wyatt. He had no place to go, other than the Saddle-brew. He'd had dinner with Dave and Aurora one night, both of whom said things like, "There are other fish in the sea," and "We liked Macy, but we really like Caroline."

Wyatt saw Caroline exactly twice after Macy told him she was pregnant. Once, to look at some land. The second time, to negotiate a deal for her. When they were done, she'd produced a bottle of champagne and after a couple of glasses, she'd kissed him. The kiss wasn't too bad, really. But it wasn't too good, either.

One night, as Wyatt wandered around the big empty house with Milo beside him, his dad called to let Wyatt know that he and his mother were leaving Laughlin, Nevada, where they'd parked the RV for a month, and heading on to Flagstaff. Wyatt drew a circle on a notepad and

raced it, around and around and around, as his father
talked about the price of gas, the day he'd won a thousand dollars at the slots in a convenience store, and how
his mother was making a scrapbook of their trailering.

"That's great, Dad," Wyatt said as he traced the
circle. He kept waiting for his father to ask about him.
He'd never told his parents about Lockhart coming
home. He wasn't sure if he'd ever told them that Macy
had been married once before. He didn't have that
kind of relationship with them.

"Everything all right with you?" his dad asked.

Wyatt hesitated. He thought about telling him everything. But then his dad said, "I better make this quick. I
don't have a lot of minutes."

"Yeah, sure. No, I'm great," Wyatt said as disappointment drew his shoulders down.

"How's that resort? Your mother and I want you to
finish that up so we can come stay," he said, laughing.

"It's off to a great start. Got a big groundbreaking
next week," Wyatt said without enthusiasm.

"That sounds exciting. Well, okay then. Just wanted
to check in. Tell Macy we said hello."

"Right. Bye, Dad," Wyatt said, and hung up the
phone. He stood there staring at it. Had he always
been so disconnected from his parents? He couldn't
really remember anymore. They'd been good parents, he guessed. He never remembered them making an effort to listen to him. They just wanted to
hear that everything was all right. When there was
a problem, they'd say, "We know you can handle it,

Wyatt," and then move on to a more pleasant subject

It would be different with his kid. He'd be an in
volved father, someone the kid could talk to. Was i
really so hard?

The more he thought about it, the more he realize
that the only person he'd ever really been able to oper
up to was Macy. He wasn't the kind of guy to have con
fidants. He had buddies, but the closest they got to talk
ing about feelings was discussing the pennant race o
the Longhorns in the Bowl Championship Series polls
The closest he'd ever come to a confidant was Tomm
Payne in high school. Tommy owned a car dealershi
in Dallas. Wyatt hadn't talked to him in ten years.

So Wyatt continued to go it alone. He spent his day
obsessing about Macy and kept imagining her with G.I
Joe. That made him crazy, so he'd try to remember he
as she'd been with him. He could see her standing ir
the kitchen, studying a recipe book as she experimentec
with some new dish. He imagined her smiling at hin
when he came home from work, or doing yoga in the
middle of the living room and warning him not to laugh

Wyatt's obsession made him angry, furious, blinc
with rage. In one of his angrier moments, he wrote
Macy a letter and told her he would seek full custody o
the baby. He heard nothing back—not that he'd really
expected to—but he'd at least put her on notice tha
she couldn't destroy his life. She couldn't take every
thing. She could take his heart and smash it to worn
food, but she couldn't take his dog or his baby. He tolc
his lawyer to go after full custody.

"You bet," Jack said. "But the first thing we have to do is file suit to have the marriage declared void. Then we can tackle the custody issues."

As strongly as Wyatt felt about the custody issues, he couldn't yet bring himself to declare his marriage void. He asked Jack to give him a couple of days. He needed to work up to it, to come to terms.

In the meantime, he tried to focus on the construction of the resort and toward that end, he put Linda Gail's excellent event-planning skills to use in setting up an official groundbreaking. He invited the mayor and the city council, all of whom were very excited about the resort and the jobs it would bring to the area. Wyatt took out ads in the local and Austin papers. He had Linda Gail send invitations to Macy and her entire family. That earned him another look from Linda Gail, but Wyatt ignored her.

The truth was that Wyatt harbored an insane hope that with the land gone, the wheels on Cowboy Bob's little chuck wagon would fall off and Macy would come back to him. Wyatt liked to pretend that he'd have to think long and hard about taking her back, but deep inside, he knew there'd be no thinking. He'd give her a good scolding, but he had another, stronger fantasy of the two of them painting a nursery together.

That fantasy kept hammering at him, pushing him to do everything he was doing. Wyatt had suffered a severe setback and he was mad as hell, but mostly, he was determined to win. He was not a man who accepted defeat.

37

It was Dr. Rock's idea that Finn put some of the coping techniques he was learning in therapy into practice in real life, particularly when it came to crowds.

Crowds were another little problem that had crept up on Finn after he'd managed to stop drinking to numb himself—he'd had what Dr. Rock said was a panic attack. It had shocked Finn when it happened, and it seemed to have happened for no reason. He'd been in Austin with Macy, where they had gone so that he could see Dr. Rock and then consult with her lawyer. They were waiting at a crosswalk for the light to turn and several people crowded onto the corner, also waiting for the light to turn. Even though Finn stood a head taller than most people, he was suddenly perspiring. Every movement, every slight jostle made him jump, and in no time at all, he was tightly wound. He felt exposed, and realized he was waiting for someone to produce a gun, a bomb, a knife—

He hadn't even realized he was breathing like he was until Macy tugged hard on his sleeve. "What's the matter?" she had asked frantically.

"I gotta get out of here," he'd said, and had started to

back up, but managed to plow into a woman who cried out. He'd really lost it then, flailing through the crowd, unable to breathe, unable to focus.

Macy had managed to get him to Dr. Rock's office. Dr. Rock had told him to lower his head between his knees and take a couple of deep breaths. When Finn had finally calmed down, Dr. Rock explained he was exhibiting classic symptoms of PTSD. Finn didn't like hearing that, but even he couldn't deny it any longer. Either he was going to lose his mind, or he was going to put his trust in Dr. Rock.

They began to work on ways to deal with his reactions.

When Dr. Rock suggested he find a small crowd and practice some of the techniques, Finn had balked. But then he'd read in the paper about the groundbreaking for the Hill Country Spa and Resort. This, he had to see—he had to see Wyatt Clark actually break ground on the land he'd stolen from him. Wyatt could damn sure look him in the eye while he did it.

Finn wasn't ready to fly solo, however, and he didn't want to appear weak to Macy. He called Brodie and asked him if he could take some time off work to go with him.

"Dude—get a lawyer!" Brodie said.

"I've got one," Finn said. "But I need money for the retainer." In the meantime, he wasn't letting Wyatt get away with it.

The morning of the groundbreaking was hot and hazy, but there was quite a little crowd gathered nonetheless—mostly retirees with nothing better to do, lots of suits, and, oddly enough, a preschool class. The kids were chasing each other in a field.

Brodie looked at the crowd, then at Finn. "You sure about this?"

"Yep," Finn said. "Let's go."

They walked down a slope to where the ceremony was going to be held. It was about a mile from the southern boundary of Finn's land. They were up on a rise, and from where he stood Finn could see that even more clearing had taken place. His throat constricted. Generations of Lockharts had owned that land. His ancestors had bought it with the money they'd brought from Scotland. They'd worked it and eked out a living, even when there wasn't much of a living to be had, and now, that land would be torn up for a line of condos.

It was painful to look at, so Finn turned his attention to where the ceremony would take place, as evidenced by eight brand-new shovels with red bows tied around the handles. A space had been cleared and fresh dirt brought in for the politicians to turn so they wouldn't risk embarrassing themselves by not being able to break ground.

A shriek of laughter caught Finn's attention and he glanced at the kids in the field. It was hard to imagine a little Macy, but he pictured a little girl with honey-blonde hair like her mother's running around that field.

Finn had thought a lot about her pregnancy. He and Macy had tried so hard to conceive a kid before he'd gone off to war. Somehow, she'd managed it easily with

Wyatt. Too easily. Finn would be lying if he told himself that at first, he hadn't been completely unnerved that she was carrying Wyatt's baby. The thought of raising another man's child—particularly when it meant he'd have that man in his life for the foreseeable future—was sobering. He'd never say so to Macy, not after she'd put it all on the line to be with him. In the end, that was the only thing that mattered. He was beginning to accept that his life hadn't worked according to his best-laid plans, and the trick to surviving was to go with the flow.

So Finn would love that child—

"Excuse me," a voice said, startling Finn. "Aren't you our local hero?"

He jerked around. "Ah . . ."

"You *are!*" The gray-haired woman beamed up at him. "Frank! Over here, Frank! It's the hero!" Several heads turned and looked at him.

"My goodness, it is!" another woman said.

"I, ah . . . I—" *Breathe. Just a bunch of senior citizens. Not enemy civilians. No guns, no suicide vests.*

"Hey, hey," Brodie said, sensing Finn's discomfort, and tried to put himself between Finn and the curious crowd.

"How are you getting on?" one man asked, sidling around Brodie.

"Good," Finn said. He cleared his throat and clenched his hands. When this happened to him, it infuriated and perplexed him. He knew it was happening, that his fears were irrational, but he was powerless to stop it. *I'm okay,* he told himself.

"We're so glad to have you back," said another woman.

"And we're so proud!" another woman trilled.

Finn felt hot and unsteady. "I . . . I, ah . . ." His throat was closing up.

"Finn's been getting back into the swing of things," Brodie said quickly.

"Well, that's to be expected after what he endured," the older gentleman said. "The local paper indicated it was pretty bad. What were the Taliban really like?"

"Hey, it looks like the master of ceremonies has arrived," Brodie said.

All heads turned to a white pickup that had just arrived, pulling right up to the rope that separated the crowd from the parking area. Wyatt got out of the truck, along with Milo. He stepped over the rope and strode to the front while Milo scampered ahead, his nose to the ground.

The assembled throng began shifting to the front, including Finn's well-wishers.

Wyatt walked up to the microphone while Milo sniffed around the shovels. "Ladies and gentlemen, if I could have your attention," he said.

People began moving forward more urgently, taking Brodie and Finn with them. Finn's pulse quickened again; to keep from flipping out, he kept his gaze fixed on Wyatt, focused on his breathing, and repeated in his head, *No one is going to kill me. No one is going to kill me.*

I am not going to kill him.

I am not going to kill him.

He didn't really hear the short speeches that every one of the politicians made. He kept his gaze on Wyatt Clark. Wyatt didn't smile, didn't make eye contact with anyone. He seemed to be looking at something in the distance. He seemed, Finn slowly realized, like a very miserable man.

The mayor was the last to speak. She had to pull the mic down and began with a thank-you for all the assembled people. She then launched into praise for Wyatt Clark. "It takes all different kinds to make a community unique and strong," she said. "It takes men like Wyatt Clark, who can see what Cedar Springs has the potential to become. And it takes people like Sergeant Finn Lockhart, whom we are so fortunate to have returned to us, who would give his life to defend places like Cedar Springs. I understand he is here today. Sergeant Lockhart, are you out there?"

Wyatt's head snapped around at that; someone pointed at Finn and a round of applause went up.

Finn tried to smile, God knew he did. But he could not unclench his fists.

"And it takes men like Simon Daniels," the mayor continued, "who has been the president of the First Bank of Cedar Springs . . ."

Wyatt did not turn his attention from Finn; nor did Finn look away. But something happened to Finn as he stood there looking at Wyatt, at the man whose life he had destroyed by living. Perhaps he imagined it, but he could see the sadness in Wyatt's eyes, the edginess in his demeanor. It surprised the hell out of Finn that he felt sorry for Wyatt. He knew how heartbroken Wyatt had to be, because he knew what a treasure Macy was.

It wasn't until a heavyset woman hurried to hand out the festooned shovels and Wyatt was forced to look at something else that their silent standoff was broken.

Wyatt and the city council and the mayor lined up, put their feet on the shovel blades, and, on the count of three, all turned dirt. The crowd applauded, the children yelled *hooray*, and the heavyset woman began to direct everyone to a tent where refreshments had been laid out.

As the crowd cleared, a few of the kids chased butterflies. Brodie and Finn remained behind, Finn watching Wyatt. He didn't see Milo until the dog came bounding up to him, his tongue hanging almost to the ground.

"Here he comes," Brodie said softly as Finn squatted down to pet the dog. "Want me to get rid of him?"

"Nah." Finn stood up. "I'll talk to him."

"Finn—"

"It's okay. I'm not going to kill him." He gave his brother a sort of half smile just as Wyatt strode over to them.

Finn looked him square in the eye. "Hello, Wyatt."

"What the hell are you doing here?" Wyatt demanded, looking at Finn, then at Brodie.

"Not much. Just watching a groundbreaking."

"Yeah, a groundbreaking. We're going to take that piece of ranchland and finally make some money off of it. What do you think about that?" Wyatt asked, folding his arms across his chest.

"Okay," Brodie said. "That's my cue to leave. Come on, Milo," he said and whistled for the dog.

"Milo!" Wyatt called. "*Stay.*" The dog sat instantly and looked up at Wyatt and Finn.

"On that note," Brodie muttered, and walked away.

"You need to leave," Wyatt said to Finn. "You're only here to cause trouble."

"I'll admit I probably had that in mind when I decided to come," Finn said calmly, "but I'm not going to cause you any trouble, Wyatt."

Wyatt looked confused. And furious.

"Look, man, I owe you an apology. I went off on you when I first got back into town, and you didn't deserve that. In all honesty, you don't deserve any of what's happened. I see that now, and I'm sorry."

Wyatt's face darkened with angry confusion. "What in the devil are you talking about?"

"I'm talking about Macy and the ranch. I know why you sold it, and I don't really blame you. I'm not going to let you get away with it, but you know what? I think I might have done worse if the situation had been reversed."

Wyatt took a menacing step forward. "Look, pal, I am looking for a reason to knock you into Travis County. You've ruined my life. Are you happy?"

"That's what I'm saying, Wyatt—I'm not happy about that at all. In fact, I am sorry to the bottom of my soul for it," Finn said, clapping his hand over his heart. "It's clear that I ruined your life, and I promise you that I never meant to. I just wanted my wife and my life back. Man-to-man here—you can't really fault me for it, can you? Any more than I can fault you for falling in love with her."

"I don't give you as much as a moment of thought, Lockhart," Wyatt sneered. "But if you think you're getting your land back, or Macy for that matter, you're wrong. I'm not through with the two of you."

"Now, Wyatt," Finn said, "you know what they say— evil deeds are like chickens in that they all come home to roost."

"Don't hand me some barnyard bromide, Lockhart. I'm not worried. Macy will come home to me once she figures out that she can't go back to her old life again, and I will build condos on that land and make a fortune, and *you*—" He snorted. "*You* should be looking for property way out of Cedar Springs because I intend to make your life a living hell."

Finn didn't like the sound of that, but he couldn't ignore the pain in Wyatt's eyes. "I don't think so," he said calmly.

"I *know* so," Wyatt snapped as the heavyset woman hurried toward them. "Get a lawyer if you think you've been wronged, but I'll guaran-damn-tee you that you won't get an inch of that land back."

"Wyatt?" the woman said, reaching them. She looked at Finn, then at Wyatt. "Everything okay? They're cutting the cake."

"Great," Wyatt snapped, and turned around. "Milo!" he called.

Milo, who had slid from a sitting position down onto

his belly, perked his ears toward Wyatt, then looked up at Finn.

Wyatt stopped and glared at the dog. "*Milo.*"

Finn watched his dog hop up and trot alongside Wyatt, who was striding so hard the woman had to jog to keep up.

Brodie, who had taken refuge under a tree, looked back at Finn. But Finn was watching Wyatt. He didn't think that even he, in his years of captivity, had known the sort of loneliness of soul and spirit that Wyatt Clark was feeling right now. At least Finn had had hope. Wyatt had nothing but empty threats to cling to.

38

Macy had naively believed that once she'd made her decision, everything would fall into place. Life would go back to normal—granted, a new normal—but at least a normal without all the drama of the last few weeks.

That was hardly the case—it seemed as if everyone in town had an opinion about what she should have done, and the running tally, as reported to her by Emma, was that about half the populace of Cedar

Springs thought she had wronged Wyatt, and the other half thought she'd taken too long to return to Finn.

"Wow," Macy said. She had her own opinions about what she'd done, and none of them were very good. It was supposed to be easier now, but it wasn't. She ached for Wyatt.

"Who cares? I know how hard this has been for you," Emma said with sisterly earnestness.

Macy looked up from writing a list of things she needed for a nursery and smiled. "Thanks, Emmie. I can always count on you. What about Mom? Is she still mad?"

"Mad is not the right word," Emma said with a roll of her eyes. "You know how she is; she gets so bent out of shape when people don't instantly agree with her. Did I tell you? One of the interviews I had last week looked really promising until I got there. It was supposed to be a finance job, but it was basically a telemarketing job. I told Mom, and she wouldn't believe me. She said I had misunderstood. Macy, I was *there*. I didn't misunderstand, but try telling Mom that."

Macy smiled.

"But hey, she'll come around to your decision."

"I don't know," Macy said. "She never liked Finn."

"That's not true! She liked Finn, but apparently she liked Wyatt a whole lot more." She grinned. "So what are you guys going to do next?"

Macy sighed and looked at her book again. "I don't know. The first thing we have to do is pay for the legal proceeding. My lawyer says it is best that Finn and I stay apart until she can get it in front of a judge. Then there is the matter of the property. Wyatt will definitely have to pay the value of it, but Lucy doesn't think we can get the land back without a lawsuit. We would need money for that, which I thought I had, but then I got this," she said, and reached across her book and a stack of magazines for an envelope that she tossed to Emma.

Emma picked it up. "The army?"

"They want back the life insurance they paid for Finn when they thought he'd been killed. Now that he's not dead, their bean counters couldn't wait to ask for it."

"You're kidding!"

"I'm not," Macy sighed. "I haven't told Finn yet."

What Macy didn't tell Emma was that things had been a bit strained between her and Finn the last few days. She couldn't put her finger on it, exactly, but guessed it was a combination of things. After all, he'd been home a month now, and he was still living with his parents. Really, who could live with Karen Lockhart without losing their mind? The money situation wasn't good, either. Macy hadn't worked in a while and was having trouble finding a job that matched her skills. Emma wasn't exaggerating—it was tough finding employment out there. The two times Macy had found a promising lead, someone with more experience had gotten the job. She had another lead for a position as a social worker—but it meant working in South Austin, which would require an hour commute each way.

Finn wanted to work, but he was struggling with some of the symptoms of post-traumatic stress. When she tried to talk to him about it, he clammed up, refused to acknowledge the difficulties she knew he was facing. He continued to do what work he could around his parents' ranch. Brodie was trying to get him on at the lumberyard with him.

The news about the life insurance money could not have come at a worse time. Macy didn't want to add to the burdens Finn already carried. She just wanted him to relax and learn to enjoy life again. She still had abundant hope that things would fall into place for them. *Everything will be all right.*

With that hope, she'd planned a little surprise for Finn. Late that afternoon, she packed up her Jeep and drove out to the Lockhart place.

When she knocked on the door, Karen Lockhart opened it. "Hello, Macy," she said tightly.

"Hello, Karen."

"Is that Macy?" Rick called from somewhere inside the house. A moment later he appeared at the door. "Hi, Macy. Come on in," he said, pushing the door open and nudging Karen out of the way.

"Thanks," Macy said, and stepped inside. "Is Finn here?"

"He's out back with my crusty old horse," Rick said. "That boy could never stay away from a horse."

"I was just fixin' to call him in," Karen said. "I'll go get him." She walked away.

Macy looked at Rick, who smiled warmly. "Don't

nind that old girl," he whispered, and put his arm
round Macy's shoulders, pulling her into the house.
She's just a mother looking out for her boy."

"I'm not going to hurt Finn."

"I know that, Macy. But Karen worries when the
aby comes, you'll feel guilty and will want to go back
o Wyatt."

God help her, sometimes Macy worried the same
hing.

Rick showed her to the living room, where a row of
vindows overlooked the back. She could see Finn strid-
ng up the back path ahead of Karen in boots and jeans
nd a T-shirt. He was wearing the straw hat again and
here were spurs on his boots. He'd been riding.

When he entered through the screen door, he didn't
peak, but strode to where she stood, wrapped his arms
iround her, and kissed her.

"Hello to you, too," she said with a smile.

"I wasn't expecting you."

"I know. I was hoping you could tear yourself
.way—I've got a surprise for you."

Finn quirked one brow. "Now that's an invitation no
nan could refuse," he said with a wink. "Where is this
.urprise?"

"You have to come with me," she said.

"And it just gets better and better. Let me grab a
hower," he said, and kissed her cheek. "Mom, don't
levour Macy or her young while I clean up," he said as
ie strode out of the living room. Rick chuckled. Karen
rowned.

"Sit down, Macy. You like baseball?" Rick aske
his attention on the enormous flat panel television th
took up the west wall.

Macy sat.

Karen did, too. She picked up some knitting an
made a halfhearted attempt to knit for about ten min
utes while Macy sat stiffly next to her. But she final
put it down and looked at Macy. "So . . . when's you
baby due?"

"Late February," Macy said.

"I can't help but feel bad for Wyatt Clark. That mu
have been a real blow to find out you were having h
baby but with another man."

The image of a devastated Wyatt flashed in Macy
mind. She swallowed and looked at the televisio
screen.

"I was down at the Envy, the hair salon on th
square, and Carol Richardson told me that your moth
thought you ought to be with Wyatt," Karen continued
"That true?"

Macy looked at Karen. "My mother has always ha
her own opinions. But I'm not my mother."

"Well, I *know* you're not Jillian," Karen said. "I'
just wondering how much influence she's going to hav
with you, because I guarantee you, Macy, when th
baby comes, you're going to want it to be with its natu
ral father. And where will that leave Finn?"

"Karen, leave it alone," Rick said.

But Karen looked at Macy, expecting an answe
Macy knew there was no answer she could give Kare

that would change her opinion. "You're too hard on me, Karen," she said.

"Amen to that," Rick muttered.

"What do you mean?" Karen demanded. "I'm only thinking of my son."

"You're too hard on me," Macy said again. "I am doing the best I know how to do. I have made a very difficult decision and I don't intend to walk away from it. You can fear the future all you like, but I won't. I cannot begin to describe how ecstatically happy I am that I can share my life with Finn. This is what I have wanted from almost the moment I met him, and I am so blessed to have a second chance. I am not going to ruin it—I'm making my life with Finn."

"Well said, baby." She turned around to see Finn standing at the door from the hallway. His hair was still wet, but he'd put on a clean pair of tight-fitting jeans, some decent boots, and a clean T-shirt that hugged his arms and torso. "You ready?"

"I am," she said, and stood up. She glanced down at Karen, who was staring hard at her cross-stitch. "There's one other thing," she said softly. "Wyatt's mother isn't around much, and this baby is going to need two grandmas."

Karen's hand froze. She glanced up at Macy wordlessly.

Finn put his hand out for Macy. She slipped her hand into his. "See you," Finn said to his folks, and led Macy out of there.

As they walked to her Jeep, he pulled her into his

side and gave her a reassuring hug. "The sooner we get out from underfoot, the easier it will get."

Macy could not agree more.

Finn paused to peer in the back window of her Jeep. "What's my surprise?" he asked, changing the subject.

"Don't look!" she cried, and playfully pushed him to the passenger door. "Just get in."

In the Jeep, she turned the radio to country music, which Finn preferred, and ignored his guesses about where they were going; when she turned on the road that led to his ranch, his smile faded. "Where are you going?"

"Home."

"It's not home anymore."

"It's not his; I don't care what he says." She pulled up at the gate and opened the driver's door.

"Macy—this is trespassing now."

Macy laughed at Finn. "What's he going to do, sue me? Wait. Don't answer that—he just might." She winked at him and hopped out.

She unlocked the gate, but Finn was out before she could push it back. "You're pregnant. Will you try to remember that?"

"I'm pregnant, not bedridden," she said with a laugh, and hopped back into the Jeep and drove through. Finn closed the gate and climbed back into the passenger seat.

Macy drove down the road, but instead of turning to the right to go to the house, she turned left and followed a very bumpy road until she got within walking distance of their favorite part of the creek. "This is it; here's your big surprise," she said, and got out of the Jeep.

Finn did, too. "What are you doing?" he asked as she opened the back hatch.

Macy's answer was to shove a pair of fishing poles at him, salvaged from Brodie's garage.

Finn looked at the poles. "Fishing?"

"Our favorite spot," she said, and tried to heave the picnic basket over the tailgate.

Finn stared at her. Macy laughed. "What's the matter? Are you scared?"

He gave her a stern look and shoved the poles at her. "You carry those. I'll carry this." He grabbed the blanket she had and stacked it on top of the basket. "You know, if the sheriff comes, I'll have to do my duty as a law-abiding citizen and turn you in," he warned her with a wink.

"Oh, yeah? I have brownies in there, the kind you like."

"On second thought, I'll take the fall."

Together, they walked down the path that led to the creek, Finn teasing her by telling her to watch out for snakes. He led her through a thicket—it amazed her that he still knew this land like the back of his hand—and on the other side, they emerged into the little green clearing where the creek turned deep enough for fishing.

He helped her lay the blanket down on the banks of the creek, then set the poles with the bit of bacon she'd brought while Macy laid out supper: cold chicken, grapes, and cheese. She'd brought beer, too, and opened one, passing it to Finn.

Finn stretched out on the blanket and propped himself on his elbow. Macy sat cross-legged, watching the tops of the trees as they brushed against the sky.

Finn took a swig of beer, then pointed the bottle neck at Macy. "You look like you've got something on your mind, baby."

She laughed. "Do I?"

"Man," he said with a shake of his head. "That laugh of yours has always made me want to do something insanely foolish, like ride a wild bronc."

"Please don't. I want you in one piece."

"So what's on your mind?" he asked.

"*Anh*," she said with a wave of her hand. "Nothing that can't wait. Next question."

Finn suddenly sat up and leaned forward. "Do you know how much I love you?" he asked, and kissed her.

Macy laughed against his mouth, put her hand on his chest, and pushed him back a little. "Do you know how much I love you?"

"I never doubted it." Finn said and pushed a strand of her hair behind her ear.

"Really?"

"Really."

"Even when you came home and found out I'd married Wyatt?" she asked dubiously.

"Even then."

Her smile faded. "Even when I told you I was pregnant?"

With a soft smile, Finn caressed her cheek. "Especially then. Anyway, the past doesn't matter. What natters is that we are here, right now—all three of us. That's all we need to think about."

She knew he was right, and that's what she wanted to think about . . . but she couldn't stop thinking about Wyatt and how she'd ruined the happiness of a wonderful man. She looked down at the blanket. "Who would have guessed your homecoming would have so many . . . issues?"

"It couldn't have been any other way except if time had stood still, Macy. Nothing remains the same," he said, and fingered a bit of her hair.

"I got a letter from the army," she said. "They want the money from the life insurance back."

Finn's hand stilled as that sank in. He sighed, let go her hair, and fell onto his back. "Figures," he said. "But I guess it makes sense. I'm not dead."

"Still . . . you'd think for all the pain you suffered, they'd let it go."

He laughed a little. "I damn sure don't want money for that." He glanced at her. "Macy, don't worry. That's nothing we can't overcome."

"But how are we going to buy another ranch so we can set up the animal rescue operation?"

"Well, I guess it's a good thing I did that interview for the *Austin American-Statesman* about the idea. We'll start by getting donations. And I've got one last trick up my sleeve."

"What?"

"A book deal."

"No, Finn," Macy said. He'd told her more than

once he didn't want to talk about what had happened
But this evening he grabbed her hand and kissed he
fingers. "I talked to Dr. Rock about it. He said he
thought it was a great idea, said it might even be ca
thartic. You know, I can get it out of my system. And it'
hard to turn down that kind of money, Macy. The guy
from New York is talking seven figures."

"*Seven* figures?" Macy said, sliding down beside
him. "Dude!"

Finn laughed as she propped her head on her hand
She traced a line down his chest. "Still—are you cer
tain?"

"For us, I'd do anything. Including accepting seven
figures to talk about my time in captivity."

"All of us?"

Finn touched his fingers to her lips. "What is the mat
ter with you tonight? Yes, all of us. Never doubt it, Macy
It's not exactly the way I wanted to start our family, bu
it's our family nonetheless. The way I see it, we're al
made up of pieces of the people who love us. That baby
will have pieces of us both . . . and of Wyatt, and whom
ever he ends up with. I don't know how that is going to
work, and I'm not crazy about it, but it's unavoidable."

Macy thought about Wyatt's angry letter regarding
custody. She could feel his pain in that letter and un
derstood he was lashing out at her in his grief. "I hope
he does find someone. I hope he finds what we have
with each other."

"Well, whatever happens, whatever our life looks
like, I want our family. Never, ever doubt that is true."

"Okay, you are making me insane with wanting you," she said, and leaned over to kiss him.

Finn shoved his hand into her hair and hungrily kissed her back. The way he touched her, looked at her, made Macy feel like she was the most desirable woman on earth. She kissed him again, this time climbing on top of him to straddle him.

"Hey, wait a minute," Finn said. "What if we get a nibble?"

"Oh, you're going to get a nibble," she said, and grabbed the hem of her peasant blouse and lifted it up over her head.

"Lord, Macy," he said, looking at the skimpy bra she wore. "You're going to give me a damn heart attack." He cupped her breasts; something flowed between them, something that only two people who loved each other as much as they did could feel, and Macy was hopelessly, utterly lost.

Finn wrapped his arms around her and pulled her down to him. He pressed his mouth against her cheek, her eyes, and then her lips. "I can't ever seem to stop wanting you," he said.

The heat of the early evening, the wind rustling the trees, the water running all seemed to fade away as Finn kissed Macy and stroked her body. His rough hand on her smooth skin excited her beyond reason; she quickly removed her bra so that he could put his hands on her breasts. She gasped softly in his ear as he squeezed her nipple between his fingers and pressed herself against him, her body stretched the length of his.

He moaned, lifted her up, and took one breas in his mouth. The sensation of it was excruciatingl arousing—Macy slid her hand down his leg and cupped his erection.

"You're beautiful," Finn said, panting a little His fingers splayed across her breast and nipple and squeezed gently.

Macy sighed with pleasure. "So are you. Now pleas take your pants off."

Finn grinned and caught her mouth with his at th same moment his hands went to his belt, fumblin with it. She rose from him, helped him shove his pant down, and, as he kicked them off his legs, took off he shorts.

He gazed at her naked body with such obvious long ing that Macy felt beautiful, especially with the sligh swell of her pregnancy. She straddled him again, rub bing against him, pressing her breasts against him. A giggle of pure pleasure escaped her, but Finn didn' seem to hear her. His hands were running over he body, making her pulse beat too fast, making her hear pound in her chest. One hand floated down her abdo men, slipping in between her legs. Macy closed he eyes and submerged herself in the sensation of his fingers stroking her. Then Finn muttered something incomprehensible against her breast and slipped his fingers deep inside her, and Macy was intensely, deeply aroused.

A moment later, she was sliding down on him, her body taking him in. Her fingers dug into his shoulder as she began to move on him, sliding up, then down, as deliberately as she might. But she was fast losing control, and Finn, who knew her body almost as well as she did, laughed breathlessly against her neck. "No, no, not yet, not that easy," he said.

He suddenly twisted her onto her back and came over her. He looked down at her, roughly caressed her hair. "You lay right there and let me show you how crazy you make me. Can you handle it?"

"No," she said honestly, but Finn just grinned and moved his thigh in between her legs, pushing them apart. He pressed himself against her, laced his fingers with hers above her head, and entered her.

Macy shuddered at the primal sensation and grabbed his hips, pulling him deeper inside her. Waves of pleasure were already rolling through her, the crescendo building. But Finn seemed to enjoy torturing her and watched her as he slid slowly into her depths, adjusting himself to her body, then sliding deeper still with small, rhythmic movements.

Macy's control was almost gone; he was so hot and thick inside her, and she arched her pelvis against him, silently demanding more as she gasped for breath. Finn at last gave in. He kissed her as he began to thrust harder and longer inside her, pushing her to new heights. As the earth began to fall away from her she cried out with pleasure and lifted her body to match his rhythm. His breath was hot on her shoulder, his grip of her hand almost painful.

The last hard wave of pleasure carried her off—he

was her river. She heard the strangled groan, felt the last powerful thrust of his body as he sank his finger into her hips.

A moment later, Macy opened her eyes. Finn was holding himself above her. His hair dipped over one eye and he had an unfathomably deep look in his copper brown eyes. He carefully lowered himself onto his elbows and cupped her face in his hands. "God, Macy," he whispered, and tenderly kissed her mouth and her shoulder before dislodging himself and lying beside her. They lay on the blanket looking up at the dusk sky, their fingers entwined, their hearts beating in unison.

A few minutes later, Finn sat up and handed Macy her clothes. They dressed quietly, their eyes on one another, their smiles warm. When they'd dressed, Finn wrapped his arm around Macy's neck and kissed her forehead. "We gotta get a place, and sooner rather than later. I don't care if it's a cracker box, and I don't care what the lawyer says—I need to be with you."

"Me, too," she agreed, and kissed his neck, tasting the saltiness of his skin. "I'll look tomorrow. Someplace small."

He chuckled. "Too poor to paint, too proud to white-wash. But it can't hurt to look. I'm going to go to New York in the morning and meet this book guy," he said. "I should be back before the end of the week. If you find something, maybe we can wrap it up then."

"Do you want me to go with you?" she asked.

"I'd love for you to go with me," he said. "But I'd rather just get in and get out, and Brodie is tagging along in case I . . . well, flip out," he said with a self-conscious laugh. "And besides, you need to find us a place before I lose my freaking mind."

Macy laughed. "Can't have that. God, Finn . . . I am so ready to be us again."

"Me, too, baby," he said softly.

39

Wyatt made a cup of instant coffee and grimaced at the taste of it. He was ashamed to admit it, but he'd never figured out how to work Macy's high-dollar coffeepot. He sat down at the kitchen bar and pushed aside a pile of mail, old newspapers, his empty bottle of blood pressure medicine, and some fast food bags, and opened the newspaper. He skimmed the front page—a lot of politics, more trouble at the border. He flipped through the paper to the Metro section when a headline caught his eye: LOCAL HERO OPENS HEART AND LAND TO UNWANTED ANIMALS.

Wyatt slowly put down his coffee cup and picked up the paper. There was a picture of Finn Lockhart, his hand on the bridle of a horse. He wasn't smiling, exactly, but there was a subtle hint of one. It almost seemed to Wyatt as if Finn were smirking at him.

Wyatt quickly scanned the article. In it, Finn talked about how he'd shared his scraps of food with a starving dog while he was held in captivity in Afghanistan. "Oh, yeah," Wyatt muttered, "a hero *and* a soft-heart." Finn said he'd always had an affinity for animals, and since he'd been home, he'd learned of several big animals that needed new homes: a pair of horses, a longhorn steer, and, of course, dogs. So it seemed "only natural" to start up a rescue ranch. When asked where and how he was going to manage it, Finn said that he was in the process of selling his story and hoped to make enough to buy land and get it started. The article concluded with information on how to donate to Finn's cause.

When Wyatt finished reading the article, he flung the paper across the kitchen. Sheets drifted to the floor. He buried his face in his hands for a moment and wondered if he would ever be able to shake Finn Lockhart from his life.

His anger and frustration and sheer helplessness were getting the best of him. Even Milo seemed depressed—he lay with his head between his paws, staring at Wyatt, as if he expected him to do something. Wyatt stood up. "Come on, pal," he said to Milo. "Let's go get a decent cup of coffee." He walked to the front door, his gaze moving over the big, gilt-edged mirror over the mantel. He'd thrown something at it one night in a fit of rage. The other stuff he'd trashed that night—a lamp, a vase, a picture of him and Macy—he'd picked up. Mostly. But the mirror he'd left hanging there like that. He liked it better. He didn't like looking at himself these days.

At the Saddle-brew, Wyatt ran into Caroline, who was a whole lot happier to see him than he was to see her. "Wyatt, just the person I wanted to see," she said, standing too close to him.

Wyatt looked behind the counter. "Sam's not working?"

"Not today. How about some coffee?"

Wyatt looked at Caroline. "Sure," he said halfheartedly. "Why not?"

Macy couldn't get hold of Wyatt. He wasn't at the office, he wasn't at home, and he wasn't answering his cell. She needed to get some things from the house, but she didn't want to go alone. She called Emma and asked her to ride along.

"Anything to get out of the house," Emma said. "If I don't get a job soon, I am going to go *nuts.*"

At the house in Arbolago Hills, Macy rang the doorbell twice.

"Just stick your key in the door and let's go," Emma urged her. "He's not home. Get in, get out."

"You're right," Macy said, and opened the door. "Hello?" she called out.

Milo was there, his paws sliding on the hardwood floors in his eagerness to reach her. She squatted down to pet him, then popped up. "I'll be just a minute, Emma."

"Cool," Emma said, and went down on her knees to greet Milo.

Macy walked down the corridor to the master suite. The door was closed, and as she neared it, she heard something like a moan. Was he sleeping? "Wyatt?" she said softly, and opened the door a crack. "Are you awake?" She pushed it open a little further. When she peeked inside, she jumped.

"Macy!" Wyatt shouted.

She was too stunned to move. Wyatt was in bed with another woman. Macy stared at the floor, trying to process it.

The next moment, Wyatt yanked the bedroom door open wearing his boxer shorts. She could see the bare legs of the woman on the bed behind him. *Caroline Spalding*. It had to be Caroline. Macy had heard about her interest in Wyatt.

"What are you doing here?" Wyatt asked, putting his hand to his nape.

"I needed some clothes. I left you a message. Apparently you didn't get it." Or maybe he did. Maybe this was Wyatt's idea of payback.

"So get them," he said, opening the door wide. Macy's gaze flew to the bed and she gasped loudly.

It wasn't Caroline Spalding in bed with Wyatt. It was Samantha Delaney. Samantha Delaney, who had been Macy's best friend, was sitting on the bed with nothing but the corner of a sheet to cover her, calmly regarding Macy.

"Oh, my God," Macy said. "*Oh, my God.*"

"What's the matter?" Wyatt asked. "Can't I move on, too?"

Macy whirled around and hurried down the hallway to Emma, who was standing in the foyer, her mouth gaping open.

Wyatt followed her. "What about your clothes?"

"I'll come back another time!" she snapped.

"Right. When you do, bring the Jeep and a ride."

Macy had no idea what he was talking about. "What?"

"That's right, I forgot to mention—I'm taking the Jeep back."

Macy spun around and stared at him.

"Oh, did you think you could just take that, too?" he asked pleasantly. "That I'd just give you a Jeep so you could leave me?"

"God, Wyatt," Emma said, her voice full of disgust.

This wasn't Wyatt. This was not the man Macy had been married to for seven months. This was a broken man, because the Wyatt she'd fallen in love with would *never* sleep with Sam. *Sam!* A dull pain started in the back of Macy's head. "Can I at least move my things before you take the Jeep?"

Wyatt sighed heavenward. "Come on, sweetheart," he said. "How long are we going to play this game?"

"*What* game?"

"Okay, maybe *game* is the wrong word," he said. "But seriously, Macy, Lockhart can't provide for you and the baby. He's living with his parents for Chrissakes. And he's obviously got some mental issues."

"Mental issues!"

"Everyone is talking about it," Wyatt said with a shrug. "How long do you possibly think it can last? You're living in a fairy tale."

"And what are you living in, Wyatt? How does sleeping with my best friend help matters in the least?" Macy exclaimed angrily. Over his shoulder, she saw Sam appear at the threshold of the master bedroom, wearing one of Wyatt's shirts and apparently nothing more. "I'll have someone bring the Jeep back," Macy said.

"Great," Wyatt said.

"Come on, Macy," Emma said, and opened the front door.

Macy had one foot over the threshold when Wyatt said, "Macy, wait." She looked over her shoulder. He was standing in the foyer, his expression angry. But it was his eyes that seared into Macy's head. His gaze was incongruently forlorn. "I shouldn't have slept with Sam, but she was there, and I—"

"I'm sorry, Wyatt," she said, cutting him off. "I will go to my grave regretting how much I have hurt you. You better go now. Sam is waiting." She walked out with Emma's arm around her waist.

Wyatt watched Macy drive away in the Jeep. In a moment of incredible stupidity at the grocery store, where he'd run into Sam, he'd made a colossal mistake. He would never be able to say why he'd done it. Because he missed Macy? Maybe because he missed sex. More likely he needed to hurt her like he'd been hurt. Whatever his reasons, Wyatt had ruined any chance of getting Macy back. He knew that. She would never get over it, and he . . . he'd only made it worse by taunting her.

With a sigh of resignation, he shut the door. Sam was standing behind him, wearing his shirt. "I think you should go now," he said.

"Yes," she said, looking at the door. "I think I should." She retreated down the hallway, and Wyatt understood that somehow, Sam had also gotten what she wanted out of this tryst.

He followed her down the hallway. "Why, Sam?" he asked as she picked up her clothes.

"Why what?"

"Why this?" he said, gesturing to the bed.

Sam shrugged and slipped on her bra.

"She was your best friend."

"No, *I* was *her* best friend," Sam said angrily.

Wyatt was starting to get it. "She was your *only* friend after Tyler died," he said. "You told me that yourself. You told me more than once how grateful you were to Macy for her friendship!"

"Oh, get off your high horse, Wyatt! Why did *you* do it? She was your wife!"

As much as he despised Sam in that moment, she was right. Wyatt felt like the scum that he was. "Go home, Sam," he said, and turned away, striding down the hallway. *What a colossal mistake.*

Wyatt never made it into work that day. And when Jesse Wheeler turned up later that afternoon with his Jeep, Wyatt told him he didn't want it.

"Dude," Jesse said. "I've got to give it back. I'll just leave the keys in the driver's seat," he said, tossed them inside, and strolled down the drive to a friend who was waiting.

Wyatt had never felt so defeated in his life. His wife didn't want him. Sam had used him. He had turned into a man he truly did not like.

That night, as the sun started its descent, Wyatt and Milo walked out of his house and got in his truck. He didn't lock the door of his house. He didn't take anything with him. He put his arm around Milo and drove down the street, away from his home.

40

Finding a place to live with no income was a difficult task. Not that people weren't sympathetic, but as one woman put it, "Rules are rules."

After a couple of days of looking, Macy went to a Realtor on the town square, thinking that she might find a small house she and Finn could rent. She was standing outside the Barbara Sullivan Realty office looking at pictures of homes for sale when Linda Gail Graeber interrupted her. "Macy, I am so glad to see you," she said, looking a little frantic.

"Hi, Linda Gail," Macy said warily.

"Have you seen Wyatt?"

Macy blushed. She could not erase from her mind the image of Wyatt and Sam in bed together. "Not for a couple of days."

"I don't know what to do," Linda Gail said. "He didn't come to work yesterday or today. I went by the house this morning and it's standing wide open, but there's no sign of him."

"Did you ask Sam Delaney?" Macy asked.

"*Sam?*" Linda Gail said, confused. "Sam's working. She hasn't seen him."

Linda Gail was obviously flustered, and Macy had to agree—this wasn't like Wyatt. But then again, Wyatt had hardly been himself lately. "What about Milo?"

"The dog is gone, too."

Macy pushed down a tic of alarm. "Maybe he's out looking at land?" she suggested.

"No," Linda Gail said. "The newspapers are in the yard and he won't answer his cell."

"Did you call the police?"

"Oh, I told Chief Ham, but he said Wyatt is a grown man and no family had reported him missing. I'll be honest, Macy—I am really worried about him. He hasn't been himself since . . . since all this happened. He just loves you something awful."

Exactly what Macy was thinking. Her tic of alarm grew to a spasm. She could not forget the look in his eyes when she told him she was pregnant but leaving him for Finn. It haunted her, made her doubt herself. What had she done? In making sure she was happy, she'd pushed Wyatt to . . . to what? To harm himself?

Linda Gail was right—this wasn't like him. He hadn't been himself in a month all because she had knocked the foundation out from beneath him. He needed her. He'd been there for her, but she hadn't been there for him.

Everything will be all right.

Macy thought of his blood pressure medicine. Reminding him to take it was one of the things she always did for him. She thought of all the things he'd done for her. Could she have been so wrong?

She looked at Linda Gail. "Let's go make some calls," she said.

At JFK Airport, Brodie came back from the gate and told Finn the flight had been delayed indefinitely. Again.

"Maybe we could rent a car and drive somewhere— Philadelphia, maybe?" Finn suggested.

"No," Brodie said. "We can't get out of there, either. There's a huge storm between us and Texas, and flights all up and down the eastern seaboard are delayed or canceled."

Finn nodded and clenched his jaw. He felt anxious in the crowded hallways and looked around for an escape. Any escape.

"Hey," Brodie said. "Nothing's going to happen here. Breathe, remember?"

Finn tried very hard to do just that, but it seemed like more and more people were streaming into the halls and milling about, and he felt utterly and helplessly exposed.

In the summer heat, sitting around the campfire in Pace Bend Park, Wyatt felt like he was sitting at the gates of hell, which he thought was an appropriate way to describe his life. And it was the best way to keep mosquitoes off of him. Not that Wyatt really felt the mosquitoes anymore—he was drunk, had been drunk the last couple of days.

Wyatt had hooked up with a merry little band of hippies at a Texaco station. He'd had a flat—probably from something he'd run over while driving all over Cowboy Bob's ranch—and D.J. had offered to help. He later learned that D.J. and Mariah, and Phil and Wendy, went back and forth between Hippie Hollow, where they would swim, and Pace Bend Park, where they camped. "It's a mellow existence," D.J., a small man who favored bandanas, had said. "Come eat some dogs with us, man."

That's exactly what Wyatt did.

The little group lived out of an old van and camped out. Wyatt had the impression they were all determined to be unemployed, but after the last couple of days of just hanging out and drinking, he was beginning to see the appeal.

They talked about moving southwest, to Garner State Park. "More for the kids to do," D.J. explained.

D.J. and Mariah had two kids under the age of ten, Serafina and Apollo. Phil and Wendy had a baby that never cried, which Wyatt thought was a little odd, but every time he saw the little thing up close— Rocky, they said his name was—he looked happy and healthy. The two families were related somehow. Wyatt was certain they'd explained how, but he didn't remember.

Wyatt and Milo slept in the back of his pickup with a borrowed sleeping bag. He'd made a couple of runs into a convenience store for beer and food. "Great!" Mariah had said, as if the Flamin' Hot Cheetos, hot dogs, and breakfast tacos solved some serious supply dilemma.

What Wyatt liked about the hippies was that they didn't ask for his story. They were content to let him just be, for which he was grateful. They could sit for many hours smoking pot. Wyatt wasn't a pot smoker, but he'd become one over those two days. He found that when he was stoned, his anxiety about Macy faded quietly and smoothly into the background.

On the third day, Wyatt was sitting next to D.J., watching Phil down at the water's edge with the kids and Milo. Mariah and Wendy were putting together the meal for the night. Wyatt and D.J. had smoked "a little weed," as D.J. put it, but Wyatt wasn't feeling quite so tranquil. He was feeling antsy and paranoid.

"We're moving on to Garner tomorrow," D.J. said. "Why don't you come with?"

"Yeah, okay," Wyatt said without thinking.

"Did you bring a change of clothes, man?" D.J. asked. "You look like you ran away from home." He laughed.

Wyatt looked down. His white shirt was filthy, as were his khakis. "I, ah . . . I was just taking a little break."

"Everyone needs a break now and then," D.J. said. "Got any beer?"

"Yep." Wyatt handed him a beer and opened one for himself.

"Hey, Mariah," D.J. called. "Wyatt's going to Garner with us."

"Cool." Mariah floated into their midst wearing a bikini top and a peasant skirt. She had a green snake tattooed around her shoulders. "You're going with us?"

"Yep. This is the life," Wyatt said, settling in. "Too bad not everyone can enjoy it."

"Ah, man, anyone can enjoy it," said D.J. "You've just got to choose this life."

"My brother can't," Mariah said. "He's in Afghanistan. What's he enjoying?"

"Right," D.J. said, and to Wyatt he said, "Mariah's brother is a big, tough Marine. He used to hang out with us before he signed up."

"He was home six weeks before he was redeployed. That's it! He could really use some downtime," Mariah said. She leaned over, picked up a beer, and wandered back to the picnic table.

"I don't know about her brother, but some of those soldiers come back and get some downtime and just milk it," Wyatt scoffed.

"What do you mean?" D.J. asked as he offered Wyatt a cigarette. Wyatt shook his head.

"I know of this one guy who came back from Afghanistan. I mean, yeah, he was a captive, but he came back, and he's done nothing but milk it." Wyatt tossed his empty beer can aside and picked up another beer. He was drinking fast. Marijuana made him thirsty. He wondered if D.J. had any more marijuana.

"That guy who was a prisoner of the Taliban?" D.J. asked. "I heard about him. How'd he milk it?"

"You know, he came back and became the big hero around Austin," Wyatt said, waving his hand. "Ma—his wife had remarried, but he didn't care. He just took her back, like he had a right. Took the dog, took it all," he said, waving loosely at *all*. "And the guy doesn't work a *lick*. He just milks it, walks around being the hero, getting everyone's sympathy."

"No, now, I heard about this," Mariah said, appearing on their right again. "That guy went through a *lot*. Give me a cigarette, babe." D.J. handed her the cigarette he'd just lit. Mariah took a drag and looked at Wyatt, pointing the cigarette at him. "He was a prisoner, and he lost his job and his land and his wife," she said, letting the smoke escape with her words. "That's not right. He shouldn't have lost all that after what he did for this country."

"If you ask me, I think she should have left that jerk she was married to right off," D.J. said.

"Jerk!" Wyatt said, quickly angered by that. "Why's *he* the jerk? What'd *he* do?"

"It's obvious," Mariah said before walking off again.

"What's so damn obvious?" Wyatt called after her.

"Hey, peace, brother," D.J. said. "It's obvious because the wife wouldn't have been with the second guy if she thought the first guy was alive."

"Yeah, well, she thought the first guy was dead and fell in love again. Is that so hard to believe?"

"No. But she obviously loved the first guy, and when he came back, she had no graceful way out of the second marriage. Think about it. There'd be no smooth way out of that situation. The second husband should have been a man about it."

Wyatt snorted. "So if Mariah's first husband came back from the dead, you'd just let her go, huh?"

"Yeah," D.J. said, frowning. "That's what it's all about. Hey, it sucks, but sometimes, life sucks. I just think if the dude really loved her, he would have walked in her shoes and let her go. That's what love is. It's letting go."

Great. Wyatt wouldn't be the least bit surprised if D.J. suddenly busted out a guitar and started singing while little flowers popped up and budded and birds gathered round to chirp along. He didn't want to hear this hippie's opinion. What the hell did he know?

The next morning, Wyatt told D.J. he wasn't going to Garner with them after all.

"No?" D.J. asked, but he didn't seem too disappointed.

"No. I think I'm done."

"Done with what?"

Wyatt had to think about that a minute. "This," he said, gesturing to the space around him. "Everything."

That afternoon, he drove up to a closed Boy Scout

camp near Pedernales Falls. It was locked up, but not too
tightly. Wyatt looked at Milo. "What do you think, boy?
Maybe this is as good a place as any to end this thing."

Macy had called everyone she could think of, had
talked to every law enforcement agency she could
find. "The problem," the police chief told her again,
"is that he's not really missing. He can go off for a few
days if he wants. His truck hasn't turned up; nothing
looks strange."

"You don't think he'd call Linda Gail?" Macy asked.
"Or lock his house?"

"Lots of people around here don't lock up their
houses, Macy. And by Linda Gail's own admission, things
really slow down in late July and early August. Now if he
hasn't shown up by Monday, we'll get worried."

"You may be worried on Monday, but I am worried
now," Macy said shortly. Something was wrong, terribly
wrong, and she felt awfully guilty. She'd done this. She
was the reason Wyatt had left. And she would never
forgive herself if something happened to him.

When Finn called to tell her they wouldn't be
able to get out of New York until tomorrow morning
and tried to explain the anxiety he was feeling, Macy
couldn't concentrate. She was thinking that Wyatt had
a friend in Dallas. What was his name? Jim, John . . .

"Macy?"

"Sorry, sorry," she said. "So the deal is a good one,
huh?"

There was a pause on the other end. "It's a good deal

I've already told you that. I was just telling you how nervous I got at the airport. Macy, what is going on?"

She couldn't hide it. "Something . . . something awful has happened."

"The baby—"

"No, no, nothing like that," she quickly reassured him. "It's Wyatt—he's missing."

"Missing?"

"He took off with Milo."

Finn said nothing for a moment. "Okay, so . . . ?"

"So it's my fault, Finn. Who knows where he is or what he's done to himself?"

"Macy, he doesn't need you to keep tabs on him."

She was really getting very tired of people telling her not to worry. She knew Wyatt better than anyone. She was becoming increasingly frustrated with the world at large. Her head was killing her, she was starving, and she had more calls to make. "This is different. I know it. Something is wrong."

"Let his family worry about it."

"I *am* his family!" she cried. "He isn't close to his parents and I am all he has, okay? And I am the reason he is out there, doing God knows what!"

"Calm down, baby," Finn said softly.

Two wishes: Finn would understand and Wyatt would come back safe and sound. "Please don't tell me what to do."

"I'm not telling you what to do."

"I need to make some phone calls. You'll be home tomorrow? Can we talk then?"

There was a long pause before Finn said, "Sure."

Macy didn't belabor the point. She said good-bye and hung up.

The first thing Finn did when they finally made it back to Austin—surprisingly, no worse for the wear—was drop off Brodie at his house. The second thing was to drive directly to Laru's house because Macy wouldn't answer her phone.

Jesse answered the door and told him that Macy was in town, at Wyatt's office. Finn turned the truck around and drove back to town.

He strode into Wyatt's offices, startling the woman behind the desk. "My name is Finn Lockhart. I'm looking for Macy Lockhart."

"Clark," the woman said. "She's in Wyatt's office. I'll let her know you're—"

Finn didn't wait for her to finish. He strode across the front office to the one in back, walking through the open door and startling Macy.

She was standing at the table, looking through some papers. "Finn!" she cried, hurrying forward to greet him. She hugged him, kissed him fully, then leaned back to look at him. "It's so good to see you."

"What are you doing here?" he asked.

"Wyatt had a friend in Dallas, but I can't think of his name. I was trying to find it," she said, and turned her attention back to the papers she was going through. "How was your trip home?" she asked absently.

Finn put his hand on her back. She looked up at

him, but Finn had the impression she didn't really see him. "What are you doing, Macy?" he asked quietly.

"I told you—"

"No, I mean, why are you doing this? Leave it to someone else."

"Finn, please," she sighed impatiently. "I'm Wyatt's wife—"

"You're his *wife*?" Finn said disbelievingly.

Macy gave him a look. "You know what I mean."

"No, I don't know what you mean. I thought we'd sorted all that out."

"I am worried to death about him. He was in bad shape and I'm afraid he might have hurt himself."

"Then the police need to find him. Not you," Finn said, but Macy moved away from him.

"The police aren't going to look for him until they absolutely have to."

Finn didn't like what was happening. He felt a strange, dark distance spreading between them. "All right. Then let me help," he suggested.

"No." Macy squeezed her eyes shut as if she needed a moment to compose herself. "Look, whatever happened to Wyatt, it happened because I pulled the rug right out from under his feet. Maybe I didn't handle it right. I probably should have told him differently."

"You don't know that anything has happened—"

"He hasn't taken his blood pressure medicine in weeks. He was supposed to play in a golf tournament but he didn't take his clubs—"

"Macy, you are not to blame for anything but telling
Wyatt the truth!" Finn insisted.

Her blue eyes were full of uneasiness. "I wish you
could understand, Finn. I *need* to find Wyatt and know
he's okay. I owe him at least that much, if not more."

"What else will you owe him?" Finn demanded.
"Will you ever stop owing him? Are you going to let
guilt rule you?"

"No! This is different—"

"Is it? Has it occurred to you that maybe he doesn't
want to be found?"

"Yes," she said weakly. "That's what scares me the
most."

"I think I found it!" the woman out front said.

"You found it?" Macy cried, and hurried into the
other room, leaving Finn with a sinking feeling in his
gut as he stared out at the stock tank.

41

The feel of a dog's tongue licking his hand woke Wyatt.

It took him a moment to remember where he was.
Oh, yeah—he'd broken into a Boy Scout camp. He was

lying facedown on a cement cot with no mattress. Beer cans littered the floor around him, and Wyatt's belly growled with hunger. He couldn't remember the last time he'd eaten.

Milo looked very excited that he was awake, and Wyatt knew why. He'd shut the door of the cabin so Milo wouldn't run off, and the dog had to go out. He pushed himself up off the cot, stumbled to the door to open it, and watched Milo bound out.

Wyatt walked outside, too, and looked around. It was a very bright day, already hot as hell. The front of his shirt was soaked with perspiration. He could smell himself, too, and wrinkled his nose. When Milo came trotting back, Wyatt gave him a healthy pat on the ribs. "You will be glad to know that I am done, sport," he said. "I've got it out of my system. We're going home, boy."

It was strange, Wyatt thought, as he picked up the beer cans from the cabin, but he was more clearheaded today than he'd been since Macy told him Finn was alive. It still hurt like hell, but at least he had accepted it.

The truth was that he'd known when he'd first met Macy that Finn Lockhart was still in her blood. He'd known it when they were dating, when he'd suffered through all of her recounting what she and Finn had done here or there, on this date or that. He'd known it when he'd found her crying one afternoon. He'd thought something bad had happened—her mother had died, his mother had died, who knew?—but she'd finally admitted that she was grieving Finn. Again.

There were several occasions Wyatt had felt completely disconnected from his wife, and he would desperately assure her everything would be all right. Then Macy would be her old self, and he'd feel that connection to her, that lifeline, and his life would be wonderful again.

But Wyatt had known, had always known in the back of his mind, that he was competing with a dead man. And he'd known, the moment Macy told him Finn was alive, that he had no hope of competing with the man in the flesh. Now that he'd come to terms and admitted it to himself, he supposed he was even a little relieved.

He didn't like the man he'd become these last few weeks. He was going to change all that, right a few wrongs, and get on with his life.

Wyatt went home to clean up before he did anything else. He was surprised to discover he'd gone off and left the house open. At least he assumed that's what he'd done, as nothing was missing. He saw the empty blood pressure medicine bottle. He really needed to get that refilled.

He showered, fed Milo, and left his house, bound for the bank.

It took Wyatt a few hours to arrange what he needed to do. When he'd finished that, he drove to the office to check the mail and found it closed. "Great," he muttered. "Go away a few days and Linda Gail closes shop."

He picked up his cell phone and called her house, but he got no answer. He wondered if she had a cel phone. He honestly didn't know—when he needed Linda Gail, he called the office.

Wyatt went in and checked the mail. There was nothing that needed his immediate attention. There were a handful of telephone messages, mostly from the contractors working on the resort. He wrote a note for Linda Gail to set up a meeting with the mayor. He hoped he'd be able to reconfigure the resort plans without any hassles, but it was best to have Nancy Keller on his side.

His last stop was Daisy's Saddle-brew Coffee Shop. He needed a major dose of caffeine to get back to normal. He walked inside and braced himself when he saw Samantha Delaney behind the counter.

Sam gaped at him.

Wyatt had mentally prepared himself. They'd used each other—there was no point in pretending it was anything but that. "Look, I deserve whatever you're thinking. I am sorry about what happened, Sam."

"They found you? I hadn't heard!" she exclaimed.

"*Found* me?"

"Wyatt . . . everyone is looking for you. Don't you know that?"

"Who's everyone?"

"*Everyone.* The whole town has been frantic about you."

"Didn't Linda Gail get my message?" he asked, confused.

"Apparently not," Sam said.

Wyatt pulled out his cell phone and dialed the office

again. Still no answer. He called Linda Gail's home
and got nothing. He thought he might have Linda
Gail's cell phone number at home.

He left the Saddle-brew and drove home, but when
he pulled into the drive, he was met with several ve-
hicles, including Macy's Jeep, Linda Gail's SUV, and a
squad car. "Hell," he muttered.

None of the people gathered in the great room noticed when he first walked in. Mark Ham, the police
chief, was there, along with Linda Gail, Macy and
Emma, and Mr. Turnbow, who owned the hubcap shop
out on the main highway. They were all talking at once.
But when Milo got up and sprinted toward him with a
bark of happiness, they all whirled around. Even from
where he stood, Wyatt could see the relief in Macy's
face. If he needed any further proof, she pushed past
Chief Ham and ran for him, throwing her arms around
his neck, and squeezing the breath from him.

Then she suddenly reared back and glared at him.
"Where have you been?" she cried, hitting him in the
arm. "Do you have any idea how worried we've been?"

"No," he said, looking around at them all. "I had no
idea. I left Linda Gail a message."

"I never got any message!" Linda Gail exclaimed.
"Oh my *God*, Wyatt! I haven't slept a wink since you
went missing!"

"I wasn't missing," he said. "What's the problem?
What are you all doing here?"

"I came by today to get the mail and found Milo, so
I knew you had to be back. We've all been looking, so

I called them, and . . . and I think I'm going to faint," Macy said.

"Don't do that," Wyatt said, and escorted her to the couch. "Look, I'm sorry I had everyone so worried. I left Linda Gail a message, but maybe the call was dropped. I had no idea anyone was looking for me— I've been out of town fishing."

"*Fishing?*" Linda Gail cried incredulously.

"Fishing," he said with a warning look for her. "I just needed a few days to clear my head is all." He looked around the room. "But I'm *fine*. This is all a misunderstanding."

"That's what I thought," Chief Ham said. He put on his hat. "I'm going to leave you folks now and go close out the report." He looked at Wyatt. "Next time you leave town, you might leave more than one message."

"I'll do that."

"I'll get back to work, too," Mr. Turnbow said. "I thought I saw your pickup in town. Guess I was right."

"I'll walk out with you," Emma said. She smiled at Wyatt as she walked by. "I'm glad you're okay, Wyatt. But don't ever do that again!"

"Thanks, Emma," he said with a sheepish smile.

That left Macy and Linda Gail. Wyatt looked at his longtime secretary. "Linda Gail, I apologize," he said. "You're a good egg. I'm glad you've got my back."

"I deserve a raise after this," Linda Gail said pertly as she picked up her purse. "I haven't slept a night since you've been gone, Wyatt, and I like my sleep."

"I'll make it up to you, I promise."

"Just where did you go fishing with Del Lago not two feet from your door?" she demanded.

"I'll fill you in later."

She frowned skeptically, but she walked to the door. "Are you coming to the office?"

"I'll be there just as soon as I have a word with Macy."

Linda Gail nodded and looked at Macy. The two women exchanged a look; Macy smiled gratefully at Linda Gail. "Thanks," she said.

"No. Thank *you*," Linda Gail said, and went out.

When she'd gone, Macy sagged against the couch. "You scared me to death, Wyatt. I thought something had happened. I've never been so frantic in my life."

"For me?" he said, inordinately pleased. "I'm flattered. Where's Farmer Finn?"

She frowned and turned her head toward the window. "He's . . . he's at home."

"Do I detect trouble in cowboy paradise?"

Macy looked at him.

"Let me make this easy for you, Macy. I've come to my own decision. It took me a while to accept it, but I have. I don't like it—it damn near killed me to admit it—but you belong with Finn. You really always did, and in a way I have always known it. I just had a hard time coming to grips with it because I love you so much. But then a hippie told me love is letting go, so—"

"A *hippie*?"

"Long story. Macy, listen—I'm sorry. I'm sorry I worried you, but I want you to know that everything is going to be all right." Macy's eyes narrowed with skepticism, and Wyatt couldn't help but chuckle. "Don't look so shocked. I'm really not a bad guy. In fact, I don't even recognize the guy I've been the last few weeks."

"Me either," she said.

He smiled ruefully. "I'm okay now. I promise you I really am."

"Are you? Are you really, Wyatt?"

"I'm still stung. And I'll always love you. But I guess I do love you enough to let go."

She blinked. Sat up and stared at him, waiting for the *but*. When none came, her features softened. "I think that is the best gift you have ever given me, Wyatt."

"There's something else," he said. "Two Wishes. I can't give back all of it because of some of the lien structures, but I've carved off most of it for Cowboy Bob's animal kingdom. It's my thanks to him for the sacrifice he made for us all."

Macy gasped. "Are you kidding?"

"No."

Affection and amazement shone in her eyes.

"But there's a catch. Farmer Finn has to consent to letting people come have a look. Maybe have a petting zoo there for the kids. I think it will make a great addition to the resort."

"My God, Wyatt . . . are you serious?"

He shrugged. "I should never have sold it. I guess I hoped he'd leave if I sold it. But . . . but I should have realized that he's too much of a man to be pushed away by something like that."

Macy stood up, pulling him along with her. She solemnly wrapped her arms around him, hugging him tight. A moment later, she kissed his cheek. "Thank you," she said. "From the bottom of my heart, thank you."

"Yeah, well, don't thank me too fast. I'm not letting you have Milo. I'm giving it all back but the dog," he said.

Macy smiled warmly at him.

"As for the baby," he said. "What about joint custody?"

"Absolutely. Wyatt . . . I love you," she said, and hugged him again.

Wyatt smiled into her hair. Strangely, those words hurt, but they didn't rip into his heart anymore.

42

Finn could see the cloud of dust rising up from the dirt road behind the oncoming car, but from where he stood in the field, he couldn't make out the car. He'd finally convinced his father to let him clear some land so he could build the folks a new barn. After some

rm-twisting, Luke and Brodie had promised to help
him.

"Finn, seriously—you have *got* to get your own
place," Brodie had complained.

Just as soon as he had a little money of his own, Finn
was going to do precisely that.

He pulled a handkerchief from his back pocket and
wiped his brow. He pulled off his gloves and stuffed
them into the back pocket of his jeans, then started
walking up the road. He hoped it was his mother bringing him something to eat.

But as the vehicle rounded the corner, his apprehension ratcheted up—it was Macy. He hadn't talked
to her since he came back from New York a couple of
days ago.

Macy's car slid to a halt—the girl drove way too fast,
but that was one of the things he loved about her. The
Jeep bounced when she threw it into park, and she got
out and marched around to the front of the hood without bothering to close the door.

He steeled himself, uncertain of her mood.

She put her hands on her hips and stared at him.
She was wearing a summer dress and her hair was moving in the breeze. Her long legs were braced apart, almost as if she expected a physical fight. Actually, Finn
could go for a little physical confrontation—damnation,
but Macy just got sexier every time he saw her.

He reseated his hat and said, "Macy?"

She made a noise that sounded like a hiccup. "I love
you, Finn."

His heart instantly rose up, and he smiled. "
wondered how long it would be before I heard tha
again."

"It's over, Finn. Wyatt came home and he's fine and
you were right, he didn't need me to worry about him
I'm sorry. I'm really sorry. I know I keep saying I an
sorry for everything, but I am."

"Macy," Finn said as he leapt over the fence and
walked toward her, "you don't need to be so sorry."

"I just want to be with you," she said earnestly. "It's
really over with Wyatt and my conscience is clear and
I . . . I just love you, Finn," she said, clasping her hand
together as if to restrain herself. "I love you. I really love
you so much, and I want to be with you."

"That is the sweetest music to these ears," he said
and gathered her in his arms and kissed her. When he
lifted his head, Macy told him about Wyatt and all tha
he'd said, about his extraordinary change of heart. Finn
was shocked by the gift of his land. It was a tough thing
Wyatt Clark had just done, and Finn's respect for the
man increased tenfold.

When Macy had finished telling him everything, he
put his arms around her and rested his chin on top of
her head. He felt more at peace than he had in years
He felt like he was finally, truly, home.

"There's only one thing he won't part with," Macy
said solemnly.

"What's that?"

"Milo," she said.

Finn thought about it a minute. Maybe his mother

was right—maybe God did work a miracle for him. "I think Milo is in good hands."

"So now what?" Macy asked.

"Well," Finn said thoughtfully as he traced his finger from the hollow of her throat to the top of her blouse, "there are a lot of things we need to do, but I think the first order of business is to get working on the family we want to have."

Macy grinned. "I think you're going to have wait about seven months to do that."

"Oh, I don't think so," Finn said, and kissed the tip of her nose. "We've got to make hay, baby, and get in plenty of practice so we can hit the ground running once the baby is born." Macy laughed; Finn kissed her laugh. He cupped her face with his hand, feeling her skin beneath his fingers, feeling her body pressed to his. This was right. This was where he was supposed to be. There was something incredibly heartening about holding his wife. She invoked all the familiar, urgent longings for her, but Finn also felt raw and powerful. He felt invincible. He believed there was nothing they couldn't achieve together.

This was why he'd survived.

"I'm all for practicing," she said when he lifted his head, and touched her fingers to his lips. "I hope we have a truckload of kids," she said. "You know what else? Cats. You never mention cats."

"*Cats?*"

"Yes, cats! At the rescue ranch," she said, and began to talk about the cruelties and indignities some cats were forced to endure and how they would be helped at their ranch.

Finn held Macy in his arms and listened as she talked about their future. He thought about the ranch. He thought about Macy and Wyatt, and the long winding path he'd taken to be standing here, right now, with the woman who had kept him going through some of the darkest days of his life.

Finn watched her eyes dancing with enthusiasm, and wished it could always be like this—that he would always be this secure in his love for her, this hopeful of the future.

And then he wished Macy would stop talking so he could kiss her some more.

43

A couple of days after Project Lifeline's big gala fund raiser, Cathy, Reena, Anne, and Linda Gail met at Daisy's Saddle-brew Coffee Shop and agreed that the event had been a smashing success. The live music had been top shelf, the dancing and casino tables the most fun, and the kid section really fabulous. Anne had heard they had raised an astonishing amount of money, especially because Finn Lockhart had been there.

"I guess you know I was right, Cathy. Having Finn Lockhart there was a huge draw," Reena said with much superiority.

"He did a great job on the silent auction!" Anne said, sounding surprised. "I'd heard all these rumors about him being a nut job, but he was just a very handsome and poised man, if you ask me."

"It was a good cause," Reena said. "That brings out the best in everyone."

Linda Gail suspected Reena was right—Finn Lockhart had been a last-minute substitute host for the silent auction when Rick Barnes had cancelled. Linda Gail had heard through the grapevine it had taken some doing to get Finn there because he was still having trouble in crowds, but in the end, he'd been a star and he'd seemed to enjoy himself.

"You can tell how much Finn and Macy love each other," Anne said with a sigh. "Did you see them dancing and kissing? They only had eyes for each other, that's for sure."

Linda Gail had seen them, and she'd wished for a little of that magic for herself, but Davis was a hopeless dancer. Nonetheless, the Graebers were happy. Her kids had had their faces painted and Linda Gail and Davis had kicked butt at the casino tables, winning two huge stuffed bears and a George Foreman grill.

"Didn't Wyatt go?" Cathy asked Linda Gail.

"Oh, no. He's got so much work he can hardly kee[p] his head above water." That was her standard respons[e] these days. Wyatt had been a bit of a recluse lately an[d] didn't go to public events. Linda Gail worried abou[t] him, but Wyatt told her not to—actually, he com[-] manded her not to, said he'd fire her if she asked hi[m] one more time how he was doing—so she didn't as[k]. But she worried about him all the same. He tried to pu[t] a good face on it, but he wasn't right yet.

"Speak of the devil," said Cathy and nodded to th[e] counter.

The Harper women had just come in—Jillia[n] Harper, her daughters Emma and Macy, and her sis[-] ter, Laru Friedenberg, who, Linda Gail couldn't hel[p] noticing, was wearing a short denim skirt, red cowbo[y] boots, and her hair in a long tail down her back. Ther[e] was one other person with them—Karen Lockhar[t,] which surprised Linda Gail. She had it on good autho[r-] ity there was no love lost between the Lockharts an[d] the Harpers, especially after this big to-do.

"I guess you all heard Laru Friedenberg kicked Jess[e] Wheeler to the curb," Cathy muttered.

"*What?*" Reena hissed. "*She* kicked *him* out? Ha[s] she looked at that man? I wouldn't kick out Jesse eve[n] if he didn't have enough brains to spit downwind."

"Laru can get who she wants," Cathy said. "But Jess[e] wasn't ready for the big *co-mit-ment*," she said, articulat[-] ing the word.

"I heard it was the other way around," Anne sai[d]. "Laru wouldn't commit."

All four women turned to look at Laru Friedenberg.

"Big baby shower next month, did you guys hear?" Linda Gail muttered behind her coffee.

"I bet that's what they're doing right now. They're out shopping for baby stuff. Nothing can unite families like babies," Cathy said with a happy sigh.

Cathy's observation wasn't too far from the truth. It had taken a few olive branches, but the Harpers and the Lockharts had found a stretch of common ground around Macy's baby.

Finn and Macy had worked extra hard to find peace for everyone. Macy had made it a point to spend some time with Karen Lockhart, and as difficult as that was, she knew she was winning the war when Karen showed up at the apartment Macy shared with Finn with a sack full of things she'd knitted for the baby.

Surprisingly, Macy's mother was a harder nut to crack, but Finn had charmed her into accepting him. He'd done it by doing some work around Jillian's house over the course of several weekends. Slowly, Jillian began to warm up to him. She even began to like the idea of the rescue ranch.

As for Wyatt . . . Macy rarely saw or heard from him these days. She knew the resort was going up and heard around town that he was very much involved with it, but that was all she knew of him. Macy thought of him frequently and hoped he was getting on with his life.

"Macy, you're up!" Emma said, moving to the side so that Macy could step to the counter.

Macy looked at Sam. "Mocha latte, please," she said coolly.

Sam didn't speak, but stepped to one side to prepare the drink. A few moments later, she set the coffee on the counter. "Four forty-nine."

Macy handed her a five.

Sam hesitated. "Macy . . . I've done a lot of thinking and I'm . . . I am so sorry. I don't know what got into me, but I can't tell you how very sorry—"

"Sorry is a stupid, empty word," Macy said, using Sam's own words. "May I have my coffee please?"

"Macy, look who's here!" Laru called from behind her. Macy gladly glanced away from Sam's stunned look and over her shoulder. She saw Linda Gail and her friends seated at a big square table. Linda Gail waved at Macy as Laru pulled up a chair. Mom and Emma were pulling a table over to join them.

"Be right there," Macy said. She picked up the coffee Sam placed before her and walked away without another word to the table where the women of Cedar Springs had gathered.

Macy stole another look at Sam behind the counter as she took her seat. She seemed so out of place. And sad. As lonely as she'd seemed the first day Macy met her. She had no one to blame but herself to Macy's way of thinking.

"Macy, boy or girl?" Reena asked, a pencil poised and ready to write in a little notebook, drawing her attention back to them.

"Honestly? I don't want to know," Macy announced.

"What?" her mother exclaimed. "You have to find out!"

As Macy and her mother argued about that, bets as to whether Macy's baby would be a boy or a girl were being fiercely debated and wagered.

Some things in Cedar Springs never changed.

Reading Group Guide

QUESTIONS FOR DISCUSSION:

1. Macy, the heroine of *Summer of Two Wishes*, is caught in an extraordinary situation—she is married to two men whom she loves. How is her love for Wyatt different from her love for Finn? What initially attracted her to Finn? What drew her to Wyatt? Which male character do you find most attractive?

2. Do you agree with Macy's approach to resolving her dilemma?

3. Wyatt finds himself in a nearly impossible position when his wife's first husband "returns from the dead." Do you think he reacts reasonably? Does he deal with Finn fairly? What aspects of his behavior toward Macy do you approve or disapprove of?

4. Finn's love for Macy helps him through some dark

times in Afghanistan. How is that love challenged once he returns to the United States?

5. Sam and Macy refer to each other as best friends. Is Sam forthcoming about her belief that Macy's treatment of Finn "had turned something sour inside Samantha"? (116) How are Sam's and Macy's ways of coping with grief similar? How are they different? Can you empathize with Sam's reaction to her friend's extraordinary dilemma?

6. Both Macy and Finn have mothers with strong personalities. How is Jillian's style of parenting different from that of Karen Lockhart? Is Jillian's reliance on the law similar to or different from Karen's belief in the power of religion? Do these women's children share their values?

7. Macy's aunt, Laru Friedenberg, is a powerful force in Macy's life. Why is Laru considered a free spirit in Cedar Springs? How does her philosophy of life influence Macy?

8. Throughout *Summer of Two Wishes*, the citizens of Cedar Springs treat Finn as a hero. Does Finn regard himself as one? Does his self-image change during the course of the novel? How does the media attention affect his sense of self? Do you think Finn is a hero?

9. Do you think that Macy should forgive Samantha at the end of the novel? Why or why not?

10. What are Macy's two wishes at the beginning of the novel? Have her wishes changed by the end of the novel? Do you believe that her most heartfelt two wishes have come true? Do you agree with the choice she makes between the two men she loves? Why or why not?

11. If you could have two wishes come true, what would they be?

ENHANCE YOUR BOOK CLUB

For your book club meeting, why not prepare a meal of regional favorites the folks in Cedar Springs, Texas, might enjoy? A great bookclub dinner menu:

Chicken Enchiladas
Perdernales River Chili
Grilled Gulf Shrimp
Guacamole Salsa
Home grown tomatoes
Texas Sheet Cake
Sangria

Julia London's favorite recipes for all of the above can be found on her website, www.julialondon.com, as well as some great links to Texas cooking.

You might play soulful country music to create the right mood during your book club meeting. Here are some of the author's personal favorites, who all call Texas home: Patty Griffith, Lyle Lovett, Marcia Ball, Shawn Colvin, Sara Hickman, Jimmy Dale Gilmore—and, of course, Willie Nelson.

If you would like to learn more about veterans' organizations, Julia London recommends the United States Department of Veterans Affairs' clearinghouse list of the many organizations for veterans at www1.va.gov/VSO/ some. She also recommends www.americanwidowproject .org.

If you want to help care for neglected and abused animals, Julia London recommends contacting the American Society for the Prevention of Cruelty to Animals at www.aspca.org and the Humane Society of the United States at www.hsus.org.

Find more links at www.julialondon.com.

What inspired you to write such an intensely emotional contemporary novel as *Summer of Two Wishes*?

The war in Iraq became personal for me when my nephew joined the Marine Corps and went to Iraq. He joined because he thought it was the right thing to do after 9/11. In addition, our local paper dedicates an issue to soldiers in the area who lost their lives in Iraq or Afghanistan. It's very sobering to see the faces of so many young men and women who gave their lives for our country, and it was hard not to imagine my nephew's face among them. Thankfully, his tour ended and he's gone on to other things. But I wondered what it would be like for people who did lose loved ones, and how desperately they must want them back. I began to think . . . what if one of those lost soldiers did come back? How would that soldier react to the way life had gone on without him? Could time be reversed?

How did the experience of writing *Summer of Two Wishes* differ from writing a historical romance such as the next novel in your Scandalous series, *A Courtesan's Scandal*?

Summer of Two Wishes is quite different in setting and tone. The historical romance novels I write are emotional love stories set two hundred years ago in societies I sometimes portray a bit whimsically. I adore writing historical romance because it is so much fun. Writing a book like *Summer of Two Wishes* was, in some respects, more difficult. One might think that the difficulty of writing a historical novel is the research involved. That's not really true—the research is fairly straightforward, and the interpretation of history is all mine. It is more difficult to convince a reader to suspend disbelief in a contemporary novel. The readers know what I know—and sometimes a whole lot more. The novel has to ring true on many different levels. *A Courtesan's Scandal* is historically accurate, but it's a flight of fancy. *Summer of Two Wishes* is a story that could, conceivably, happen today, so it must pass a different sort of test in the reading experience.

What aspect of writing a novel set in modern times did you find most enjoyable?

I especially enjoyed the dialogue. The characters in *Summer of Two Wishes* sound like my friends and family; I can relate to them immediately.

In *Summer of Two Wishes* you created two strong, dynamic yet very different male characters—Finn Lockhart and Wyatt Clark—who are complex and seem so real. How did you gain such insight into the male psyche?

This question makes me laugh because I don't think I have any particular insight into the male psyche, and I think my husband would agree. However, I have studied men in their natural habitat over the years and through various relationships, both familial and romantic, so I guess I've picked up a thing or two.

You live in Texas, where *Summer of Two Wishes* is set. Why did you choose this setting for the novel? You write about the town of Cedar Springs as if it's a real place. Is it modeled after a specific town? Have you ever lived in a small town?

I chose this setting because I am a fifth-generation Texan; I grew up on a ranch in West Texas, and I still live in Texas. The setting is very familiar and comfortable to me. Cedar Springs is not a real town, but it is modeled on several small towns around Austin, where I live now, such as Marble Falls, Fredericksburg, and Georgetown.

How did you manage to endow the canine character Milo with so much personality? Do you have a dog?

I am definitely a dog person—I have always had dogs and I am sure I always will, because there is nothing in life quite as sure and steady as a dog's affection. I do not have a dog presently; I dedicated the book to my two labs, who I lost in the last year. Hugo and Maude were my faithful companions for fourteen years, and I am still mourning their loss. But recently I saw a couple of happy dogs with a rescue organization, and they've been in my thoughts. I wouldn't be surprised if we have a new dog in the next year.

Macy loves two men at once—do you think that is really possible?

I do think it is possible, but I think it is unlikely a woman would love two men like Macy loved Wyatt and Finn. Or perhaps I should say I'm not sure my own heart would work that way. I think one would be in my heart and the other I would love more like an old flame. I hope I never have to find out, because one man is more than plenty for me!

You present six different marital or romantic relation ships in *Summer of Two Wishes*. What are the essential ingredients of a happy love relationship between a man and a woman?

Romantic love goes through so many cycles over the long run, doesn't it? A very wise woman once told me that a person can put up with a lot in a marriage or relationship if she feels as if she is heard and appreciated. I think that i true.

Finn's return from the dead could be considered a miracle. Do you believe in miracles? In wishes coming true—even if their fulfillment leads to more wishes?

Miracles are those things I only see once they're behind me. I believe in miracles, but I never recognize them without years of hindsight to aid me. I definitely believe in wishes coming true. There is a reason the phrase "be careful what you wish for" is in our vernacular.

Will you write another contemporary novel? What are you writing now?

Definitely! I hope to write many more contemporary novels. There are so many life issues in twenty-first-century America and so many people I've met that inspire me. I am currently writing another book set in Cedar Springs, so I hope you will come back and visit the town again.

Enjoy the following preview of

A Courtesan's Scandal

the next passionate novel in

Julia London's

captivating Scandalous series,
coming from Pocket Books in November 2009.

On a snowy Christmas Eve, as the most elite ranks of the *haut ton* gathered at Darlington House in London's Mayfair district to usher in the twelve days of Christmas, an annoyed Duke of Darlington was across town, striding purposefully down King Street through a light dusting of snow, studying the light fans above the town house doors in search of the intertwined letters G and K.

He passed a group of revelers who called out "Happy Christmas" to him, but it irritated the duke, as they blocked the walkway. He curtly tipped his hat, stepped around them, and continued on, looking at every fan above every door in the line of tidy, respectable townhomes.

He found his G and K on the last town house, a large red brick building. Quite nice, actually. The duke could not help but wonder what salacious little act the resident had performed to earn a house of this quality.

He stepped up to the door, lifted the brass knocker, rapped three times, and stepped back. His hands clasped behind his back, he waited impatiently. He was in a ve[ry] cross mood to be sure. He'd never been so exploited, s[o] ill-used—

The door swung open and a swarthy-looking gentl[e]man in a rumpled suit stood before him. He looked th[e] duke directly in the eye and offered no greeting.

"The Duke of Darlington." His voice was gruff [as] he reached into his coat pocket and withdrew a callin[g] card. "I have come to call on Miss Bergeron. She is e[x]pecting me."

The man held out a silver tray. Darlington tossed h[is] card onto it. "I'll inform her you're here," the man sai[d] and moved to shut the door.

But Darlington had been vexed past all civility; h[e] quickly threw up his hand and blocked the door to pr[e]vent it from shutting. "I'll wait inside, if you please."

The man said nothing, but shoved the door shut, lea[v]ing Darlington standing on the stoop.

"Bloody outrageous," he muttered, and glanced up th[e] street. It was Christmas Eve, and in spite of the inclem[ent] weather, people had set out to various gatherings. H[e] himself was expected on the other side of Green Park [a] half hour ago to preside over the annual soiree held f[or] one hundred and fifty of the family's closest friends.

The door abruptly opened, startling Darlington. Th[e] man said, "Come."

Darlington swept inside and removed his beaver ha[t,] which he thrust at the man. "What is your name?" h[e] demanded.

"Butler."

"I do not mean your occupation," he said shortly, "b[ut] your name."

"Butler," the man responded just as gruffly. "This way," he added, and carelessly tossed the duke's hat onto console. He walked on, lifting a candelabra high to ght the way.

He led Darlington up a flight of stairs, then down corridor that was lined with paintings and expensive hina vases stuffed with hothouse flowers. The floor covring, he noted, was the finest Belgian carpet that could e had in London.

Miss Bergeron had done very well for herself.

Butler paused before a pair of red pocket doors and nocked. A muffled woman's voice bid him enter. He ooked at Darlington. "Wait," he said, and walked in hrough the doors, leaving them slightly open.

Darlington sighed impatiently and glanced at his ocket watch again.

"Here now, darling," he heard a feminine voice say ilkily. "Tell me, how do you like this?"

"Mmm," a male answered.

Darlington jerked his gaze to the pair of doors and tared in disbelief.

"And *this*?" she asked with a bit of a chuckle. "Do you ke it?"

Her response, from what the duke could gather, was a igh of pleasure.

"Ah, but wait, for you've not lived until you've—"

"Caller," Butler said.

"Not *now*, Kate," the man objected painfully. "Please! ou leave me with such hunger."

"Please show him in, Aldous," the woman said. Digby! Keep your hands away!"

Darlington started when Butler pushed the doors

wide open. He quickly glanced down, almost afraid to look into the room, afraid of what lewd act he was interrupting.

"Your Grace?"

Darlington looked up. Whatever he might have expected, it was not what greeted him. Yes, the room looked a bit like a French boudoir with peach-colored walls, silken draperies, and overstuffed furnishings upholstered in chintz. There were magazines, hats, and a cloak carelessly draped over a chair. But the woman inside was not lying on a daybed with a man on top of her as he'd suspected.

He was surprised to see her standing at a table piled high with pastries and sweetmeats. Moreover, there were Christmas boughs and hollies adorning the walls and the mantel, a dozen candles lit the room, and a fire was blazing in the hearth.

There was indeed a man, as well, a portly fellow who weighed eighteen stone if he weighed one, but he was holding nothing more lurid than a teacup. On his lip was a white substance, which, judging by the look of things, was the remnants of a pastry.

Darlington was stunned, first and foremost because he had supposed something entirely different was occurring in this room. But perhaps even more so because the woman, Miss Katherine Bergeron, was breathtaking.

Darlington had known this woman was unusually beautiful. He'd heard it from more than one quarter, and he'd seen it with his own eyes not two nights past at the King's Opera House, when he'd attended the first London performance of Mozart's *La clemenza di Tito* at the behest of his friend George, the Prince of Wales

He'd sat with George in the royal box, and it was George who had pointed her out, seated two boxes away. She was in the company of Mr. Cousineau, a Frenchman who had made a respectable fortune from selling fabrics to wealthy London society. Miss Bergeron was infamously his model and his mistress.

As he observed her that evening, she'd leaned slightly forward in her seat, enraptured by the music. She'd worn a milky white silk gown trimmed in pink velvet that seemed to shimmer in the low light of the opera house. Pearls had dripped from her ears, her wrist, and, more notably, her throat. Her hair, pale blond, was bound up with yet another string of pearls. She did not wear a plume as so many ladies seemed to prefer, but instead allowed wisps of curls to drape the nape of her long, slender neck.

She'd seemed to sense his gaze, for she'd turned her head slightly and looked at him. She did not glance shyly away when she discovered him observing her, but calmly returned his gaze a long moment before turning her attention to the stage once more.

The duke had found her boldness mildly interesting. Nevertheless, he had not anticipated seeing her again . . . until George had summoned him. Now he was standing in her private salon.

But she looked nothing like she had the night at the opera. She was beautiful, astonishingly so, but a simpler, natural beauty, free of cosmetic. She wore a rather plain blue gown with a shawl wrapped demurely around her shoulders. Her hair was not dressed, but hung long and full down her back.

"Your Grace," she said again, smiling warmly. She

picked up a plate of muffins. "May I entice you with Chrismas treat? I just made them," she added proudly.

"They are divine, Your Grace," the portly man said coming to a pair of small feet and bowing his head.

"No," Darlington said incredulously. Did they thin he'd come for tea? He looked at Miss Bergeron. "A word madam?"

"Of course," she said, and handed the plate of muffin to her companion. "Please do go with Aldous, Digby and mind you don't eat them all."

"I shall endeavour to be good," he said jovially, "bu you know how wretched I can be." He patting his enor mous belly. He took the plate from her, gave the duk another curt bow, and followed Butler out.

When they had left the room, Darlington looked a Miss Bergeron. "I regret that we've not had the courtes of a proper introduction, but it would seem the situation does not lend itself to that."

"Yes," she said, eying the rest of the food on the table "I had not expected you so soon."

"Your patron was rather insistent."

She gave him a wry look and gestured to a chair nea the table. "Are you certain I cannot tempt you to tast a muffin? I confess, I am just learning the art of bakin and I am not certain of the quality."

No, she could not; Darlington did not move.

"Please," she said again, gesturing to the chair. " hope you will be at ease here."

"Miss Bergeron, I do not find the circumstances th least bit easy."

"*Oh*," she said, lifting a fine brow. "I *see*."

He rather doubted she did. She was a courtesan

ardly accustomed to the pressures of propriety he faced
every day. "I have come as the prince has demanded to
make your acquaintance and to mutually agree on an appearance or two that will serve his . . . purpose," he said
with distaste.

She smiled then, and Darlington knew in that moment how she had captivated the prince. "Very well."
She folded her arms across her middle and moved away
from the table, that lovely, captivating smile still on her
face.

If she thought that he could be so easily seduced,
he was very much mistaken. And pray tell, what was
that just above the dimple on her cheek? A bit of flour?
There is the Carlton House Twelfth Night ball," he
said, a bit distracted by the flour.

"That would do," she agreed. "Shall I meet you
here?"

"I will come for you."

Her smile seemed to grow even more enticing.

"There is an opera scheduled shortly thereafter. Will
that suit?"

"I adore opera," she said smoothly.

"Very well," Darlington said. "That should suffice for
the time being. Furthermore, I will remind you that in
the course of this *ruse*," he said with an angry flick of his
wrist, "I expect you to defer to me as one would defer to
a peer. We are merely to be seen in public together and
rely on the usual wagging tongues to do the rest. Therefore, I see no reason to touch or otherwise engage in any
untoward behavior that might be remarked upon by my
family or close acquaintances. When these public events
have concluded, I will see to it that you are escorted

safely home, but I see no point in prolonging our conta[ct]
any more than is required. Are we are agreed?"

She smiled curiously. "Are you always so officious?"

Officious. If only she knew what sacrifice he was ma[k]-
ing at the prince's behest. "Do not mistake me, Mi[ss]
Bergeron. I have been coerced into this . . . charade," [he]
bit out. "I take no pleasure in it. I would not give you th[e]
slightest cause for false hope of any sort. Now then—
we are agreed, I shall take my leave," he said again, an[d]
turned toward the door.

"If by false hope you mean that you will not taste m[y]
muffin and pronounce it very good, you must not fre[t,]
Your Grace," she said, drawing his attention back [to]
her. "I had no hope of it, I was merely being civil." Sh[e]
picked up a delicacy and walked toward him, her gaz[e]
unabashedly taking him in. "There is just one sma[ll]
matter," she said, pausing to bite into the delicacy. He[r]
brows rose, and she smiled. "*Mmm.* Very good, if I do s[ay]
so myself," she pronounced, tilting her head back to lo[ok]
up at him, her pale green eyes softened by the length [of]
her dark lashes.

The duke frowned suspiciously. He had an insan[e]
urge to wipe the flour from her cheek. She was de[li]-
cate, her height slightly below average. She had a soft[ly]
regal bearing, an elegance that set her apart from mo[st]
women. And her hair . . . her hair looked like spun silk.

"I should not like to give you cause for false hop[e]
either. Therefore, I should like to make it perfectly clea[r]
that this arrangement is not *my* preference any mor[e]
than, apparently, it is yours. I am not yours to use, You[r]
Grace. You may not touch me, or otherwise take libert[ies]
with my person."

The duke cocked one dark brow above the other and smiled wryly, his gaze on her lush lips. He certainly understood what pleasure a man would find in kissing that mouth. "You may rest assured, Miss Bergeron, that neither my desire nor my intent. I find the suggestion quite distasteful."

Something flickered in her eyes, and she smiled with relish. "*Really*? No man has ever said that to me." She popped the last little bite into her mouth.

Did this chit not know who he was? What power he wielded in the House of Lords? In *London*? He shifted slightly so that he was towering over her. She did not seem the least bit cowed.

"*I* am saying it, Miss Bergeron. I am not the prince. I am not bowled over by your beauty or your apparent bedroom charms."

"Splendid! We should get on quite nicely then, Your Grace, for I am not a debutante yearning for your attention or a match."

For once, the duke was speechless. "Is there anything else?" he asked curtly as she calmly . . . and provocatively . . . used the tip of her finger to wipe the corner of her mouth.

"Yes. You may call me Kate," she said pertly. "What may I call you?"

"Your Grace," he snapped, and strode out of that French boudoir with an uncharacteristically hot temper.